Beautifully WOUNDED

Secrets & Scars Series

— Book One —

SARAH JD

To those who have had their power taken from them.
To those who denied consent and was ignored.
To those who have had to fight for basic human rights.
You are not alone.
We see you.
We hear you.
And we stand by you from every corner of the globe.
Be the kickass FMC in your story and never give up fighting!

CONTENT WARNING

The Secrets & Scars Series is a dark MF contemporary MC age gap romance that contains subjects that may be triggering to some readers, including but <u>not limited to</u>:

- Emotionally dark and traumatic.

- Abuse from a parents,

- Graphic violence,

- Non-consensual acts including rape outside the relationship,

- Demeaning acts,

- Suicidal thoughts & self-harm,

- Kidnapping,

- Trauma from Religious Extremism,

- Exposure to cultish situations,

- Emotional & physical blackmail,

- Explicitly detailed sex scenes,

- Killing, brutality and gore.

1

ABBEY

"Let me out!" My fists pummel my bedroom door, the timber rattling under each blow as I scream. "You can't do this!"

I'm about to bash my fist again when a loud hum stays my hand mid swing, and it takes me a moment to recognise the sound. A loud sob escapes me as I spin to face my window, blinking to clear the wet blur of my tears.

"No!"

I stumble towards the window, testing the lock, already knowing it's secure.

It's always fastened, just to ensure I can never escape.

Spinning on my heel, I spot my chair at my desk and run for it.

"You can't do this!" I scream again, my voice barely sounding like my own, having taken on an animalistic rasp.

Gripping my chair, I hoist it up to my chest before darting back towards the window, desperate to escape this prison my parents have forced on me.

I need to get out.

I need to get out, now.

As the hum continues and the setting summer sun gradually disappears from the lowering security shutter, I force another animalistic scream, and launch the chair towards the window.

The shattering of glass and the crash of the chair are loud as it breaks through and skims the lowering shutter, landing on the path outside my window. A glimmer of relief rushes through me at feeling the gentle evening breeze flow in and hit my sweat-soaked skin, teasing me with hope.

Hope that I can escape before it's too late.

Hope that I can disappear and never be found again by these people.

My family.

The shutter is closing faster than I'd like, which kicks me into action, and despite the shards of glass protruding around the framed edges and the fact I know I'm going to get cut, I leap for the opening.

I have to get free. I can't stay here anymore.

Rough hands grab me from behind, tugging me away from my only escape.

"No!"

"You can't stop this from happening, Abigail!"

The screech of my mother is loud and menacing as she and my dad drag me kicking away from the opening as I watch, as if in slow motion, as the shutter finally seals shut, locking me in.

"Maggie, get the pills from the kitchen!" my mother demands of my sixteen-year-old younger sister as Mum and Dad wrestle me to my knees.

"No! No pills! Please!" I plead, my arms burning under my parents' tight grips as they try to force me to stay still.

I don't, and I won't ever stop fighting them. Not now. This isn't right. They can't do this.

"I'll get them, Mum," Maggie calls enthusiastically, dashing from the room as I plead with her.

"No Maggie. Stop. You know this isn't right!"

"Maggie, no!" my littlest sister, Tahli cries, her voice trailing off as she chases after Maggie.

Damn it. I don't want Tahli going against my parents. She's only twelve, and so much like me. I fear what they might do to her if she's seen to be siding with me.

But Maggie, they love her. She's their favourite. She never does anything wrong in their eyes. If only she'd talk to them. Try to get through to them on my behalf, I may have a chance of getting out of this unscathed.

But Maggie is nothing like me. She's my mum in a nutshell. Practically a clone. And deep down, I know she'd never help me. After all, tonight's drama started with her and her hatred for me. She didn't have to tell my parents what she found, yet she did, with a sinister grin on her smug face.

"Daddy. Please." I sob as his face comes into view, hoping he'll still see the little girl in me. The same little girl that he used to adore. "Don't let this happen, Daddy. It doesn't have to be like this. I know you know that."

"Shut up, Abigail!" my mother hisses, her hand fisting in my hair and tugging my head back so I'm forced to take in her furious brown eyed glare. "Don't try and get your father to side against me. My beliefs are his beliefs." She snarls in my face, baring her smoke-stained yellow teeth.

Why does she hate me so much?

Why does she choose her beliefs over everything else?

Over her child?

"Your mother is right, Abbey. Stop making this harder for yourself by fighting. You need to accept the consequences of your actions."

I try to tug against my dad's firm grip as I glance up at him, noticing how tired he looks, but I barely move. His strength alone has me trapped here.

"But Daddy. I didn't—"

"Stop!" he roars, cutting me off as his free hand grips my jaw so hard, I have no choice but to open my mouth.

"Take out two pills," my mother demands, which is when I realise Maggie has returned.

"I brought a bottle of water too, to make sure they wash down properly, like last time."

"Good girl, Maggie," my mother praises, and I start struggling profusely, a wild and monstrous screech ripping from my throat as I fight harder, trying to get free.

"Stop hurting her!" Tahli screams from somewhere behind me, but no one pays her any attention, their focus on me as the three of them work together to control me.

No. No. No. I scream in my head as I try to force my mouth closed, but my dad's grip is firm, and Maggie, the little bitch, shoves two pills into my open mouth before she starts filling it with water.

I try to cough, but my mum releases my hair and pinches my nose, even as my dad forces my mouth shut.

I flail like a crazy woman to no avail, their strength overpowering until my body begins fighting my own instincts, and I swallow the damn pills and water.

When my dad notices, he forces my mouth open again, and Maggie, the traitorous evil cow, starts filling my mouth with more and more water.

The fight leaves me, knowing it's too late. They did what they set out to do. Lock me in here. Drug me so I'll stop fighting, all so they can control me better.

I know what's coming. More drugs, I'm sure. How else will they keep me compliant in the morning when they dress me in white, pay off the minister, and force me to marry one of the cruellest people I know?

Yes. Even crueller than my mother.

The moment my parents release me, I tumble to the carpet on my bedroom floor, sobbing, curling in on myself as I stare at their feet exiting my room.

"Thank you for your help, Maggie. You honour our family." My mother's words float to me right before my door closes, and I hear the latches click into place as they lock me in.

One. Two. Three. Four. Five.

I count in my head until I reach ten, and then leap up off my floor, knowing they are no longer on the other side of the door.

Scurrying over to my desk, I pull out the small trash can and shove my fingers down my throat.

I can't let the drugs work. If I do, I won't be able to fight.

I gag a few times before I force my fingers so far into the back of my throat that it hurts, and finally my attempt works.

I heave up the water with force into the can, frantically look-ing for the two white pills.

Nothing.

"Shit. Come on. Come on," I whisper-cry to myself, before repeating the process and inducing more vomiting.

Again, I heave, purging more of my stomach contents, and this time, one pill comes up too.

"Yes." I quietly celebrate and yeah, I know how utterly crazy it is for me to be cheering myself on for hurling. I hate doing it. It's horrid, yet right now, it's what might save me.

I try again to induce more vomiting, and after three attempts with little results, I know the second pill isn't coming up.

Dammit.

I don't know what drug it is, but my parents have done this before, when they told me I would be spending the long week-end with Daniel and his family at their holiday house. They did it again for New Year's Eve, knowing I'd do anything not to be alone with that monster.

Last time, the two pills made me lethargic and eventually knocked me out for the night, and in the morning, as I woke, still affected by the drugs in my system, my mum shoved another pill down my throat, my body too lethargic to fight her off.

By the time Daniel and his family arrived to pick me up, my steps were heavy, my speech was slurred, and my eyes lazy, drifting shut on their own accord.

They controlled me those nights so I'd comply the next morn-ing, and they are trying to do the same thing now.

I plan on giving them a very rude shock when they come to re-drug me in the morning.

Even as I think it, I can feel an unwelcome lightness washing over me.

Dammit. The pill still inside my gut is starting to work.

Slowly, I start crawling across my carpet towards my window where large shards of glass remain scattered.

A soft manic giggle rumbles in my chest as I realise the irony of this situation.

My parents removed all sharp objects from my bedroom last year when they feared I'd use them to harm myself.

Not gonna lie. I thought about it.

So why now, have they left me with hundreds of sharp splintered shards at my disposal?

Are they just dumb, or will they be back to clean it up?

Knowing it's likely they'll be back, I quickly snatch up a large shard that's big enough to grip, and long enough to do real damage and I hide it under my mattress.

Never have I wanted my mum to come back into my bedroom more than in this moment.

She'd never expect me to really hurt her, which is exactly how I'm going to escape, even if I have to kill her.

2

RINGO

The house is dark. From outside, nothing looks amiss, just like the other houses on the street. It makes me wonder what goes on inside all the other houses, or if it's just this one.

"You ready to do this?" JD sidles up next to me, taking one last drag on his dart before dropping it to the path and stubbing it out with his booted toe.

"Yep," I respond, watching to make sure he does the right fucking thing, which, of course, he does.

Bending to pick up the remains of his cigarette, he shoves it in his zip pocket inside his jacket, making sure to remove any evidence that can be linked to us.

"No names." Trunk grunts, as if we need to be reminded, but we all nod anyway.

"The mum van is ready to go," Jols states, shooting me a smile and I nod, fucking glad she's in Fox Pines with us tonight. Having a chick with us may come in handy, given what we're about to do.

"Stocky, you stay out here and look for signs of any witness-es," I gesture to the big guy, who nods, his expression serious and already on task. "Murf, I want you on the dad. Trunk, you take the mum." When they nod, I glance at the only female in our crew. "Jols, I want you on the sisters' bedroom. If our infor-mation is right, they are in the same room tonight and one will be passed out, but the other won't be expecting us. If she hears a female voice, she may not panic as much."

Jols nods, her gaze shifting to the house.

"I'll get the girl?" JD asks and I nod.

"Yes. I'll be busy having a little fucking chat with the parents." The growl in my voice gives away the fury bubbling in my veins.

I may be a fucking prick that only abides by the laws of my club, but when it comes to harming innocent women and chil-dren, I draw a big fucking line. The motherfuckers who dare to hurt the innocent come to regret their decisions when the Southern Sadists get a hold of them. A quick death isn't some-thing we do well.

No. Long, drawn out, gut wrenchingly painful deaths are what we like to deliver. It's something I've come to enjoy a little too fucking much.

After a quick weapon check, we pull on our balaclavas and move stealthily across the front yard, approaching the house as Stocky keeps watch.

With gloved hands, I locate the pot plant by the door and lift it to find the spare key just where we were told it would be.

Fucking idiots. Can they be any dumber? Why not just leave the fucking front door wide open so anyone can walk in off the street?

A round of quiet grunts sound behind me when I pull out the key and unlock the door, the others likely coming to the same conclusion as me.

Yes, we might be the ones entering without being fucking invited, but really, do people have to make it so easy for us?

Pushing the door open, I take a step in and wait for an alarm.

We were told there wasn't one, but you never fucking know, so I wait, and move further inside when nothing happens.

The image of the hand drawn layout of the house is fresh in my brain, and as my team fan out to do what they were tasked, I flick the hall light on and study the family portraits that adorn the walls.

What fucking lies they tell.

"What are you doing?!" a woman screeches from the end of the hall. "Get out!"

"And so it begins," I mutter to myself, leaning closer to study the three sisters in a framed picture.

The oldest and youngest look very similar. Blonde hair. Big brown doe eyes. Sweet innocent, heart-shaped faces.

"Sarg. Roadblock," JD calls, and I drag myself away from the fake happiness of the portraits to peer up the hall.

Jols is closest to me, standing guard outside a door. She holds up two fingers and points to the door, telling me that two of the sisters are behind it.

Giving her a nod, I make my way up the hall, ignoring the yelling coming from the parents' room as I approach JD. He's standing outside a door, studying something.

"What's up?" I keep my voice quiet, my eyes finally landing on the roadblock.

Fucking hell.

Latches.

Three of them.

All with locks.

"These folks aren't fucking around," JD mutters.

"Yeah, no shit. What the fuck goes on in this house?" I hiss, fucking disturbed by this sight alone.

My best mates' hazel eyes peer at me past the knitted mask hiding his identity, and I don't miss the concern swimming in them.

"She's eighteen," I remind him.

"It doesn't make it right." He hisses, and I nod. This is hitting a little too close to home for him. I know that.

"I know, man. It's never okay, no matter how old someone is, but we have to be thankful it's not a minor behind that door."

The words taste foul on my tongue, the image of the oldest blonde girl from the portrait flashing through my mind. She looked like she wouldn't hurt a fly. Why would anyone lock her up like this?

"Find the key," he snaps, his eyes turning to slits, and I know he's pissed at me for sounding so fucking cold hearted. He knows that's the way it has to be though, which is why he's not arguing with me.

You can't do the shit we do and let fucking feelings get in the way. That's how accidents happen and innocent people get killed.

Storming up the passage, I enter the parents' bedroom to find them on their knees at the foot of the bed, their hands and feet bound behind them as Murf and Trunk stand over them, watching them both sob.

Finally letting my anger surface, I storm towards the father, gripping his thinning hair and tugging his head back as I snarl in his face. "Where are the fucking keys to open your daughter's door?"

"I-I-I…" He starts fucking crying even more, and I'm about to bitch slap the fucker when the wife speaks.

"Stop being so pathetic, Colin. Your sixteen-year-old daughter has more balls than you."

Slowly, I release Colin's hair and turn my attention to the wife. "Sounds like you're not the one who wears the pants in this house, Colin," I mutter, and the wife sneers at me.

"God will damn you for breaking in. He will banish you to hell, where you'll be punished by the devil for all eternity."

My brows shoot up in surprise, and I glance at Trunk and Murf, who return my shock.

Now I get it.

We're dealing with religious radicalists.

Fucking great.

Leaning down to stare in the face of the woman, I flash her a smile. "I look forward to the day I go to hell to party with the devil. But just so you know, believing in God doesn't mean you're going through *his* pearly gates, woman. You're a different kind of evil, and I'll be seeing you in hell, where fuckers like me will entertain themselves by tormenting fucked up cunts like you."

A loud gasp leaps past her lips before she makes a raspy noise in the back of her throat, and knowing what's coming, because this isn't my first fucking rodeo, I move away in time to dodge the blob of saliva she tries to spit at me.

"Where are the keys?" I snap at her, but she seals her lips shut.

"Tear this fucking room apart until we find the keys," I order my men, and they hurry into action, pulling open drawers and emptying the contents as they rifle through it while I watch on.

There's a high chance the keys could be somewhere else in the house, but I get the feeling mummy dearest would keep them close. If for no other reason than to be able to access her daughter faster to torment her even more.

"Found some keys," Murf calls and I glance up in time to see them flying towards me.

Catching them, I dangle them before the woman's face. "Are these them?"

"Why are you here?" she snaps in response, curling her lip.

"Why is your daughter locked in her room like a prisoner?" I counter, but the woman simply scoffs as I move to the doorway.

"She is none of your concern," the woman yells, her tone panicked.

"Cap," I call to JD, and he turns. "Catch." Tossing the keys in his direction, I watch him catch them and immediately try one of the keys in the bottom latch. When the first one doesn't fit, he tries another, and thankfully, the first lock clicks open.

Moving back into the parents' room, I ignore the useless husband as he sobs, lowering to my haunches in front of the woman and staring into her eyes for a long moment before I speak.

"Your daughter is no longer any of your concern. She is mine now. I'm taking her for myself, to do with as I please." I chuckle as she gasps, leaning in closer to her trembling body. "And she will love it."

"Ahhhhh!" the woman screams, and I stand, chuckling, knowing just how to annoy the religious types.

They want their daughter innocent. Kept that way until she marries, but now she knows I'm going to do everything in my power to corrupt her little girl.

Well. That's what she thinks anyway, and I'm not about to fucking correct her.

"Uh, Sarg?"

The uncertainty in JD's tone is what has me moving back out of the room, my eyes latching onto him as I enter the hall, watching as he stares into the now open door of the bedroom.

"What?" I snap, but he just points and steps aside so I can see for myself.

As I step into the open doorway, it takes me a moment to make out what I'm seeing.

The room beyond is pale pink, the furniture white… well, what's left of it. Most of it has been trashed, except for the bed.

There's a small trash can on its side, with what looks like a puddle of vomit spilling out. The glass in the window is shattered with shards of glass everywhere, and a security shutter is all the way down, keeping the outside world out… or the inside of this house in.

These aren't the things that keep my feet glued in place, though.

It's the girl standing in the corner by the window, her baggy white t-shirt torn at the shoulder and stained in blood, as too are her arms. Her cheeks have smears of the thick crimson too, and her blonde hair is tinted red at the ends, making her look like something from a horror film.

If it weren't for those big brown doe eyes, I wouldn't know it's the same girl from the portrait in the hall. She was neat. Proper. Innocent. But this girl, with her chest heaving, her head tilted down, so she peers at me through her dark lashes, and her hand wrapped firmly around a large, and very deadly shard of glass, as droplets of blood drip from her hand onto the carpet below, I have to wonder if this girl is someone else?

"Abbey?"

My voice is raspier than usual, deep and demanding, and it causes the girl to flinch and take a step back.

"Are you Abbey?" I ask, and her top lip curls as she bares her teeth.

"You can't force me to marry that monster. I won't do it!" Her last words come out as a piercing scream before she lifts the shard out in front of her. "I'll kill you! I won't let you take me to him!"

Fucking hell.

I want to give her the benefit of the doubt and assume she's not a fucking nut job given the sight of her. Surely, it's her environment that has pushed her over the fucking edge, and the locks on the door weren't actually there to keep the world safe from her.

"Sarg?" JD questions from behind me, and I turn back and shrug.

"The job is to take her, so I'm taking her." Then I turn back to the girl and step into the room.

3

ABBEY

He's coming for me. Oh my god. What do I do? Why isn't he scared of me? I look like a crazy woman. Surely, he should be running.

As the hulking man stalks into my room, tall and looming, his black mask and clothes remind me of lethal mercenaries from movies, sending a chill down my spine.

Why would my parents send this man in to take me to Daniel? Are they scared of me?

Are there cameras in here and they saw me paint myself in my own blood, so they called in reinforcements?

My gaze darts around my room, looking for said cameras, but it's too late. The man is closing in.

"Put the shard down," he demands, and hell, I almost drop it. Not from fear, though. More like the tone in his voice has some sort of control over me.

"N-no." I shake my head, holding the shard out further, readying myself to stab him if he gets any closer.

"Don't make this harder than it needs to be. Drop it."

Again, I shake my head but freeze when a second man steps into the room.

"Right behind you, Sarg," he calls, and shit. I can't take on two of them.

"P-please. D-don't." I start sobbing, desperate to get free. Why won't they just let me go?

"We're not here to hurt you. Just put down the glass," the first man orders, his hands held up in front of him as if he's trying to calm a beast.

"Stop!" I scream, and without second guessing myself, I press the tip of the shard to my neck. "I'll do it! I swear I will!"

Both men freeze in place, and the guy at the back shoots his gaze to the back of the other guy's head as he speaks. "Sarg. What do we do?"

The other man, Sarg, doesn't answer him, instead he speaks to me.

"You don't really want to do that. What you want is to escape this house. Am I right?"

My chest heaves as my hand trembles, and I feel the sharp tip scratch the surface of my skin.

"Think about it. If you hurt yourself, you'll just end up in hospital with doctors telling you what you can and can't do. Maybe they'll even put you in the looney bin. Is that what you want?"

My head shakes in answer, but no words leave my lips. I can't make sense of this situation.

What's happening here?

What's right and wrong in this moment?

"Then put the glass down."

The deep baritone of his voice keeps me in place, my eyes locking with his as we stare at each other. When did he get that close?

I blink a few times, trying to rid my eyes of the tears as his intense gaze stays on mine. His eyes are brown too, but maybe slightly lighter than mine. They remind me of the whiskey my dad swirls in the bottom of his glass when he's deep in thought. Like a rich and vibrant amber.

"Put it down. Now!"

The demand is loud, falling from Sarg's lips as he lunges for me. I'm so shocked by the abruptness that on reflex, I drop the shard, lurching backwards so hard I practically wind myself on the wall behind me as I collide with it.

In a matter of seconds, he and the second man are on me, strong hands cuffing my wrists so I can't fight them, and even though I struggle with everything in me, I'm no match for their brute strength.

I scream as the three of us go crashing to my bed, and I hear them grunting orders to each other as they wrangle me. But really, there's no need. I'm helpless to fight them.

Somehow, I end up face down on the bed, the heavy weight of one of the men on my back, pressing me into my mattress.

Memories start rushing to the forefront of my mind, and I squeeze my lids shut.

No. Don't think about it, Abbey. Don't think about it.

I try to ward off the trauma I have no idea how to deal with, willing the flashes of memory determined to force their way in and consume me to stay back. They aren't welcome here.

"Please d-don't." I beg, hoping he's not here to do *that*. Please, anything but *that*.

"Here's what's going to happen." The deep rumble comes from the one called Sarg, his rasp against my ear, his breath warm across my cheek as he speaks. "We're going to go and see your parents. And then we are going to leave. You will do everything I tell you, without argument. Do you understand?"

I nod into the mattress, even though I want to defy him and say no.

Suddenly, the heavy weight is off me, and I go to push myself up, but realise my hands are tied behind my back.

My heart thrashes wildly, terror washing over me at being bound, the beating organ in my chest pounding so violently I fear it will stop at any second.

This can't be happening.

Why is this happening?

With two firm hands gripping my upper arms, I'm hauled off my bed, the sudden movement forcing a gasp from my lips.

"Jay!" He booms from behind me, and I whimper, shrinking in on myself as he holds me back against his chest.

The other man, who was doing nothing but staring at me, quickly moves out into the passage, gesturing to someone else, and he steps out of the way as another man steps in.

"Sarg?"

Wait.

That's not a man, I realise, the voice feminine, and that's when I notice the shorter stature of this black clad person, who definitely has boobs under those clothes.

"Find a bag and pack her stuff. Make sure you get all the girly shit you chicks like. We leave in five."

"Yes, Sarg." She nods, her gaze lingering on me for a moment before she heads for my wardrobe.

I don't get a chance to see what she's getting as Sarg urges me forward and I stumble over my feet when he tries to move me.

"Ouch," I cry as a splinter of glass stabs into my bare foot, and the man curses before sweeping me up in his arms.

I'm trembling in his hold, terrified of what's about to happen. Terrified for the moment he delivers me to Daniel. Because when that happens, my life will be over.

I was so close to getting out of here. Another two days and I would have been free. Another two days and I would have had the safety of my Uni accommodation to protect me while I prepared my final escape plan, but thanks to my sister, everything has changed.

The man's thick arms feel strong as he carries me, and I hate how I get the urge to curl into his hold, exhaustion starting to make itself known, probably an effect of the one pill still in my system.

When I'm carted through the doorway of my parents' bedroom, it takes me a moment to comprehend what I'm seeing.

My parents, on their knees. Black smudges of mascara have run down my mum's face, and dad's cheeks are nearly purple as he sobs. Beside them, are two other men, tall and strong, dressed all in black with their faces covered as well.

What the…

"Put her down!" my mum screeches, snapping her teeth like a rabid dog. "You can't have her!"

The man carrying me chuckles, even as he lowers my feet to the floor.

"Oh, I can, and I will," he snickers, and I don't miss the insinuation in his tone, my head snapping in his direction.

"What are you talking about?" I ask, confused as hell.

"Nothing. Just reminding your mummy dearest that she can't have you anymore. You're mine now."

"W-what?" My mouth drops open as I turn my gaze to my parents. "Daddy?" I beg, hoping he'll fix everything, just like he did when I was little.

Sarg chuckles again. "Sweetheart, the only man you'll be calling Daddy from now on is me."

What?

"No!" My dad roars as my eyes widen and I take a step back, only to crash into the other man that was in my room before.

"Steady," he says quietly, not sounding as menacing as the huge man they call Sarg, who I'm pretty sure just said I'll be calling him Daddy.

Uh-uh. No way!

I spin on my heel, trying to make a run for it, but strong arms wrap around my waist and haul me backwards, my legs kicking out as I panic.

"Calm down, kid. We ain't gonna hurt you."

I want to scoff and argue with the man pinning me to him, but his hand slaps over my mouth, stopping any words from coming out as he turns back to face us towards Sarg and my parents.

"Mr Delany. Mrs Delany. I hereby relieve you of your duties of the care of your daughter. She is now my responsibility. I will be the one to discipline her from now on."

"No! You can't have her. She belongs to me. She's to be married—"

Sarg lurches forward, fisting the top of my mum's hair, much like she did to me earlier tonight when she forced pills down my throat. I can't help it, when he tugs her head back and my mum cries out in pain, I start to relax, and I even think I smile behind the hand still covering my mouth.

Not like a lot. Just a bit.

And shit. What does that say about me?

Am I just as evil as she is?

"You will not be choosing who she marries. I will," Sarg hisses in my mum's face. "And if I find out either of you so much as try anything similar with your other two daughters, I'll make sure the both of you go missing. No one will ever find your bodies, or what's left of them, anyway."

My dad's sobbing should upset me, but a part of me just doesn't care if he's scared right now. After the things he's let my mum get away with, standing back and watching her dole out her punishments. I suddenly feel safer with these brutes trying to kidnap me.

They're still men, Abbey. They can still do all that stuff Daniel did to you.

Even as I tremble knowing that's true, in a strange way, I'd rather they do those vile things knowing they are people my mum doesn't want me to go with. No, she'd rather send me to Daniel, knowing how he treats me. Knowing what he does.

"You brought all of this on yourself, Abigail. If you spread your legs like a whore, of course he's going to treat you like one. You reap what you sow."

I'll show her reaping what I sow.

Okay, so maybe I won't, but going with these men, even if it is unwillingly, feels like a big fuck you to my parents. And an even bigger one to Daniel.

"Time to go," Sarg calls, shoving my mum sideways to the floor, and for the first time, I notice her hands and feet are bound behind her.

A gasp flies from my lips when the other guy is the one to hoist me in his arms this time, and my parents disappear from view as I'm carried down the hall, past my open bedroom door, towards the front of the house.

As we pass by Tahli's room, her door opens, and I see the flash of her blonde hair, panic slamming into me as I fear for her safety.

These men might hurt her.

I start to struggle in the man's hold, desperate to get free and protect her.

"Abbey!"

Her voice, so scared yet somehow strong, shows me she'd do just about anything to help me if she could. She's so little, though. I couldn't bear it if she got hurt because of me.

"Tahli!" I call back, wanting to reach for her, but with my hands bound behind me, I'm absolutely useless.

The man carrying me stops and turns, though, and I see Tahli take a step back just inside her doorway as Sarg looms over her.

"Stay away from her!" I protest, trying to wriggle free, but the man holding me is too strong. I can't get to my little sister.

To my surprise, Sarg lowers down onto one knee, and pulls up his mask, revealing his face to her. A sob escapes me when I think maybe he's about to kill her, but then I see her nodding, and she speaks quietly to him as he does to her.

They both glance at me then, and for the first time, I get a glimpse of the man's face.

I'm not sure what I expected, but a beard definitely didn't even register as a possibility. Nor is how soft the flushed skin on his cheeks appears.

"Love you, Abs," Tahli says softly, and hell, my lower lip starts trembling.

"L-love you too, Chook." I use the nickname I gave her when she was first born. "Stay out of t-trouble, okay?"

She nods, not shaken by the way I sob through my words, and then as if I haven't been shocked a thousand times already in the last twenty-four hours, my twelve-year-old sister shifts closer to the man and gives him a hug.

What the hell is going on?

"Go back to bed, okay?" Sarg says, ruffling Tahli's hair. "Your parents are okay. They've just been put in the naughty corner for a while."

She nods, like that's totally acceptable, before stepping back into her room and closing the door.

All of a sudden, with my little sister now out of sight, I'm scared shitless again. I just want to be left alone to live my life, yet I can't escape people that feel like they have a right to control everything I do.

"P-please," I whimper, watching Sarg rise to his towering height as he tugs his mask back down. "Just let me g-go. I'll run away. I won't bother anyone, I s-swear."

Stepping closer, his height forces my head to crane back, before he hooks his finger under my chin, his whiskey-coloured eyes hard and piercing as he leans in closer.

"My orders were to get you out of this house and take you with me, Angel. You best believe that's what's happening."

I part my lips to argue, but a second later he reaches forward, his big hands peeling me from the arms of the other man to cradle me against his chest before he carries me out into the night.

4

RINGO

S he smells good. Too fucking good for someone practically painted in her own blood. The metallic scent should turn my fucking gut, yet a sweet fruity scent emanating from the top of her head overpowers everything else. It must be her hair. Although some of the strands are painted crimson as well, the hair at her roots appears and smells clean and fresh.

I have the strangest fucking urge to press my nose to her crown and inhale.

Jesus fucking Christ.

Is this really what happens when I get too close to a chick now?

Have I really reached a new low of pathetic-ness?

All it takes is fruity fucking shampoo to have me thinking thoughts I shouldn't, especially given who it is on my fucking lap.

She's the victim. My fucking mark. The package I was sent to collect.

Clearly, I need to listen to JD and just let one of the Doxy girls suck my cock once and for all.

Fuck. I wish it were that easy.

The girl in my arms, Abbey Delany, trembles on my lap in the back seat of the van Jols is driving. She's only tried once to scramble free, but she quickly realised I wasn't loosening my grip.

She's so small. Thin. I can feel her bony arms and legs under her clothes, like there's not enough fat on her body to keep her warm. I could fool myself into thinking that's why she's trembling, but every one of us in this stolen silver mum van knows she's terrified.

I probably should have told her she doesn't have to fear us, but the truth of it is, she does. I may have saved her from one set of evil fuckers, but she's about to step into a whole world of crazy fuckers, so there's really no use in lying to her.

"Rest stop," Jols calls from the front of the cabin and my captive stiffens in my arms.

What does she think is going to happen?

I can only fucking imagine. She was sure we were there to take her to her future husband, who she clearly didn't want to fucking marry.

It's an age-old tale. Parents arranging marriages for their children. Not so common here in Australia, but the general public would probably be shocked to know how often it happens.

This situation, though, is a little different. Some may say arranged marriage, but it was clearly a forced marriage, and given the girl was willing to stab herself with a huge fucking shard of glass to avoid being taken to her fiancé, tells me she wasn't just trying to rebel against her parents' desire for her to marry someone they chose for her.

That and a few things her mother said.

What a fucking piece of work she was.

As the van pulls off the road into the rest stop parking lot, my captive's muscles bunch under my hold as she lifts her head to look out the window.

"Calm down, Charity. It's a piss stop."

Her big eyes dart to me as she rears back a little to get a better look at my face. I fucked the mask off as soon as we were on the highway, leaving Fox Pines behind us. She couldn't really see much then, but now, the light from the toilet block shines in through the windows, and she's studying me really fucking closely.

"Like what you see?" I smirk, chuckling when her eyes round in horror and she quickly glances away.

As the car comes to a stop, I shift her on my lap and start un-tying the cord I bound her wrists with earlier. It's satin. Probably the cord for her bathrobe or some shit. Whatever it is, I knew it wouldn't hurt her skin.

Physically hurting her is the last thing I want to do.

"We need to get you cleaned up," I mutter, watching as she brings her wrists to her chest, her breathing quickening. "Your hands are cut up from the glass. Jols can put a dressing on them to protect the wounds."

"J-Jols?"

Her voice is so husky, cracking a bit as she speaks, but it sounds so small. Like a baby fucking mouse.

"I'm Jols," Jols speaks up, flicking on the interior light and turning in her seat to peer back at us.

"I-I thought h-he c-called you J-Jay?"

A smirk pulls at my lips at Abbey's words. I don't know why, but for some fucking reason, I like that she paid attention earlier.

Jols nods. "Yeah. Jay, as in the letter J. J for Jols. We don't use real names on a job."

"A job?" Abbey asks, shifting on my lap to turn and face me.

"Yeah." My grin grows. "A kidnapping job."

My words widen her eyes, while the fellas chuckle and get out of the car, and Jols just shakes her head at me.

"Stop being a prick."

"What?" I shrug, my tone all innocent, but Jols just scoffs and gets out of the car too, leaving me and my little captive alone in the van.

"We are going to get out now, Charity, but just in case you need the warning, you don't want to know what will happen if you try to run."

She shoves back off me, her arse falling to the seat next to us, those brown eyes wild with fear as they glass over.

"W-why do y-you keep calling me C-Charity?"

Leaning in close, I hook my finger under her chin and tilt her head back until she resists a little. "From now on, you won't be known as Abbey. No one can know your real name, unless, of course, you want your fiancé to find you?"

She shakes her head as much as she can under my touch. "Can I have a d-different name?"

Releasing her chin, I grumble, "no," before opening the door and slipping out.

I'm expecting her to argue, but when she doesn't, instead, simply slipping out of the car behind me, I'm a little disappointed.

As Jols grabs some stuff out of the van, I lead Abbey up the path to the toilet block.

"All clear, man," Murf mutters as we near, holding a door open. "No shower, though."

Glancing back at Abbey, her eyes dart around frantically, giving away her panicked thoughts as she takes in the situation. When she glances into the dark bushland to our left, I have to wonder if she's contemplating running.

Sighing, I reach back and fist her upper arm, dragging her to my side as a fearful squeak passes her lips.

"Inside," I snap, hauling her into the fluorescent lit facility that's surprisingly well maintained.

Glancing around, there are three toilet cubicles, a paper towel dispenser on the wall, and a small counter with two hand basins and a dingy mirror sitting behind them on the brown brick wall.

Releasing her arm, I test the hot water tap, relieved when the cool water turns warm.

"I've got this," Jols announces as she steps inside with us. "You can wait outside."

Turning my raised brow on her, she rolls her eyes at me.

"Seriously, Ringo. You don't think I can handle a teenager that's scared of her own shadow?"

Abbey frowns at Jols' words, but I ignore that and give Jols the bad news.

"No, actually. I think as soon as I step outta here, she's gonna give you her sob story, and you're gonna feel all fucking sorry for her and then work up a plan to help her escape."

"Fuck you, Ringo. When have I ever gone against your orders?" Jols sneers, tossing down the bag and towel hard to the tiled floor.

"There's always a first time," I mutter. "Besides, I was told to get the girl and not take my eyes off her until she's safe, so guess fucking what? I'm not leaving this fucking room. You can clean her up with me here, or you can step out and I'll do it myself."

Abbey whimpers, sidestepping closer to Jols, and I chuckle.

"She can't help you, Charity. Best you learn that now."

"Stop calling m-me Charity." Abbey tries to snarl, but in the end, it sounds more like a fucking suggestion than a demand.

"Not gonna happen," I snicker, before gesturing to Jols and the bag by her feet. "We don't have all night. Are you doing this, or am I?"

Huffing, Jols sticks her middle finger up at me and bends to pick up the bag before placing it on the bench and rifling through it.

"Ab… Charity." Jols corrects herself. "Come over here and start rinsing the blood off your arms."

Abbey's dark gaze remains on me as she slowly makes her way to the sink beside Jols, her distrust obvious.

I give her a wink.

Her lips part in an aghast gasp, and when I don't look away, she turns her back to me, as if she can fucking hide from me.

For fuck's sake, why did I agree to this job?

Scrubbing my hand down my face, I lean back against the wall, my mind drifting to my little brother.

My dead little brother.

He was a piece of shit. Got in with the wrong fucking crowd. And yeah, I get that my crowd are no fucking saints, but we have morals and rules and there's typically a reason we do what we do. We honour the patch we wear, the fat boys we ride, and the hierarchy in our ranks.

My little brother joined a gang. A crew of thugs whose only purpose was to party and destroy lives. Even the innocent.

He got heavily into drugs, and I was waiting for the day the call would come to tell me he'd been killed. I never imagined his end would be because he was trying to save someone else. Someone innocent.

As fucked up as it sounds, I'd never been prouder of him than the day he died. Fuck, for the first time, I know he was proud of himself.

Which leads me to why I just busted into a stranger's home, in an area we don't rule over, to kidnap an abused girl in the dead of night.

A favour.

Yep. A fucking favour, and there's no other fucker roaming this earth I'd do this for, but for the innocent girl my dead brother died for.

"Is his name Ringo or Sarg?"

Abbey's hushed question draws my attention as she looks at Jols, and I notice that her trembling has increased as Jols helps to wash off the dried blood coating her arms and hands.

Fucking hell, if she shakes any more, she's gonna fucking hurt herself.

"I'm known as Ringo," I answer for Jols, stepping up behind Abbey and placing my hand on her shoulder. "Calm down, Angel."

Abbey stiffens under my touch, and my eyes meet Jols' briefly before she returns to her task.

"Are you cold or nervous?" I already know the answer. It's February. The height of our summer and the night is balmy, so there's no chill in the air to cause her tremors.

"I-I don't know."

Appreciating her honesty, I step up closer behind her, deliberately letting my breath fan over her ear.

"We aren't going to hurt you, Charity. Relax."

I'm surprised when she does. It's just a fraction, but noticeable enough. Clearly, she's scared of me, yet for some reason she responds to me. Maybe it's out of fear, but I don't think that's it.

"Lean back," I order, and only after a brief hesitation, she does, relaxing back against my chest as Jols works on patching up the cuts on her hands. "Close your eyes," I rasp quietly next to her ear and watch in the reflection of the mirror as she does as I ask.

Interesting.

She remains like that while Jols works. I ignore the weird glances Jols shoots my way, rather enjoying watching Abbey in the mirror.

Once Abbey's hands are patched up and her arms are clean, Jols gets to work on cleaning her face, wiping away the deep crimson to reveal soft creamy flesh underneath. I have the strangest urge to reach out and touch it, but thank fuck Jols speaks, shaking me out of whatever the fuck that was.

"We have to rinse your hair now, and then get you changed."

Stiffening under my hand, Abbey's lids fly open, her gaze wild like she's just woken from a dream.

Or a nightmare.

Was she really that relaxed, leaning against me, that it's like she's been startled awake?

Her big doe eyes meet mine in the mirror, and for a long drawn out beat we stare at each other. Her face is free from smears of blood now, her appearance more in line with the teenage girl I studied in the family portraits back in her home. That girl was a year or two younger though, and this one here, wears dark shadows under her eyes. She's experienced more heartache than the younger version of herself, and it's clear things have been rough for a while.

Her cheekbones are too prominent. There's no plumpness to her cheeks like there was in the portrait. Instead, they seem to hollow a little. Kind of like the life has been sucked out of her.

Heat washes over me as anger towards something I don't have a clear picture of ticks in my jaw.

Maybe I shouldn't have left her parents alive. Maybe I should have killed them and taken the three sisters.

Once again, it's Jols that breaks through the weird fucking thoughts in my head, and she starts giving Abbey directions, so I take a few steps back while they get started on rinsing out some of the blood from Abbey's blonde hair.

She's not trembling as much now. Hopefully, because she feels a little safer. I should probably remind her not to get too comfortable, that she has plenty to fear, but for some reason, I like that those deep brown eyes don't look at me with as much trepidation as they did ten minutes ago.

Once they've rinsed out most of the blood staining the ends of Abbey's blonde hair, Jols moves to the bag and pulls out some clothes.

"We need to get you changed."

Abbey's frantic gaze locks on mine in the mirror, and yeah, I could be a prick and fucking watch, but despite what I said to Jols when we first stepped foot in here, I decide to stop being a prick for a fucking minute.

"I'll step outside."

My grunted words are met with a relieved sigh from both women, so with one last warning glare at them, I leave them to it and step back out into the balmy night.

"She okay?" JD asks, and I nod.

"As okay as she can be in this situation."

"What's the plan? She coming back to the Western?" Murf asks, a dart hanging from his lips as he unzips his fly and flops his dick out.

"Seriously?" I snap and his bushy dark brows hitch as he steps closer to the shrub by the path.

"What?" is all he says as he starts pissing.

"Dude, there's a pisser right through that fucking door." JD points out but Murf just shrugs, continuing to piss.

"This bush was looking thirsty. I'm just trying to keep it alive."

"For fuck's sake," I grumble, tipping my head back to look at the stars above.

They are brighter out here in the country.

"What is the plan?" Stocky asks, just as curious about the blonde angel we stole earlier.

"She's coming with us, yes." I drop my gaze back down to earth to see JD staring at me.

"She coming in as a mouse or Doxy girl?"

Fuck. I've been avoiding this part.

The job we did tonight wasn't for the MC. It was for me. Well, not *me*, but a personal favour I owed, and when I got the call for help, I couldn't say no. It was a pure fluke we were even in the area, having just left an informal meet up with Griffin Marx at the Red Room in Redfield.

I didn't even run this personal job past Smitty, our President, and to make matters worse, I used a chick to help complete the job.

Like most MC's, we don't have female members, but Jols is Smitty's stepdaughter, and she's been a part of the club for years. It's not out of the ordinary for her to tag along for a casual catch up with fellow organised crimers in the state, and hell, she's even been a lookout and getaway driver a time or two, but since Stocky had shoulder surgery last month, I wasn't going to risk him inside Abbey's house, so I tasked him as the lookout, and Jols inside with the rest of us.

Since taking Abbey was not official club business, our Prez and Vice don't even know we are coming back with a guest. And guests aren't typically allowed, so it's not unusual that JD is asking what role she's going to be playing inside our club.

"Neither," I snap, answering JD's question.

Four sets of eyes land on me, brows high on their foreheads as JD, Murf, Stocky and Trunk look at me as if I've grown two fucking heads.

"For now, I'll keep her hidden in my room until I can find somewhere to relocate her."

"You're gonna break club rules for her?" JD snaps, anger contorting his face.

He looks fucking weird since he shaved his beard off after losing a bet last week. I've known the fucker for close to twelve years, and I've never seen that fucking baby face under the facial hair he's been rocking ever since he's been old enough to grow it.

"In case you've forgotten, we already did that tonight by taking her without approval. You all agreed you wanted to help. I didn't make any of you." I shrug, running a frustrated hand down my face.

"So you're gonna sneak her in and we're just supposed to keep our mouths shut?" Trunk asks, a deep frown furrowing his brow.

"Do as you please. I'm not ordering you to do anything. But we saved her tonight. You saw how she was being kept. You saw the state she was in. I'm not taking her to the Western to be fair fucking game."

"I won't expose her," JD announces unsurprisingly. Not just because he's my best mate, but because he has a soft spot for saving girls in need. He would have saved his sister if he could have. He'd never wish that fate on anyone. Even a stranger. "But what if someone stumbles upon her?" he asks.

"I'll deal with that if and when it happens," I state. "But just in case, from now on, only refer to her as Charity. Don't say her real name or mention where she's from. If anyone asks, tell them I found her and to speak to me."

"You got it," Murf agrees, his dick now tucked back in his pants as he draws in a lungful of smoke from his cigarette.

The others nod, but Trunk has more to say.

"If she's found, you know Prez will decide what to do with her. Making her a mouse would be kindest, but he's likely to declare her as a Doxy, or fuck, even a pass around."

A low growl rumbles in my chest. Not because Trunk is wrong, but because he's right.

"If Smitty finds out I have her there, then I'll claim her as mine."

A gasp coming from behind me has me gritting my teeth before I force a smirk and turn to see sweet little Charity balking at me with her mouth wide open and fear etched across her face.

Then, before I even realise what she's about to do, she runs.

5

ABBEY

Before I can second guess my reaction, I run.

"I'll claim her as mine."

His words echo through my head as I force my legs to move as fast as I can, bolting into the darkness towards the trees surrounding the rest stop. Shouts come from behind me, but the rushing torrent of my blood whooshing past my ears is almost deafening, making it impossible for me to know who's yelling.

Thanks to Jols' packing skills, I now have on clean clothes, which includes my old runners, making it easier for me to hurry over the twigs and scrub as the bushland engulfs me.

I have to get free.

I can't keep letting people do this to me.

The snap of twigs behind me sends a fearful whimper past my lips. Someone is chasing me. Someone is closing in.

My foot catches on a fallen branch, and I squeal as I start hurtling forward, the bed of the bush floor coming at me fast.

"Stop!" The growl is loud, a strong arm hooking around my chest just in time to save me from face planting, my trembling body crushed back against a broad chest.

"What the fuck did I say earlier?" Ringo sneers into my ear, his breath so close, so warm that I'm sure his lips must be a mere fraction away from my lobe. "I thought you understood my fucking meaning when I said you don't want to know what will happen if you try to run."

"P-Please. L-Let me g-go. Y-you don't w-want m-me. I'm not w-worth it," I beg, stuttering my way through the words as I sob.

"Someone thinks you're worth it. Someone thinks you are worth kidnapping in order to get you away from your family." Lowering my feet to the ground, Ringo releases me, only to spin me to face him.

It's dark out here, the only light is from the half moon above, and the lights from the toilet block at the rest stop filtering through the trees. His silhouette is huge. A looming presence in itself, but I can just make out one side of his face in this light, his stare hard and annoyed as he glares at me.

"Believe it or not, I am trying to protect you," he snarls, sounding pretty unhappy about being put out.

"I don't believe you." I force the words, determined to not let my fear continue to allow other people to control me. "You said you are going to claim me."

My words cause his lips to kick up in a smirk.

I think.

I can't be sure in this dim light.

"That's right, Charity. I did."

"How is that any different from what my parents were forcing on me?" I take a step back, shaking my head. "I refuse to marry you or anyone else."

"Who the fuck said I wanted to marry you?" he asks, his tone now sounding amused.

Great. Now he thinks this situation is funny.

"You said you were going to claim me as yours." I rebut, my tears no longer falling but my cheeks flaming in anger. Why is this guy such a… a… dick?

"I did. Yes. That's not a fucking marriage proposal. In my world, we don't need shit like that to own something."

"W-what? Own something?"

Did he really compare marriage to ownership?

I shouldn't be surprised. It's the way Daniel saw it, too.

"You find her, man?!" a male voice yells through the trees.

"Yeah. I fucking found her!" Ringo calls back, not taking his sight off me for a second.

"I'm not going to have sex with you," I blurt out, and this time, his smirk grows as he chuckles.

"I wasn't planning on fucking you, Charity." He takes a step closer, and when I go to step back, my calf hits the trunk of a tree behind me, showing me I have nowhere to go.

Shifting closer, he does that thing he keeps doing, pressing his finger under my chin and forcing my head back to stare up at him. "Unless, of course, you want me to fuck you?" He leans down closer, hovering his lips right before mine, and I hold my breath, my heart tripling its speed. "But if you want that, Angel, you'd better ask really fucking nice."

I swear I stop breathing. Is he going to kiss me? Why would he want to do that? Is he going to rape me?

Bile rises up, burning the back of my throat, and my heart starts pounding again before Ringo takes a step back, releasing my chin.

"I really am trying to protect you, Charity. How about you fucking let me?"

Let him? This is all so messed up. I can't make any sense of why I'm here with him.

"Who wanted you to kidnap me?" I ask, trying to force a level of confidence in my voice that will make me sound strong.

I fail.

"That is for me to know, and you to find out when I get the green light to tell you. Now, are you going to walk back to the van willingly, or do I have to carry you?"

"I'll walk," I snap quickly, shoving past him and hi-fiving myself, in my head of course, for being so ballsy.

His deep chuckle rumbles behind me as I head back towards the light of the rest stop, Ringo's heavy feet snapping twigs as we go.

When we emerge from the thick of trees, the four men and the one woman, Jols, turn to watch us return, and given the way they nod as we approach, I guess Ringo gave them a gesture or silent order from behind me, kicking them into action, all of them climbing into the vehicle.

When Ringo gestures for me to get in through the open door, I reluctantly step up into the van, only to find one seat left.

"You can come snuggle between us." One of the guys snickers from the very back seat which Ringo and I were on next to one of them earlier.

I stare back at him and the other big guy, their legs manspread so far apart there's no way I can fit between the two of them. Not that I want to, and I'm pretty sure the blond guy that just spoke knows that.

"Shut the fuck up, Murf. She's not sitting with anyone but me."

Ringo's words are part welcoming and part terrifying.

I don't want to sit between those men who resemble the big tatted up biker dudes I've only ever seen in movies. But I also don't want to sit with Ringo, because that would mean I have to sit on his lap again.

The sliding sound of the door closing draws my attention, right before Ringo folds himself into the last seat and reaches out to snatch my wrist, dragging me to him.

I try to snatch it back, but I'm weak against his strong hold, and before I can figure out a way to get myself out of this situation, he has me sideways on his lap, stretching the seatbelt around both of us before clicking it in.

"Relax, Charity. I won't bite," he mutters quietly so only I can hear, while Jols starts up the van, and music I don't know begins playing through the speakers before she drives us back onto the highway.

I'm so rigid on this rough man's lap, my spine stiff, and my hands tremble.

It could be worse, Abbey. You could be with Daniel.

The thought sends a shiver up my spine, and oddly, Ringo's arm supporting my back squeezes me a little tighter. He probably thinks my reaction is because of him. I want to tell him it's not, but why should I? This man kidnapped me. Yeah, he said he's trying to protect me, but what sort of saviour saves the damsel the way he did?

Oh, my goodness. I really am a damsel.

I hate the thought of that. It makes me feel weak, but as I cast my eyes over the huge men and kick-ass woman, all squeezed into this car, there's no use lying to myself.

I am weak.

Weak and pathetic, just like Daniel reminds me every time before he…

No. I can't bear to think about that. The things he's done to me over the last eighteen months are things I want to forget.

My lower lip wobbles as I fight off the memories. And then it wobbles some more when I think about what my parents had planned for the morning. How everything I've been working towards has been ripped away before I had the chance to escape.

But I have escaped.

The thought is jarring. Yes, I have escaped. Not the way I had planned. Being kidnapped by a gang of thugs isn't anywhere remotely what I had planned, but… I have escaped that fate my mother had planned for me, at least.

There will be no wedding tomorrow between me and Daniel. I bet he'll be relieved. He never actually wanted me, also forced into this situation by our parents. But he sure liked owning me. Forcing me to behave a certain way. Do what he wanted. He used the wedding as a threat to make me comply, knowing our parents were determined for us to marry, but were happy for us to wait until we finished University, unless Daniel or I misbehaved. Unless one of us went against their wishes or did anything else to shame them.

That was their condition. Comply, or be forced to marry sooner.

I'd nearly gotten away. I was so close, but then my parents found out my secret, and within minutes, the wedding was being brought forward to tomorrow.

"Charity?" Ringo's gruff whisper snaps my eyes to his. "Are you prone to seizures?"

His face is so close that I nearly bump my nose into his, so I shrink back to try and focus my eyes on his shadowed expression.

"What? No," I whisper back, and this time his large hand reaches up to my face.

Naturally, I flinch, which causes him to growl, and I want to ask him if he's part bear with the way he does that, but when he reaches forward again, he swipes his thumb across my cheek, and I remain stock still.

"You're trembling so much I wasn't sure if you were seizing. And you're crying again. Have I not made it clear that I'm not going to hurt you?"

I scoff loudly, but then slap my hand over my mouth, my eyes wide as the light filtering from the front dash illuminates how he lifts a single brow at me. And then he slowly smiles.

"See, I'm not so scary."

I scoff again, this time dropping my hand away, and he does that growly thing.

"Now that your seizing is slowing, do you want to tell me why you're crying again?"

"I'm not crying," I mutter, swiping at my wet cheeks.

"You *were* crying," he counters. "Do you want me to take you back home?"

His question stiffens my spine again, and I try to stare into his eyes to gauge his seriousness, but in this light, it's hard to tell.

"If I said yes, would you?"

He doesn't answer me.

"That's what I thought," I mutter.

"Wanna tell me about your parents? Why were you locked in your room?"

His question feels too personal, and I cross my arms over my chest and try to turn away from him, but I literally can't move any further with us both squeezed under the seatbelt.

"Come on, Charity. Help me understand what's going on."

"Call me Ell," I interrupt, relaxing back into his arm a little more. I may as well, since I have no idea how long we'll be driving for.

"Ell?" he asks, sounding confused.

"Yes. Short for Eloise. It's my middle name."

He chuckles. "Your name from now on is Charity."

"But I don't like Charity. It makes me sound like a charity case," I whine.

"Exactly." He nods, and I have the urge to punch him.

Do it, Abbey. What's he going to do? Hit you back?

Well, duh. Isn't that what men do?

"You think I'm a charity case?" I snap, trying to sit taller and not lean against his arm this time.

"Yes. Because you are a charity case," he says so matter-of-factly that the urge to punch him turns into wanting to bite his nose off.

And I would, but then there'd be blood and I'm not really good around other people's blood.

"I'm not a charity case," I hiss.

"Yes, you are."

"No, I'm not," I snap, louder than I should, and the man sitting next to us peers over, but I pretend to ignore him, as does Ringo.

"The definition of a charity case is someone that needs help," Ringo explains, sounding annoyed. "And you needed help. Still do. I'm here to help the person that needs help. The charity case. Therefore, your name is fitting, and this fucking weird conversation is over."

Something in me snaps. His words. His honesty. Everything that's happened in the last twenty-four hours comes to the forefront of my mind, and I see red.

"I hate you!" I scream, my fists flying out to swing punches at him, but his hands shield his face before they grip my wrists, and the van swerves on the road as the others around us mutter curses.

"You got the fucking wheel, Jols?" Ringo snaps as I try to pry my wrists free of his vice-like grip, releasing another scream as I start kicking my legs.

"STOP!"

His boom is loud in the confined space, and I instantly still, my head dropping as I cast my eyes to my lap.

"Fucking hell, woman. Was that really called for?"

"She clock you or what?" JD asks from the front seat while the others snicker.

Ringo doesn't answer them, instead leaning in close. "If you hit me again, Charity, I'll consider it foreplay."

I don't say anything to that. I can't. I just nod, my heart racing as I keep my eyes cast down, not interested in seeing his face or the smug look I bet he's wearing.

I want to go home.

The thought is weird, because I don't want to go home. Not to my parents. My little sister, yes, but everything else in that house can rot in hell as far as I'm concerned.

So really, I think I just want to be somewhere safe. Somewhere I don't have to look over my shoulder. Somewhere I can trust people.

Does such a place even exist?

I remain quiet for the next forty or so minutes, hating how as each minute passes, I start to relax a little more on Ringo's lap.

He seems unbothered by my presence on him as well, his head tipped back, his eyes closed, and even though I'm so exhausted, I stay awake, glancing around the van at each person, even though I can hardly see them.

When the car starts to slow, and Jols turns it off the highway onto a side road, I stiffen again, anxious for where we are going.

Is he taking me to someone that wants to hurt me the way Daniel did?

I don't really know many people, especially outside of Fox Pines, so I'm absolutely baffled as to who on earth wanted Ringo to steal me away.

We drive for a while more before turning onto a dirt road, and my heart starts to race again, fear chasing away any semblance of calm I had as a parked truck comes into view.

Sitting taller under me, Ringo peers through the front windscreen, and I notice the others shift in their seats, too, as if preparing to get out.

Are we here? Here being the destination.

When the car stops and Jols shuts off the engine, the others climb out while Ringo unclips our seatbelt, but doesn't move.

"Are you gonna try to run again, Charity?"

"If you keep calling me that, I will," I snide and he chuckles.

"Foreplay. I knew you had the hots for me."

Gasping at his audacity, I rear back, but this time, I don't fall off the seat. No, this time, hands grip me from behind and lift me out of the van with ease as Ringo follows.

"Get her bag and put her in the truck," Ringo orders JD, who just manhandled me out of the van.

"She riding with me and Stocky?" JD asks as he rounds the back of the van and takes my bag out.

"Nah, man. I'll ride with her and Stocky. You take my hog back to the Western. Stay with Jols."

Hog? Western?

I have no idea what Ringo is talking about, but JD beams as he moves back to us with my bag.

"You really gonna leave me in control of your ride?"

"Yes," Ringo hisses, stepping forward and pointing a stern finger in JD's face. "Don't put a fucking scratch on it or I'll feed your balls to Molly."

JD rears back. "Bit fucking harsh."

"What the fuck are you talking about? That's going easy on you. Fucking look after it," Ringo barks before gripping my upper arm and passing me to JD.

"You're such a fucking Grinch," JD whines, leading me away from the van, towards the truck.

"Who's Molly?" I ask JD, as we move away from Ringo's earshot.

"Molly's the fucking queen. You'll meet her soon enough."

I'm so confused. Hog. Queen. Molly. Western. Are they all people or…?

I consider asking JD, but then we are at the small truck and he's unlocking it, helping me up into the cabin and directing me to sit in the middle and as I do what he asked, clipping my seatbelt in place, JD's attention remains on whatever is going on behind the truck.

From up here in the cab, I see four motorcycles parked in front of the truck, just under some bushes partially hidden away.

Damn. Was my assumption correct? Are these guys bikers? Do we even have them here in Australia?

A bright light snags my attention to the driver's side mirror to see a ball of flames behind us, a gasp flying from my lips as I stiffen in panic. My gaze darts to JD, half expecting him to be readying himself to go and save someone, but when I realise he's too calm, leaning against the open door watching the fire engulf the van, I start to relax.

They are burning the van.

Shit. How many times have they done this? Everything they've done tonight seems to come so naturally to them that I have to assume they do this a lot.

After a minute, the others move to the motorcycles, and JD talks quietly with Ringo outside the truck before he, too, moves to the last motorcycle.

I jump in my seat when the driver's side door swings open abruptly, and one of the bearded men climb in, shooting me a wink.

"I'm Stocky."

His voice is deep, just like Ringo's, and they look a similar age. I have no idea what age that is, though. Old. Not my parents old, but still old all the same.

I don't say anything to him, wrapping my arms around my waist as the night air finally cools, sending prickles of goosebumps to scatter across my skin.

"Put this on."

Ringo's demand draws my attention to where he's climbing up into the truck on my other side. He's holding out a black hoodie, and when I just stare at it, he gives it a shake.

"Put it on, Charity."

I roll my eyes, but snatch it off him, unclipping my seatbelt to slip the hoodie on, before clipping myself back in.

Suddenly, I'm engulfed in Ringo's scent. I've smelt it numerous times since he entered my bedroom earlier tonight, but this time, it's wrapped around me, and I'm honestly disturbed by how relaxed it makes me.

A yawn escapes my lips as the truck starts up, and Ringo's eyes meet mine as he fastens his own seatbelt.

"We still have a bit of a drive. You should try to get some sleep."

Sleep. Hell, it sounds good in theory, but how will I ever sleep while these thugs are around? I can't take my eyes off them for a second. What if they try something? What if they…

Nope. Not going there.

As we drive off, following behind two of the motorcycles, while the other two follow behind us, I get a better view of the fire burning in the reflection in the side mirror, the van fully alight as it burns wildly.

I've heard about this on the news. The police said burning the cars used in crimes is common practise for organised crime in Australia.

Which begs the question.

"Am I the crime you committed? Is that why you're burning that van?"

My question doesn't even surprise Ringo, and he shoots me a sinister smirk, leaning in to bring us close again.

"What do you think?"

Shrugging, I lick my dry lips, suddenly feeling parched. "I don't know. That's why I'm asking."

Even in the dull light, I don't miss the way Ringo's eyes dart down to my lips, watching as I lick them again, and when he answers, his eyes linger there briefly before he locks his gaze with mine again.

"Kidnapping is a crime, Charity. How does it feel to know all of this effort has gone into stealing you away?"

My cheeks feel hotter than they should. I'm not entirely sure what's happening. Maybe I'm falling ill. I mean, it would be my luck.

I take a moment to try to compose myself and consider his words, and my brows hitch when I realise I'm kinda happy that there's been so much fuss. Something I'm not used to.

Ringo takes that moment to lean closer, his lips hovering just by my ear before he speaks.

"That's what I thought, Charity case."

6

ABBEY

At some point, I fall asleep, no longer able to keep my eyes open as the music in the truck reminds me of the music my best friend, Lexi, listens to. Well, I guess I'm not really her best friend anymore, not after what I did. She has a new best friend now, and me? Well, I only have me, and my littlest sister, Tahli. And hell, right now, I don't even have that.

When my lids flutter open again, my head is resting on Ringo's arm, so I sit up in a hurry, mortified I did that.

The prick just chuckles quietly next to me.

The truck has slowed. We are no longer on a highway but driving in what looks like a metro area of Melbourne. A little rush of excitement has me sitting taller, my eyes scanning everything I can see to find a sign that gives away our location.

I'm happy to be away from Timber Valley, where my hometown of Fox Pines is. I used to love the regional area, but now, the things that happened to me have poisoned any love I have for that place.

My family never ventured into the city much. My only taste was the few times a year I went and stayed with my Gran, but she got sick a few months back, and my mum was quick to shove her into an aged care facility.

I don't even think she's been to visit her since the day she moved her in.

I hate my mum. She was always hard on me growing up, but her true colours didn't show until I committed an irreversible sin in the eyes of the Lord.

"We're nearly there. Pull your hood up," Ringo orders, not even bothering to look at me, so I poke my tongue out at him.

"I like this one," Stocky says from my other side, a deep chuckle rumbling from his chest, and my eyes widen.

Did he just catch me sticking my tongue out like an immature brat?

Whoops.

I have no idea what's gotten into me. I would never normally act like this.

Maybe it's because I'm so tired. Or perhaps something in my head snapped tonight, and now I'm a little unhinged.

I smile inwardly. I'm barely unhinged.

What I think I'm feeling is a sense of freedom. Which is weird, right? Because I'm not free. I've been kidnapped by people who I'm pretty sure belong to one of those lawless motorcycle clubs given the motorbikes, and just their general demeanour.

Of course I could be stereotyping.

I have no idea who wanted me to be taken, so I could be trading one prison for another, but what if this prison isn't as bad?

And how crazy is that thought? Thinking like that is all sorts of messed up.

"Hood, Charity," Ringo barks, so I reluctantly do as he demands and pull the hood up over my head, covering my blonde hair that still has a tint of pink on the ends from my blood.

The truck starts slowing some more, and the motorcycles in front of us indicate right, and Stocky follows suit.

It's then that my eyes snag on what looks like an old motel, with a half shattered Best Western sign hanging haphazardly off a tall pole.

This must be the Western they were referring to.

"Get down." Ringo points to the floor between his legs, and I'm quite certain my brows shoot up into my hair.

"What?"

"I need you to get down here." Ringo points again to the floor between his legs. "Just until we get parked."

I'm about to ask why again when he reaches across me and unclips my seatbelt.

"Hurry up," he snaps, manoeuvring me even though I want to protest, and before I know it, I'm pushed to the truck floor between his legs.

Staring up at him in disbelief, I part my lips to ask him what the hell is going on, but he shakes his head, his eyes remaining on mine as he speaks.

"Keep quiet and don't fucking move. I'll tell you when it's safe."

Safe?

What?

Suddenly, any excitement I had flies away like a bat out of hell.

I'm still not safe.

Just that thought has me curling in on myself, trying to make myself as small as possible.

The tall doors and dash of the truck hide me huddled on the floor, and I draw the string of the hood tighter, trying to hide more of my face.

As the truck turns, I'm jostled a little as we drive over what must be a driveway entrance, and Ringo's legs close tighter around me to hold me in place.

This position is weird, which seems to be the theme of the night. But here I am, sitting on the floor between a stranger's legs, and as the streetlights illuminate the inside of the cabin, I force myself to keep my eyes on Ringo's, instead of venturing south, because oh my goodness, his junk is right there.

My cheeks flame at the thought, and I can't make sense of why. This man is a… man. Like an older guy. Who kidnapped me. And in my experience, a man's junk has been used as nothing but a weapon against me.

Holy shit. This isn't that Stockholm syndrome thing, is it?

The thought tugs at the corners of my lips, a smile threatening because I immediately think of One Direction and their song.

I love 1D.

As the truck slows to a stop, Ringo's legs press tighter around me before he speaks. "Head down. Don't let your face be seen."

My eyes widen, but when I hear the window of the truck sliding down on Stocky's side, I hurry to lower my head, curling in tight like a toddler that thinks that because I can't see them, then they can't see me.

"Hey man," a gruff voice comes from outside. "Everything run smoothly?"

"Yep. Got a lap dance off a Marx dancer earlier," Stocky says with pride in his tone.

"Really? Fuck, Ringo, when are you gonna let me come on one of your rides?" the outside voice asks, sounding younger than I first thought.

"When you finally get patched in," Ringo mutters, like he doesn't care for the conversation.

"Feel free to hurry that along." The outside voice laughs, before Stocky starts driving the truck again.

"You can look up, Angel," Ringo says quietly, and I glance up to see his face is closer as he leans down. "I have to sneak you in. I'll explain later, but once we are parked, I need you to do everything I tell you until I get you to my room. No questions. No trying to run. No bratty comebacks."

I nod, but squeak when we're jostled, and I realise we are going down an incline and rolling over a speed bump. Without thinking, I latch onto Ringo's leg, trying to keep myself in place.

Even though he sits tall again, Ringo's eyes stay focused on me. I should be more scared of him than I am, I know that, but for some reason I'm not.

Is it weird that despite everything that's happened that I feel safe with him?

As I clutch onto his leg, I notice in my peripheral vision that we are now in an underground garage, and after a short drive, the truck stops, and Stocky shuts off the engine.

It's then that I hear the loud rumble of the motorcycles, obviously from the others, as they park in the underground garage as well.

"You want us to shield?" Stocky asks, and I peer over Ringo's knee at him to see him looking at Ringo.

"Yeah. We need to get her to my room. Then you guys are done." Ringo nods, before his eyes shift back down to me.

"Got it. I'll word up the others," Stocky announces, and then he opens his door and slides out.

I have so many questions, but I keep them in, doing as he asked.

No questions.

No trying to run.

No bratty comebacks.

"This place isn't for sweet girls." His voice is raspy as he keeps it quiet. "I need to keep you hidden to keep you safe until I can work out a new plan. I want you to get out of the truck. Stay attached to me like your life depends on it. Keep your hood on and head down, and if we come across anyone, don't fucking look at them or say anything. Got it?"

Nodding, I keep my voice in, suddenly wanting to leave here.

This doesn't feel safe.

All I want is to feel safe.

The rap of knuckles on Ringo's window draws his attention, and he nods at whoever it is before opening the door.

"You need to let go of my leg now, Angel."

Why does he keep calling me Angel? I thought he decided my name to be Charity. While Angel isn't exactly a name I'd choose, it's a lot better than Charity.

Slowly, I release his leg, staring up at him to await my next instruction.

"Slide up here. Onto my lap."

Why is his voice so husky? He must be tired. I know my voice goes like that when I'm really tired.

Doing as he asks, I ease up between his legs, my cheeks flaring to life at how close I have to get to his private parts in order to squeeze out of the space. It didn't seem that hard to get into, but then again, he did kind of drag me. This time, he's letting me make my way out.

As I rise up, he helps me onto his lap, and gestures for me to climb down out of the cab, which I do to see the others waiting.

"Remember. She's not here. If she's found…" Ringo doesn't finish, but they all nod before he closes the truck door, having climbed out behind me. "Let's go."

Ringo sidles up beside me, wrapping his arms over my shoulders and squeezing me close, as the others fall in around me, making a barrier as we start to walk.

I do exactly as Ringo asked of me, keeping my head down, my eyes on my feet, having no idea of our surroundings, other than the old concrete path that turns into a paved red brick path.

We come to a door, and the others part so we can step forward, Ringo unlocking it with a key.

"Head inside. The bathroom is at the back of the suite if you need it. I'll be right in."

When he urges me to step inside, I do so reluctantly, my eyes scanning the space he calls a suite, which is nothing more than an oversize motel room with a bed, a small kitchenette, one of those old brown round tables and chairs, and a tattered old couch sitting in front of a TV.

It reminds me of something out of an eighties movie. Dark woods. Green carpet. Creamy coloured walls that were probably once whiter.

The door closes behind me, and I spin in panic, scared I'm being locked in, but notice it's still slightly ajar, and I can hear Ringo talking in hushed tones to the others outside it.

Calm down, Abbey. He said he's trying to protect you.

I want to trust him, but everyone I've trusted has betrayed me in some way, making it hard to accept that this stranger doesn't have an ulterior motive.

He wants to have sex with you.

Ugh. I tip my head back, annoyed with my inner voice. I'm so sick of feeling like this. Always in flight mode.

I'm just so exhausted.

There are noises coming from either side of this room. Muffled noises that resemble a loud TV, some music, and someone clearly having sex.

Oh, my… This is a seedy motel. I already know that, but is it like one of those motels that hookers work out of? I know the Foxy Pine Motel in my town is known for that. Not that I know for sure, but I've heard my mum talking with her church friends, signing petitions to get the place shut down.

She's such a prude. Why can't she just mind her own business and stop forcing her religious bullshit onto everyone else?

Needing to pee, I sigh and move to the rear of the suite, noting the wardrobes no longer have doors on them, making it look like a walk-through wardrobe as I round the corner and reach for the bathroom door.

I'm so preoccupied as my eyes latch onto the black leather vest hanging next to me with the words Southern Sadists MC on it that I don't hear what I'm walking in on until it's too late.

A gasp lodges in my throat, my eyes widening as I see a man, covered in tattoos, completely naked as he thrusts his… appendage into a naked woman's mouth as they stand in the bathtub shower.

"Oh, fuck yes. The more the merrier, sweetheart."

His voice is a strangled laugh as his face contorts painfully, his eyes raking over me while he grips the woman's head and forces her hard against his crotch, choking noises coming from the woman as she struggles to push free.

"No!" I squeak loudly as the man roars in pleasure, and I stumble back through the door, crashing into a chest behind me. "No!" I yell, my eyes wide as I see a gush of vomit spew from the woman's mouth around the man's… thing… and I gag.

With my arms flailing, I try to fight, try to push away the danger at my back.

"Fuck!" Ringo's voice meets my ears as he releases me with a shove to the side, dashing past me and into the bathroom. "Get the fuck out, Brody!"

"You brought a toy." The man, Brody, singsongs, laughing.

"You didn't have to hold my head, Brody." A woman's voice whines as she gasps for air. "I wouldn't have moved. I told you I could last."

As the woman's voice floats out to me, I cringe, sinking backwards into the wardrobe space with the hanging vest as Ringo comes charging back out to the mouth of the wardrobe area. His furious glare directed towards the motel room door.

"JD, get the fuck in here!"

"Bring the girl back in here, Ringo." The man's voice, who I assume is Brody, floats from the bathroom. "Stop being greedy. Sharing is caring, you moody fucker."

I squeak and shrink back even further when Ringo's looming presence stops in front of me as he points a stern finger into the bathroom.

"Don't mention her again. You didn't fucking see anyone."

"Who are we talking about?" the woman asks, and Ringo snarls.

"Darla, get dressed and get the fuck out."

"Ouch. Someone's grouchier than normal." She teases, before clearly addressing the man that choked her with his penis. "You owe me fifty bucks, Brody. I took your whole cock."

"You hurled on it." Brody counters and Ringo steps aside, backing into me as the naked woman stops in the bathroom doorway and glances back at the man.

"You didn't say I couldn't upchuck on your dick. You simply said I couldn't take the whole thing until you came. That horse cock was so far down my throat you tickled my stomach. I expect the cash by lunch tomorrow."

"Hurry the fuck up," Ringo snaps but stiffens as the woman sets her sights on him.

I can't see her face, but I can see the top of her black hair, wet and wavy.

"You know, if you'd just drop those iron walls, Ringo, and let us Doxies service you, you'd be less moody. I've learned this new trick with my fingers and tongue that'll rock your world."

"If I have to ask you one more fucking time to get out of my room, Darla, you'll find your arse out on the fucking street."

"Jesus, fine. I'm going." Darla huffs before greeting JD with a jiggle of her tits as he rounds the corner to take in the scene.

"Are you fucking serious, Brody?" JD roars, pushing past Ringo.

"Seriously satisfied. Yes." Brody chuckles, right before a loud skin on skin slap sounds. "Ouch. What was that for?"

"The fuck are you doing in our Sargeant's room?"

"Well, you changed the lock on your door, so I couldn't get in, and I still have the spare key for Ringo's—"

"Give it to me," Ringo barks, stepping into the bathroom with JD, and I'm tempted to peek around the corner, but I'm also tempted to bolt.

I can't do this. I can't do this.

As Ringo and JD yell at Brody, I slide down the back of the wardrobe wall to the floor, underneath the hanging vest, and pull my knees to my chest, burying my head.

Memories swarm me. Rough hands. Violent shoves. Feeling like I couldn't breathe. Like I was going to die.

"Take it like the slut you are."

"When you bleed, it only makes it better."

"This is what you were made for. Taking cock."

"Who is she?"

The voice, so much closer now, snaps my attention up, and through the blur of my tears, all I see is the long dangle of a trunk-like penis right at eye level.

I whimper and tuck my head back in, more memories coming at me and all I want is for this to be over.

No more. Please. No more.

A loud crash makes me jerk, but I keep my eyes closed as Ringo snarls.

"What did I fucking say? Don't look at her. Don't acknowledge her. Are you fucking deaf?" There's a slap and then Ringo continues. "You're still a fucking prospect, Brody. If you wanna get patched in anytime soon, you'll forget seeing her. Don't even fucking think about her."

"Don't fucking look at me, little brother," JD hisses. "You got yourself into this mess. Don't fucking think I'll save your arse just because we share blood."

"Fine. Whatever. I saw nothing," Brody concedes.

"Make sure you don't fucking forget. Now get the fuck out," Ringo booms, and I hear a grumble and footsteps before the door opens and closes again.

"Get your little brother under control. He's on his last fucking legs," Ringo snaps at JD, who sighs.

"Sorry man. I'll have another word with him tomorrow," JD mutters. "She going to be okay?"

"I don't know," Ringo says quietly. Softly.

I want to believe he means well, but how can I with what I just saw? Why would he bring me to a place like this?

I hear them move away, and when I know I'm alone, I let my walls down and the dam of emotions bursts free.

I cry.

I cry so hard, trying to stay quiet, my chest aching like a phantom hand is reaching inside and trying to pull my heart free.

What am I going to do? I can't stay here with these animals, but where am I going to go after what just happened at home?

I still can't believe my sister Maggie helped my parents drug me.

"Hey." The deep voice is close, and I hold my breath, willing my tears to dry up so I don't look so pathetic.

"I don't want to be here."

"I know."

"Please, just let me go." I beg into my hands, still not looking up at Ringo.

"I will."

That gets my attention, and I peek through my fingers to see Ringo sitting on the worn green carpet in front of me, his knees up and his arms resting on them.

"Y-you'll let me g-go?"

He nods. "Yes. When the time is right."

"But I can't stay here," I snap, dropping my hands to reveal my tear-stained cheeks. "I can't be around that. Around… abusers."

Ringo's shoulders rise as he sighs, his whiskey-coloured eyes almost looking sympathetic.

"I know it seemed like abuse, Charity. But Darla consented to what happened. And Brody, well, he's just an immature idiot. I'm sorry you had to see that."

I stare at him for a long moment, so many questions swirling through my head, and for the life of me, I don't know why I ask this question first.

"Is that what you do? To women, I mean."

Ringo's brows shoot high, and for a moment, the hardness that masks his face seems to slip away.

"I'm not into puke play, Charity. Or choking chicks on my cock."

My lip wobbles as memories of Daniel's fingers digging into my head painfully beat their way to the forefront of my mind.

"Talk to me, Angel. What's going on inside your head?"

I shake my head, not ever wanting to admit to the things that were done to me.

"Look, I know you don't know me, and I know I'm an arsehole, I'm not sure I'll ever be able to change that part about myself, but I can assure you, I will never hurt you, or stand by and let someone else do that. I'm sorry that I don't have somewhere nicer to take you, but I promise I'll get you out of here as soon as I can. Until then, can you try to trust that I'm doing everything I can to protect you?"

I shrug, because I can't find the words he wants to hear, but it doesn't make him angry.

"The bathroom is clean. I made Brody wash the shower down. How about you use the facilities and then try to get some sleep? You've been through a lot tonight. Some rest will help."

I nod, because sleep does sound good. I'm so damn exhausted, so when Ringo stands and moves back to give me space, I crawl out of the open wardrobe.

For now, I'll rest, but tomorrow, when I can think straight, I'll figure out a way to run. Ringo may want me to trust him, but experience tells me that the only person I can rely on is me.

7

RINGO

The fuck was I thinking bringing her here? Not that I have anywhere else to take her, but maybe I could have reached out to some contacts to take her. The Angel sisters would help. I know that for a fact, but my instructions were clear. Take her and keep her safe. Don't let anyone else near her.

Fuck.

FUCK!

The moment I saw her painted in her own blood, I knew she'd been through something, and I kinda thought it was all related to her parents and their religious bullshit, but her visceral reaction to seeing Brody and Darla made it clear.

Someone has hurt her sexually. Raped her maybe. Whatever it was, I now feel like a cunt for teasing her and being suggestive with her.

Fuck.

Dragging my hand through my hair, I glance at the old digital clock on the bedside table. It's just ticked past five in the morning. Abbey has been in the bathroom for over thirty minutes. I've tried to be patient and give her the space she needs, but what if… What if she's trying to hurt herself?

Remembering the way she was willing to stab herself with a shard of glass earlier, I storm to the bathroom and shove the door open, knowing there's no lock on it. And then I still.

Shit.

Slowly, quietly stepping into the room, I see the blonde of her hair in the bathtub and my heart sinks as I prepare to find her laying in a pool of her own blood.

Only, I don't.

I blink a few times to make sure my fucking exhausted eyes aren't fucking with me.

Nope. They aren't. Abbey has made a bed from the towels in the bottom of the bath, and she's asleep.

Shit. She obviously didn't feel safe coming out into the bedroom. Probably thinks I was going to force her to fuck me.

Jesus fucking Christ. I'm not the right guy for this job. I should have said no.

Should I leave her there? It can't be comfy.

Turning, I storm back into the main room, going to the bed on the side closest to the wall, and pull the covers back. I fluff the pillow a bit and momentarily realise that I've never shared this bed with anyone. I usually sleep in the middle, but this side doesn't normally get used.

Well, it does now.

Moving back into the bathroom, I gently remove the towel she has draped over her as a blanket, and reach down, scooping my hands under her, and lift her in my arms.

A small whimpery moan falls from her lips, even as she curls into my chest, and fuck, for a moment I just stand there in my shitty bathroom staring down at her.

She's still wearing my hoodie. It's fucking huge on her, thoroughly engulfing her, and I have to wonder if its size helps her feel safer somehow.

Without the fear etched across her face, she looks so sweet and innocent. How could anyone want to hurt her?

Fuck.

My head is all messed up right now. I need to get this situation with her sorted as quickly as possible and get my head back in the game.

Moving out into the main room, I lower Abbey to my bed, and as soon as she's on the mattress, she curls on her side, some mumbled incoherent words slipping past her lips before she snores faintly.

I grin.

I might have to give her shit about snoring tomorrow.

Maybe.

Moving through my room, I make sure the door is locked and slide the couch against it to stop any fuckers trying to get in, and then I peel off my jeans, leaving my boxers and tee on, and slip into my bed.

I should probably sleep on the shitty couch, or even the floor, but for some reason, I need to be close in case she needs me. And hopefully, if she wakes, she'll realise I'm not trying to do anything untoward to her.

As the rising sun filters in past the cheap thin curtains, I stare at this little blonde angel in my bed. She's only eighteen. Barely an adult, yet the things she's experienced make her seem so much older.

My sisters would like her. Alana would likely set out to corrupt any religious beliefs left in her, but I don't think that would be a bad thing.

My ma would adore her.

Shifting closer to her, I settle onto my pillow, fucking happy to finally be in bed after a long arse day. I thought it would be weird having Abbey in my bed, but her faint snores are comforting, and before I know it, my lids are falling shut.

When I wake later, I find myself pretty much in the same position, but this time, Abbey's big doe eyes are staring at me.

"You're being creepy," I rasp, my voice husky from sleep.

"I think it's creepy that I fell asleep in the bath and woke up in your bed."

I smirk at her comment.

"I think it's funny how you snore."

Her brows hitch. "I do not."

"Sorry to tell you this, Charity. But you do."

She narrows her eyes.

"How did I end up in this bed?"

I shrug one shoulder. "No idea. Weren't you sleeping in the bath?"

She rolls her eyes. "You're kinda annoying."

"And you kinda like me. Admit it. I'm not so bad. I didn't hurt you. Did I?"

Her playful expression falls, and her soft pink lips part. "Not yet."

Her words are barely a whisper, but they pack a punch.

I try not to take it personally. She's speaking from her experiences, and clearly, she hasn't been able to trust anyone. Or men, at least.

"I'm not sure exactly what happened to you. I have a fair idea, but I want you to know I'm sorry it happened. You don't deserve the bad things people have done to you."

Her eyes well with tears, and she tugs the blankets up higher, nearly covering her head, but she leaves her eyes free so she can keep a watch on me.

"Have you killed people before?"

Her question is a surprise and I consider lying, but she needs honesty. She deserves that, at least.

"Yes."

"How many?"

"Charity, I don't keep a head count." I admit, annoyed, and she shrugs under the blankets.

"More than ten?"

"Yes," I admit.

"More than twenty?"

"I don't know. Maybe."

She studies me for a long moment before she speaks again. "Do you enjoy it?"

"This is a weird morning conversation. I haven't even had my coffee yet."

"I feel like I would enjoy killing Daniel."

Her admission would sit me on my arse if I were standing. There's no way I ever expected those words to fall past her lips.

"You might, for a second," I agree quietly. "But then you'd realise what you did, and that you can never take it back. Living with it is the hard part."

She shakes her head. "The hard part is knowing he's still walking around, free to…" She trails off.

"Free to do what, Charity?"

This time, when she shakes her head, she covers it with the blanket and mumbles, "I'm tired."

"Then sleep."

"Okay," she whispers, like it's that easy to just fall asleep, so I'm shocked when I hear her breathing deepen a few minutes later.

Kidnapping Abbey was my job. Getting personally involved wasn't part of it, yet I want to get involved so fucking much. I want to hunt down this Daniel fucker and make him suffer through everything that he's done to her, and then I want to torture him some more until he's begging for death. And even then, I won't kill him. I'll keep him alive for years if I have to just to make sure he experiences everything one hundred times worse than what he's done to Abbey. Maybe then I'll finally kill him.

My MC isn't in the business of conducting hits. Mostly we are middlemen, and when there is a death involved, it's usually because someone tried to cross us, or another club is trying to encroach on our area, which typically turns into an all-out MC turf war. What I did by taking Abbey wasn't part of the MC, yet I involved some of our members and brought her here, risking getting caught with her.

Maybe I shouldn't have agreed to it, but I'm glad I did now. I'd hate to think what would have happened to her if we hadn't swooped in to save her from her crazy fucking parents.

When I can hear that Abbey is sleeping deeply again, I pull back the blankets so I can see her face. I feel like a fucking creep laying here watching her sleep. She's so young and innocent and I'm an old fucker that lost any hint of innocence when I was a few years younger than she is now.

Thump. Thump. Thump.

I jerk up in bed at the banging on my door, the move jolting Abbey awake to sit up in a gasp, and I lurch toward her, slapping my hand over her mouth.

Her chocolate eyes are wide, terror already trembling through her body, so I release her mouth and press my finger to her lips.

"Shhh, Angel. Stay quiet for me."

Thump. Thump. Thump.

"Wake up, Ringo. Let me the fuck in."

"Fuck," I hiss.

"Who's that?" Abbey whispers, clutching the blanket to her chest.

"My Prez," I whisper as I tug the blankets from her grip. "The President of the Southern Sadists MC. Smitty."

"Oh." She mouths as I stand from the bed and point towards the back corner.

"I need you to go into the bathroom and don't come out until I say you can."

Thank fuck, she nods, not feeling bratty enough to protest, and she hurries from the bed and into the bathroom.

"Get the fuck up!" Smitty yells, so I yell back.

"Hang the fuck on, you grumpy fuck!"

I hear him chuckle as I look around the space to see if there's anything out of place, and once I'm satisfied it looks just as boring as it did yesterday, I move the couch and throw open the door.

"The fuck, man. You're interrupting my beauty sleep."

Smitty chuckles, shoving past me as he strolls in and flops back to sit on my couch.

"No amount of sleep is going to help your ugly mug."

"Whatever." I chuckle as I move to the kitchenette and switch on my jug. "What was so fucking urgent you had to wake me?"

"I just wanted an update on your meeting with Griffin Marx."

As the electric jug does its thing, I get a clean mug and dump in a heaped teaspoon of coffee followed by two sugars.

"It wasn't a meeting, remember?" I turn to Smitty, leaning back against the counter. "Just a chat."

"Whatever. Tell me what he said."

"He's on board," I explain, crossing my arms over my chest. From this position, I can keep an eye on the bathroom door. "Says there's a property we can get cheap enough on the outer fringe of Fox Pines. The old Hill estate. Vixen's Lodge."

"Ain't that the place that burnt down after a girl was assaulted?" Smitty asks, looking lazy as fuck with his foot propped up on his opposite knee and one arm stretched out along the back of the couch.

"Yeah, it is. After the shit that happened there, they're finding it hard to sell. Should be big enough for what we need. We'd have to build everything ourselves. I think there's still a barn."

"Sounds fucking perfect. Did Griffin mention what Ewan's thoughts on it might be?"

"Griffin doesn't think his old man will be on board about sharing the trade in that area, but seems to think what he doesn't know won't hurt him."

"Fucking Griffin. Cheeky fucker." Smitty chuckles. "Let me handle Ewan Marx. What about Barrett Marx? Had any contact with him?"

As the jug starts to boil, I turn and flick it off before pouring the scalding water into my mug and then stir the coffee.

"I spoke with him last week. He's still overseas. Not planning on touching Aussie soil again for a while. I get the feeling there's some sort of family drama there," I admit, moving to my fridge and getting out the milk.

"He got some connections for us?" Smitty asks and I nod, pouring a dash of milk into my coffee.

"Yeah." I turn back, holding my steaming mug of coffee. "He's got some decent contacts in Peru that could help get some candy past our borders once they open up again."

"Fucking COVID," Smitty mutters and I nod.

"Yeah, fucking COVID."

Standing from the couch, Smitty checks himself out in my mirror over the counter, combing his fingers through the sides of his still damp hair. "Get me more info on the Fox Pines property."

"Already on it."

He grins at me, and I can tell by his expression that the business side of our chat is over.

"What the fuck happened over here last night when you got back?"

I cringe. "You heard that?"

"Everyone fucking heard it. What did Brody do?"

"Aside from breaking into my room? Caught him getting a puke blowy from Darla in my fucking bath." I shake my head as Smitty chuckles. "I swear that fucker has no boundaries or sense of personal space."

"Want me to bounce him?"

I'm tempted to say yes. If he were anyone else, he'd probably already be gone, but he's JD's little brother, and he's trying to get him under control. I know from experience how fucking hard that can be. I still wonder if Muz would be alive now if he'd joined the MC instead of the street gang he was in.

"Nah." I sigh. "Not yet. But one more strike and the fucker is out. We can't carry wayward fuckers that don't know how to respect orders."

"Deal," Smitty says, stepping forward and gripping my shoulder. "It's Spud's birthday. I'm sending some guys to the warehouse to get some grog and the Doxies are gonna cook up a storm. Try and show your face later."

I roll my eyes. He knows I always show my face, but it's with reluctance. I'm not a drinker or a substance user, so being around fuckers off their face is nothing short of annoying.

"You know I'll be there. I'm gonna take the day, though. I'm fucking exhausted."

Smitty frowns. "You crook?"

"Maybe. Dunno."

"Want me to send in some Doxy girls to clean up a bit in here?"

"Fuck no." I hiss. "After Darla's attitude last night, I want them to stay the fuck away from me and my room until further notice."

"Yeah. Okay. No problem." Smitty nods, moving to the door. "Would you get back in bed already? Your ugly face is offending me." He chuckles, throwing the door open again before slamming it shut behind him.

"Prick." I chuckle quietly to myself, finally taking a sip of my coffee.

Mmm. Fucking good shit.

I take a moment to sip more of it before putting the mug down and shifting the couch back to the door to create the barrier, and then locking the door for extra measure.

My eyes dart to the bathroom where Abbey is hiding. She probably heard all of that. Not that it matters, but if Smitty found out, I'd be in deep shit.

Fuck, what am I doing taking these risks?

Fuck it. Deciding to find out, I beeline for the bathroom to where Abbey is hiding.

8

RINGO

Stepping into the bathroom, I find the shower curtain drawn around the bath.

"You asleep?" I ask, moving to the toilet and flipping up the seat.

"Nope." Her voice comes from behind the curtain, and for some reason a grin tugs at my lips.

Since I have no jeans on, I easily slip my cock out from the top of my boxers and start taking a piss.

"Oh, my god. Are you really… weeing?"

Chuckling at her words, I release a slow moan to show her how fucking satisfying taking this piss is.

"Couldn't you wait until I was out of the room?"

"Nope," is all I say as I finish up before flushing the toilet and lowering the seat.

I don't know what it is, but for some fucking reason, I love tormenting her.

Should I do that after everything she's been through? Maybe not, but if she can't learn to laugh at least sometimes, then she's never gonna survive this.

I wash my hands quickly, and then turn to the closed curtain, fisting it and reefing it open. A small, surprised gasp flies past her lips, and fuck, when her caramel doe eyes meet mine, staring up at me from where she's huddled, my mind conjures images of her naked. My dick in her mouth as she stares up at me just the way she is now.

Fucking hell. What the fuck, Cam?

"You gonna stay in there?"

"Yes," she mutters and my lips spread wide in a grin.

"What if I need to take a dump? I highly recommend you clear out for that."

"Oh, my god!" she squeals, leaping up and scurrying from the bath and back out into the main room.

My chuckle follows her as I do, and I watch her hurry back to the bed where she sits on top of the blankets but clutches her pillow to her stomach over the top of my hoodie she's still wearing. She must be getting hot by now.

"You okay? Hungry?"

She shakes her head. "I feel a bit off."

"Eating might help. I'll send JD to grab us something," I mutter, moving to my phone and snatching it off the charger.

As I type out a message to my best mate, I keep my eyes on Abbey, noticing that she looks a little pale.

"You drink coffee?" I ask, and when she shakes her head, I send the message to JD and pocket my phone. "You got Rona?" I ask, referring to this fucking virus that's sweeping the world.

"I hope not." She frowns, keeping her gaze cast to her crossed legs.

I fucking hope not, too. So far, I've managed to dodge it. I can't afford to get sick. Not in my role in the club.

"So how much of my conversation with Smitty did you over-hear?" I ask, hoping the change of subject will take her mind off the possibility that she's picked up the virus.

"All of it," she admits, her doe eyes darting up to mine as if she's trying to gauge my reaction.

I smirk. "You have questions, don't you?"

"So many."

Her response has me throwing my head back, laughing, and I catch sight of a small smile pulling at the corner of her lips.

Fuck. I think that's the first time she's smiled. I want to see more of it.

"I'll let you ask three questions for now."

She rolls her eyes, but when I don't say anything, she sighs.

"Who's Griffin Marx?"

Moving to the bed, I sit on the end, in front of her but far enough away that it's not too close to make her uncomfortable.

"He's the new player in the Timber Valley district," I answer honestly.

"New player?" She frowns, her fingers fidgeting together in her lap, only just peeking out from the sleeve of my hoodie she's still wearing.

"Yeah. Organised crime. Drugs. Strippers. Whores. He's a new player in Timber Valley's crime scene."

"Oh."

"Next question." I urge and she thinks for a moment, her eyes travelling over my beard before her gaze meets mine.

"Is candy drugs?"

She really did hear everything.

"Yes. Next question."

She rolls her eyes again at my attempt to hurry this along.

"That property you were talking about in Fox Pines. Why do you want it?"

Now I wasn't expecting that question. I should probably lie. No one but me, JD, Spud, Tups and Smitty know about that. But fuck, I can't seem to lie to her, so instead, I keep it vague.

"We're looking for a new place to have more room to do bad shit."

"That's vague," she deadpans and fuck, I throw my head back, laughing again.

"Depends who you ask."

Nodding, somehow satisfied with that response, she falls quiet for a few beats, her eyes on her fingers again before she works up the courage to speak.

"If I tried to walk out the door, would you stop me?"

My brows shoot up. "Yes. And that's four questions."

"I'm a rule breaker." She shrugs. "Why would you stop me?"

Wow. It seems like a good sleep has given her a little more courage today. I don't hate it. In fact, I fucking love it. I wonder what a full night's sleep would do for her?

"I'd stop you because the people in this place are just like that kid from last night. If they find you, they'll think you're fair game."

Her face falls, leaving behind pure disappointment and a little fear again.

Fuck.

"Why did you bring me here, then?"

Sighing, I drag my hand over my face, tugging on my beard as I go. "I don't have anywhere else to take you. I could take you to my ma's but she's sick and I don't want the cops raiding her and my sisters if they get wind you're there." I shrug. "It's just for a few days. I'll figure out something else, so you don't have to be stuck with me and my kind."

"But… I could just go." She points to the door standing from the bed, pressing herself to the wall as she goes to move past me. "I really do appreciate what you've done to help me, but I can figure it out from here."

As she goes to slip past me, my hand darts out, slamming to the wall to block her path, and even though I hate the fearful gasp that flies from her lips, I don't fucking tone my pissy attitude down.

"How? You got money, as in cash? Using your bank card will just alert cops to your whereabouts."

I watch as she visibly gulps, her eyes trained on my hand where it's pressed to the wall, keeping her caged in.

"Charity? Answer me."

"No, I don't have any cash," she snaps, her angry glare turning to face me, and fuck her rosy cheeks are begging for me to touch them. Graze the backs of my fingers over the searing heat. "I was meant to go to Uni in two days. In the northeastern suburbs, to study nursing. I could go there," she shrugs, "and I don't know, hide away in my room in the share house and not answer the door if my parents show up."

"You know that won't work. You either go to the cops about them or you have to go into hiding until you can be sure they won't try to take you for whatever fucking god worshipping shit they are tied up in."

The telltale sign that she's about to cry starts with the wobble of her lower lip, and she ducks her head as the first tears burst free.

"I can't go to the police. I just want to be free."

"Fuck," I whisper, dropping my hand from the wall, only to take a risk and gently clasp her fingers, pulling her towards me a little. "I realise I'm no fucking superman. I'm a prick wound up in Melbourne's underworld. I'm the man you've always been warned about, but one thing you can be assured of is while you're here with me, I'll protect you. You have my word on that."

With her closer, I lift her chin, urging her to look at me, but unlike the other times I've done this, this time, she keeps her gaze cast down.

"What do you get out of it?" she asks, her voice so gentle it sounds fragile like a thin sheet of glass. "What do I have to do in exchange for your protection?"

"Fuck, Charity. This isn't transactional." I push under her chin again, trying to get her to look at me, and when she still refuses, I lose my patience. "Eyes on mine." And just like that, her doe eyes fuse with mine, her submissive nature unable to go against my demand. "It would be good if you stop trying to fucking run and swing punches at me."

"I only did that once," she whispers, and I smirk.

"Once too many, Angel."

"Why can't my name be Angel instead of Charity?" she asks, and for a long moment, I can do nothing but stare at her plump lips, wondering if she can handle the truth, because frankly, it's fucking with my head.

And then I admit the truth.

"Because Angel is just for me."

9

ABBEY

Ringo's chest rises and falls as he sleeps on top of the blankets next to me. I've barely spoken to him after he admitted that the term Angel is just for him, but I also haven't been able to stop watching him, and now that he's asleep, all I can do is study everything about him.

I've been feeling so sick, my tummy churning at times, and when JD dropped some food in earlier, I was only able to nibble on some of the fries. My throat feels a little scratchy too, and I'm worried that I may have finally picked up the virus sweeping the entire world. I'm hoping it's from the screaming and crying and all-round chaos of the last twenty-four hours, but I guess time will tell.

"Angel is just for me."

Damn, I can't get Ringo's words out of my head.

It's weird. I'm not sure how to take them. What did he mean by that? It kinda sounded like he meant it as an endearment, but that's ridiculous, right? He's like, old. Not as old as my parents, and honestly, I don't know exactly how old he is, but he has to be closer in age to them than me. He's such an… adult.

I inwardly shake my head at that thought.

I'm an adult. Or so the law says. I've been eighteen for basically half a year. So why do I feel like a child? A useless, helpless child dependent on other people to take care of me. I have no money. No job or job skills. No home. No nothing. I have no idea how to be an adult. No idea how to navigate the world, especially away from the rigid religious beliefs my parents have been inflicting on me for the last eighteen months. But what I do have is an opportunity to try and change all of that. I don't know how, but I do know I have to try.

I'm so confused. So scared, and I really do feel so unwell. And yet, the one thing I've felt for so long now has gone.

I don't feel so lonely anymore.

I'm not an idiot. I know I'm a prisoner here. Ringo won't let me go. He says things to make it seem like he has my best interests in mind, but I don't know this man, and the people he lives with here are extremely questionable.

Even so, it's the first time in a long time I don't feel so trapped. Which makes no sense since I'm barricaded in a cheap motel room with a beast of a man surrounded by an outlaw motorcycle club.

Maybe all the trauma has messed with my rational thinking?

Ringo's been asleep for a while now. I got up and walked around the small space before and even peeked through the curtains to see what all the noise was outside. It looks like there's a group of people playing cards in the centre of the courtyard and others are swimming in the pool that from here looks like it could use a good clean.

There are a few women walking around. They aren't wearing many clothes, and most of the men grope them as they pass by. I spotted that Brody guy kissing a different girl from last night. And another guy sitting at the table playing cards pulled one of the women's tops down and started sucking on her nipples.

That made me feel funny between my legs and reminded me of the time, before everything went wrong with Daniel, when he made me feel good. Then that thought made me feel nauseatingly sick, so I slipped back under the covers and have been watching Ringo ever since.

He's wearing a black t-shirt and a pair of shorts that he slipped on over his boxers earlier. He's so big. Muscley. He makes me feel so tiny, like he could snap me like a twig with his bare hands. He's such a… man. Not the teenage guy that Daniel and his friends are with barely any body hair and their skin free of any wear and tear.

Ringo is the opposite, his skin bronzed, black ink covering his arms and disappearing under his shirt. His dark hair is long and wavy, some strands curling at the ends. He wears a hair tie on his wrist, and I've noticed that sometimes he ties his hair back, but it must annoy him because it's back down soon after.

I've never stared at a man so closely before. I have this strange urge to reach out and run my fingers over the thick veins in his forearm. They are so prominent, barely hidden by the thin layer of hair that covers his arms.

I wonder if the hair is soft or coarse.

The loud shrill of a phone ringing makes me jump and Ringo's eyes snap open to catch me ogling him. My cheeks flare to life even as he smirks before rolling to his side to answer his phone.

"This better be good. I'm trying to sleep."

Ringo's voice is raspier than usual, probably from being asleep, and I can hear a male voice talking to him, but I can't make out what they are saying.

"Seriously?" Ringo snaps, before ending the call and swinging his legs over the side of the bed.

He doesn't say anything to me, so I stay put and watch him shift the couch away from the door and unlock it. A moment later, JD slips inside before locking it behind him.

"Turn on the TV," JD barks, not even waiting for Ringo to do it before he's got the remote in hand and doing it himself.

Sitting taller on the bed, I lean to the side to see around Ringo's broad shoulders as the voice of the Chief Medical Officer fills the room.

"Oh no. Not again," I say quietly, and Ringo peers back to me before stepping aside so I can see the screen properly.

"Fuck's sake," he mutters as the words, five-day snap lockdown spoken by the Chief Medical Officer cause us all to stiffen.

I thought we were out of the woods. I thought there would be no more lockdowns, but here we are again, watching our government enforce restrictions to stop us from leaving our homes.

Last year, when we first went into lockdown, and I had to start remote learning to finish off my final year of secondary school, I was terrified, but I quickly realised that although it meant I was trapped in the house with my family, it also meant, I wasn't exposed to Daniel. For a brief time, there was a shred of hope. Some peace.

By mid-year, though, my mum was concerned that Daniel and I being apart so much wasn't good, and Daniel's parents agreed, so they started breaking the rules.

When the August lockdown started, I was relieved. I looked forward to celebrating my eighteenth birthday at home, but Daniel came around. His family too, and we were forced to spend some time alone. Something about making sure our bond was maintained.

Bond? Seriously? What bond? There's only ever been torment.

Watching the screen now, and the headlines in bold red font run across the bottom, I feel fear, but also relief.

At least I'm not back in Fox Pines, married to Daniel, trapped with him alone.

The thought sends a tremor up my spine.

"We were meant to go on a run this weekend," JD mutters to Ringo as they both stand with their legs wide and arms crossed over their chests, watching the screen.

"Smitty will call church. Word Murf and Trunk up. We'll need a team to get supplies. And ask Jols to tee up the Doxies to go to the store and get enough food."

JD nods. "Will do. Anything else?"

"Remind the girls to go to different stores," Ringo orders. "I'll message Stoner and up the security at the warehouses."

A few more quiet words are shared between them, and I find myself a little fascinated by what they are talking about.

Church. Doxies. Security at the warehouses.

I'm not sure what I thought an outlaw motorcycle club would be like, but I didn't consider they'd run like a well-oiled machine.

Even the conversation I overheard while I huddled in Ringo's bathtub about buying property. It's all business.

"What are you gonna do with Charity while church is on?" JD's question has my ears pricking up, and I watch as they both glance over their shoulders at me.

"You go to church?" I ask, finding that hard to believe.

"What? Law breakers can't worship God?" Ringo smirks, lifting a brow as he turns fully to face me.

"The Devil maybe," I say with more confidence than I've had in days, and his smile grows, his white teeth making an appearance past his dark facial hair.

"You already know us so well."

Chuckling, JD shoots me a wink. "I like her, Sarg. I think she'll fit in here just fine."

Even though JD is laughing, Ringo shoots him a glare.

"What? It's true."

"She doesn't have to fit in here. She's not staying," Ringo snarls, and ouch, why do his words sting?

I don't particularly want to stay here, but I kind of hate being dismissed so easily.

"Exactly," I snap. "I'm not here to stay. In fact, I'm happy to leave right now."

I don't know why I say that, or why Ringo turns his glare to me, but JD still chuckles and excuses himself, leaving me and Ringo glaring at each other.

"Someone has more sass today."

I nod at Ringo's words. "I'm feeling more myself."

His eyes narrow. "You still look pale."

"Way to make a girl feel pretty."

He smirks. "Even pale, you still look pretty, Angel."

Oh.

My gaze darts down to the bed as my cheeks heat, and I know he's only trying to get a rise out of me. A reaction to stir me up. He doesn't actually think I'm attractive, yet here I am, acting like an inexperienced teenager that clings on to any compliment I can get.

Stop being pathetic, Abbey.

"This snap lockdown is going to extend your stay here. Sorry," he mutters, moving to the bathroom, and a moment later, I hear the shower turn on.

I glance at the door separating me from the outside world. It's locked, but Ringo didn't shift the couch back into place, and I could so easily sneak out while he's in the shower.

I should go. Try to run. Try to escape.

But where would I go?

I'm somewhere in metro Melbourne. Depending on which side of the city I'm in, I could be up to three hours drive away from Timber Valley. I have no friends. My Gran used to live near the city, but even her house had been sold as soon as Mum moved her into the home.

What do people like me do? Go to shelters? Do they still have them during lockdown? They'd have to, right?

I wouldn't even know where a shelter is. I have no idea where I am. I don't have a phone, my ID, or any bank cards to get cash out. Not that I would. Ringo was right about that. My parents would have gone to the police by now, and if I used my card to get money out, the police would know.

Standing from the bed, I walk towards the door, but I don't get too close. I just stare at it, wondering what would happen if I open it and step out.

"You planning your getaway?"

I spin, my hand pressing to my chest as I gasp, only to find Ringo a few feet away, beads of water trickling down his bare chest, with the only thing covering him, a grey towel.

I shake my head quickly, my eyes glued to his bronzed skin, travelling over his broad chest, his pecks, and his nipples. His tattoos continue down his chest onto his abdomen, and there's a thin trail of dark hair leading from his navel and disappearing under the towel.

"Eyes up," he demands, and I snap my gaze to his. "Out that door is the rest of my MC. If they see you here, in their home, they will assume you are here for a reason." He leans in closer. "To party. With them. Do you need me to explain how they like to party?"

"No." I shake my head, remembering what I saw earlier.

"So you understand why stepping out that door is not in your best interest right now?"

"Yes. I wasn't going to, I was just…" I trail off.

What was I doing? Was I considering leaving? Yes. Would I have tried? No. Because I'm too scared. Too weak.

"I have to go out for a bit. Can I trust that you will stay put, or do I have to arrange a babysitter for you?"

"I'll stay put," I admit, eyeing his phone on the counter behind him. "Can I use your phone?"

His brows hitch. "Who are you going to call? Your mum?"

His teasing words sting a bit and I shoot him a glare.

"Yeah sure. I'm going to call her and tell her how well my kidnappers are treating me."

Ringo smirks. "Best behaved kidnappers you'll ever come across."

I roll my eyes. "I'm bored. I was hoping to listen to some music or play a game."

He stares at me for a long moment, right before he grips the top of his towel and pulls it free.

Spinning, a squeal flies from my lips as I cover my eyes with my hand, hearing him chuckle behind me.

"Not so boring now, is it?"

"Oh, my god! I don't want to see your penis!" I squawk and he roars with laughter.

"Penis? Angel, this thing isn't a penis. It's a cock." I feel him step closer behind me, and a moment later his words come right at my ear. "And when it's hard, it's a beast."

Lurching to the side, I squeal again and bolt for the bed, throwing myself down, face first, so I don't risk seeing said beast.

When the bed dips beside me, I rear up and scurry to the head of the bed, pressing myself up hard against the cane frame, my eyes wide with fear as I prepare for him to finally take payment for kidnapping me.

"Relax, Charity. I'm only messing with you." He leans down, tugging on some socks. He has a pair of boxers on. When the hell did he put them on?

"Why would you do that?" I ask, timidly.

Sitting tall, he glances at me, his face more serious than moments ago. "I get that what you've been exposed to was traumatic, but since you're going to be here for the next week, and I know you'll probably sneak a peek out the window, you'll likely see some crazy shit fit for the filthiest porn sites that are legal to visit. I'll make sure you're not threatened in any way, but you'll need a thick skin and to know you'll likely see a whole lot of dick through that window. Especially later tonight, when Spud's birthday celebrations get a little crazy."

"I won't peek."

He smirks. "You will. Eventually. The things you'll hear will pique your curiosity. But I want you to know that the women here consent to everything. Sometimes things can get a little hardcore. Rough even. But it's all consensual, and no one is really getting hurt."

"Like what happened in your bathroom?" I whisper, before worrying my lip.

"Yes. Just like that." He reaches to the floor and picks up his jeans and then proceeds to feed his feet into the legs. "But you're safe with me. Okay?"

My brows shoot up. "Until you want to flash your penis at me again."

Standing to pull his jeans up, he grins and shoots me a wink. "I had my boxers on under the towel. And for the love of anything, stop calling it a penis."

"But that's what it is."

He slips his t-shirt on. This one is light grey. "Technically, yes, but *that* word is not sexy."

"Newsflash. I'm not trying to be sexy," I counter and his eyes lift to mine, a sinister look flashing in his eyes. He looks like he wants to say something, but whatever it is, he keeps it to himself, instead sitting back on the bed to pull on his boots.

"I have to go to church. I'll be about an hour. Can I trust that you won't try to run?" He moves around the corner to the wardrobe and reappears a moment later as he shucks on the vest that was hanging there.

"When will you tell me who wanted you to kidnap me?" I ask instead of answering him, and his eyes narrow before he sighs.

"I'm waiting on a call. As soon as I get it, I'll have more information for you."

I can't tell if he's being honest or stalling, which means I have no other choice but to trust him.

"What if someone tries to get in here?" I ask, genuinely concerned.

"They won't. Everyone will be busy getting ready for tonight and the lockdown. But if you really are concerned, use that phone," he points to the old, corded phone sitting on his bedside table, "dial six and let it ring once and hang up. I'll hear that and come back straight away."

"Oh. Okay."

"And before you go thinking you can use it to call someone on the outside, think again. The old phones only work internally."

My heart sinks because I was thinking maybe I could call someone. An old friend that may or may not take my call.

Ringo rounds off a few more rules before he leaves. Don't open the door for anyone. Don't make it obvious if I try to peer out the window. Don't make too much noise to draw attention. And of course, once again, don't run or I won't like what happens.

He then lets me know that even if I do leave the room, I won't get past the security on the gates, which settles any more ideas I have of trying to run as he leaves for whatever the hell church is.

Finally, alone in the room, I let my curiosity get the better of me and snoop through the few drawers in the room. I find his boxer and sock drawer over by the hanging clothes. I snoop through the pockets of his jeans and hoodies, but there's not much else.

Doesn't he have stuff?

There's not a single thing in this room that looks personal. No picture frames with friends or family. No trophies. No posters. It just looks like an old shitty motel room used by a guest.

Glancing around the space, boredom creeps in, so I decide to clean myself, taking a quick shower, struggling a little with the dressing on my hand before redressing in some more of the clothes Jols packed for me. Another pair of gym pants, a white tee, and I redon Ringo's hoodie despite how warm it is in here.

Rifling through my bag, I check to see if there's anything Jols packed that can keep me occupied, like a book, or even some nail polish, but I don't find anything but my clothes.

Ugh.

I stare at myself in the mirror for a bit. Ringo was right. I look pale. Sickly. It's fitting with how I feel, although my boredom has given me restless energy that I don't know how to deal with.

Leaning closer to the mirror, I study the darkness sitting beneath my eyes. It's not new. I've had it for months. Lack of sleep most likely the cause. That and my crippling anxiety making it hard to stomach food.

Glancing down, I pinch the fabric of my leggings, pulling it easily because they're no longer skintight on my bony legs. I'm sure I look like I have an eating disorder, and I guess I do if you consider how little I can manage to stomach, but it's not on purpose. It's from the fear I carry. It's made me so sick over the last year.

Sighing, I use the comb I found with my clothes, and detangle my hair, parting it down the middle and braiding my hair on one side. After securing the hair tie I found in my bag, I braid the other, but since I don't have another hair tie, I go hunting for Ringo's. He's always got one on his wrist. He'd have more around here somewhere, surely.

The bathroom cupboards come up empty, so I move to the bedroom and glance around.

Ah. The bedside table.

Moving to it, with the end of my braid pinched between two fingers, I pull open the drawer and immediately spot a handful of hair ties.

"Yes," I whisper, smiling over the small win, and secure my second braid.

I'm about to close the drawer when the book underneath the hair ties catches my eye.

The Forgotten 500.

Curious, I brush the hair ties to the side and pick it up, flipping it over to read the blurb to find it's about World War II.

Huh. I never considered Ringo would be into reading war history.

I'm about to put the book back when I freeze with the book mid-air, my eyes locking onto a large black cylinder that reminds me of a torch. Only the end has a fleshy coloured tip.

Slowly, I reach down and grip it, lifting it out to examine it, before a strangled choke comes from my throat.

"Oh, my…" I whisper, gazing at the very clear looking vagina.

Is this?

I'm about to throw it down, but then, against my better judgement, my curiosity gets the better of me and I press my finger to the surface.

Oh wow. It's soft. Almost like silky skin, and I find myself gliding my fingertip over it.

It kind of feels real.

Does Ringo use this? Does he put his penis in there?

Needing to know if it has a hole to slide something into, I use my thumb to part the… uh… labia, and then I push my finger in.

Oh… Flutters of arousal grow between my legs, and I'm shocked to feel it for the second time in the last twenty-four hours since it's been so long that I've felt anything remotely arousing after Daniel started treating me like a disposable whore.

As I ease my finger out and then slide it back in, I picture Ringo's face. His broad chest and those rippling abs. I try to wonder what his face would look like as he slides himself inside this… thing.

Would his face contort?

Would he moan?

Does he fill it full of his—

"A-hem."

The sound of a throat clearing behind me has me stiffening, and I pray to a god that has done nothing but let me down, that my ears are playing tricks on me, and Ringo isn't standing right behind me as I hold this sex toy with my finger inserted deep inside it.

10

RINGO

"**W**hat are you doing, Angel?"

Not in a million fucking years would I have thought this sight is what I'd walk in on.

I fucking debated for a split second, not letting her know I was there watching her just to see what she'd do next. I mean, slipping her delicate finger inside my sucking fleshlight pussy had me instantly hard, a feat no other woman has been successful in doing for three fucking years now.

No one but an eighteen-year-old emotionally wounded blonde angel that I kidnapped.

Well, fuck me.

If this isn't a fucking dilemma.

That innocent little gasp she does so often flies from her lips as she spins, holding my fuck toy, her caramel eyes wide with fear as she starts shaking her head.

"I… I… Um…"

I chuckle.

"You want me to show you how it works?"

Her brows shoot high.

"What?" she squeaks, and I step closer, backing her up until her legs hit the bed and she falls back on her arse.

"It has a few functions," I say, taking it from her trembling grip. "I can simply fuck it myself, or use the vibrating mode to give me some extra sensations." I press the button on the end, and it comes to life, vibrating in my hand.

I watch Abbey closely, the way she still trembles but also the way her eyes dart from my face to the toy in my hand, taking it all in.

"Or I can use the suction function," I tell her, pressing the buttons to change the mode, and fuck me. Her cheeks flare redder than before as she squirms.

Is she aroused?

Fuck. My cock jerks at the possibility.

I shouldn't fucking do this. She's barely an adult. She's been through so much, yet for some reason, I don't think her trembles are from fearing me entirely. I think she fears the way she's feeling. And fuck if I can turn my back on her.

I hardly know this girl, and I swear she's fucking bewitched me.

Leaning closer, I use my finger and slowly insert it in between the folds of my toy, letting her hear how it sucks my digit. "Do you want to feel it?"

Her doe eyes dart back to mine, her lips parting to answer, but nothing comes out.

"You don't have to," I tell her and her brows furrow.

"Don't I?"

"Fuck, no." I pull it away from her, and her eyes drop to her lap. "Eyes up," I tell her, and just like the other times, her eyes meet mine.

I wonder if she knows she's a submissive? Or even if she'd want to be. I'm sure she's that way from her upbringing. Maybe she'd want to rebel against it if I point that out. So, like a dick, I don't because I like her this way.

"Why would you think you have to?"

Sucking her bottom lip into her mouth, her teeth momentarily make an appearance as she bites down before she answers with a shrug. "I'm still waiting for the other ball to drop, I guess. The ultimatum. The moment you demand payment for taking me away from my family."

I flick the device off and raise a brow at her. "I've already told you there's no exchange required. Can't I have kidnapped you out of the goodness of my heart?"

A small smirk tugs at her lips, pulling one side up higher.

"There are so many things wrong with that sentence."

I grin back. "There are, you're right. But even though I kidnapped you, I didn't do it to do anything sinister. Only to remove you from an awful situation, so when I ask you if you want to feel what it's like," I shake my pocket pussy before her eyes, "I'm genuinely just giving you an option. It doesn't mean by doing that I want more from you. That I expect you to spread your legs for me, Angel."

This time, as she studies me, she chews the inside of her mouth. "But you're... hard."

My brows shoot high, and I want to curse my hard cock for being so fucking prominent.

"I am, yes. I walked into my room to see a beautiful angel poking at the thing I fuck on the daily. I can't control my body's reaction any more than you can control the flush on your cheeks." I grin as her cheeks flush hotter, and she ducks her head. "So, I'll ask you again. Do you want to feel it?"

Flicking the switch on the device again, the sucking sound fills the space, and I study Abbey's downcast head as her faint words meet my ears.

"Is it weird that I want to?"

I have to admit, I was sure she was going to decline even if she did want to.

"Curiosity about anything, whether it's sexual or not, is not weird. So if you want to see what the suction feels like, then that's okay. If you don't want to find out, then that's okay, too."

Her caramel eyes dart up, and for a long beat, she keeps her gaze locked on mine, her stare no longer so fearful as she studies me, and then, as if she hasn't already knocked me on my arse numerous times already, she holds her finger up.

"I want to feel what it's like."

Fuuuuck. My cock is as hard as stone, fucking aching to sink into a tight hot hole, but this isn't about me. I can fix that later. Right now, all I want to do is make sure she gets what she wants.

Biting back my smirk, I point the silicone pussy in her direction. "Just slip it in," I say, my fucking voice huskier than normal, giving away how this whole fucking scenario is affecting me.

With her eye on the prize, Abbey presses the tip of her index finger to the lips of my toy, and then slowly sinks it in.

"Oh!" she yelps, her lips spreading wide in a smile as her eyes dart back to mine. "It's stronger than I thought it would be."

"It's my favourite setting," I admit, and her cheeks flush again.

Biting her lip, her brown pools remain locked with mine even as her finger remains embedded in my masturbation device before she speaks.

"You prefer the sucking?" she asks, but then gasps and pulls her finger free, slapping her other hand over her mouth. "Please ignore that question. I've invaded your privacy. I'm sorry. But in my defence, I was looking for a hair tie, and well I found one, and then spotted the war book and was reading the back and that's when I saw your… toy. See, I told you I was bored."

Huh. She's a rambler.

Turning off my toy and dropping it back into the open drawer, I lower to my haunches in front of her, wanting to be eye to eye.

"I already told you it was my favourite setting. So yeah, the sucking action is my preferred mode because it gets me over the line pretty fucking fast. And your questions are fine. I prefer questions rather than beating around the bush." I hook her index finger with mine, watching how she glances down at where we are joined. "As for the boredom, I'll try to figure something out." Then I tug on her index finger, gaining her eyes again. "You probably wanna go wash your hands since you put your finger where my cock usually goes, and I'm not that good at washing things thoroughly."

"Oh, my god!" she squeaks, flying up from the bed, nearly knocking me backwards as she runs for the bathroom, and I throw my head back, laughing.

Fucking hell. I never in a million years expected this conversation. And fuck me if I don't enjoy her curiosity and the fact she actually isn't that scared of asking the questions. It gives me hope that she does actually trust me, that her fear is really just from her past trauma and something she'll be able to get a better grip on over time.

"Do you have any hand sanitiser?" She calls from the bathroom, and I laugh even more, moving to join her.

Those doe eyes widen as they lock with mine in the reflection of the bathroom mirror, and I shoot her a wink before leaning down and opening the drawer in the vanity, pointing to the hand sanitiser.

"This isn't funny," she grumbles.

"Isn't it?"

Huffing, she makes use of the sanitiser, shooting daggers at me.

"Did you pray for forgiveness in church?" she sneers as I lean back against the tiled wall, crossing my arms over my chest.

"Church is what we call a members' meeting."

She frowns. "That makes no sense. Why not call it a meeting?"

"Well, I guess because the meeting itself happens in a place we declare as a sacred space. Only members can enter. No women."

She rolls her eyes. "So you kidnapped me and brought me to a man's club? That's great."

"Someone's a bit moody. Are you sexually frustrated, Angel?"

She glares at me and huffs. "No. I'm sick of feeling unsafe."

That wipes my smirk right the fuck off my face.

Fuck.

Stepping forward, I turn her to face me, my eyes locking onto hers as I try my fucking best to make sure she can see how serious I am now.

"Do you feel unsafe with me? Honestly?" I ask. "Tell me the truth?"

She thinks over my question for a few beats before she shakes her head. "I mostly feel safe with you."

"But there's still a part of you that doesn't?"

She shrugs. "You're still a man. Someone I hardly know. I'd be a fool to trust you completely."

I smile at that. "Very true."

"But despite the fact I feel somewhat safe with you, I don't feel safe in this place."

I get it, because she fucking shouldn't. The men here aren't about hurting women, but they are still men, and sometimes, they get carried away.

The Doxy girls can handle it, but Abbey isn't, nor will she ever, be a Doxy girl. She's the kind of girl the boy next door pines over, spends years trying to win the affections of, and one day gets down on one knee to ask her to be his wife.

It pisses me off that life has been stolen from her by her fucking parents.

"You're safe in this room."

"But not outside it?" she asks, and I shrug.

"It's not that you aren't safe, it's just that in my world, you'll likely be mistaken for something you're not, and I don't want you to have to deal with that, which is why I keep reminding you to stay in the room."

Brushing past me, she leaves the bathroom, and I follow behind slowly, watching her pace the small space.

"I'm bored. I'm not trying to be ungrateful, but you don't even have Pay TV or PicFlix. What am I meant to do?"

This must feel like a prison to her. A safer one than the one I stole her from, but a prison all the same.

"If I give you my phone, can I trust you won't make a call? Because you know I can go online and check."

My question stills her feet, her body still engulfed in my hoodie despite the warm afternoon.

"Of course I wouldn't. I won't message anyone or anything, but do you have an account I can buy an eBook from? I can read on your phone. That's what I really need right now."

I actually believe she won't do the wrong thing. If anything, breaking the rules is not in her nature. It's the way she's been raised, and my guess is the few times she has broken the rules, she's paid the consequences dearly.

"You don't want to read my World War II book?"

Her lips thin in a yeah-nah smile as she shakes her head. "I think I'd rather stare at the wall."

I can't hide my smirk. "You enjoy reading?"

She nods. "It's been the only thing that's held me together over the last couple of years."

Fuck. Pain slices at the centre of my chest at her words, the ache in her tone so brutal that I know any thoughts I've had of what she may have been subjected to probably don't even touch the surface of the harsh truth.

"I'm expecting a call. A very fucking important call. One I will need to return within minutes of receiving. If I place someone outside my door until I'm back, can I trust that you will subtly let them know when the call comes in, so they can get me, or bring my phone to me? You'll have to let them know without letting anyone see you."

She nods quickly. "Of course."

I should just go and tell Smitty what I did last night and be done with it. Tell him I did a favour that involved our club members and that I smuggled an unapproved guest in without his knowledge.

Will he deck me? Most likely, but that doesn't fucking worry me. What does worry me is what he'll decide to do with Abbey. As the club President, he has the power to kick her out on the street and demand I stay away. He also has the power to declare her a mouse or Doxy, in which case, Abbey's worst fears will come true.

Why the fuck didn't I think over the consequences before I said yes to this job?

Because you'd do anything in memory of your dead brother, you moron.

Fuck.

"Don't fucking make me regret this, Angel." I point sternly at her, and she shakes her head, her eyes wide with what looks like a glimmer of happiness.

I pass her my phone, and help her navigate to the online store, telling her to order whatever digital books she likes, and while she does that, I hunt down Brody, finding him sitting on the edge of the pool getting a fucking blowjob off Georgia.

"Hey shitface, get your dick outta her mouth and come with me," I snap, but Brody stays put, tipping his head back to look up at me as he fists Georgia's hair and starts thrusting into her throat.

"Give. Me. One. Sec…ahhhhhh."

I want to punch the fucker for making me wait, but his orgasm is quick, and he's shoving Georgia away as she spits out the mouthful of jizz she just received.

"Jesus, Brody. You said you'd pull out. You know I don't drink spunk." Georgia splutters, shifting back in the murky pool water to get away from Brody, so I pull the prick up by the nape of his shirt, dragging him away from the pool as he tries to tuck his dick back in.

"Hey, take it easy, man."

"You want to earn your way in faster?" I snap, shoving him hard, nearly making him fall on his face as we reach the centre of the courtyard that the Doxy girls are decorating for Spud's birthday.

"Fuck yeah. What do I gotta do?" he says with excitement, not even acknowledging the fact I shoved him.

"You know that thing that you didn't see last night?"

Brody stops, shooting me a toothy smile as he waggles his brows. "Yeah?"

"I want you to guard my fucking door from the fucking outside and make sure no one goes in or out except for me. And when she asks you to get me for an important phone call I'm expecting, you will come and get me straight a-fucking-way."

"Yeah. Yeah. I can do that." Brody nods.

"You can't leave your post unless you are coming to get me. Are you sure you understand what the fuck I'm asking of you?" I hiss, curling my lip as I loom over him.

"Yeah, I get it. Stay outside your door. Don't let anyone in or out and come and get you when she tells me to."

"You know what will happen if you fuck this up?"

"I don't get fast tracked in?" he asks, sounding really fucking sure.

"Actually, it'll mean you never get in. It'll mean that before the night has ended, you'll be out on the street, on your own, never permitted to step foot inside these walls again."

He gulps. "Never?"

I lean forward, coming nose to nose with him. "Fucking nev-er."

"I won't let you down." He assures me, so I point to my fucking door.

"Aside from me, no one in or out. Time starts now."

He gives me a mocking salute and takes up his post just out-side my door as I ignore him and re-enter to go over the rules one more fucking time with my angel.

11

ABBEY

Temptation is evil. I've been taught that all my life, and I know from experience how true it can be, yet I war with myself over the desire to go against Ringo's wishes and make a call on his phone. How easy it would be to just dial the number I've had memorised for years. To make the call and speak to the girl who is my very best friend, even if I'm not hers.

Instead, I lay on the bed, trying to block out the thumping music from outside the door and window and pretend I don't hear all the giggling and squealing women who sound like they are having the time of their lives.

With my gaze cast to the screen of the phone, I reread the same sentence in the eBook I read only moments ago, and finally make it to the next paragraph before chanting from outside distracts me.

"Ugh," I sneer, dropping the phone to the bed and rolling off to hurry over to the window.

I can't help myself. I want to see what's going on.

Slowly, and gently, I pull back the thin scrap of fabric they call a curtain, just enough to peer out to the party happening beyond.

There has to be close to fifty people out there. The men outnumber the women, but I don't think that matters by the way they all seem to share the females.

My heart picks up pace in my chest, and I can't tell if it's excitement or nervousness causing it. I try to spot Ringo in the crowd, but I can't see him anywhere, and a jarring thought hits me.

Is he in another room with a woman… having sex?

I shake my head at the thought, because it's simply none of my business or my concern. What he does is up to him. He's only my babysitter, after all. Or perhaps captor?

Ugh. I have no idea what he is exactly, and it irks me that I even care.

He was aroused earlier. I saw it. The very hard bulge in his jeans. I tried not to look, but when I pretended to look at the sex toy he and I were discussing, which now seems so strange that I even had that conversation, instead of focusing my gaze on the vagina thingy, I stared at his hard junk straining against his jeans.

He wouldn't have known I was doing it with the angle my head was in, but it sure helped to add that embarrassing heat to my cheeks.

The funny thing is, it's been such a long time since I even remotely considered a penis to be something of interest. Part of me had it in my head that perhaps it was safer for me to be a lesbian, even if I don't really like the idea of being intimate with a woman. It just seemed like a safer option, and I had thought that if I could get away from Daniel and my family, then perhaps I'd cut my hair off and simply hang around with females for the rest of my life.

I bite my lip as I remember watching Ringo slide his finger inside the hole of his toy. The sound of it sucking his digit caused a flutter between my legs, not for the first time since being in his company.

Which is weird, right?

He's like, so old. My reaction must have to do with my new-found freedom, or at least partial freedom. I may be locked in this seedy motel with a biker gang, but I feel freer than I have in so long, it almost makes me happy.

Deciding that watching the chaos outside the room is more interesting than reading right now, I move to flick off all the lights and drag one of the flimsy dining chairs to the window where I draw the curtain back just enough that I can see out, but not so much that it will be obvious to those out there that someone is inside here watching.

At least, I hope not.

The same flutter between my legs returns when I see a heavily inked man with a short beard tear off his shirt and start kissing one of the women. She instantly wraps her arms around him before he lifts her, and her legs do the same.

As they kiss, he walks them over to a table where he lays her out and starts removing her clothes. I can feel my cheeks flare hotter at the sight of her bare flesh and the way she arches her back off the table. It sends her boobs higher. The golden light from the courtyard, which must have once been where cars parked, is just bright enough to show me a glimpse of her hard nipples before the man starts sucking on them.

I shift on the seat, rubbing my thighs together as the flutter increases.

I shouldn't be watching their private moment. I know that. It's a sinful act, yet for some reason just knowing that makes me not want to look away.

Besides, others are watching. Some have pulled chairs up as if they are watching a show. There are a couple of women grinding on men's laps doing some sort of lap dance.

I spot one of the men that was with Ringo when they kidnapped me. The one that drove the truck. I think his name is Stocky. Like Ringo, he's not a bad-looking man for someone that looks like he hasn't done his hair today. He has a cigarette hanging from his lips, and as he stands watching, he begins to undo his jeans.

He's not going to…

Oh.

Heck. He is. He just got his penis out.

Ringo's words come to me from earlier.

"This thing isn't a penis. It's a cock."

My lips part as I take in Stocky and the way he wraps his hand around his appendage.

Ringo is right. Penis just isn't the right word for something that looks like that.

"It's a cock," I whisper to myself, the word feeling weird to say. "Cock," I say louder, before snickering to myself.

I'm losing the plot. Now not only am I spying like a peeping Tom, but I'm talking to myself about cock.

When one of the women steps up in front of Stocky, I'm almost annoyed that she's blocking my view, but then, he points to the ground, his lips parting as he speaks to her, and the next second, she drops to her knees.

Bad memories try to rush me, but even as my lip trembles, I will them away because even if what I'm doing right now is wrong, I don't care. It's the most normal I've felt since I first got together with Daniel, back when I thought he actually liked me.

Maybe I shouldn't be watching like a creeper or feeling that flutter that I never thought I'd feel again, but I need this. I don't know why, but I just need to see these acts happening with both parties willing. Both parties getting pleasure.

As the woman wraps her lips around Stocky, I take a risk and move my hand to press between my legs, desperation guiding me to see if I can ever feel pleasure again.

The shrill of Ringo's phone ringing forces a squeal past my lips, and the chair nearly falls backwards as I leap up and spin to face the noise.

Over on the bed is Ringo's phone screen, lit up brightly as the ringing sound increases.

Shit.

He's waiting for an important call.

Dashing forward, I scoop the phone up to see the name flashing across the screen.

IMPORTANT.

That's it. No other name to say who it is, and I guess names probably aren't used so much in organised crime.

Placing the phone on the table as it stops ringing, I move to the door and lift on my tiptoes to see through the peephole. I can't see anyone immediately in front of the door, but Ringo said Brody, the crude guy that I walked in on yesterday, was the one he tasked to stand by the door, so I carefully unlock it before gently cracking the door open just a smidge.

The sounds of the party flow in loudly through the small crack, and so do some moans of pleasure so close I can't help but see who they are coming from.

Brody. He's just outside the door, his jeans around his ankles.

He's having sex right there, pounding into a woman up against the wall.

"Oh my god," I whisper and hurry to close the door again, spinning to press my back against it.

He's such an animal. Couldn't he have waited until later to do that? Like once Ringo had returned?

The phone lights up and starts ringing again, and my heart begins to thrash in my chest with anxious energy.

Ringo said the call was important. He needs to return it soon after. I need to get the message to him that it's ringing.

Spinning again, I crack the door open again, a little wider this time, and work up the courage to use my voice.

"Brody," I whisper, and then want to slap myself because, as if anyone would have heard that. I could barely hear my own voice.

FML!

"Brody." I hiss louder this time, but still, he continues to thrust between the woman's legs as she makes muling cries.

Ugh. This guy!

"Brody!" I snap louder, and this time I get a grunt of acknowledgement from him. "Get Ringo. The call he's been waiting for is happening now."

"Yeah." Brody pants, pulling back enough so I can see his pleasure-pained expression, but he doesn't stop, his eyes dropping to watch where their bodies join.

The phone stops ringing again, so I close the door and start pacing.

I don't know what the urgency is with this call, but Ringo was dead serious about needing to take it, and he was doing me a favour by leaving his phone with me, so I had something to do.

I feel bad now for that. If he didn't have to worry about my bitching about being bored, he'd have his phone and he would have taken the call by now.

Normally, people would be patient and just wait for them to call, but what if it's his mum? He said she was sick. What if something has happened? Or what if it's a crime lord, and the call was part of some sort of deal they made that will fall through if he doesn't take the call?

What if… My thoughts trail off as the phone starts ringing again.

Hurrying to the door again, I crack it open and snap louder. "Brody, stop doing that and get Ringo now."

"Who's in Ringo's room?" the girl asks, trying to pry her head from the brick wall to look in my direction, but Brody's hand wraps around her throat, baring his teeth as he thrusts harder and faster.

"Focus on fucking me like a good whore."

His words stir my memories again. The urge to scream at him for saying such crude things to the woman who is giving herself to him is almost too hard to resist, yet I do.

He's not going to stop what he's doing until he's satisfied, and like Ringo said, she is consenting, although I have no idea why a woman would let a man speak to her like that.

Hot tears pool in my eyes as I close the door again and stare at the phone as it rings a few more times before stopping.

What do I do?

Moving to the window, I take stock of the situation out there.

Everyone is busy. The sex scene I was watching before has grown with more women and men now partaking, all preoccupied.

I still can't see Ringo, though.

Once again, the damn phone starts ringing, so I decide I must make an executive decision.

I need to find Ringo myself.

Moving to the bathroom, I check over myself. I'm wearing black leggings and Ringo's huge black hoodie. It's like a dress on me, and even though it's too hot for these clothes, they bring me a sense of comfort.

My hair is still in braids, so I lift the hood and tug on the cords, drawing the hood tighter around my face a little before slipping on my runners.

"You can do this," I tell my reflection, before spinning and snatching up the phone again.

At the door, I open it a little wider to see Brody has changed position. The girl now bent over a chair by the door, facing the other direction as he pounds into her from behind.

My heart races and I suck in a deep breath and step outside, forcing myself to ignore the fact this douche of a guy is busy having sex right in front of me.

"Brody. Where's Ringo?"

My words have him grunting again while waving a dismissive hand at me. "Prez's room."

"Where is that?" I snap, my eyes darting around even as I keep my head cast down, hoping to avoid becoming an interest to anyone watching on.

"Across the lot." He grunts, before slapping the woman's arse. "The main house by the pool."

I gulp.

Across the lot. He means this courtyard packed with bikers and practically naked women.

The phone starts ringing again, and a quick glance shows *'IMPORTANT'* flashing across the screen again, so I flick it to silent and hurry forward into the crowd of people.

RINGO

No matter how many fucking times I tell Smitty that I'm not interested in the fucking Doxy girls, he still insists on parading them and their so-called skills in front of me. My gaze travels over Wendy, one of the more senior Doxies who has spread herself out on the table before me, legs wide, muff bare, her fingers sinking inside herself as she moans like it actually feels good.

Maybe it does. Who fucking knows, but it's of no interest to me.

"We are going to help the Marx crew break into the warehouse north of the city," my Prez mutters, his eyes dropping to his lap as Celina, one of his personal Doxies, grinds her bare arse over his hard-on hidden behind his jeans.

Thank fuck.

I've seen his dick enough over the years, and I really don't want to see that fucking thing tonight.

"The Triad warehouse?" I ask, my brows shooting high.

"Yep. Those fuckers have the state's supply of dunny roll. It's about fucking time they share."

I chuckle. "Not just that. I'm certain they are behind the haul of PPE gear stolen last year."

Smitty nods, his hands gripping Celina's hips as he grinds up against her, while Molly, his real queen, an eight-year-old rottweiler, sits by his feet. "Yeah, those fuckers are stealing our business."

It's fucking true. They are.

In a time where people are forced to remain locked inside their homes, our regular trade of drugs and guns has practically dried up. We've had to think fucking quick, and what everyone was after became what we traded in. Essential items. Medical resources. And fucking dunny roll. Who would have thought toilet paper would become so fucking valuable?

A loud moan floats from Wendy, like she's trying to gain my attention as I lounge back in the chair and sip my fucking Sarsaparilla.

Yep, just like every other time there's a celebration in the MC, I'm on the hard stuff. The guys used to give me shit over it years ago, like my decision not to intoxicate myself with drugs and alcohol somehow made me weak, but when they realised that in fact, while they were all fucking useless, I was still on my game, alert, present and ready just like a sergeant-in-arms should be.

A role I take fucking seriously.

After all, I'm basically the closest thing to law these men have. We have rules and bylaws, and it's my job to fucking ensure the members adhere to them.

Fucking pity I'm the one who has broken the rules by involving other members in a personal job and then sneaking an outsider into our compound.

Fuck.

"Ringo. You look hungry," Wendy purrs, spreading her legs so wide that her feet now hug the outside of the table. "Come a little closer and have a taste."

For fuck's sake, why does Smitty insist on humiliating the Doxies like this in front of me?

She knows, and he fucking knows, I'll reject her. It's not like after three fucking years of saying no that I'm just going to suddenly change my fucking mind and want to fuck one of them.

I go to shoot my Prez a fucking glare to remind him I'm not into this shit, when I notice his frown, his eyes taking in something behind me.

Then I hear it. A small gasp from behind me.

"Who's this?" Smitty asks, sitting taller in his seat, Molly standing to attention next to him, and my head snaps over my shoulder to see Abbey staring wide eyed, her big doe eyes practically the only noticeable thing about her as she hides in my hoodie.

FUCK!

Why the fuck is she here?

Spinning away from me, even as I go to stand, she makes a run for it, only to slam into Brody as he comes rushing in like a fire is lit under his arse. "Fuck, I wasn't meant to let you out."

A fearful whimper flies from Abbey as she shoves Brody aside and bolts out the door.

"Who the fuck was that?" Smitty asks over Molly's barking, shoving Celina off his lap, and I hesitate for a fucking moment, not sure if I should answer him first or go after Abbey first.

Fuck.

I decide I can answer him later, and instead I lurch forward, grabbing Brody by the scruff. "You're fucking out!" I boom before shoving him backwards out the door, where he falls on his arse.

"Ringo!" Smitty yells as I take fucking chase, needing to find Abbey before she gets found by someone else.

As I clear the pool area, I skid to a stop at the edge of the courtyard, my gaze racing over the crowd just in time to spot her slight frame engulfed in my black hoodie, disappearing into the crowd before it absorbs her.

My feet move instantly, heading towards the place I lost sight of her and unfortunately, the savage growls of an unhappy Molly follow. I shove through the crowd, my club brothers already in full fucking party mode as they mess with the Doxy girls, unaware of the building drama.

My eyes rake over everyone as I try to spot her, but it's her cries that draw me to the side of the crowd where I see the big burly back of one of our older members, Fryer, as he cages someone in against the brick wall.

I see fucking red!

My feet pound heavily as I storm forward, watching as Abbey's small hands try to push him back, and as I get closer and her terrified face comes into view, I hear her repeated words over and over.

"No. No. No."

Fryer fucking palms her tit before his words meet my ears. "Who brought in a new toy? Fuck yes."

"The fuck!" I roar, my fingers digging into his cut as I drag him off her before I pull back and clock him in the jaw with a loud crack.

"What the fuck, Ringo!" he sneers, stumbling back into a nearly dead shrub as Abbey presses herself so close to the wall it's like she's trying to disappear through it.

I can't tell who she's scared of. Me, Fryer, or Molly standing off to the side savagely barking like she's gearing up to attack.

"Keep your fucking hands off what's mine!" I roar, balling my fist in his direction and, unfortunately, catching the attention of others behind me.

"What do you mean, she's yours?"

Fuck.

Smitty.

I spin to see our club President, my friend, looming behind me with half our fucking members at his back.

He followed me.

Fuck. Fuck. Fuck.

My eyes catch sight of Jols and Trunk, their concern evident, although I'm not sure if it's for me, Abbey, or the fact they may be implicated.

"Molly! Quiet!" Smitty hisses and the dog instantly stops barking, moving to his side but keeping her eyes trained on Abbey.

Turning back to eye my captive, I move to her, noticing how she tries to shrink back further as I approach like she's fucking scared of me.

Maybe she should be. I'm not good fucking people.

Stepping forward, I grip her arm, ignoring the way she tries to pull away as I tug her to my chest where I roughly hold her, unsure how to fucking rein in my temper.

Fuck. What do I do here?

Ignoring everyone else, and knowing I need to give Smitty some fucking answers, I tug Abbey back just as forcefully and snarl in her face.

"The fuck did I tell you?"

She flinches at my harsh tone, her eyes pooling with tears as her lip trembles and fuck do I want to punch myself in the fucking head.

She doesn't deserve to be treated like this.

"Y-your phone rang," she stutters quietly. Timidly like a little mouse. "I t-tried to get B-Brody to find you but he was b-busy and the p-phone rang so many times. I knew y-you needed to take the c-call."

Shit. The fucking call.

I shouldn't have left my phone with her. What the fuck was I thinking?

She was bored and looked so helpless… fuck.

"Ringo, who the fuck is this? What's going on?" Smitty's angered tone makes me stiffen. He's clearly had enough of waiting for me to fucking clue him in.

Jesus fucking Christ.

I shake my head, knowing I only have one choice, so I lean closer to speak to the scared angel trembling in my hold, so only she can hear.

"If you want to get out of this unscathed, Angel, go along with every-fucking-thing I say. You got it?"

Her caramel gaze locks with mine, glassy from unshed tears, and even though she whimpers, she nods, so I nod back and release my grip on her arm, spinning to face the fucking music.

"She's mine," I declare.

Smitty frowns, while feminine gasps come from the Doxy girls watching on, and a few hoots come from some of my club brothers.

"Since fucking when?" Smitty snaps, taking a step forward, his glare hard and his tone accusing. "You haven't claimed a woman since—"

"I said she's mine." I cut him off and his eyes narrow. Even though my tone is laced with menace, Abbey shifts closer at my back, so I reach for her and tug her to my side before wrapping my arm over her shoulders, holding her close.

"She's not wearing your patch," Smitty points out as his gaze rakes over her.

"Not yet. I was hoping to announce it on the weekend, but then the snap lockdown happened."

His eyes snap back to mine. "You been hiding her?"

"I've been enjoying her. There's a fucking difference." I counter and for a long drawn-out moment, we both glare at each other.

Then, my Prez smiles.

"About fucking time you got some action. I was beginning to worry you'd turned into a eunuch."

"Shut the fuck up." I smirk back, and the tension starts to ease from the onlookers as they begin to talk amongst themselves.

"How long has this been going on?" Smitty asks, and I gesture my head to the crowd of men and Doxy girls eating up all the drama.

"Can we talk about this somewhere else?"

Smitty chuckles and claps me on the shoulder. "Yeah, back in my room."

As my Prez turns with Molly guarding his side, the crowd disperses and I keep Abbey tucked to my side, following Smitty, weaving through the crowd as they try to get a glimpse of the woman I've just publicly claimed as mine.

For fuck's sake. They are going to make a big fucking deal about this. I just fucking know it.

How am I going to explain when she leaves?

Fuck.

As we break through the crowd, heading to the main house, I lean down and whisper against the hood still covering Abbey's head. "Only talk when I say you can."

She nods against me, so I give her a little squeeze, still feeling her tremble slightly, and we all step back inside Smitty's house.

Wendy, still fucking perched on the table with her legs spread, takes one look at the scared little mouse tucked into my side and glares like she has a fucking right to.

"Why don't my two favourite girls enjoy each other on the couch?" Smitty suggests, thank fuck, and while Celina seems all for it, giggling and bouncing her tits as she does a little jump and excited clap, Wendy rolls her eyes and drags herself off the table like she's just been asked to scrub a fucking shitter.

As I retake my seat, I pull Abbey onto my lap, and much like I did in the mum van after stealing her, I pull her legs up and cradle her to me, hoping it looks like she's precious to me.

She stiffens.

"Relax," I whisper against her hood, my words seeming to do the trick as she does what I ask, some of the tension easing from her shoulders.

"Let's get a look at the woman that's caught our man's eye." Smitty insists, gesturing his hand to Abbey, which only makes her stiffen again.

Reaching up, I hook my fingers in the fabric of the hood, and her fearful eyes meet mine as I start to ease it back to reveal her white, blonde hair in those plait things, her big doe eyes going wide, and I can tell she's internally panicking.

So I do the only thing I can think of to remind her that I'm not a monster, while at the same time showing my Prez that she does, in fact, belong to me.

I lean forward and press my lips to her temple, lingering there for a beat longer than necessary when I see her lids flutter closed and feel her shoulders relax again.

Interesting.

"Hmmm," Smitty mutters, "Not a woman, I see."

Pulling back from the display of affection, I glare at my Prez.

"She's of fucking age."

"Hey, I'm not judging." He raises his hands in surrender, shooting me a smirk.

"You fucking know me, man. I'm not like that. This club isn't like that." I remind him and he snickers while nodding, relaxing back in his seat, his hand dangling over the side to scratch Molly's head.

"You don't need to remind me of our fucking morals, Ringo. But it's been a fucking while since you showed an interest in pussy. You'll have to forgive me for wondering if perhaps your taste had changed since Kylie."

"Attraction to a minor is not a fucking taste. It's a fucking sickness," I hiss, and Smitty nods before turning his attention back to the timid girl huddled in my lap.

"What's your name?" he asks her, but she doesn't answer, doing exactly as I asked of her and not speaking.

Smitty's brow hitches, probably assuming it's a display of disrespect.

"I told you she's mine, man. She only talks for me," I state, which brings back his smirk before I press my lips to her ear, this time no fabric of a hood acting as a barrier.

"Answer him, Charity," I say the name slowly as a reminder that she's not to use her real name.

Those big doe eyes lift to meet mine before she visibly swallows and clears her throat, turning her gaze to Smitty.

"I'm Charity."

Smitty's lips spread wide in a grin, and the foreplay that was taking place on the couch off to the side ceases as both women turn their attention to the timid girl on my lap.

"How old are you, Charity?"

I growl under my fucking breath at his question, like he doesn't fucking believe me when I said she's old enough.

"Eighteen," she answers, a little more steel in her tone this time.

Good girl.

Slowly, Smitty's grin contorts as he throws his head back in a roar of laughter, his hand slapping to his knee. "Eighteen. Fuck, man. She's only just scraping over the line of being legal."

"Legal is fucking legal," I snap, and he nods, even as he reaches for his smokes and taps out a durry.

"True." He chuckles again, lighting up and taking in a deep drag before blowing the smoke up in the air between us.

"So, how did this all happen?" Smitty gestures with his cigarette to me and Abbey and I ease her back to relax against me, placing my hand over hers resting on her thigh.

"Well, I came across her in Timber Valley. It's made my trips to see Griffin worth it." I lie easily and chuckle, shooting Smitty a wink which pleases him if his grin is anything to go by.

"I bet. And you brought her back just in time for the five-day snap lockdown."

I nod, "Yeah. Gives me more time to enjoy her."

I ignore the way she stiffens at my words, and I hope she remembers that this is all a ruse.

"No wonder you were antsy to get back to your room." Smitty chuckles, taking another drag of his cigarette. "She a sub like Kylie?"

For fuck's sake. I wish he'd stop saying Kylie's fucking name. He knows how much I hate hearing it.

"She is." I grit out, keeping up the fucking ruse. "And if you don't mind, I'd like to take her back and punish her for leaving the room when I explicitly said not to."

"By all means," my Prez gestures with his durry between his fingers to the open door, "Have at it. And enjoy."

"Oh, I fucking will." I lace my tone with fucking anticipation, trying to put on a good fucking show, even as my captive whimpers from the abrupt way I stand, letting her slip off my lap and scurry to stand.

Smitty's chuckles follow us out as I lead Abbey with a tight grip on her arm, like she's in fucking trouble.

While part of me wants to scold her for leaving the fucking room when I told her not to, my anger is better directed towards Brody, who had one fucking job to do, and like always, fucking failed.

"Ringo." Abbey's timid tone meets my ears, but I hiss in response.

"Don't say a fucking word."

The crowd parts when they see me approaching, dragging the blonde beauty I just declared as mine across the fucking courtyard.

Jols steps up at our side, hurrying beside us and goes to speak, but I hold a finger up to stop her.

"I'm fucking busy."

"But I need to know," Jols snaps, hurrying to keep up.

"You don't need to know shit. Nothing has changed." I spit, getting more and more furious with every fucking step I take that brings me closer to my shitty motel room.

"You didn't tell him about…" she trails off as I stop at my door, spinning to face her with Abbey's arm still caught in my firm grip.

"I told him about meeting Charity in Timber Valley when I went to meet Griffin. I told him how she's fucking mine. How I've claimed her. Now, if you'll excuse me, I have to make fucking sure it appears like I'm telling the fucking truth."

Jols frowns. "What do you mean?"

I reach back and open my door before snarling in Jols' face, letting her take the brunt of my rage, even though Brody is the only one that deserves it.

"Now I get to spend the rest of the night fucking the woman I've claimed."

A whimper flies from Abbey even as I spin her, slap her arse hard, the loud clap so audible that anyone nearby won't have been able to not hear it, and shove her in the room, following in after her and slamming the door in Jols' face, cutting off her protests.

Then, out of nowhere, a fist slams into my face.

13

ABBEY

"**O**uch," I cry, pain shooting from my knuckles to my wrist and then right up my arm as I stumble backwards, my eyes going wide as a trickle of blood oozes from Ringo's lip.

"What the fuck was that for?" he snarls, and I scurry backwards as he stalks forward.

"You slapped my arse. What else would it be for?" My words are firm, but my heart is anything but strong right now, fear wrapping around it like a thick blanket of frost.

My feet hit the wall by the wardrobe entrance, and as he continues forward looking everything like the madman that stole me from my parents last night, I'm reminded of the words he hissed at Jols.

"Now I get to spend the rest of the night fucking the woman I've claimed."

"I don't give you permission to have sex with me," I blurt, stumbling into the wardrobe opening, still trying to put distance between us.

"Darlin, I don't have sex. I fuck. And I never said I wanted to." He reaches for me, and I squeal, spinning and dashing towards the open bathroom door, gripping it as I step in and try to force it shut.

Ringo's too fast. His big hand stops it, his towering height and broad shoulders filling the doorway, trapping me.

"Y-you did. Y-you told Jols you were going to spend the night…" I trail off, my cheeks heating at the thought of repeating his words.

"Say the words I said, Angel. I said the word *fuck.* I said I get to spend the rest of the night fucking the woman I've claimed." He smirks cruelly as he tilts his head. "Can you even fathom saying such a crude word?"

Tears prick at the back of my eyes as my shoulders drop, shame washing over me.

"There's no need to be a prick and tease me about it," I snap, feeling the familiar prickle of humiliation Daniel enjoyed tormenting me with so often. "You know, for a minute there, you fooled me into thinking you were actually a decent man."

My words cause his smirk to fall, and I almost feel bad.

"Don't ever forget that I am *not* a good man, Angel. At the end of the day, I'm a part of that world." He points to the wall, but I know he means to the chaos happening outside his room.

I stare at him for a long beat, my mind like a busy concert hall filled with hundreds of voices making it hard to hear myself think.

"Look, I'm sorry about the arse slap. I was playing a part. A necessary part to make everyone think you're mine."

"Why do I have to be yours? What does that mean?" I ask, and when he takes a step closer, I take another step back.

Sighing, Ringo rakes a rough hand down his face before his eyes meet mine again, their whiskey colour looking a little drained.

"It means they won't touch you."

I wait for him to say something else in explanation, but when he doesn't, I push for more information.

"But why? What does me being yours really mean to them?"

"It means that upon knowing this, they will leave you alone. They won't touch you. That's all you need to know."

I roll my eyes at him, and he smirks, which makes my lips twitch too.

Ugh. I'm trying to be angry here. Why am I fighting a smile? *Focus Abbey.*

"Why is it such a big deal that I be yours and not just a guest? Isn't that enough, just knowing I'm a visitor?"

"We don't do visitors here, Angel. Crime world, remember?"

"How could I forget," I scoff, and this time he rolls his eyes.

"Look. None of this was planned. I got a last-minute call, was asked to take you and keep you with me. To protect you. I did that without the permission of my club President, and not only that, but I also involved other club members. Then, as if that wasn't bad enough, I brought you here secretly. If I had told Smitty about you, he could have ordered you away, and that I not help you. Or he could have ordered you to be something else within the club. Declaring you as mine is the only way to keep you from being used as something you're not."

I take a moment to consider his words. They sound genuine enough, I guess, considering I hardly know this man, but they still leave me confused.

"What could your President order me to do if I wasn't yours?"

My words are timid. Too soft for the world we are in, but fear over the answer has its claws in me, digging in, reminding me I'm still not safe.

"It doesn't matter." He waves a dismissive hand, and I stomp my foot, annoyed at being treated like a child.

"It does matter. Tell me!" I yell, and this time, even though his brows are hitched, he looks amused.

"Fair enough. I'll tell you, but then this fucking conversation is over."

"Fine," I snap, crossing my arms over my chest, exhaustion tugging at me.

"There are four reasons why females are in our space here at the Western. The women here are either old ladies, Doxy girls, mice, or pass arounds." Ringo steps backwards out of the doorway and gestures his head as he starts walking, so I follow behind, and sit on the end of the bed when he points at it, giving me a silent order.

"A pass around is someone that comes into the club as a brief visitor. Sometimes just for a night or a week or two. Sometimes a little longer. They never last much more than that."

"Why are they called a pass around?" I ask, watching as he drags the chair I'd placed in front of the window earlier, over to me before he straddles it backwards, resting his thick corded arms painted in intricate tattoos on the top of the chair, watching me.

"They are used as fuck toys, Angel. Passed around between the men. They are usually up for anything. Many have it in their head they are here to find a member that will claim them, but the fact they are used for nothing but sex and a good time turns any members off wanting to keep them. Others are happy to be pass arounds, riding on the coattails of the free food and a place to crash until they are kicked to the curb."

I can feel the way my face drops. I can't do anything to stop it. Being a pass around sounds awful. I don't know why anyone would choose to do that.

I swallow thickly before clearing my throat, hating the way Ringo is studying me so closely.

"You can see how I didn't want that fate for you, right?"

I nod at his words, my eyes dropping to my lap and my fiddling fingers.

"Eyes up, Angel."

In an instant, my gaze is locked back on his, and I want to slap myself.

Why do I do that? Why do his simple demands have me obeying so quickly?

"A mouse is different. Usually someone younger, much like yourself that needs shelter. They are usually claimed by a member and their wife or old lady to live with them in exchange for domestic duties. Help with cooking, cleaning, looking after children."

My brows shoot up. "That doesn't sound so bad."

"I guess not, except for the fact I would lose control of watching over you, and once you are in, Angel. You are in. You don't just get to leave the household you're placed in. And you'll likely end up being a Doxy girl in the end. Since keeping you hidden is temporary, making you a mouse would be a bad idea. There's no walking away when you're ready to return to your life."

"Oh."

"And as for the Doxies, well, given where this chair was, I'd say you have a good idea what the Doxy girls do."

My cheeks flush at being caught spying.

"What's the difference between the Doxy girls and the pass arounds?"

"Doxy girls aren't members of the MC, but they live within our walls. They cook for us. Clean for us. Shop for us. And, if they feel inclined, they give us access to their bodies for pleasure."

I don't miss the way he uses the word us. So that means he has sex with the Doxy girls too. Probably the one that was on the table when I found him earlier. She was pretty. A little older than some of the other women, but she looked at Ringo like she wanted to devour him. Maybe he'd already had sex with her before I found them.

But then, is that right? Some things Smitty said made me think Ringo didn't have sex with anyone.

"Last is the old ladies." He continues. "They are the property of a club member. Owned by them, and therefore off limits to anyone else. Old ladies get treated with more respect. They have the protection of the club at all times, and some members make them their wives, while others have a wife on the outside of the club, and an old lady on the inside."

My mouth drops open at that. The entire meaning behind an old lady sounding dreadful. Well, I guess except for the respect part and the club protection.

"Which part about that is shocking?" Ringo asks, smirking at my reaction, and I snap my mouth closed and shrug.

"Oh, I don't know. Maybe the part about being property. Owned. Or maybe the part about being the other woman to a married man."

He chuckles. "It's not always the case that a member has both a wife and an old lady. But it does happen, and I can assure you, both women know about each other most of the time."

I scoff. "And you think it's alright for a man to own a woman like a possession?"

"Yes." He answers faster than I'd like, and I get a sinking feeling deep inside my chest.

Stop thinking he's a good guy, Abbey. He's a criminal.

"I see you don't like my response." He chuckles, tilting his head to study me further.

"No, I don't like your response. As someone that was about to be forced into marrying a monster, only to be owned by him, I absolutely do not like your response."

His smile slips away, and his expression turns serious. "Shit. Angel, I'm sorry. You're right. A woman should not be someone's property."

The familiar feeling of threatening tears pricks at my eyes, and I will them to hold off. I'm sick of appearing weak. Helpless. Naïve.

"Don't pretend to mean that for my sake. I'm nothing more than a job you're doing for someone else's agenda. I haven't forgotten why I'm here."

The neutral expression that masks him now hints at no emotions or reaction to my words. If anything, I'd say the closest emotion affecting him right now is indifference.

"You're right." He holds out his hand. "My phone."

I hesitate for a moment. For some stupid reason, I don't like the chill that's just settled between us. Which makes no sense. We are strangers. He's lived through years of experience in this world, and I am yet to find any semblance of hope or happiness coming my way. I know nothing of what lies out there in the real world. I only know the vile dark acts that have been forced on me, my life always at someone else's mercy.

Slowly, I reach into the hoodie pocket and pull out the phone, noticing a number of missed calls before I reach out and place it in his hand.

His gaze dismisses me instantly, turning to the phone as he curses under his breath, standing while he taps on the screen and then holds the phone to his ear.

Then he starts pacing.

"It's me," he says into the phone, pausing as whoever it is speaks before he responds. "It's okay. I got her. She's safe."

I straighten at his words, realising that the call he was waiting for had to do with me.

Who's on the other end?

"Honestly? Worse than you thought. Not a good situation at all. It's lucky we went in when we did."

I stand, approaching him slowly as I listen, and when he turns in his pacing, his eyes find mine.

"She was a bit cut up, more self-inflicted in an attempt to protect herself, but other than that and her distressed state, she seemed okay. I did notice some bruising on her arms and her face."

He drops his eyes as he listens to whoever is speaking and then spins and steps outside to take the rest of the call.

My heart races as he closes me off from the conversation. I want to hear it. I want to know who it is, so without thinking, I hurry to the door and tug it open in time to hear his words.

"She'll need to be relocated after the snap lockdown. She's not safe here."

I can't contain my gasp, and he spins, glaring at me as he points over my shoulder back into the room.

I shake my head.

"Look, I can't really talk now," he mutters, moving forward to back me up as he steps back inside and locks the door behind him. "Yeah, I'll put her on."

I still at his words, watching as he mutters something else and then holds the phone out to me. "It's time to find out who ordered me to kidnap you."

My hands start trembling as I reach out, Ringo's eyes not missing my reaction, so he passes me the phone and walks me backwards, sitting me back on the end of his bed.

Stepping away from me, he moves to his little kitchenette, opening the fridge and pulling out a Coke as I slowly press the phone to my ear.

"Hello?"

"Oh my god, Abbey! I'm so sorry it had to go down the way it did, but I didn't know how else to get you away from them and also teach them a fucking lesson."

Tears flood my eyes instantly at the familiar voice, a sob escaping me in response.

"Abbey?"

"Lexi," I cry, or perhaps it's more of a wail, as I slip from the end of the bed, landing on my arse on the grotty looking carpet where I start sobbing uncontrollably.

"Oh Abs. I'm so sorry. I wish you had told me how bad it had gotten. I wish you had let me help you sooner."

I try to speak, but my words are incoherent as I try to tell her I'm sorry.

My childhood best friend from Fox Pines is the one that saved me. I don't deserve her kindness after the horrible things I did to her all to protect my own arse, but she's never given up on me. Hell, she would have come in guns blazing all by herself if she could have. And I bet she wanted to, but her boyfriend Ayden most likely would have locked her away before letting her put herself in danger. Not after everything they've been through. What Lexi's been through.

Strong yet gentle hands slide under me before I'm lifted against Ringo's hard chest, and I continue to sob as Lexi talks me through it, telling me that I'm safe now. That my parents and Daniel can't get to me. That I never have to see them again if I don't want to.

With me still cradled in his arms, Ringo lowers us to the bed, and he holds me tight as I cry and listen to my best friend until my sobs subside enough for me to put words together.

"H-how did you k-know?" I ask Lexi, and she instantly understands what I'm trying to ask.

"Tahli. We've been chatting for months on that game app. Koala-roo. I ran into her in the supermarket one day while she was with your mum. She was in a different aisle, getting things off a list, so I was able to talk to her quickly without your mum noticing. She's the one who mentioned the kids' game, telling me she can talk to me on it without your parents knowing," Lexi explains. "I've never downloaded an app so fast, Abs. By that night, I was chatting with her, and she started telling me things.

She said she just wanted you to move away to University so you could be away from your parents. She'd been counting down the days with me. I'd planned to come and see you once you left. She said you got into Nursing."

I nod, even though she can't see. "Yes. I know it can be studied locally, but I kept telling my parents about a specialty program I wanted to do, saying I would likely be able to earn more money while still having time to raise a family. And they fell for it. I was surprised my mum didn't look more into it. I just wanted to get away from them so I could figure out a way to run."

"Shit, Abs. What changed? Tahli was frantic last night when she messaged me. Said Maggie dobbed you in about something and then all of a sudden there was chaos, the wedding was being planned for the next morning, and how terrified she was when she had to watch Maggie help your parents force some sort of meds down your throat."

Unable to hold back my tears again, another sob escapes me, and Ringo's large hand starts rubbing my back, offering me comfort he doesn't have to give me. It's the only thing that helps the words to come.

"The pills were a sedative. They've done it before. They do it when they want to control me. Make sure I do what they want. They would have dressed me in white the next morning and taken me to marry Daniel while I was in a near catatonic state. But they didn't get to do that, thanks to you."

"Well, I couldn't have done it if it weren't for Ringo. I knew he had the skills to do what I asked, and the ability to make you disappear without a trace so your parents can't find you."

My eyes dart up to Ringo, his face kind of blurry given its close proximity. He glances down at me, pulling back a little so we can see each other, and I continue talking while he stares down at me.

"How do you know him?"

"Long story short, you know the guy that took a bullet for me when my brother…" She trails off, "Well, yeah, you know that guy?"

"He died, didn't he?" I was sure he died.

"Yeah. Muz died. Ringo is his older brother."

"Oh." My lip trembles again and I study this big lethal man holding me as a flash of pain passes his expression before he tries to hide it.

Can he hear what Lexi is saying?

I suppose he might be able to given how close we are right now.

"I know he probably seems scary, and not the sort of man you're used to associating with, but he's a damn good man, Abs. He really is. Don't let his moody attitude fool you."

A grin pulls at my lips, and when I notice Ringo trying to hide his own behind his beard, I know for sure he can hear Lexi, too.

"Lex. Is Tahli alright?" I ask, my thoughts going back to my twelve-year-old sister, so sweet and innocent that I hate the thought of her being in that house alone with those monsters.

"Yeah, we were chatting in the game app before. She's doing alright. Just worried about you. If you download the app, I'll send through her username and mine too, and we can all communicate."

"Yes. Yes, please do that." I practically beg, desperate to chat with Tahli myself.

"She's a strong kid, Abs. Much like you. Do you know she even drugged Maggie last night?"

"What! No, I didn't. How?"

Lexi giggles. "She said she got one of the pills your mum forced on you and crushed it up in Maggie's hot chocolate before bed. She was annoyed that your mum was making them sleep in the same room because she knew it was so Maggie could keep an eye on Tahli so she couldn't try to help you."

I start giggling too. "I love my little sister."

"You'll love her even more when I tell you she went back to bed after Ringo left with you. She ignored your parents' calls for help and left them to figure a way to get themselves out of the situation they were left in. She said it took them three hours."

"Oh, my god." I slap my hand over my mouth. "I wish I was a fly on the wall for that."

"Right. Me too. Tahli is fine, trust me. She's just worried about you."

"I can't wait to hug her when this is all over," I admit, and Lexi sighs through the phone.

I can picture her sitting in her bedroom, her blonde waves wild and her blue eyes bright. I bet Ayden is there with her, probably hugging her close as she speaks.

"Abs. What happened that made your parents rush the wedding forward to the next morning? Tahli really wasn't sure why."

I stiffen at her question, my gaze darting back to Ringo's as he watches on silently.

I can't say it.

I can't tell her.

I can't tell anyone.

What will she think?

What will Ringo think when he finds out?

I need to leave here as soon as I can. Make a run for it and figure it out on my own.

My eyes sting with the heat of my tears once again, and I force out the words. "I can't say right now."

She falls quiet, probably hurt that I'm still keeping secrets from her, but what other choice do I have? She will never understand. If the truth comes out, no one will understand.

The heaviness of it all feels suffocating, and all of a sudden, I can't seem to get air into my lungs.

I gasp, trying over and over, yet nothing works, and before I know what's happening, the phone is pulled from my grip, and the deep baritone of Ringo's voice cuts through the air before I'm being carried somewhere else.

14

RINGO

"Come on, Angel. Breathe for me."

With another chilled can of drink from the fridge, I press it to the back of Abbey's neck, hoping the shock will startle her out of her panic.

I'm not sure if it's my words or the cold can, but she manages to gasp, taking in a deeper breath.

"Yes, that's it, Angel. Try again."

Again my words spur her on, those big wide eyes glassed over as she struggles, locked onto my face like I'm her lifeline.

Her lips part, and she manages another deep gasp as I hold her cradled to my chest, keeping the cold can in place.

"More," I demand, and that's when her airways finally open, and the much-needed oxygen starts rushing back in.

"Thatta girl," I rasp, moving back to the end of the bed, sitting with her still in my arms as she takes in breath after breath of air.

"I-I'm s-sorry." She manages to get out on a choked sob, which is when she completely breaks.

Her heart wrenching cries fill the room, her face contorting in agony that tells a tale of the internal pain she's been suffering. Wave after wave of pain pierces the air, the anguish so intense that I feel it to my bones.

I know this pain. The undeniable crushing feeling of loss.

I don't know what it is she's lost. Did someone close to her die?

I fucking hope not. Being left behind by someone that makes up the other half of your heart is an excruciating death of its own. But if it isn't that, then I'm almost too afraid to consider what has transpired to cripple her like this.

Whatever she has gone through is undeniably unbearable.

Her dainty hands clutch onto my shirt like she's barely able to keep her head above the torment drowning her.

"I've got you, Angel. I've got you."

I squeeze her as tight as I can, holding her to my chest as she unleashes the pain within, not knowing what else I can do but hold her through it.

And fuck, I'd do just about anything to get her to stop crying like this. To stop enduring whatever trauma she is reliving in her head.

"I'll protect you. They can't hurt you anymore," I rasp against her hair, hoping my words break through enough that she believes them.

It's a long time before her cries lessen, eventually shifting into painful sobs, but I keep holding her, rocking a little, trying anything to soothe her pain away.

I still when I find myself pressing my lips to her hair.

Did I just fucking kiss her?

If she noticed, she mustn't care because she doesn't stiffen, or shift, or even make a noise, which is when I realise Abbey has cried herself to sleep in my arms.

Well, fuck.

That's just as heartbreaking.

Brushing her hair back off her tear-stained face, even in sleep she's frowning, like the nightmare she's lived has followed her there.

"If I could take away your nightmares, Angel, I would."

Fucking hell, now I'm talking to a sleeping woman.

Sighing, I tip my head back to look at the paint peeling on the ceiling. I've stared at that fucking patch of peeling paint for months, wanting to fucking fix it, yet not really having the desire to waste my time on this fucking dump.

It's not my real home. It belongs to the club, and is the best way for us to remain a unit with all these fucking lockdowns, but one thing is for sure, this fucking place isn't good enough for Abbey.

I need to get her somewhere safer and fucking cleaner.

I stay sitting on the end of the bed for so long, staring at her, barely noticing the party still in full swing outside. The celebrations are out of place compared to the darkness staining the four walls of this shitty room tonight. I have to stop myself numerous times from opening the door and demand every fucker shut the hell up and have some respect.

It's not their fault, though. They don't know what's happening in here. They don't know that the female, barely a woman, that I snuck into the compound is a girl I stole. They don't know that she's been abused by her parents and her fiancé, and just like me, they don't know the extent of the abuse. They don't know the pain she is suffering. The agony tearing shreds off her soul.

After about an hour of just holding her and watching how her tears dry on her cheeks, and how her frown smooths out to finally show gentle peace, I carefully move her to the bed, laying her on top of the covers before draping a spare sheet over her.

Not that she needs it with that fucking hoodie still on, but I'm not about to disturb her to remove it. She'll wake up and take it off if she gets too hot.

Joining Abbey on the bed, even though it's late, I redial the number of the burner phone I arranged to be sent to Lexi, and she answers on the second ring.

"Yeb?"

I frown. "Who the fuck is Yeb?"

Lexi giggles. "Oh hi, Ringo. Sorry, I thought it was Abbey."

"But you called her Yeb?"

"Well, yeah. I can't say her real name until I know it's her calling. What if the cops had gotten your phone and called me? I can't let them know I'm in on Abbey's kidnapping."

"True," I say, relaxing back against the shitty cane bedhead, glancing down at Abbey's sleeping form, her lips parted as she snores quietly. "But why Yeb?"

"Yeb was her code name when we were kids. We wrote our names backwards and took the first three letters to make our code name." Lexi giggles. "Genius, right?"

I chuckle. "Sure."

"You're just jealous you weren't as cool as we were when you were little."

"You have me there. I was nowhere near *that* cool," I tease sarcastically.

"Especially since your name would have been Nor."

"Fucking hell." I snarl as Lexi laughs uncontrollably. "Why do you know so much about me?"

The fact that she knows my real name is annoying. Not that it matters, but in my line of work, we stick to road and nicknames.

Lexi sighs, turning serious. "I visit Muz's grave every month, Ringo. Your name is on his headstone."

I forgot about that.

Shit.

"Every month?" I ask and she sighs.

"The stupid lockdowns have made it harder, but I try."

Shit. I don't even go to his grave that often.

I'm a crappy brother.

"Is Abs okay? The call disconnected earlier."

Reaching out, I stroke back some of Abbey's blonde strands that have escaped her braids. "I think she had a panic attack. I managed to get her to breathe properly again, but then she just broke."

Shit. My voice cracks as I speak, and a moment later, I hear Lexi sniffling on the other end of the line.

"Ringo, she's a good person. She's going to tell you she isn't. Be hard on herself for some of the shit that went down eighteen months ago, but you have to remind her that she's still a good person for me, okay?"

"I can try, but I don't know if I'm helping her or making it worse. There's a fucking orgy happening outside my room right now, and given her reaction to some of the stuff that's happened…" I trail off, not able to finish, but Lexi already knows.

"She may be fragile, but the girl I knew before all this stuff happened was excited about life, about love, was super curious about sex. Hell, she lost her virginity before I did. Yes, she's been in a really fucked up situation, but if you give her time, she'll learn who she can trust again."

"I don't know if I'm the man for the job, Lex." I remind her, my gaze never wavering from the angel asleep next to me.

"You're the only one that can help her. The only one with the skills to keep those people away from her."

"Why can't she go to the police?"

"I'm not entirely sure," Lexi admits. "But I believed her when she told me she can't trust the cops. And when you can't trust the cops, who can you trust?"

Fuck.

She's right.

"I'll do what I can."

"Thanks, Ringo." Lexi's tone is nothing but sincere. "Oh, and if you really want her to trust you, tell her your real name. That way, you'll appear more human than thug."

I chuckle. "Goodbye Lexi."

"See ya," she giggles before ending the call.

Shit.

Now I'm even more confused.

I'm inclined to think I shouldn't be the one looking after Abbey, but after speaking with Lexi, I suddenly feel like I'm the only person for the job.

Lexi does have a way of making me feel like some sort of God.

Maybe it's because I helped her and her boyfriend when my dick of a little brother put them in an impossible situation. Or maybe it's because she knows I'm the one who made a secret deal with her mum and burned down her childhood home and all the darkness it carried for the both of them.

Or maybe, it's because I encouraged her to visit Muz in the hospital before he died, and then invited her to the funeral, even though she blamed herself for his death.

Whatever it is, Lexi trusts me. She trusts that I'll take care of her friend, so that's exactly what I'm going to do.

Staring at my phone for a long moment, I consider who my next call should be to.

I could reach out to the Marx family, the heavy hitters of Melbourne's crime world, but that means bringing in more men, and I get the feeling Abbey could use more women around her. Women who aren't here to flop a nipple out on demand for one of my club brothers.

Opening my contacts, I select The Angel Sisters, and hold the phone to my ear as it rings.

"Well, well, well. If it isn't one of the Southern Sadists most notorious." Amanda teases before her sister, Bec adds her two cents worth.

"Oh, I don't know. President Smitty is a lot more badass if you ask me."

"Hmmm." They both hum in agreement and I roll my fucking eyes.

"You two done?"

Bec laughs. "Not nearly, but to what do we owe the pleasure?"

"Abbey Delaney," I say quickly, and the two women's humour falls away.

"What about her?" Amanda asks abruptly, and I frown.

"You know her?" I ask, my gaze darting down to her sleeping form once again.

"We know *of* her, and that she went missing two nights ago."

Normally, I'd be surprised the Angel sisters already know of Abbey, but after their secret weapon, Hush, turned up in Fox Pines a year ago, I'd already assumed Abbey would be on their radar.

"She didn't go missing," I deadpan. "I took her."

"Damn." Amanda draws out the word. "You'd better start talking really fast, Ringo, because I'm about to send a whole lot of trouble your way."

"Calm the fuck down. I took her as a favour to Lexi West. Abbey's situation exploded, and I went in and did a snatch and grab."

I'm glad for Amanda's reaction, although it shouldn't surprise me.

The Angel sisters run an organisation called Angel Org. They help vulnerable people escape their situations. Mainly women and children, but that's the main part of what the world thinks they do.

Underneath their well-run organisation are two very power-ful women, who help dole out justice. They have contacts all over the world. Control most of the east coast of Australia. And have a list of secret assassins who make people disappear, along with some super creative suffering beforehand.

They are vigilantes, and the Southern Sadists, along with the Marx crew, often work alongside them when needed.

We all commit crimes, but there's a moral code we stand by.

"Huh. Hush didn't have that intel," Bec says, and I nod, even though they can't see me.

"Doesn't surprise me. Lexi has been tight-lipped regarding her involvement."

"Well, I think that's something to celebrate. What an awful situation that poor girl has been in," Amanda says, and I hear rustling down the line like they are moving or walking. "So, how can we help?"

"I need intel. What do you know about her situation and family?"

"She grew up in Fox Pines. Her family has always lived there. Her parents were part of the main Catholic Church until a couple of years ago. It took us a while to find out where they moved their worshipping to."

Sitting taller on my bed, I frown. "And?"

"They moved to the Valley of the Trinity and Merciful Fellowship."

I stiffen. "Hold the fuck up. Didn't Hush and the Marx crew eradicate that group after finding they were linked to Carnal Unicorn?"

Carnal Unicorn was a dark web syndicate of predators and paedophiles. A sick group of men and women I thought were dealt with.

Amanda sighs. "Yes… well, that's what we thought, but it turns out new ministers stepped in to take over the church aspect of it. Those cultish churches are popping up faster than this annoying virus is spreading. Our teams have been watching on, but as far as we can tell, Carnal Unicorn hasn't resurfaced, and the church sessions seem just as normal as regular church."

Bec scoffs. "How would you know what regular church is like? We've never been."

"That's what our intel says," Amanda snaps as Bec laughs.

I can imagine they are pulling faces at each other on the other end of the line.

"So, they are a religious family, which I already picked up on, but how does Daniel fit into all of this?"

"He started off as a nice guy, luring Abbey in, but once they got sprung playing hide the sausage, Abbey's mum went bananas." Bec rushes out, the anger in her tone evident. "The next thing you know, Priscilla, that's her mum, has arranged for the two kids to be married, had Daniel's parents sign a contract, which is when Priscilla started controlling just about every aspect of Abbey's life."

"Daniel the pin dick fucker turned into a real piece of work after that," Amanda snaps. "Didn't like being forced into an arranged marriage, and instead of blaming his parents or even himself, he made Abbey the focus of his rage."

"Yeah, like her parents, mainly her bitch mum, used the pending nuptials as a way to make Abbey obey, threatening that if she misbehaves, the wedding will happen immediately." Bec growls and does an angry screech afterwards.

"But why would Daniel's parents agree to this?" I ask, fucking confused. It all seems very far-fetched, yet I know it's real.

"That's what we don't know. We think Priscilla has something over them. They also go to the same church, so maybe it has something to do with that," Bec states.

Fucking hell. There's so much we don't know.

"Do you have any idea why the wedding was moved up?" I ask, and Amanda hums.

"So that's why things exploded? Something must have happened. Abbey must have done something wrong in her mother's eyes, if that's the case."

Glancing down, Abbey shifts, curling in closer to my legs, but she remains asleep.

"I need to get Abbey out of here. After everything she's been through, living in an MC compound isn't the right place for her."

"Oh, my god! You took her to the Western?" Bec screeches.

"Where the fuck else was I meant to take her?"

"Uh… your house. You have a house, don't you?" Amanda asks.

"Yeah, where my mum and sisters live. I can't take her there."

"Why not? Too personal for you?" Bec teases.

"I was actually hoping *you'd* have somewhere for her," I snap, ignoring Bec's dig.

"Shit, no. Not unless you send her to Devon. Otherwise, we are at full capacity. The lockdowns have increased the domestic violence in the state."

Shit. I'd been relying on them having space for Abbey. I don't have a fucking backup plan.

"I'll figure something out." I sigh.

"Sorry big guy. The best we can do is help you get across the border. If you need to get out of the country, Barrett Marx is your best bet."

"Thanks." I grunt, raking my hand through my hair, feeling like I'm back at square fucking one.

Ending the call, I toss my phone on my bedside table and shift to lay down next to Abbey.

"Looks like I'm it," I whisper to her sleeping face, feeling the weight of my words.

I'm all she has to keep her safe from her parents and her fiancé.

But who the fuck is going to keep her safe from me?

15

ABBEY

The last few days are a blur. I spent them in bed sleeping, dreaming, crying. My limbs felt like they were bound in concrete, and my eyes stung from the never-ending flow of tears. I barely ate, and my gaze never landed on Ringo's when he tried to get me to fill my belly.

I just couldn't.

The pain of everything hit me like a freight train. It was overwhelming. Suffocating. All-consuming.

I didn't actually think I'd ever resurface, to be honest, and for a time there, I don't think I cared.

But then I remembered why I wanted to escape, and now, today, I've dragged myself out of Ringo's bed with a new sense of purpose.

To live.

To survive.

Approaching Ringo where he's sitting in the sun in the court-yard with Jols and JD, his eyes find mine, and he sits a little taller, a flash of surprise flicking across his expression.

"You're up."

I nod, offering him a half smile.

"Can I use your phone, please?" I ask, and his brows furrow as he grips the paper plate on his lap, the remnants of barbequed meat grease staining the surface.

"You want to use the app?" he asks, already figuring me out, so I nod. "You know the deal, Charity."

Ugh, that stupid name.

"Fine. What do I have to eat?" I ask, glancing over my shoulder at the table packed with an array of salads, barbequed meat, and bread rolls.

To try to get me to come out of my depression coma, Ringo had offered me his phone, telling me he'd downloaded the app that Lexi had been using to contact my little sister. That was the only thing that sparked an interest in me at the time, but then he'd gone and tried to blackmail me into eating something first if I wanted to use it, so I sunk back into my comatosed state preferring the numbness I felt there.

"Let's get you a plate," Ringo states, standing from his chair, his towering height dwarfing me as he passes by.

I follow, watching as he puts a sausage, some salad and a bread roll on the plate before holding it out for me.

My stomach roils.

"That's too much."

He shakes the plate. "Nope. It's hardly anything. Just try."

My eyes meet his, mine pleading, his unwavering.

"You have to eat, Charity."

"I'll eat if you stop calling me that," I whisper snap, and one corner of his lip twitches.

"Never. Now fucking eat, or no phone."

I roll my eyes and snatch the plate from his grip. "Anyone ever tell you, you're an arsehole?"

This time, his smirk shows. "Every fucking day." He gestures to the chair he was sitting in, so I move to it and take it, ignoring JD staring at me on one side, and Jols on the other.

Did he tell them what he overheard on the phone?

Do they all know now?

Heat flushes my cheeks at the thought. I hate people knowing my business. Mainly because I feel so ashamed. It's embarrassing. No one understands why a mum would do that to her daughter. Even I don't understand why either, other than I bring shame on the family.

Balancing my plate on my lap, I start picking at the food. I suck in a deep breath when the nausea hits again, but will it away so I can handle a little sustenance.

"Hey kid. When's the last time you took a shower?" JD's question has me snapping my head in his direction, and Jols scoffs.

"Leave her alone, JD. She's had a tough couple of days. Showering would be the last thing on her mind."

Shit.

Ringo must have told them.

I have no idea to what extent, but just knowing they know something has my emotions reappearing.

I stand quickly, nearly losing the food on my plate, but Ringo leaps forward and catches it before it's too late.

"What are you doing?" he asks, his presence looming, yet I don't look up to meet his eyes.

"Going to shower," I say quietly.

"Ouch," JD mutters behind me after a loud slap fills the air. "What the fuck was that for?"

"Just the fact you asked that means you deserved that slap," Jols snaps, but I don't hang around to hear anything else, high-tailing it back to Ringo's room.

Hurrying inside, I go to close the door behind me, but Ringo is right there, my plate in hand, following.

"Eat first. You're withering away. You'll never get strong and healthy if you don't give your body what it needs."

I still at his words, knowing he's right.

If I'm going to live and survive, then I need to get strong and healthy.

I need to look after myself, because no one else will do that for me.

I've wanted that for so long. To be left alone by my family so I can just be me.

Well, here's my chance. It's time I started acting like I can actually do this.

"If I eat this and shower, you'll let me use the Koala-roo app, right?" I ask, finally meeting Ringo's stormy brown eyes, and he nods.

"If you eat, you can have my phone until dinnertime."

Slowly, a smile tugs at my lips.

I'm going to get to chat with Tahli and Lexi today. Just the thought has my mood lifting.

I nod, taking the plate from his grip, and taking a bite of the sausage.

Even though my stomach roils again, I force it back, sucking in deep breaths as the flavour hits my tongue and explodes. I swallow the first bite and then have another, closing my eyes as I try to rush my chews before swallowing.

Holding up the sausage, my lips part as I go to take another bite, but then, my gaze locks onto Ringo as he watches me, his focus not on my eyes or hand, but on my lips.

I frown, and he doesn't even notice.

Slowly, I close my lips around the sausage and sink my teeth in, watching how his eyes and nostrils flare.

Oh.

My.

God.

Is he…

Heat flushes my cheeks, and the bite of sausage nearly chokes me, a cough bursting from my lips as I try to stop the meat from flying from my mouth.

"Shit," Ringo hisses, moving to me and patting me on the back, but his nearness just makes my skin flare hotter.

What the hell is happening right now?

"I'm okay," I snap around the mouthful of food and another cough, shifting quickly away from his touch.

He frowns, and I realise he noticed me shift away like I'm scared of him.

Shit.

I'm not scared of Ringo. If anything, I feel safer with him than anyone I've ever met.

What I am scared of is the way my body is reacting to him. It's not repulsed by him at all. Quite the opposite, and I don't know what to do with that information.

"I'm going to take a shower," I rush out, but he holds his hand up to stop me.

"Hold up." He steps closer, pointing at me. "You've been wearing the same damn clothes for days. Please tell me you plan on changing them today."

My brows crease as my gaze drops to the hoodie swimming on me and the black leggings underneath.

"I guess I could change the bottoms." I shrug, glancing back up to meet his piercing gaze.

"What about my hoodie? Can I have it back?" he asks, and I frown, even as I clutch the neckline, taking a step back.

"No."

I can tell he's biting back a smile. "You're not going to give me back my hoodie?"

I shake my head. "I'm claiming it as mine now," I admit, the thought of him taking it sounding more terrifying than the way my body reacted to him only moments ago.

"Fine. You can have it, but can you go a day without it so I can give it to the Doxies to wash?"

What the hell?

"No." I wrap my arms around myself this time, holding the fabric close. "They aren't touching it."

Ringo's smirk is huge as he chuckles. "Charity, come on now. It's starting to smell. Surely you can go a day without it—"

"No. No, Ringo. I'm not giving it to them," I snap, anger contorting my expression as I point a stern finger to the floor.

His brows hitch as his smirk grows and he just stares at me for a few long beats before talking.

"Fine. No Doxies, but what do I have to do to fix this? It smells," he steps forward and jabs the centre of my chest with his finger, "therefore *you* smell, and not in a nice way."

Horror takes over my expression. I can feel my heated cheeks and the way my mouth parts in disbelief, even though it was clear I smelled a few minutes ago when JD called me out on my lack of showering.

"I don't have a hoodie like this."

Oh, my god… am I pouting?

Given the dimple appearing in Ringo's cheek, I'm going to say yes.

He finds my discomfort really damn funny, doesn't he?

"You don't have a sick hoodie like mine?"

I roll my eyes. "Old men don't speak like that. Don't try to act cool, Ringo."

He beams. "I don't have to try, darlin'."

Once again, my cheeks are flaring to life, this time at his endearment, which I'm sure he meant nothing of, but holy crap. Hearing it roll off his tongue directed at me has me reeling.

"Perhaps you love the hoodie so much because it smells like me. Well, it used to." He teases, and shit, he doesn't realise how close to the truth he speaks.

"Ew. No," I gasp, curling my lip in disgust.

Hey. Ten points to me for my convincing acting skills.

"Well, Charity," he approaches, forcing me to lift my gaze to his looming height. "If it's not for any of those reasons, how about you tell me the truth? Why are you so attached to my hoodie?"

My lashes flutter as my mind races for a reason, a lie, but as I try to conjure something to tell him, his finger hooks under my chin and lifts, drawing my gaze to meet his.

"It makes me feel safe." The truth tumbles from my lips before I even realise I've spoken, and I expect him to look surprised, but he doesn't.

He just keeps staring at me like my admission is totally fine.

"What about my hoodie makes you feel safe, Angel? The feel of the fabric? The size of it? The smell of it?"

Jesus, he's really asking me that?

Biting my lower lip, I consider the lies I can muster, yet when I finally answer in another whisper, it's with the truth again. "Yes. All of those reasons."

Ringo nods, like he thought as much, completely accepting my reasoning as if it's not creepy.

"The weather is so stifling. Don't you get hot wearing it?" he asks, and I shrug.

"I like the heat. I've felt cold for so long. I can't seem to get warm enough, but when I'm wearing it, I feel comfortable."

A frown flickers across his expression before he hides it.

I'm not sure how my words made him react that way until he speaks.

"My ma once told me that when someone is anxious, their brain is never at peace, so instead of the heart focusing on pumping blood throughout the body, it focuses on pumping most of it to the brain because that's the part of the body that needs the help." He shrugs, his eyes going distant for a moment before returning to meet my gaze. "I don't know how true that is, but it could be what's happening here." He gestures to me, and for a moment I can't speak.

That statement is so profound.

Ringo clears his throat, taking a deep breath.

"Can we swap it out for another?" He points to the hoodie and my brows shoot up.

"Swap it?"

"Yeah." He finally releases my chin and turns to the wardrobe, finding another hoodie, this one green. "How about you put this one on instead?" He holds it up. "And give me that one so I can wash it."

"I thought you said the Doxy girls will wash it." I frown.

"I did, but I can do it if you'd rather?"

Ringo doing washing?

Now there's an amusing thought.

"Maybe I can help? If you show me where the laundry is, I can wash our stuff."

Our stuff.

Shit.

Why did I say it like that?

There is no *our* or *we*.

I'm a damn guest, or prisoner.

"I mean… you know… if you'd like me to wash your stuff." I quickly add, waving a dismissive hand, my eyes darting around the space, avoiding his face.

Really smooth, Abbey.

"I'd fucking love it if you washed my things, Angel."

My eyes dart to his, a smirk tugging at his lips.

"So what do you reckon? Swap this hoodie for that one?" He gestures his head down at my body, and I consider it briefly before nodding and snatching the clean hoodie from his grip before spinning and rushing into the bathroom.

His chuckle floats through the closed door as I shut myself in, pressing my back to the thin timber separating us.

I wait until I hear him open the external door and leave before I strip off and take the much-needed shower. I have to admit, it feels good to have the warm water rushing over my skin, rinsing away the sweat that's built on my skin from days of keeping myself hidden away.

I peel off the now soaked bandages on my hands to see the cuts are healing well enough that I can probably go without them now, and I take extra time, washing my hair and shaving my legs with the disposable razors Ringo left for me days ago.

By the time I get out and dry myself, I feel more human than I have in days, and manage to nibble on the bread roll when I re-enter the main room, fully dressed in clean underwear, clean red bike shorts, and a white tee underneath Ringo's green hoodie.

When I step outside the room a few minutes later, my gaze lands on the lady that was sprawled out in front of Ringo on the table in the President's room the other night. I think her name is Wendy, and as I take her in, I can see her sights are clearly set on Ringo as she stares at him across the courtyard.

That is until she notices me.

Her dark glare shoots my way, which seems to get Ringo's attention because his eyes find me as I slowly approach, as do a number of other men lazing about on chairs in the sun.

For the first time in days, instead of leaving my hair down or putting it in braids, I've tied it up high on my crown, my blonde strands still wet as droplets soak into the green fabric of the hoodie.

Normally I'd hate the attention, but something about the way my mere presence annoys Wendy has me walking taller, my chin high, shoulders rolled back with a level of confidence I haven't felt in a couple of years.

"Someone looks happy today." Smitty, the President, chuckles from next to Ringo, nudging him with his elbow as I approach.

Ringo holds his hand out as I near, my eyes falling to it and I hesitate slightly, my gaze darting back up to lock onto Ringo's.

Oh right. The ruse. I'm playing the part of his girl.

Reaching out, I slide my fingers into his open palm, and he pulls me to him, leading me down onto his lap.

"Hi," I say sweetly to Smitty, trying to sound as confident as I pretended to be moments ago.

"Hey there, pretty girl. You feeling better today?" Smitty asks, and when I tense a little, Ringo links his fingers with mine, giving my hand a gentle squeeze.

"Yes. Sorry, I haven't been a very pleasant guest." I smile. "I haven't been feeling well, but feel much better today."

"Better not have been Rona." Wendy, the cow, snipes as she comes to stand next to Smitty, draping herself over him like she's about to start dry humping his thigh.

"If it was the virus, I can assure you Charity wouldn't be out here spreading it around." Ringo snaps at Wendy, as he absent-mindedly pulls me closer on his lap.

"Charity is an interesting name." Darla comes up behind Wendy, propping her hand on her hip as she gives me the once over. "Why'd your parents call you that? Because you're a charity case?"

"The fuck!" Ringo bolts up, nearly sending me flying as he lunges for Darla, and it's Smitty who blocks his path.

"Back the fuck down, Ringo." Smitty sneers as he holds him back, but Ringo ignores him, stabbing a finger in Darla's direction. "Fucking apologise. Now!"

His boom is loud, and regret washes over Darla's expression as she nods. "I-I'm sorry."

Ringo shoves Smitty back. "Don't fucking apologise to me!" he snarls, turning to glance at me a few feet away as I wrap my arms around my middle.

Reaching out to me, Ringo's stare is firm and commanding as he waits, and even though I eye Darla and Smitty, my hand finds Ringo's before I let him tug me to his side.

Turning to face Darla again, Ringo glares at her. "Apologise to *my* woman."

Oh.

Oh.

His woman.

Darla visibly gulps, but I don't care much for her discomfort.

"I'm sorry, Charity. That was so rude of me. I don't know what I was thinking."

"I fucking do," Ringo mutters quietly before his gaze shifts to Wendy, who looks nothing but smug right now.

Did she put Darla up to this?

The last thing I need is a bunch of high school bitchiness from grown women who should know better.

"It's okay," I say to Darla despite how I feel. "I actually joke about being a charity case myself. I don't know what my name givers were thinking when they named me that. I've been considering changing it."

When Ringo glances at me, I can tell he's biting back a smirk at the way I so easily go along with the lie.

"Name givers? Is that what you call your parents?" Wendy sneers, like she's about to cause trouble, but I simply shrug.

"The people who gave me life aren't worthy of being called parents," I declare before glancing up at Ringo, offering him a smile. "I might change my name to Angel, since that's what you like calling me."

Oh damn.

Who am I right now?

Even though Ringo grins, his tone oozes seriousness.

"I thought I told you that name was just for me."

I shrug innocently, but then let loose my devious expression, feeling playful. "I thought you liked calling me your sex goddess. At least that's all you managed to mutter last night when I—"

"Don't fucking say it," Ringo snaps, his lips tugging at the corners at my sudden, mischievous playfulness as he leans closer so only I can hear. "You're playing with fire, Angel."

I know I'm only acting a part, but I'm pretty sure I'm playing it a little too well right now. I'm almost convincing myself.

Smitty and a few of the other men are chuckling, while Darla is smiling, and Wendy is scowling.

"Ahhh, Beatle, weren't you going to show me where the laundry is?" I ask, since I'm already playing with fire, I may as well toss fuel on the flames.

"Oh, he told you how he got his nickname, did he?" Smitty chuckles as Ringo glares at me. "Who would have thought this fucker was in a band back in the day?"

So that's where the nickname Ringo comes from.

I nod like I have a clue when really I'm just making up crap as I go. "I know, right? It's hard to believe he has a musical bone in his body with his inability to dance."

Smitty loses it then, clutching at his chest as Murf approaches us wearing a huge grin, while Ringo shoots daggers in every direction of laughter.

"Well, if you'll excuse us," he states so everyone can hear. "She wants to see the laundry room, and not for the purpose of washing our clothes."

I frown, unsure of his meaning before he reaches down and grabs a handful of my arse, giving it a squeeze until a squeak flies from my lips, shock widening my eyes.

"What did you say earlier, Angel? You want me balls deep inside you as you sit on the washer during the spin cycle?"

Roars of laughter fill the air, as well as hoots as Ringo scoops me up in his arms cradling me to his chest, and with purpose in his strides, heads straight for the laundry room across the courtyard.

16

ABBEY

My arse hits the washing machine, a gasp flying from my lips as Ringo sits me on the cool surface. My frantic gaze darts around the dingy space, shock and a little fear seeping in as I realise my mistake.

I poked the bear.

"I'm sorry. I was just going along with things. I didn't mean to make you look bad or…" I stop blabbering as Ringo steps closer, shaking his head as a smooth chuckle floats from his lips.

"You didn't make me look bad, Angel." His large hands come to rest on the tops of my thighs, and a jolt of something I don't want to admit shoots straight between my legs, startling me.

What the hell?

"What I said about dancing… I have no idea if you can dance or not. I'm sure you're a great dancer."

Oh hell. Why is his smile so… sexy?

Wait.

No, it's not.

It's definitely not.

Oh, my god.

What is happening?

I stiffen as his large hands give my thighs a gentle squeeze, and then slowly part my knees further apart.

"W-what are you doing?"

"Just playing the part, darlin'." He drawls, "How many eyes are on us right now?"

Frowning, it takes me a moment to realise what he means, but then my gaze shoots over his shoulder, to the open door, where multiple sets of eyes are cast in this direction from the courtyard.

"Um… A lot."

He chuckles. "Should we give them a show?"

My eyes nearly bug out of my head. "No. No. No way." I repeat my words, hoping it's really damn clear that I'm not doing… that.

"Relax, Angel. It won't hurt."

Ohhhh no. Why am I feeling hot? Like all over. This hoodie is suddenly way too hot. My clothes suddenly too much to bear on my skin. Why is there an ache building between my legs?

Dammit. This is embarrassing. I tried to ignore it, but it was there the moment I woke this morning, in addition to teasing me in some of my dreams over the last couple of days. When I dream, they are usually nightmares, but for some reason, I had a sex dream for the first time in over a year, and now… I ache.

Ringo leans in, getting close and I stiffen, all while I have the urge to lean in closer.

"Wait," I mutter breathlessly, feeling confused and scared and way too turned on to make any sense of anything, but then Ringo steps back quickly, turning and slamming the door closed.

A round of boos and disappointed awes meet our ears from the other side, and Ringo chuckles, turning to face me and leaning against the door.

"Don't worry, Angel. I won't touch you unless you beg me to."

My mouth drops open, and I glare at his smug expression as he crosses his arms over his chest.

"You're a prick."

He wags his brows. "You already knew that."

"I actually thought…"

I can't finish the sentence, both from embarrassment and fear.

"What? That I was going to fuck you?" he snaps, dropping his arms and closing the space between us. "Just like you were doing out there, I was playing the part. It was nothing more than a show in order to fool them all into thinking you're actually mine."

Stepping between my legs again, his bearded chin brushes closely to mine as he hovers a breath away, and for a moment we just stare at each other, breathing the same air.

"Just for the record, Angel, because you clearly need it spelled out for you. I *will* never and *have* never forced myself on a woman. If you want me between your naked thighs, I can assure you, it'll be because you asked."

A whimper escapes me, and not because I'm scared or hate his words, but because I'm fighting the urge to lean in. To see what it would be like to feel his lips against mine. What it feels like to kiss a man with a beard. To simply kiss a real man. Not a boy. Not a teenager. But a man that knows how to please a woman.

"Are you afraid of me?" he asks, misunderstanding my whimper. I don't respond, and a deep growl rumbles in his chest. "Answer me, Angel."

"No." I give him what he asks for, not able to refuse him when he asks me like that. It makes no sense to me.

"Hmmm, then perhaps you're afraid of the way you're feeling?"

Shit. How does he know?

Oh god. Am I that readable?

"Angel. When I ask you a question, you answer me."

"I…" My cheeks flare to life, and he pulls back a little to study my face.

"Are you afraid of the way you're feeling?" he asks again, and I nod.

He considers that for a moment, before putting a little more space between us and reaching up to tangle his fingers in my ponytail.

"Do you feel achy? Hot? Sensitive…" he leans closer, "between your legs."

All I can do is whimper again.

"Why are you scared of that feeling?" This time he tugs on my hair tie, loosening my ponytail.

"I don't want to say," I rush out, studying his gaze, which is focused on my hair as his fingers mess my styling up.

"You've felt that way before, right?" he asks, ignoring the fact I said I didn't want to say.

"Yes." I breathe, and he nods, his dark gaze locking with mine.

"When was the last time you felt like that?"

I shake my head. "I don't want to have this conversation with you."

"Why?" he asks, his expression neutral, telling me he won't be angry if I want to end the conversation now.

"Because it's weird. I don't know you. And you're like old."

He chuckles. "How fucking old do you think I am?"

I shrug. "Like, forty."

His head tips back as a laugh leaps from his mouth, his deep rumble sending my lips north.

"What?" I ask as he continues to laugh. "Are you older than that?"

"No." He grips his middle, his smile so wide that I can see the flash of his white teeth past his beard. "Fuck, maybe I should look into getting Botox if I look forty."

My shoulders sag. "I'm sorry. I just really don't know many people that aren't either my age or my parents' ages. And I never knew the real ages of the teachers at school. I don't really have anything to compare it to."

Slowly, he nods, a grin still tugging at his lips. "You remember the big guy that bailed you up the other night when you left my room when you shouldn't have?"

Even though I roll my eyes, I still nod.

"Well, that was Fryer. For reference, he's forty-two." Then he jabs his thumb to his chest. "I am thirty-three."

"Oh," I say, a little stunned. Thirty-three isn't that old… right?

I mean, yeah, I'm still in my teens, so the age difference between us is big, but not parental big. Not unless he was a father at fifteen.

"So now that we've established I'm not *that* old, is this con-versation still weird?"

I shrug. "Kinda. I'm not used to talking to… well, anyone, about stuff."

"That's because you were in a place where you couldn't trust anyone. I hope you'll eventually learn to trust me."

I don't know why I want his words to come true so badly. I'll be gone soon, and this man will be nothing but a memory of the time I got kidnapped.

I nod, because I don't know what else to do, and Ringo sighs.

"My name is Cameron. Cameron Musgrove."

My brows hitch. "Your real name is Cameron?"

When he nods, my shoulders relax.

"Do you have a middle name?" I dare to ask, and his lips thin like he is struggling with my question.

"If I tell you," he points a stern finger at me, "you'd better not fucking laugh."

Still with a wide smile, I sign a cross over my heart, waiting for him to divulge the name that he's clearly embarrassed about.

"My full name is Cameron Eugene Musgrove."

My smile drops.

My lips snap shut.

I hold my breath.

Oh, my god.

Don't laugh. Don't laugh. Don't laugh.

"Don't fucking do it." He hisses, which breaks my dam.

Throwing my head back, my giggles are loud, happy tears forming in my eyes for once as he broods before me, throwing up his hands.

"Fine. Laugh all you want," he snaps before muttering quietly. "I bet Lexi knew this would happen."

"Wait, what?" I snicker, trying to calm myself down. "You spoke to Lexi again?"

He nods, crossing his arms over his chest, his legs wide as he watches me, not looking very impressed.

"When? What did she say?"

"It was the other night after you spoke to her and…" He trails off, his expression morphing to pity before he waves a hand between us. "Anyway, she thought if I told you my real name, which cannot be fucking repeated to anyone, that you might see me as more human than thug."

Still smiling, I nod. "She was right. Cameron Eugene definitely makes you more human."

He rolls his eyes at me. "Are you done?"

I shrug. "I guess."

He sighs again. "I guess you want my phone now that you've eaten and washed?" When I nod quickly, he continues. "Will you at least spend the afternoon in the sun with me while you use my phone? The vitamin D will do you good."

I nod, even as I speak. "I suppose I can do that." I tease. "Can I use your phone again tonight?"

His smile is gentle and genuine. "Of course. As long as you eat."

I roll my eyes, and he steps forward, tipping his head towards me. "Mess up my hair."

"What?" I squeak, leaning back a little, but he chuckles and takes my wrist, guiding my hand to his head.

"Mess up my hair. We gotta make it look like we fucked, Angel."

My cheeks and between my thighs flare to life simultaneous-
ly at his words, and a moment later my fingers are threading
through his longish dark strands, which is softer than I imagined.

"Ohhhh yeah." He groans dramatically, and when I go to pull
my hand back, his vice-like grip around my wrist stops me as he
leans in more. "Don't stop."

I can't help it. The need to obey him and please him is ridiculous, yet it controls me as I do as he asks, my fingertips scratch-
ing into his scalp.

"Fuuuuck, Angel. You know how to make a man hard."

One of those embarrassing squeaks flies from me again as
this time, I successfully pull my hand free, and Ringo's chuckle
fills the space of the laundry room as I shove him back.

"Stop." I order, yet I can't hide my smirk and his eyes, light
from laughter, lock with mine.

"Darlin', I'm a man, locked in a room with a beautiful woman
who smells fucking intoxicating, makes the sexiest little whimpers, and scratched my head. I can't control my reaction."

He thinks I'm beautiful? That I smell… intoxicating? And he
thinks my pathetic whimpers are sexy?

Oh shit. Why did he have to admit that to me?

*Don't be that girl, Abbey. Compliments don't mean I should
spread my legs. Been there, done that. Was the worst decision of
my life.*

"Can we go?" I ask quietly, and he turns, pulling back the
curtain covering the window to peer out.

I don't miss the way he rearranges his junk in his jeans. I guess
he wasn't kidding when he said he was hard.

"Yeah, I guess enough time has passed for a quick fuck." He turns back to me. "Are you good? Do you need to go back to the room and take a minute?"

I frown, confused by his question. "A minute?"

"You know." He shrugs. "To scratch that itch you were feeling."

Itch?

Oh.

OH.

"No." I shake my head quickly, my cheeks flaming with heat once again.

The smart thing would be to try and scratch that itch, but I already kinda tried when I woke in bed earlier, and the moment I touched myself, the ache went out like a bucket of iced water was thrown on me.

Yeah, it probably had to do with the memory of Daniel creeping its way in, but still. If I need to go back to the room for anything, it's to douse the fire, not let it build until it explodes.

Offering me his hand, Ringo helps me down from the washer, and I realise as we rejoin the others, that he was messing my hair up before to make it look like we… well, you know.

We're met with some hoots and hollers, and everyone seems to forget about it within minutes of us sitting back down with the group.

Ringo hands me his phone, opening the app and quietly tells me the info for Tahli's and Lexi's usernames, and the moment I set up my profile and create a new message to my little sister, she responds.

Tears fill my eyes, my smile wide, and I duck my head, hoping no one sees it, but a moment later, Ringo's large hand takes mine, urging me up off the seat next to him and onto his lap.

"Just relax, Angel." He rasps quietly, and he positions me to rest against him, my ear pressed to his chest where the loud thrum of his heart somehow soothes me.

I curl into him, focusing on my phone as I chat in text to Tahli, finally feeling some peace that she's okay.

We spend a couple of hours in the sun, the men and women in fits of laughter as some of the men do what they call, Rona Olympics, which consists of doing stupid stuff, either blindfold-ed, or with their arms tied behind their backs, or after downing six shots of whiskey and then seeing who can run the longest without throwing up.

That was when I excused myself, because, *ew*.

Tahli had gone offline about thirty minutes before that any-way, and the hot sun was making me tired, so when I excused myself to go back to Ringo's room, he followed.

We both laid on the bed, the ceiling fan on full blast as we tried to cool off.

Not for the first time, Ringo insisted I take the hoodie off, but I just shook my head and focused on his phone to chat in the Koala-roo app with Lexi this time.

I can't even begin to explain how good it is to be chatting with Lexi again. The fact that she was the one that arranged my kidnapping, even after everything I did to her, speaks volumes about the person she is.

She assures me Ringo is what she calls 'good people', and something she said to me via chat really resonated with me.

He may be a criminal, but he doesn't lie about who he is. It's the people that lie and do the most heinous things that are the real monsters.

That really hit hard, because I realised it was one thing I already appreciated about Ringo. He didn't try to pretend he was this good guy. He didn't try to coax me into going with him by lying about who he was. He knew I wouldn't have gone with him either way, so he told me exactly who he was, took me, and was unapologetic about it.

Why can't more people be like that?

Why can't I be like that?

I want to be. I really do, but with everything that's happened, I don't know that I'll ever be able to reveal things to the people that know me.

That's why I need to leave. Go far away and start over somewhere new. Build a new life and embrace the questionable decisions I've made.

At some point during my text chatting with Lexi, Ringo's long, even breathing draws my attention, and I notice he's fallen asleep.

I find myself watching him. The way his normally hard expression has softened. The way his toned abdomen is noticeable through the fabric of his grey tee as he takes each breath. And I really can't stop looking at his crotch, especially now, as it seems to grow before my eyes underneath the denim.

My eyes dart back to his face, but he's still asleep, and I almost wish I could see inside his head to reach his dreams.

Who is he dreaming about? What is he doing? How does he feel?

Stop it, Abbey.

I mentally scold myself, my head way too deep in the gutter today for my own good.

I contemplate sneaking into the bathroom to touch myself just to scare the ache away, but think better of it and shift my gaze to the ceiling as I go over in my head what Tahli told me earlier.

She told me that Mum and Dad went to the police, and that when the police wanted to ask Tahli and Maggie questions, our parents wouldn't allow it.

When I chatted with Lexi, she said the police had come to question her a couple of times, my parents apparently adamant that if it was a ruse, I'd be hiding at Lexi's house.

Ringo shifts on the bed next to me, a moan of sorts slipping from his lips as he palms his penis from the outside of his jeans.

It's a cock, Abbey. Say it. Cock.

Ugh.

As his hand moves away, I can see the very clear, firm outline of his hardness, and the ache between my legs grows.

I shouldn't do what I do next, but arousal I'm not used to having is controlling me, and I place the phone down and dis-creetly ease my hand under the hoodie on the opposite side from Ringo, moving to press my fingers between my legs over my bike shorts.

Unlike this morning, there is no invisible bucket of ice water, only enraging heat as I part my legs a little, my eyes cast on Ringo's large bulge as I try to picture what it looks like in my head.

Long, thick, straining with veins, and… a foreskin.

Wait what?

Ugh. No. Stop.

My brain is being a bitch. There's no way Ringo has a foreskin. Not like Daniel.

A wave of nausea rolls through me at the reminder of what his penis looks like, and a vile shiver runs down my spine.

Taking in a deep breath, I glance at Ringo's face again and press my fingers to my needy bud through the fabric of my leggings.

What if he woke up right now and dove his face between my legs?

A ripple of arousal flutters through my core, and I keep pressing, circling, letting myself feel the pleasure that has been gone for so long.

I need more. I need more than my hands. I need someone else's hands. Lips…

A moan escapes me, and my hand slaps over my mouth right as Ringo's eyes snap open.

17

RINGO

I f she thinks I don't know what she was doing, then she's dead fucking wrong. There was no mistaking what that moan was, and the fact she's hightailing to the bathroom just fucking confirms that my Angel was touching herself.

Sitting up, I palm my hard cock through my jeans, wondering if she saw it while I was napping.

I'd been dreaming, but man, it felt so fucking real.

We were on the bed, just the way we were when I must have fallen asleep, and she kept rubbing her thighs together, just the way she was beforehand as well.

It's clear she's horny. Aroused and aching, and my dream state took me there.

I'd asked her if I could touch her, and dream Abbey said yes. She'd spread her legs for me, an invitation to access her body, and I'd rolled over to situate myself between her legs, although suddenly, her clothes were gone, and her cream skin led a trail to the pink flesh between her thighs.

Fuuuuck the way dream Abbey looked down her body at me, biting her lip just like she does sometimes, her caramel gaze lust drunk, as she rolled her hips, trying to get her needy little bud closer to my lips.

Then, I blew hot air over it, and she moaned, but the moan was so loud, it woke me.

And here we fucking are. Me hard as fucking stone on the bed, with her, probably mashing away the ache in the bathroom.

Fuck.

Why do I want to go into that fucking bathroom so much?

If it were any other woman, I'd be kicking that fucking door down and claiming her sweet cunt in a heartbeat.

But Abbey isn't any other woman. It's clear her fear of the way she's been feeling relates to whatever has happened in her past. The last thing she needs is a fucking brute biker mauling her.

Needing a fucking minute, I get up off the bed, shove my feet into my shit kickers, and head outside.

"You okay, man?" JD asks, offering me a dart, which I accept, lighting it up and savouring the first few drags. "Blondie keeping you busy?"

There's amusement in JD's tone, and I can't help but smirk, even as I shrug.

"Just trying to keep up the ruse," I say quietly, and he nods.

I haven't seen much of my closest mate over the last few days, but that's not unusual after what we did the other night.

Going in to kidnap Abbey—or rescue her, depending on how you look at it—would have really hit home for JD after what happened to his sister.

"Are you good?" I ask him, watching his expression as I take another deep drag of my cigarette before blowing the smoke off to the side.

He nods, not making eye contact. "Going into her house really kicked my arse."

"Yeah, I figured. I'm sorr—"

JD holds his hand up, rounding on me and keeping his voice low. "No. We did a good thing. Don't apologise for asking me to help you."

Reaching out, I grip my best mate's shoulder, and with the cigarette between two fingers on my other hand, I point at him. "You are a good fucking man, but that doesn't mean I don't feel fucking bad for putting you in that situation."

"I know." JD nods, dropping his gaze to our feet, and I know he's taking a fucking moment to compose himself. "What did you say to Brody that has him pissing his pants?"

When JD's troubled gaze peers back up to mine, I can't help but smirk.

"I noticed that fucker had gone quiet."

"Quiet is an understatement. He's been offering to fucking clean and wash my clothes like I can somehow save him from his fate."

I chuckle. "Stupid fucker."

"So what did he do, aside from the whole thing with Darla in your room?"

Releasing JD's shoulder, I take another long drag, holding the toxic smoke in my lungs as I answer. "I tasked him to watch my fucking door while I hung with Smitty. The fucker was too busy railing a Doxy outside my door to notice Charity fucking leaving to find me."

"Oh, shit." JD's brows shoot high.

"Yeah. Oh, fucking shit." I nod. "Told the fucker he was out and haven't seen him since."

JD chuckles. "Explains why he's been hiding."

"Hmmmm," I mutter, turning back to my door to see if, by some miracle, Abbey has decided to come out from hiding too.

"So you've claimed her?" JD asks, and I turn back to see he's watching my door as well.

"Apparently," I mutter.

"You don't sound happy about that." JD Points out, and I fucking sigh, pressing the smoke to my lips for one last hit before dropping it to the ground and stubbing it out with the weight of my boot.

"I just didn't expect..." I trail off, frowning.

What the fuck didn't I expect? To be attracted to her. To want to do things to her I know she's not ready for? To protect her from the entire fucking world, even every bastard in this club?

"Bro. What's got you so fucking twisted up?" JD asks, and I lock my gaze with his, knowing if I want to say any of these thoughts out loud, he's the only one I'd trust with them.

"She has me riled up," I admit, and his brows shoot high.

"As in... a good way?"

"As in, I want to rip her fucking clothes off and devour her," I snap between clenched teeth, barely able to keep my clipped tone quiet.

"Fuuuuck. That's new."

"Yeah, no fucking shit," I mutter, looking back at the gathered men already blind drunk, trying to play poker off Nola's naked body as she giggles.

"What's it been? Three years since you've been interested in pussy."

A low growl rumbles in my chest as I shoot a death glare at my best mate. "Don't refer to her as pussy."

His brows fucking disappear under his shaggy brown hair.

"Fuck. This is more than getting laid."

That's what I'm fucking worried about.

I spin, giving the pissheads my back as I stare at my closed door. "It's wrong, right?" I ask. "She's so fucking young. Naïve. And so fucking damaged."

Taking a step back so he's still facing our club brothers, but so he can see my face too, JD shakes his head. "Tell me about her."

"What? Why?"

"Just fucking do it," JD snaps, and a grin tugs at my lips.

"Fine. When she's not terrified, or walking around like a numb zombie, she's kinda sassy. Quick-witted. I can tell she's smart, too. I can see there's this whole other side to her that I haven't met, but I just fucking know will blow my fucking mind. Which makes no fucking sense, since I really don't know her." I shrug, dropping my gaze to the ground. "She's strong, though. She's been through something, man." I glance up at JD, shaking my head. "Something really fucking bad, and she's been trying to get by, biding her time until she could escape, but I can see that whatever she's running from, it'll never leave her."

"Damaged." JD nods and I nod in return. "Do you think that maybe you see Kylie in her?"

"The fuck?" I hiss, glaring at my best mate, who doesn't even flinch. He knew I'd react that way.

"She was pretty fucking damaged." He points out.

"That was fucking different. She had an addiction. A fucking disease. And what for? She never experienced the crap Abbey has had to."

"Don't you mean Charity?" JD reminds me, and I fucking rake my hand down my face, trying to calm my growing rage.

Shaking my head, I look up at the sky, pinks and purples washing over the top of us as the summer sun sets.

"I'm not trying to be a prick. What sort of friend would I be if I didn't ask?"

"Yeah, I know." I sigh, dropping my gaze back to my mate. "Maybe it's just because I'm forced to be around her basically twenty-four seven. Maybe I just need to fuck a Doxy and this fucking weird infatuation will vanish."

"Maybe," JD shrugs. "It's worth a try."

I nod, even though the thought of touching anyone makes me want to swing fists.

"I need to get out of my own funk, too," JD states. "Was thinking of giving Helina a ride tonight. You feel like a show?"

I smirk. This fucker. He's such a fucking exhibitionist, and as fucking weird as it sounds, the only other time I've gotten off in the last three years with someone else in the room has been while watching him and his fucking antics.

There was a time I'd considered that maybe I was gay, or bi, since I enjoyed watching him. I quickly learned that it was more about the act being displayed right in front of me, and the way he involves me by asking what I want him to do to whichever girl is at his mercy.

Yeah. I fucking like that.

But never have I joined in. Never have I let anyone else touch me, not since Kylie.

"I could use a show." Jols interrupts, shouldering me as she joins us.

"You wanna be part of the show?" JD asks with a smirk, knowing too fucking well she'll say no.

"Oh sure. Daddy Smitty would love to see his men rail his stepdaughter." Jols rolls her eyes, and we chuckle.

"I gotta say, as much as I like you Jols, I don't wanna see that either, so I'm with Smitty on that one." I grin and she shrugs.

"Whatever. If these fucking lockdowns don't stop, I might say yes one day. A girl has needs, after all."

JD's fucking eyes light up. "Say the word, Jols, and I'll rock your world."

She scoffs. "I'm not so sure you would, tiger."

"The Doxies don't complain."

"The Doxies teach each other how to fake it and look real." Jols deadpans and JD's smile falls.

"They do fucking not."

She shrugs. "What the fuck would I know? I only hang with them eighty percent of the time."

JD's expression is priceless, mortification contorting his features as his eyes dance between me and Jols.

"She's just fucking with me, right?" he asks me, and I chuckle, holding my hands up.

"Don't fucking bring me into it. I wouldn't know since I don't fuck them."

JD's eyes darken and he gets in Jols' face as he points at her. "I fucking challenge you."

"To what?" Jols giggles.

"To come to my fucking room and see if I can't make you cream so much, you need new panties."

Jols stops giggling, her spine straightening as she makes herself taller, which effectively pushes her tits out, right against JD's chest. "Jimmy Dean, if I come to your room, you'll be lucky to last a minute before you're shooting your jizz in your boxers."

I throw my head back, laughing, but JD doesn't fucking move, his nostrils flaring.

"You just said my real name."

"I did." She smirks, cocking her hip, her claw-like nails resting over it. "Jimmy. Dean." She drawls each name nice and slow, fucking asking for trouble.

"No one says my name," JD growls, and my smile falls as I consider that perhaps my best mate might truly be pissed.

"Really?" Jols gives him a one-shouldered shrug. "Because I just did."

In an instant his hand is fisting in her hair, and a faint whimper escapes her as he holds her captive against him.

"Hey man." I reach forward, ready to stop him, but then he grins.

"I knew you had a thing for me, Jols. There's no hiding it now." He shoves her back, shooting her a wink. "I dare you to come to my room later and find out which one of us is right."

For the first fucking time ever, I see Jols' cheeks turn red.

Fuck. I never thought I'd see the day.

Sighing to try and cover up the way her body reacted, Jols flips her long dark strands off her shoulder. "I would come to your room later, but I'm all booked up for tonight. I hear your little brother has a pierced cock. Looks like tonight's my turn to find out."

Jols spins and hurries off, even as I hold JD back, his hands outstretched to grab her.

"Calm fucking down." I chuckle, and when JD relaxes, I release him.

"Fuck. My dick is iron hard."

"Looks like you'll be giving a good show later, then." I chuckle and JD nods.

"Too fucking right, I will. And you know who will be watching like she doesn't want to join in?" He wags his brows at me. "Jols."

Murf takes that moment to come over with a tray of barbequed food, offering us some, so I grab a plate off the nearby table, and pile some snags, chops, and corn on, and head back to my room, determined to get Abbey to eat.

Inside, I find her sitting cross-legged on the bed, her slight frame still drowning in my green hoodie, her hair tied up high on her head again, having tidied it up after I messed it earlier.

Her caramel eyes shoot up to see who's entering, but just as quickly return to the phone where she must still be chatting to her little sister or Lexi.

"Hungry?" I ask, and she shrugs.

For fuck's sake. How can she not be starving? She hardly eats.

Placing the plate on the table, I move to the bed and quickly swipe the phone.

"Hey!" She hisses, lunging for me, but I pull back, lifting my hand high, even as she stands on the mattress and tries to reach for it.

"Uh-uh, Angel. Eat first. Then you can have the phone back."

"Ugh." She growls, balling her fists at her sides as she glares at me. "Just give it back. I'll eat while I chat."

I shake my head. "Nope. Eat first. Chat after."

"You know, you really are irritating." She glares, both hands on her hips now as she still stands on my bed.

"I've been called worse." I shrug, and she nods.

"I can just imagine."

"Stop being a brat and get down here." I point to the shitty green carpet, but she shakes her head.

"No. Give me the phone first."

So, this is how she wants to play it?

Fine with me.

"You're not getting the phone until you've eaten. Now get down here."

"No." She pronounces the word like I'm hard of hearing.

"Down! Now!" I boom, and in an instant, her eyes drop to the floor as she quickly gets off the bed, coming to stand before me.

Fuck.

I knew she was a submissive, and I know she doesn't know she's one, but right now, as she stands before me, her eyes cast to the floor between us, I wish she did know. I wish she knew so I could command her to kneel. To open her pretty mouth wide and take my cock deep into the back of her throat until she gags.

Fuck, she'd be such a good girl.

I consider if this is perhaps what has me so captivated with her. The fact she is a natural submissive. She never chose to be like this. She was raised that way, and it makes me wonder if she wouldn't, in fact, enjoy that in the bedroom.

Considering her past, and what I think may have happened to her, my guess is she may not be so keen to give up her control, since it most definitely was taken away from her.

"Eyes on mine." I command, and just like I thought, her caramel pools dart up to meet mine. Fuck me. She's even standing with her hands clasped together in front of her.

"Eat a snag or chop, and a corncob, and you will be rewarded with the phone."

Slowly, she nods and when I step aside and gesture to the table, she quickly takes a seat and starts nibbling on a snag.

I sit too, taking a chop and using my fingers like a caveman, and eat as I watch her.

She frowns a little as she eats, a cringe crossing her expression before she places the snag down and starts on the corn. I bite back a smirk as she sinks her teeth in, her lashes fluttering as she closes her eyes and starts chewing.

"Are you vegetarian?" I ask, noting the difference between her trying to eat the meat and taking a decent bite of the corn.

She shakes her head, but then shrugs. "I don't know. Maybe?"

I chuckle. "Isn't being vegetarian a choice? You either like eating meat or you don't."

She shrugs again, her eyes on me as she takes another bite of her corn.

"There are more veggies out there." I point my thumb over my shoulder. "Would you like me to get more for you?"

"Yes, please." She nods with a mouth full of corn, some of the juice running down her chin.

I can't fucking help it. Before I realise what I'm doing, I reach forward and wipe up the escaped juice with my finger before licking it off. Her eyes go wide, and I chuckle, more to hide the fact that I'm just as shocked, before I stand and leave the room to gather more vegetables.

Casey is a big believer of salad and vegetables with at least two meals of the day, so it's no surprise there is an array of options on the trestle tables by the barbeque. I get another plate, filling it with potato salad, peas, beans, broccoli, and a garden salad, before snatching up a couple of bread rolls and butter, too.

When I return to Abbey, her eyes go wide at the large plate piled high, and she immediately starts with the green vegetables, eating quickly like she's starved.

Has this been her problem the whole time? I just wasn't offering her the right food?

Whatever it is, I'm fucking happy she's finally eating. Warmth fills my chest, and I feel like beating it and yelling, "I man, feed woman!"

It's weird to feel like this over simply getting her to eat, but fuck, I think I'll make it my mission to see her eat like this for every fucking meal.

I watch her in silence, leaving her to enjoy the food, loving how she sometimes has her mouth full, the fork piled with food ready to go, and her other hand picking up whatever it can to shove in her mouth before she's even finished chewing.

It's not long before she's full, and even though there's still a lot of food left, I don't force her to eat more since I'd over piled the plate.

Leaning back in her chair, Abbey presses her hand to her chest, and she sighs, a small smile tugging at her lips.

"That good, huh?"

She nods. "Delicious."

Placing the chop bone back on my plate, I use a napkin to wipe my fingers clean. "In future, if you want something in particular to eat, tell me. I don't care what you're eating, just as long as you are. You're too skinny."

A single brow shoots up as she studies me. "What if I want a big bowl of French fries and a tub of cookies and cream ice cream?"

"Then that's what I'll get for you."

She rolls her eyes. "We are in lockdown."

"And?" I ask. "You do remember who I am. I don't exactly obey the law if it gets in the way of what I need or want."

Something about what I said causes her to blush, and she starts nibbling on her thumbnail.

"What?" I ask, and she shrugs.

"If I really wanted those things, and they weren't here, would you really break the law to go out and find them?"

I nod. "Of course."

"Why?" She frowns, and I consider lying, telling her that Lexi demanded I take care of her, but again, I find I don't want to do that. I want her to know the truth.

"I want to make you happy."

This only makes her frown deepen. "But why? We aren't friends."

"Aren't we?" I ask, and now she looks more confused. "Did I not hold you when you fell apart a few days ago? Have I not offered to keep you safe? Have I not protected you, fed you, made sure you changed out of your smelly clothes? Isn't that what friends do?"

"In all fairness, the changing clothes thing was probably more for your benefit." She deadpans, and I chuckle.

"Good point."

"And you're keeping me safe and all that stuff because Lexi asked you to."

"Fine, but what about the part when I held you until you cried yourself to sleep in my arms?"

She shrugs, her eyes turning glassy. "You have a conscience." It comes out more like a question, and I shake my head.

"Nope. Try again."

"You don't want Lexi to think you're being a prick?"

I chuckle at that. "Nope. Not even close. She already knows I can be a prick, and so do you."

"I don't know then," she whispers, her eyes falling to her lap where her fingers are fidgeting.

"Eyes up." I demand, and there they are, flecks of gold amongst the caramel, as she looks at me with uncertainty. "I may be a prick, and a monster to some, but to you, well... I'd consider you a friend. Especially since we've been sharing a bed and a bathroom, and well, I'm pretty sure you were checking out my dick earlier."

"Oh, my god!" She squeals, shooting up from the chair as my chuckle fills the space. "You're an animal." She declares, hurrying to the other side of the room, putting space between us.

"You're right. I am an animal. Which I happen to think you secretly like."

She sighs. "You have to stop with that nonsense, old man."

I shake my head. "Nope. I know what you were doing in the bathroom, Angel, and I know you're scared of the way it makes you feel, but when you're ready to have that itch scratched, let me know."

Her cheeks flare to life like two red beacons in a dark sea, and I point to the window.

"Things are heating up out there. If you feel brave enough to get a closer look instead of watching from the window, come outside. Watching is half the fun."

I leave the room quickly then, letting my words sink in and curiosity fills my mind.

Will she make an appearance?

Time will tell.

18

ABBEY

I'm burning up from the inside. It's like lava is flowing through my veins, and every stitch of clothing is too hot. Too much. Just the press of the fabric between my legs is making it unbearable to resist touching myself, yet the humiliation of knowing Ringo knew what I was doing earlier stays my hand.

What the hell is wrong with me?

It has to be this feeling of being free that has my body reacting this way. Knowing my parents can't get to me. Knowing Daniel can't put his slimy hands on me, is a huge relief.

But what? As soon as I'm free, I turn into a horndog?

I consider calling Lexi. Maybe she can help me figure out why I'm so desperate to fill the emptiness between my legs.

Never in the early days with Daniel did I feel like this.

Sure, he made me feel good a time or two, but this… I think there's something seriously wrong with me.

The music is loud outside, so too is the laughter and the moans that occasionally break past the barrier of the closed door.

I stare at the window, desperate to turn the light off and move to it to watch what's happening beyond, yet the fact Ringo knows I do that, and knows what I did earlier is making it hard for me to move.

"I'm pretty sure you were checking out my dick earlier."

Dammit. His words keep replaying in my head. I'd hoped he didn't notice what I was doing when he woke up, but he obviously did.

How mortifying.

He must think I'm some sort of perverted creep.

Ugh. Maybe I am, because all I want to do is go to that damn window and watch the porn scene unfold.

The moment I hear cheers, I'm moving, shutting off the lights and easing the curtains open to see out into the courtyard. It's dark now, but the lights around the building's edge and the two large spotlights shining into the centre of the yard illuminate the crowd.

I can see one of the men that was with Ringo when they took me. JD. I'm pretty sure he was the one that broke into my room. It was hard to tell who was who with the black balaclavas they wore.

JD is completely naked, and heat pools between my legs as his peni—cock, standing tall, comes into view. My breathing quickens as I watch his fingers press between the girl's legs.

She's on top of a table, completely naked, and there's a man standing near her head, pressing his tip against her lips.

Memories come rushing in, and nausea rolls my stomach, a cry lurching from my lips as I force myself to keep watching.

No. Stop. I tell myself. *I'm not there. This isn't that.*

I'm trembling, sweat running down my back as I fight off the vile images I fear I'll never be able to forget.

"This isn't that," I whisper to nobody, taking a step closer to the window to force myself to watch. "This isn't that," I say louder.

I drag my gaze from the man at her head feeding his dick into her mouth, back to JD who is… oh… his fingers are inside her, and she's thrusting up to meet his touch.

A gasp lodges in my throat as my eyes find their way past JD and the girl, to see Ringo, his gaze trained on the window as if he can see me.

Can he see me?

I don't know if he can, and I don't know if I care because… Oh… My… In his hand is his dick. No, not a dick. Absolutely nothing less than a cock.

More heat pools between my legs as I nearly press myself to the glass, desperate to get a closer look.

He should be watching the pornographic scene before him, yet his eyes are cast my way as his hand slowly moves up and down his shaft.

Oh wow. It's so *big*.

I lick my lips, almost drooling from the sight before me, and I find I'm desperate to go outside, like Ringo suggested.

Should I?

No. That would be wrong… wouldn't it?

You're an adult Abbey. You can make your own decisions.

Shit. Can I though?

I've never been able to before, so just the thought of having this option makes me want to do it.

In fact, doing anything my parents would oppose makes me want to rebel.

My feet are moving before I can second guess myself, and I open the door, determined to just do something, anything that is a decision I've come to on my own.

The music is so much louder out here, and the men and women are either moaning, laughing, or talking amongst themselves as I slowly approach.

Reaching the back of the pack, I casually walk around the group to stand in the gap I could see through from the window, and the moment I do, Ringo's eyes are on me.

My breath quickens as I take in his subtle smirk, almost like he knew I wouldn't be able to resist, and when his eyes drop from my face to his lap, mine follow.

Squeezing my thighs tight, the ache gets almost unbearable as I watch, easily able to see his large hand, fingers curled around his length, squeezing as he slowly pumps his length.

My lips part and I release a breath, my feet shuffling as need shoots to the apex between my thighs. I lick my lips, then bite down as I watch, but then a naked female arse moves in front of Ringo, blocking my view.

Um… excuse me.

I want to say the words out loud, but keep them in, momentarily disappointed as I watch Wendy touching herself, trying to gain his attention.

The moment Ringo's large hands grip either side of her hips, I stiffen.

A feeling, much like dread, settles in my gut at the sight, and heat pricks the back of my eyes.

Wait. What is wrong with me?

What is this feeling?

Jealousy.

Do I want to be the one he's touching?

That's wrong, right? Because I'm only eighteen and he's in his thirties.

It probably is wrong, but I can't deny that what I'm feeling is jealousy.

A second later, Wendy stumbles to the side and I pick up Ringo's growl as he shoves her away.

"How many fucking times do I have to tell you, no? Now get the fuck outta my way so my girl can watch me."

Holy cow.

My girl.

Ugh… stop being so naïve, Abbey. He's playing his part. You're not really his girl.

When his dark gaze locks back on mine, I feel the threat of tears fall away, replaced by searing heat.

I have no idea what JD and the other man are doing to the Doxy girl on the table, because I can't take my eyes off Ringo, my hands coming to the tops of my thighs as he settles back in his chair and starts pumping his hard length once more.

Again, I watch in fascination at how tightly his fingers grip, and wonder if that might hurt. Surely it mustn't if he's still doing it.

When his other hand moves into my line of sight and two fingers lift up in a gesture, my gaze finds his as he stares at me.

"*Come here,*" he mouths, and oh hell, I have to force myself not to move as I subtly shake my head.

"*Please,*" he mouths, and ohhhh myyyy goooood. I really want to go to him.

My gaze darts around the yard. Some men are watching the two guys and woman in the centre, and most of the women are in some sort of compromising position with the male onlookers. As drawn to Ringo as I am, I can't go to him like this, with people everywhere. With people that can see. People who might want to join in.

My eyes find his again, and I gently shake my head, emotions stronger than the arousal that gave me the courage to come out here, and I find myself stepping back.

I can't do this.

One foot after the other, I put distance between us, and then I turn and run back to the room. The moment I close the door, I press my back against it, my chest heaving as the burn of tears threaten again.

What is wrong with me? Why can't I just let go?

I hurry away from the door, using the light shining through from outside to guide me when the door quickly opens, and I spin, gasping.

Even though I can't see his face, the broad silhouette can only be that of Ringo, and a whimper escapes me as he steps inside and closes the door behind him, and the lock clicking into place is louder than it probably should be.

He's locking me in.

This is it.

This is when he takes what he wants.

I shake my head as he steps forward, his gruff voice quiet.

"Don't run from me."

I shake my head again. "No."

"What do you think is happening here?" he asks, and I frown as my heels hit the wall that runs along my side of the bed. He still continues forward.

"I can't. Please don't make me."

I hate the fear in my voice.

I hate how weak it makes me sound.

I hate the reason *why* I'm like this.

I hate it all.

"Angel, I would never make you do anything you didn't want to do."

He steps up before me, and I press myself back into the wall, trying to see his face, but all there is, is a dark shadow.

Shaking my head again, I squeeze my lids tight, repeating over and over, *no, no, no.*

Light filling the room catches my attention, and I pry my lids open to see Ringo moving back towards me from the bedside table where he just turned on the lamp.

The concern etched over his features stuns me. I wasn't expecting that. I was expecting anger. Frustration. Even hate. But not concern.

"I want to help you, but I don't know how," he admits as he drops his arse to the end of the bed, defeat dragging his shoulders down.

I'm still pressed against the wall like he's about to attack at any moment, and the humiliation of it all is just too much. Hot tears burst from my eyes and I slide to the floor, bringing my knees to my chest.

"I'm sorry," I whisper through my tears, and a moment later, Ringo is there on the floor with me, shaking his head.

"No, I'm sorry. I shouldn't have done that out there. Fuck," he rakes his hand through his dark waves, "I shouldn't have brought you to a place fuelled by sex when clearly it's been used against you."

A sob leaps from my throat, and I hide my face behind my hands. "Will I ever be normal again? Will I always see those monsters?"

"Those?" Ringo asks, and a moment later, his hands come to mine, gently peeling them from my face. "Angel, you said those."

Even though my tears still fall, I remain as still as I can, unsure of what to do.

Do I tell him the truth? If I do, will he still look at me the way he did outside?

"Angel, please talk to me. If not me, talk to Jols or Lexi. Don't carry this on your own."

I shake my head, because I just don't know what to do. It's been so long since I could trust anyone.

"I'll go and get Jols," he says with an edge of disappointment in his tone.

Would he rather I tell him and not her?

When he goes to stand, I reach out quickly, latching onto his hand, desperate for him not to leave.

"I'm scared," I admit, and slowly, he lowers back down, moving closer again, not letting go of my hand.

I stare at his huge hand engulfing mine. His skin is so much darker than my paleness, his fingers older, showing signs of wear and tear, and even as strong and masculine as they are, their hold is gentle and warm, and I find myself scared he'll let go.

"You're scared of me?" he asks, and I shake my head, but then I shrug, my actions making no sense.

"I'm scared of what you will think when you find out."

"Find out what, Angel?"

"What they did," I whisper, tears blurring my vision as I stare at our joined hands.

"Hey," he rasps, hooking his fingers under my chin to lift my head and gaze to his. "Look at me."

I do.

"Do you think I will think less of you?"

I nod, "amongst other things."

His lips thin. "I can assure you, there's nothing you can say that would make me want to turn my back on you. Nothing would stop me from wanting to protect you."

My lower lip trembles as I work up the courage to ask something I'm not sure is even there, yet I'm so drawn to this man, I just have to know.

"But it might make you stop looking at me like you did outside."

A deep growl rumbles in his chest, and before I know what's happening, Ringo's big hands are cupping my face, his forehead pressed to mine, bringing us so incredibly close.

"Nothing will make me stop wanting you, Angel. Not even the fact I probably shouldn't, given everything you've been through."

With a shaky hand, I reach up and press it to his chest, right over his strong peck. He hisses in a breath, his hand coming to rest over mine as he speaks. "You're trembling so much. You don't have to touch me, Angel."

"I-I want to. I just." I shake my head, which breaks the intimacy of his forehead pressing to mine, and I want to slap myself because I really loved having him that close, feeling the heat of his breath over my lips.

"You just what?" he asks, and my eyes drop to his chest as shame laces my words.

"I can't get the images out of my head. The memories. Every time I feel… something, it's like a swarm of bees honing in on me to attack. They just come at me from out of nowhere."

Ringo's breathing deepens, even as he urges my head back up so I have no choice but to look at him.

"I'm no counsellor or psychologist, but I hear talking can help. I promise nothing you say will change the way I feel about you."

I stare into his stormy eyes for a long beat, wanting to open up to him, but still scared that when I do, it will change everything.

"Will you do something for me first? Before I tell you?" I ask, and he nods quickly.

"Of course. Anything."

Can I really do it? Ask him for what I really want? What I really need right now?

It takes me a moment to work up the courage, and even though I want to squeeze my eyes shut so I can't see his reaction, I force myself to witness it all.

"Will you kiss me?"

19

Did I hear her right? She wants me to kiss her?

Fuck, I wasn't expecting those words but I'm glad she said them.

"I'd love to kiss you, Angel, but why do you want me to kiss you now before you tell me?"

I study those big doe eyes glassed over with intense emotion, wishing I could see into her soul. Her pink tongue darting out to lick her lips draws my attention, and I watch as she wets them, perhaps in anticipation, which has me distracted until she speaks.

"Because I'm scared it will be the only chance I'll get to feel the kiss of a real man."

Fuck. A real man? She thinks *I'm* a real man?

I'm a man, yes, but not a good one. Maybe I should tell her in detail about all the bad shit I've done. Maybe that will help to remind her who she's talking to right now.

Yet I can't bring myself to do it.

Selfishly, I want to shield her from that darkness. I want to pretend I'm a better man than I am, but fuck, if she asks me, I'll tell her the truth. I have a feeling I'd do just about anything for her, which once again is a really fucking weird notion. I've known her for a whole what? Five days?

Fuck.

Did I ever feel this way with Kylie?

Just thinking about my dead ex feels wrong while I'm with Abbey, so I push all thoughts of her away and concentrate on what Abbey said. She's scared that kissing me now will be the only chance she'll get to kiss a real man.

"You don't think I'll want to kiss you afterwards?"

She shakes her head.

Shifting closer, I hate that we are huddled on the filthy green carpet, but love how close she's letting me get. With my palm cupping her cheek, my gaze roams her face for any last signs of fear before I speak.

"I *will* kiss you, Angel, but just so you know, it won't be the only time. Once you let me kiss those pretty plump lips, I'll want to keep kissing them until you ask me to stop."

Her caramel eyes widen a little at my words, but I don't hesitate for a second longer, closing the small gap and pressing my lips to hers.

She's trembling under my touch, and I consider if I should stop, but the moment I shift back the slightest, she follows, her hands fisting the front of my shirt like she can't bear the thought of me moving away.

I part my lips, needing to taste her, and when hers part too, I gently brush my tongue between her lips, and feel her moan around it.

Fuuuuck.

In a flash, my other hand comes to her nape, my need to control her and keep her in place taking over. Instead of fighting me, Abbey's trembling falls away as she melts against me and deepens the kiss.

The moment her tongue brushes against mine, a growl rumbles from my mouth into hers, the animalistic part of me wanting to truly claim her. To make her mine. To never let her go.

That fucking thought startles me, and I pull back, because what the fuck?

Five fucking days.

Five.

Fucking.

Days.

How the fuck can I be feeling like this after only five fucking days?

It has to be because I haven't been this close to a woman in three years.

But that's not right, is it?

How many times have Celina and Wendy attempted to seduce me? How many times have I let them grind their arses over my crotch, and rub their tits in my face, just for my cock to remain flaccid?

Then there was that time up in Sydney when the bar chick caught my attention. She got me hard, and even though I didn't fuck her, I about came in my fucking pants, but then my mind went back to Kylie. To that day. That awful fucking day.

The worst day of my life.

"I'm sorry." Abbey's timid apology shakes me out of my thoughts, my eyes refocusing on the here and now and the sweet-looking angel in my clutches.

Shit.

She's not the only one that's damaged.

"Why are you sorry?" I ask breathlessly, stroking back some blonde flyaways that frame the side of her face.

"I didn't mean to get carried away. It's just…" She trails off, her trembling fingers coming up to touch her lower lip and I watch in awe as she traces her fingertips over the beautifully plump flesh. "I've never been kissed like that before."

Her words are a whisper, and fuck if they don't twist me up on the inside in the best kind of way. I can't hide the fucking shit-eating grin that tugs at my lips as I chuckle.

"You think I'm a good kisser, then? Good to know, but why are you sorry?"

"Oh… uh… You stopped so suddenly. I really didn't mean to make you feel uncomfortable."

Jesus. What I'd give for her just to let go and take. Be selfish. Worry about herself and her needs instead of pleasing everyone else.

"Actually, I'm the one who has to apologise. That wasn't on you. It seems I have my own demons." I point to my head, and the most fucking adorable frown brings in her brows.

"You do?"

Cupping her face again, I nod. "I do. I'm sorry. And for the record, you're an amazing kisser, and I can't wait to do it again."

Her cheeks flare to life, even as her lips pull up in a smile that nearly fucking floors me.

Fuck.

Seeing her happy, even if it's for a moment in time, is truly a fucking sight to beholden.

I should back away and put space between us, and not just because I'm having some sort of possessive attachment issue to Abbey, but because she is here to be protected. She is here to be given a new start away from the toxic life she's been stuck in. She's here only for as long as I can find somewhere more suitable for her.

I hate the thought of her leaving, but this place is no place for someone like her. She deserves better than a compound filled with a bunch of rough men that drink too much, kill on command, and sink their dicks in whatever holes are being offered.

"You should smile like that more often." I point out, and her eyes drop to my chest as the smile slowly falls away.

"I'd like to. I hope that one day, it's all I can do."

"Hey." I urge her eyes back to mine, stroking my thumb over her cheek. "You will. It's just gonna take time. But you have to tell someone what happened."

Holding my gaze, her doe eyes turn glassy, and she nods. "Okay."

"Come on." I ease back and stand, offering her my hand. "Let's move to the couch."

She takes my hand and lets me pull her up and lead her to the tattered piece of furniture, and once she takes her seat, I move to the kitchenette to get us a cold drink each and some chocolate.

I hear girls like chocolate.

We each take a sip of our drinks, and I sit next to Abbey, angling myself towards her, feeling fucking nervous for what I'm about to hear. I know it isn't going to be good, and I already want to kill her fiancé and parents, but fuck, when she mentioned more than one person, she didn't mean just those three. There are more people involved in what's happened to her, and I need to keep fucking calm so I can take mental fucking notes of all the people I'm going to kill.

We sit in silence for a few more minutes, and I realise she's stalling. She wants to have this conversation as much as she'd like to eat a bar of soap. I have no fucking idea what to do, but I need to get this conversation started, and not just because not knowing is eating at me, but because keeping it in is destroying her.

"You asked before if you'll ever be normal again? If you'll always see those monsters. Do you mean your parents and your fiancé?"

Her lower lip trembles, her eyes darting to her fidgeting fingers in her lap as she shakes her head.

I fucking knew it.

"Can you tell me who you mean?"

Her tear-filled eyes dart up to mine as her lips part to speak, but a sob lodges in her throat, and she shakes her head as she pulls her knees to her chest and lifts my huge hoodie over them to hide nearly her whole body.

"Okay, let's start with something easier. What's your fiancé's name?"

"Daniel," she whispers, but then angry heat fills her eyes. "And as far as I'm concerned, he isn't and never was my fiancé."

Ahhh, there's the fire I want to see.

"How did things with you and Daniel start?"

She sighs, her expression turning bored. "He showed an interest in me, and I fell for it, basically." She shrugs. "He was nice in the beginning. Patient with my inexperience." She sighs then, resting her head to the side to lean against the back of the couch. "I remember thinking it was perfect. I thought we had this really strong connection, and when we were around each other, we couldn't keep our hands to ourselves." Her expression falls. "It all started around the time Lexi began spiralling." Her lip starts to tremble again as her gaze locks with mine. "I swear I had no idea what was happening to her at home. She never said anything to me. I really thought her hate for her brother was just sibling rivalry."

Reaching out, I rest my hand on her knee, which is hidden away by the hoodie. "No one's blaming you for what happened to her."

She scoffs. "Well, they should. What sort of best friend am I if I never noticed?" She shakes her head, her self-loathing evident in her expression. "A bad best friend. That's what I was. What I am."

Lexi's words come back to me.

"She's a good person. She's going to tell you she isn't. Be hard on herself for some of the shit that went down eighteen months ago, but you have to remind her that she's still a good person."

"Hey. Stop," I demand, and her hatred falls away as her eyes round at the tone of my command. "I won't let you speak badly of yourself, Angel. You need to remember that Lexi deliberately kept that secret, probably because she was ashamed. Does that remind you of anyone?" I point out and she shoots me a *'really'* look with raised brows.

"Whatever," Abbey mutters, and I give her knee a squeeze.

"So, you and Daniel were in a relationship?"

She nods. "Yeah. I was worried about my parents finding out, but when he told me his parents were members of the same church my parents joined earlier that year, I knew that perhaps I didn't have to hide my relationship from them." She shakes her head in disgust. "The stupid church. I don't know why they moved from the one we'd been at for years."

"What's the name of it?" I ask, already knowing and hating this fucking story. There have been hundreds of random churches popping up across the country over the last few years, and not your basic Christian or Catholic church, either.

"It's the Valley of the Trinity and Merciful Fellowship."

Even though I already know, just hearing her confirm it has me rolling my tongue in my mouth to bite back the rage I want to start spewing.

Those fucking churches are run by cult like groups who like to enforce sick and twisted beliefs and make money off trafficking.

Knowing they are a part of that church explains a lot about Abbey's mum's extremist ways. Unfortunately, since Abbey has obviously attended that church and knows some inside information, it does put a bigger target on her back.

I'm going to have to tell Smitty the real reason Abbey is here.

Fuck. I should have already done it.

"Is something wrong?" Abbey asks, and I sigh, realising my expression must be giving away the fucking chaos in my head.

"No, sorry. I'm just processing everything." I gesture my hand in a wave for her to continue. "So, was your mother happy about the relationship?"

She nods. "Happier than I thought she'd be. It's all she could talk about with Dad, and before I knew it, she was having lunch with Daniel's mum, and giving me permission to go away for the weekend to their beach house with them." She shudders, and whispers, "I hate that place now."

"Hey. Come here." I offer, patting my lap, and a small grin tugs at her lips as she unravels herself from hiding in the hoodie, and crawls onto my lap, getting comfy and stretching her legs out on the couch.

"Am I squashing you?" she asks shyly, and I can't help but chuckle.

"Angel, you're as light as a feather."

She grins back before her eyes fall to her lap again, where those damn fingers start fidgeting again.

"So when did things change with you and Daniel?" I ask, weaving my fingers through hers to stop the fidgeting… and also because I can't fucking help myself.

"It was just after I spent the weekend away with him and his family. My parents were out. Weren't meant to come home for ages, and well… ummm."

I already know the story from the Angel sisters, but I want Abbey to think she's the one that told me. I need her to trust me.

"Angel. Were you a naughty girl?"

Her big doe eyes meet mine, amusement dancing in them at my question, and I can tell she's not thinking about what she and that fuckwit did, but rather what she wants to do with me.

Just to test my theory, I dart my tongue out to wet my lips, and she instantly tracks the movement, her lips parting as her breathing grows heavier.

I have to admit, I feel fucking invincible that I can get such a visceral reaction from her despite the conversation we are having. She's clearly in need of a release, and one I'm determined to help her with, but first, she needs to lift this weight off her shoulders.

"What did you and Daniel do?" I ask, and the mention of his name severs the trance she was in, making her spine stiffen.

"Ahhh, well. You can guess." She shrugs. "And my mum came home early and walked in to find her sweet innocent daughter with her legs spread and her cherry obviously already popped." There's so much hate in her tone, her lip curling as she speaks. "That was the moment everything changed. She lost her shit, got on the phone to his mum, and before either of us knew what was happening, we were told we were to get married." She waves a dismissive hand. "There was a whole lot of talk about bringing shame to the families, and me being a whore, which I found utterly rude since no one called Daniel a whore. Just me for being so easy and giving it up to him."

I can't fucking wait to gut her mum.

A low growl rumbles in my chest, and Abbey's unsure gaze meets mine.

"In my defence, I really did think he loved me. He told me he did."

"Angel. There is no defence needed. None of what you just told me is alright, nor is it your fault. You did nothing wrong."

She shrugs like it's neither here nor there. "I guess it doesn't matter now. It happened, and then my life changed."

"How so?" I ask, needing more details.

"My mum was adamant that Lexi was the one to lead me astray. They used to feel sorry for her, you know, because her parents neglected her so much. They didn't mind that she stayed over a lot when she was little, or that they had to feed her. But when we turned into teenagers, things changed. They no longer liked those things about my best friend. Hated her music choices. Hated her messy hair, and that she didn't carry herself like a lady. Hated when I went to her house for sleepovers while her mum was so spaced out."

Her voice cracks then, and she takes a moment, clearing her throat like something is lodged in it.

"I didn't help with how my parents felt about Lexi. I used her to cover up my own lies." She shakes her head, dropping her chin to her chest. "When they smelled smoke on my clothes, I said it was from Lexi. When I got home past curfew, I said it was Lexi's fault. When they found a love note in my school bag back in year nine, I said it was Lexi's…" She trails off, a quiet sob escaping her. "It was no wonder when the shit hit the fan about Lexi's home life that they refused to help. And the stuff with Daniel meant they used my pending marriage against me. If I put a foot out of line, the marriage would happen sooner. If I associated with Lexi, the marriage would happen sooner. If I disrespected them again, the marriage would happen sooner."

Fuck. There's no doubt in my mind that I'm going back to Fox Pines as soon as the lockdown is over to fucking slaughter her parents.

"Daniel's feelings for me changed after we were sprung. It was clear he never really had feelings for me, and admitted later that being with me was a bet with his mates. They each had to make a girl fall in love with them and get the girl to give up their virginity within three months, at which time, they were to dump the girls and find a new one. The winner would get five grand at the end of the year. I was lucky number four for Daniel."

"I'm going to kill him," I mutter, not able to keep my thoughts in, and slowly, Abbey's caramel pools lift back to mine.

She studies me, no fear in her gaze, but more curiosity than anything.

"You're going to kill him?" she whispers, and I nod.

"Yes."

She stares at me so intensely, for so long, that I start to fucking squirm under her stare, and then she says something I never thought I'd hear.

"Make it hurt."

Fuck.

"I will, Angel. That's a fucking promise."

Her lips part and her eyes drop to my lips again, that need inside her once again taking over.

"There's something wrong with me," she whispers, and I frown.

"What do you mean?"

Her gaze shoots back to mine as she whispers again. "I ache."

Fuuuuck. Even her tone sounds like it's in pain as she admits to the arousal coursing inside her.

"I know you do, Angel. And I promise to help take it away as soon as you're ready."

She rubs her thighs together, the movement making the globes of her arse rub against my crotch, and my cock instantly awakens.

"Maybe I'm ready now," she whispers again, and the edge of unsureness in her tone tells me everything I need to know.

"Not just yet. But I think you'll be ready soon."

She chews on her lower lip, keeping it trapped under her teeth for a few long beats, but then she snaps herself out of it, releasing her lip and sucking in a deep breath.

"You doing okay?" I ask, and she nods.

"You're a distraction."

Her admission has me throwing back my head, my laugh loud in my room, and that pretty fucking smile quirks up her own lips.

"I'm not the only one that's a distraction."

She blushes, ducking her head, and a moment later, all the colour drains from her face.

"Angel?"

"There's so much more," she whispers, shaking her head.

"Just take your time." I suggest, hoping it prompts her to finish telling me what happened to her.

"Daniel was mad about being forced into an engagement with me, naturally. So was I." She explains, watching her fingers fidget again. "I wondered why I was the only one asking why it had to be that way. Why he wasn't arguing or fighting the decision our parents were making?" She shrugs as she scoffs. "Turns out he's fuelled by money. There's a trust he gets access to when he's twenty-one, but his father threatened that he won't get a cent of it if he doesn't fall into line and do as he's told." Her eyes come back up to mine. "So, he fell into line."

She takes a moment, her eyes going distant, like she's trying to recall a memory.

"I can't actually remember the first time it happened. Daniel had turned so much hate towards me, that I figured he'd never want to touch me again, but our families kept forcing us to spend time together, and eventually, he decided that if he was being forced to marry me, then he owns me, and can do as he pleases." She sighs, dropping her gaze to my chest. "So he started forcing me… you know… in the bedroom."

"He raped you," I state, and she shrugs, so I jut her chin up with my fingers and catch her gaze. "He raped you, Abbey."

"Mum said it wasn't rape because I was to be his wife, and part of my duty to him was letting him have his way with me. She asked me why it matters when I'm already so good at being a whore that it shouldn't bother me."

She chokes up then, and I pull her to me, wrapping my arms around her slight frame as she cries into the crook of my neck, while I try to keep my fury reined in.

I should have killed that fucking bitch. She is so much worse than I realised.

"Why does she hate me so much?" Abbey chokes out through her sobs, and I hold her closer, her head in the crook of my neck as I press my lips to her hair again.

"Fuck, Angel. Your mum is messed up." I try to make excuses for the bitch of a woman just so Abbey doesn't think there's actually something wrong with her. "She doesn't deserve your tears."

"I know, but it just hurts so much, knowing how she used to be with me, and how she is with me now."

"I know it does," I say, not knowing what else to fucking say.

This is so fucking messed up, and I know we haven't even touched the surface yet. It fucking kills me to see, hear, and feel the pain emanating from this sweet soul.

I hold her for a long time, until her tears stop falling and her cries fall silent, and just when I think she must have fallen asleep, her whisper meets my ears.

"It happened three times."

I stiffen.

"What happened three times?" I ask, shifting to tug her back so I can see her face, but she doesn't let me move, obviously wanting to keep her face hidden in my neck.

"The first time was my birthday, when I turned eighteen. My birthday was during one of the lockdowns, so I thought it would be nice and quiet, but then, despite the rules set in place, my mum gave me a pill and told me to take it."

A shudder ripples through her, and I know she's reliving that day in her head.

"I did, not knowing what it was, but I took it because she's my mum, and she told me to." She shrugs against me. "Soon after, I felt really relaxed and tired. She put me in the car and drove me to Daniel's house on the outskirts of town. She didn't even take me into the house, just told me to get out and she drove away. I wasn't sure what was happening, but then Daniel appeared and led me to their big shed. Half of it is decked out as a party space, and inside, were his friends…" She trails off, and I swear my fucking blood turns to ice in my veins.

"What happened?" I whisper this time, and a sob leaps from her throat right before she lurches off me and runs for the bathroom.

20

ABBEY

I welcome the burn of the vomit. It feels better than having to say the words out loud. It feels better than thinking about the day I turned eighteen, or the other times after that. It feels like a purge, and one I'm desperate for.

As I heave over the toilet, I feel a warm hand at my back, circling, giving me the type of comfort I haven't received in so long. It feels so nice. I almost want to ask Ringo to stop, because I know that eventually, I'll be alone again, with no one to look after me, and I don't want to remember how good it feels to have someone care.

When the purging subsides, Ringo urges me back and flushes away the delicious food I'd eaten for dinner, before helping me stand and wetting a washer to offer me while he gets a glass of water.

Shit.

I'm exhausted.

Telling him all of that stuff about my family and Daniel has left me drained, but also kind of relieved.

It feels good to tell someone, even if it is a summarised version of the last eighteen months, it's still a relief.

Maybe Ringo was right. Maybe talking does help.

Even so, I know he'll want to know more about what I was trying to tell him before I got sick. I don't know if I have it in me to say the words out loud.

I tried once.

After my birthday, I tried to tell my mum, but she told me to stop being dramatic and lying. I came to believe she already knew, and when she dropped me off, I think she knew exactly what Daniel had in store for me.

We move back to the main room, and even though Ringo sits on the end of the bed, I can't seem to sit still. I start pacing, back and forth, back and forth, trying to figure out the best way to just get the words out and be done with it.

"Angel," he starts, but I shake my head.

"I don't know if I can say it. I mean, you know, right?" I ask, glancing up as I continue to pace back and forth. "You already know what happened. I don't really have to say it, do I?"

Sympathy washes over his features, and I kinda hate seeing it. "How many friends did he have there?"

Oh yeah. He knows.

My stomach roils again, but my anger keeps it at bay. My anger is making me feel alive right now, pumping my life source through my veins, setting my adrenaline alight, preparing me for war.

"Including Daniel?" I ask, but it's really just an acknowledgement. "There were five the first time. Six the other two times."

"Fuck!" The animalistic boom flies from Ringo, scaring the life out of me, a squeak leaping past my lips as I jump.

Now he's pacing, raking his hand through his hair and looking like he's going to pull the strands right out.

My breathing is fast. Shallow. Almost painful. My heart thrashing, yet almost feeling like it's about to stop.

"Five? Six?" he snaps, in question.

"I shouldn't have said anything. I knew I shouldn't have said anything." I start rambling as I back away, tears blurring my vision, my head shaking at the sheer anger in his voice.

No one wants to know this about the girl they are interested in. No guy wants to know you were used as the whore at the end of a train line.

I need to run. Where can I run? What will I do if I leave here?

"Angel. I'm sorry." His tone is less savage this time, and I see his blurry silhouette coming towards me, but I back up against the door, reaching back to find the lock. "Hey, what are you doing?"

I shake my head, not able to speak as I fumble blindly, trying to get the damn thing open as he looms over me.

"Angel, I can't let you leave," he rasps, his hand slapping against the door to stop me from opening it.

"But you said I'm not a prisoner." I manage to mutter, tears searing my cheeks as I keep trying to blindly get the damn latch unlocked.

"You aren't, Angel. But you're in no state to go anywhere, and we are locked down. Let's not forget that I want to keep you safe."

"B-but you're angry at me. I told you—"

"I'm not angry at you, Angel. I'm angry at those fucking cunts that…" he chokes on his words before he finishes his sentence, "I'm angry at your rapists."

Two large, yet gentle palms come up to cup either side of my face, his thumbs swiping at my falling tears as his face unblurs in my vision.

"You did nothing wrong. You hear me? You are the victim. Everyone else has done wrong by you, and mark my fucking words, Angel, they will pay. They will pay severely for what they did. That's a fucking promise."

If I know anything is true in this world, it's the conviction in his tone. He'll follow through on his promise.

"I don't want to talk about it anymore," I whisper, and he nods, pressing his forehead to mine.

"You don't have to. I'm sorry I made you."

"You didn't make me. You encouraged me, and you were right. I feel a bit lighter."

"Jesus, any lighter and you'll blow away on the breeze." He jokes, the long facial hair on his upper lip quirking up with his smile.

"I'm sorry you got lumped with me and my problems," I admit, feeling the niggle of being a waste of space creep in again.

"Don't talk like that. I'm glad Lexi called me. I just wish she'd done it earlier. Like a year fucking earlier."

"In her defence, she had no idea what was really happening. She still doesn't know. I've never told anyone else what I told you, and honestly, I never want to say the words again."

"Then you won't have to." He declares, easing back to give me more space. "But there's one thing I need from you. Not now, but before the lockdown lifts."

Curious, my brows shoot high. "And what's that?"

"I need the names of the six guys. Not spoken, but written down, and if you have their addresses, then I'll take that too."

"Are you really going to…"

"Fuck yes I am. And I get it if you don't want me to. You're a good person, Angel. I don't expect you to agree with my methods, but the fact of the matter is, they don't get the privilege of going to prison and having a trial. They don't get to breathe and live full lives. In fact, the remainder of their lives will be so fucking bad, they will beg for death."

A shiver ripples up my spine, and prickles of electricity tingle over my skin from head to toe. His eyes are fierce and are nothing but determined and I feel so alive at his words that I almost wonder if perhaps I should check myself? Remind myself to pull my head in and manifest the good parts of me that cried when my friends flooded an ant nest when we were little, killing the innocent insects just going about their day.

I decide, after what I've endured, that I'm allowed to feel good about the thought of revenge.

"I'll have the list for you by the morning," I tell him, and he nods, satisfied, before he slips his hand into mine and leads me away from the door and over to the bed.

I have no idea what time it is, nor do I care, and I happily slip under the thin blanket we've been using despite the sultry nights.

I can't seem to get warm, my feet and hands feeling the coldest, so when Ringo eases under the blanket too, and reaches for me, dragging me closer so I can tuck myself into his side, I welcome the warmth. It's like his touch, the press of his body against mine slowly thaws me out, and before I know it, I drift off to a dreamless sleep.

When I wake next, it's to the chirp of birds, making the early morning hour almost as loud as the partying going on last night.

Shit.

Last night.

What was I thinking going out there while they were all…

This place, well… it's different. From my brief time here, I've observed a bunch of scary men and a handful of scantily dressed women party like there's no tomorrow and engage in sex acts fit for an X-rated website.

I know that there's not a whole lot to do during lockdown, but I get the feeling the way they kill time here is normal, even if there's no lockdown.

Seeing all that sex has to be the reason why I'm so horny.

Oh man, under different circumstances, if I told Lexi about all of this, she'd be in fits of laughter.

That thought tugs at the corner of my lips, and I pry my lids open to make sure Ringo is still sleeping and not watching me be weird.

Nope.

He's still sound asleep.

Like I seem to do a lot, I study him while he sleeps. I enjoy seeing this side of the big bad biker who busted into my house and threatened my parents. His expression is so soft while he sleeps. It's like all the hardness he carries throughout the day falls away, and in its place is this gentle man, or perhaps gentle giant better suits him.

I can't believe I watched him… wank.

My cheeks flush at the thought, and the ache intensifies between my legs.

Dammit. Why am I like this?

It's confusing as hell, especially given what I admitted to Ringo last night.

The ache between my legs vanishes, replaced with an ache in my chest, and the threat of tears.

I'll never be the same.

For weeks now, I've daydreamed about hurting them. The six guys that took advantage of my drugged state. Sometimes the thoughts scare me, because never in my life have I ever imagined hurting anyone the way I want to hurt them.

I want to make them quiver in fear and beg for mercy. I want them to feel what it was like to endure the things they did to me, and while their gender prevents them from truly knowing, the fact that there's still a way to do… *that* to them, has fuelled my appetite for revenge.

But, let's be honest. I'm me. I could never…

I slowly sit up on the bed and stare down at Ringo.

He could. I know it in my bones that if I asked him to do that, he'd make sure they know what it's like to have their body used, their limbs stretched every which way, to have their hair pulled so hard, that clumps get torn from their scalp. He'd make sure they couldn't breathe and know what it feels like to choke as someone shoves something so forcefully down your throat that you can't help but vomit. He'd make sure their skin is left with bruises in the shapes of gripping fingers, and that their most intimate places are abused in such a way that sharp pain and bleeding will linger for weeks.

It may be wrong of me to want Ringo to do that, but as I ease from the bed, careful not to wake him, I don't even hesitate when I pick up the pen and notepad off his bedside table, and write down the names of the monsters that took everything from me.

Daniel Stone – 11 Mackery Lane, Fox Pines.
Craig McRoe – 261 Commercial Road, Fox Pines.
Michael Berry – 22 Landrey Place, Fox Pines.
Tim Beck – address unknown.
Donny Allen – address unknown.
Darnel Rivers – address unknown.

I shed a single tear as I place the notepad and pen back on Ringo's bedside table, but it's not for them. No. They will never get my pity.

The tear is for me. The old me. The person I was before all of this happened.

She was nice. Sweet. Smart. But ultimately, naïve.

I can't say I'm none of those things anymore, but what I am now, that I wasn't back then, is damaged. Wounded. Ruined. So broken that I know this simmering hate I feel brewing will never leave me. It will always be a part of who I am now.

And I don't even know who that is.

After I have a quick wash, I rummage through Ringo's wardrobe and find another hoodie, swapping it out before I gather up my dirty clothes, and his, and slip from the room to do our laundry.

It must be pretty early. There's not a sign of anyone awake.

There are a few men passed out in various locations around the courtyard. One of which is sleeping soundly in the small garden bed outside the laundry room.

I smile.

He kind of looks comfy. It's like he fell there and just decided it was as good a place as any to sleep.

These people... well, they are so far off even being remotely like the people in Fox Pines or at the church that I find it refreshing.

They are rough. Inappropriate. And probably the happiest bunch of blokes I've ever met.

In the laundry room, it doesn't take me long to figure things out. After all, this is what my mum has been training me for. Or perhaps grooming me is a better term for what she's been doing.

Now that I've been away from her for a few days, I feel like a blanket of manipulation has lifted and I can see everything clearer. I don't know why my mum is the way she is, or why my dad just lets her control everything, but what I do know is that they are both monsters for standing back and allowing their daughter to be treated the way I have.

Even though I don't particularly like my sister, Maggie, I worry about what will become of her given how brainwashed she is.

And Tahli... Well, I need to find a way to get her away from them as soon as possible.

Just as I turn from the large washing machine now doing its job and washing mine and Ringo's clothes, a startled gasp flies from my lips as I come face to face with a glaring Wendy.

"You won't last. You know that, right?"

My brows hitch at her words. I don't even know what to say to that, but before I can even form a word, she continues.

"He'll get bored with you. You're not exactly his," her disdained glare looks me up and down, "flavour."

"Whatever." I manage to mutter, taking a step forward in the hopes she backs up and lets me out the door.

She doesn't.

"Ringo doesn't do sweet. Whatever fascination he has with you will likely vanish before the week is through." She curls her lip in disgust. "You're simply too vanilla for a man like him."

"Can you please move?" I snap, which just makes her scoff.

"Unless you're willing to let him do the things he truly desires to your little fragile body." She shrugs, lifting her hand to study her nails before glaring back at me. "He's such a man, you know. He can't help it if he likes it rough." Her claw-like fingers wrap around her neck and she pretends to choke herself. "He likes to choke his women until they stop breathing."

My heart starts thrashing in my chest, as her actions and words evoke a memory that I never want to remember before her lips spread wide in a sinister smile.

"He likes to fuck his women after they pass out. He likes being in full control of their body, able to do to it whatever he wants without them…" she leans forward, and I now regret stepping closer as her cigarette scented breath heats my face, "saying no."

"You don't scare me," I hiss, trying to find my lady balls, but unfortunately, my voice still resembles a mouse.

Wendy throws her head back laughing. "Oh, dear sweet Charity. I'm not trying to scare you. I'm simply giving you a heads up for what's in store for you if you want to stick around." She shrugs like she doesn't care, but obviously she does. "Besides, it's no skin off my nose. He still comes to me and begs to sink his big cock deep into my cunt."

"You're vile!" I snap.

"And you're delusional if you think you can make him happy!" She snaps back, shoving my chest and making me stumble back into the washer. "You stupid, naïve little girl. You know nothing about our world. Don't come crying to me when you marry him, thinking you've nailed him down, only to find out that I'm his old lady. So while you might end up playing house with him, just remember when he comes to the club, he'll be balls deep in my arse."

"Piss off, Wendy."

The additional female voice snaps my attention over Wendy's shoulder to see Jols standing there, glaring at the back of Wendy's head.

Spinning on her heel, Wendy faces Jols but says nothing, the two of them seeming to have some sort of telepathic argument before Wendy huffs and shoves past Jols, storming off.

"Are you alright?" Jols asks, and I let out a breath I didn't realise I was holding, slowly nodding.

"I-I think so."

"Just ignore Wendy. The dumb bitch has been pawing at Ringo for years, and not once has he taken her up on her offers. She's just jealous that you got what she could never get."

I shake my head. "But I don't have… that. Me and Ringo… we're fake. It's not real," I whisper, my heart hurting at the truth of my words.

Yeah, we shared something last night, but Wendy is right. I'm not Ringo's type. I could never let him choke me.

"If you say so." Jols grins knowingly, and my brows hitch, but she doesn't notice because she's stepping out of the room and gesturing for me to follow.

When I step outside, I watch as Jols kicks the booted foot of the man slumbering in the garden bed.

"Hey Barts. Wake up." She kicks his foot again, and as I approach, I hear him groan in protest.

"Stop Natasha. I got up for the baby last time."

I frown at his words while Jols sighs, her hands on her hips as she shoots me a sympathetic look. Then she kicks the guy's foot again.

"Barts. It's Jols. You're at the compound. Not with Natasha."

This time, his eyes snap open, and he peers up at Jols with the saddest lost puppy look I've ever seen.

"Shit. Sorry. I must have been dreaming," he mutters, pushing himself up to reveal the crushed flowers underneath.

Whoops.

"You know, if you want her back, you gotta quit Jimmy and Molly."

He nods, running his hand over the blond mess on his head. "Yeah, I know. I'm gonna—"

"No, you're not," Jols snaps, leaning down to get in his face. "If you were going to, you'd already be sober and tucked up next to her in her bed." She straightens. "But instead, you're…" She doesn't end her sentence, but rather gestures to his state, and his shoulders slump.

Damn. I kind of feel sorry for him.

"Come on." Jols nods her head at me, and I follow, avoiding Barts' lost puppy eyes. "You want to talk about what happened last night?"

"What?" I ask confused as I hurry to Jols' side. "What happened last night?"

Jols stops abruptly, so I skid to a stop and turn back to look at her.

All I see is sympathy.

"Ringo messaged me last night. Told me a very brief rundown of what you told him about… well, what happened to you."

He what?

No.

I don't want people to know.

Suddenly, my breathing quickens as humiliation flushes over my skin in raging heat, and I ball my fists, ready to punch something.

Why would he tell her? How could he do that?

I trusted him.

More than ever, I know I can't stay here. My need to run from this place is so overpowering that it's like an impulsion I can't control, and I stiffen as my body prepares to do just that.

21

ABBEY

"Hey, calm down," Jols offers soothingly, her hands held up as she steps closer, but I take a step back and shake my head, getting ready to run.

I can't believe he told her. Why would he do that? Am I gossip to him?

Oh my god, I asked him to kiss me!

I have to go.

There aren't many men around right now. I could probably get away easily enough.

I take another step back, my eyes scanning the space.

"He only told me because he knew that I might be able to help." Jols continues, but her words only fuel my anger.

"Help?" I snap, shooting her the glare I can't contain. "How the hell can you help? How the hell can *anyone* help?!"

I watch as Jols visibly becomes uncomfortable, her eyes dropping, her confidence slipping, and her feet shuffling.

"I guess he thought because I've been through something similar that perhaps I could relate, and it might help you not feel so alone in your suffering." She shrugs, her pained expression meeting mine again. "He never meant any harm. He just wants to help you."

Burning pricks at my eyes as they begin to flood with tears, and as the hot droplets burst over, I bat at them, quickly looking around the courtyard to see if anyone is watching, but it's still quiet.

Did she really just admit that she's been through something similar to me?

The thought makes me queasy. How can people do such heinous things?

As I study her through my tears, I can see it. The way her shoulders have rolled forward a little, closing herself off. The way her fists are opening and closing like she's struggling for control.

She's telling the truth.

"You… That happened to you?" I ask, feeling like a bitch for jumping down her throat.

"Yes." She nods, having to clear her throat before speaking again. "It's not something I talk about, and it's something I've worked hard to overcome, but I see what he sees in you, Ab—Charity," she corrects herself. "I'd like to help if that's something you'd be open to."

My lip quivers as I stare at this beautiful woman before me, her eyes so blue that I swear she must be a mermaid born in the prettiest of tropical waters. Her dark brown hair is simple, long, straightish with a slight wave, and although she has some tattoos—one on her hand, and a couple on her arms—and wears leather pants and a simple white singlet while spending her days with the roughest of men, and sassiest of women, she seems so… decent.

Just like Ringo.

"Are you Ringo's sister?" I blurt, and her brows shoot up.

"No." She laughs. "Why? Do we look alike?"

"No." I shake my head, smiling and willing away my tears. "But you seem alike. In morals and personality."

She nods in understanding. "Ringo took me under his wing. He *is* like a big brother to me, but we definitely aren't related. If it weren't for him, JD, Murf, Stocky and Trunk, I don't think I would have ever gotten through the aftermath of what happened."

I nod. "They seem… nice."

Jols throws her head back, laughing. "I wouldn't use nice to describe them." She shrugs. "But decent, they are."

"I'm confused. I didn't think they allowed women to be members in the club."

She nods. "They don't. I'm not a member."

"Oh. Are you a Doxy?" I ask, confused, knowing she doesn't seem like one of the women who aim to please the men of this club, and she scoffs.

"Fuck no. I ain't spreading my legs for the likes of these fuckers."

I giggle, and she grins. "Let's grab some breakfast and I'll fill you in."

Jols smiles warmly at me, and I realise then that she kind of reminds me of Lexi. Just older. And with darker hair.

As Jols starts walking again, I briefly glance at the end of the courtyard to the mouth of the driveway where I know the manned entrance is. I probably wouldn't make it far by foot, but maybe by car.

I glance at the doorway that leads down to the parking garage and frown. There was a truck, some vans, and a heap of motorcycles, but I didn't see any cars down there when we came here the other night.

Not that it means there aren't any. I was tucked down on the floor between Ringo's legs, so I couldn't see out the window, and when he escorted me inside, I was surrounded by his men and Jols, ordered to keep my head down.

"You coming?" Jols calls, shaking me out of my thoughts.

"Yeah." I nod, spinning to follow her, even as I glance back over my shoulder in the direction of the entrance.

Ringo says I'm not a prisoner, so that means I can just leave when I want to, right? After the lockdown, I can just walk out.

After grabbing some breaky, I nibble on a piece of toast, not feeling much like eating as Jols eyes me, and I know she wants to ask me about what I divulged to Ringo last night.

We sit quietly for a few minutes at the table closest to the room that looks like it used to be a dining room for the hotel guests. It's set up like a bar now, from what I can see. I guess they use it more when the weather isn't so great since they seem to be doing all their drinking activities out in the middle of what used to be a central carpark in the middle of the buildings.

"I was twenty when it happened," Jols says quietly, snagging my attention as she plays with the crumbs on her paper plate. "A guy I grew up with had joined the Red Eights. Do you know what that is?" Her blue gaze darts up to meet mine, and I shake my head. "It's a street gang in the city. One of the many." She shakes her head. "My mate, Kyle, got mixed up with them, and I could see him slipping away from reality, using too much."

"Using? That's drugs, right?" I ask, hating how dumb I sound, but when she nods, her eyes don't portray thoughts of how naïve I am. Just pain from her memories.

"I stupidly thought I could stop him. Change his mind and get him to come back to the burbs with me."

"Burbs?" I ask, still hating that I don't seem to know much of anything.

"Suburbs." She offers me a warm smile. "We lived in the Eastern suburbs of Melbourne, and it was normal for teens and young adults to want to venture to the city more as we got older, but Kyle stopped coming home, and I could see how distressed his mum was over it. And well…" she shrugs, "I missed him too."

Jols shifts in her chair, clearing her throat, and I can tell she's struggling with her emotions, so I keep quiet, waiting to see if she'll tell me more.

Not that it matters if she doesn't. That's her prerogative, but a part of me aches to know if someone will truly be able to understand.

"I walked into the dingy club at the wrong time, because as soon as G-Wack saw me trying to convince Kyle to leave, he chose me for his new initiates."

"What is G-Wack?" I ask, shifting forward in my seat.

"G-Wack was the Red Eights gang leader."

"His name is G-Wack? Who the hell came up with that?" I scoff, and Jols smirks, her shoulders relaxing a little.

"He did. Named himself because his real name, Theo Anderson, just didn't seem threatening enough."

I giggle, "Neither does G-Wack."

We both laugh at that, the act making me feel temporarily light. Free.

"Long story short," Jols continues as she eyes me. "There were ten initiates who spent the next nine hours using my body non-stop, after drugging me and tying me down so I couldn't fight back."

My lip wobbles and the little food I ate threatens to come up as her words sink in.

Ten of them.

Nine hours.

Drugged and tied.

There's no further warning, my stomach rolling as I heave, quickly leaping up from the chair just in time to reach the dying bushes to the side. Tears pour from my eyes in hot rivers, and a gentle hand rubs over my back as my body controls me, purging the vileness from within.

"How long has she been like this?"

The deep baritone of Ringo's voice meets my ears, and it's like a blanket of warmth and safety floats over me.

"Just now. I was sharing my past," Jols admits, and Ringo curses, his fingers brushing some of my escaped hair off my dewy forehead.

"Angel," he rasps, close by, and I suck in a deep breath as the forceful waves subside. "What can I do?"

"T-tell me you k-killed him."

My words cause him to drop his hand from my hair, and I wipe my mouth as I straighten and turn to face him and Jols.

"Who?" he asks.

"G-Wack. Tell me you killed him."

Ringo's brows hitch, but my eyes find Jols, who is grinning.

"Not only did Ringo kill him, but he made him suffer for days."

I nod, forcing a half smile at Jols before glancing at Ringo. "Good. People like that deserve to die."

Ringo smirks. "That they do, Angel."

The way he stares at me, his dark stormy eyes somehow looking like they soften as he takes me in, does something to me.

I know I'm only young. I know I'm naïve. And I know we are complete opposites, but there's something about the way he looks at me that makes me feel… like I'm more.

Of course, it could be just the desperate part of me wanting someone to at least like me a little. Just enough to want to fight for me. And yes, I know he's been doing that, but it's only because Lexi asked him to. If it weren't for her, he'd never have come across me, let alone gotten involved with me.

It's at that moment that some of the men start stumbling from different rooms, followed by the Doxies too, so any conversation about Red Eights and the attack Jols survived ends quickly.

"I need to help the Doxies with brunch," Jols says, dragging her gaze to the hungover men, slowly staggering closer to where we are.

She's not a Doxy, but she helps around here, and I guess I should be too since I'm eating their food and using their water.

"I'll come and help." I offer Jols a smile when her eyes dart back to me.

"That would be great." She beams, and I wonder if perhaps I've made myself a friend.

"You sure, Angel? You're a guest. You don't have to." Ringo steps forward, stroking back more of my hair.

I grin. It's like he can't help but touch me.

Of course, I'm likely wrong, but I'm going to let myself think that since it makes me feel warm and fuzzy on the inside.

"I'm sure." I nod, leaning into his big palm when he cups the side of my face. "I want to help."

"Of course you do." Ringo smirks, leaning closer and pressing a whiskery kiss to my forehead.

I notice Jols grinning from ear-to-ear as she watches us, and behind her some Doxies stare at us for a little too long.

Do they have the same opinion as Wendy? Do they think I won't last?

I decide I don't care, and follow Jols where we spend the morning helping the Doxies prepare brunch for the club members.

Using my hands and keeping busy is good, and even though I was sick just before, I feel like I have more energy than I've had in weeks. Plus, the mundane activity helps me to not think about last night's or this morning's discussions.

Ringo watches me most of the morning. Each time I glance over at him as he chats with the President, or his mate JD, his eyes remain locked on my every move.

When one of the younger members challenges anyone that will say yes to a bottle flip competition, Ringo mouths, *"come here"*, much like he did the night before when his hand was wrapped around his… um… dick.

Immediately my cheeks heat, remembering the look in his eyes and how hard he was. I thought I'd be more terrified of seeing his…

For Christ's sake, Abbey. Even in your own head, you have trouble thinking the word.

Dick. IT'S A DICK!

Ugh.

Dammit. Focus.

Where was I?

Oh yeah, I thought I'd be more terrified of seeing his *dick*, not to mention all the other dicks that were out. For the briefest of moments, I wanted to go to him so badly. I wanted to have the courage, just like the Doxies, to stand before him, and touch it.

I wonder what he would have done if I had.

The two of us are playing a part, after all. Did he want me to go to him because people may have been watching? Or did he just want me to go to him simply because he wanted me near?

It unsettles me a little how much I want it to be the latter.

Do I really want his interest?

Do I really want to feel his hardness and see what happens when I wrap my hand around it and—

Ringo, still watching me as I stare at him, raises a brow and mouths again.

"Come here, Angel."

Oh.

Angel.

Why does he call me that?

"Because Angel is just for me."

He said that to me when I asked if Angel could be my name instead of Charity. His reason left more questions than I began with, because it kind of felt like he meant it as an endearment, and not simply a name, and well, despite him being scary as hell,

I liked the thought that perhaps the term, Angel, meant more to him.

Which is why I'm pathetic.

We don't even know each other and the first hint of someone showing an interest and I'm practically drooling. It's probably why Daniel thought I was a sure bet in the beginning.

Needing that prick's name out of my head, I slowly start to walk across the courtyard, making my way to him as I pass the big burly man that cornered me the night I left Ringo's room to find him.

I duck my head, not wanting to look at him, yet always on alert, my eyes darting back to the man just in case he pounces.

To my surprise, his eyes meet mine and he gives me a warm smile, if that's what you can call it under all the bushy hair covering his jaw and upper lip. He gives me a nod, kind of like people give as they pass each other on the walking track around the pond in Fox Pines.

I don't smile back. I can't. He terrified me the other night, and I don't trust him one bit. But he doesn't call me out on it, and I continue towards Ringo, finally reaching him where he still watches.

"What were you thinking about over there?" He gestures his head back towards where I'd been standing, and I shrug, not wanting to reveal my inner thoughts. "You know, I've noticed something about you, Angel." He reaches out, gently gripping my wrist and tugging me closer, guiding me to sit on his lap.

"What have you noticed?" I ask quietly, feeling my entire body flush with heat as I settle on his lap.

We are so close now, his scent wrapping around me, a mixture of spice and wood, and our faces are mere inches apart. I'm entrapped by his eyes, so dark, yet hypnotising as he stares back, making me feel… seen.

"Well, it seems that your creamy skin, right here," he reaches up, his fingers grazing over the side of my face and into my hair before his thumb brushes over the apple of my cheek, "goes bright red quite a lot. Just like it is right now."

My lips part as I suck in some air, having forgotten how to breathe for a moment there, but the action steals his gaze from mine, to drop to my lips, and holy hell, my heart flips inside my chest.

What is happening right now? Does he want to kiss me again?

It's the ruse, Abbey. The role he's playing to keep you safe.

"And your cheeks were flushed moments ago when you stood over the other side of the yard. So, what I want to know is, what were you thinking about then?"

I shake my head just a fraction, his hand still cupping the side of my head, his thumb still brushing back and forth over my cheek. My very flushed cheek.

"I… I don't remember."

He chuckles. "Yeah, you do. You just don't want to say."

His hand drops away, and I instantly miss it.

There's no way I'm telling him what I was thinking about, which is certainly something out-of-place given everything that is happening.

I'm here because he kidnapped me from my abusive situation. A situation that also involved a fiancé that likes to rape me. How on earth can I be thinking about this man who I hardly know, and his… dick?

Ugh, I've been nothing but a horndog lately.

Could it be from being around people that have open sex so freely, or is it just him?

Maybe it's from the kiss we shared. It was a kiss I asked for in a moment of desperation, and even though he said he'd love to kiss me, he could have said that to be polite.

Are motorcycle club members normally so nice?

Ugh.

"Brunch is ready!" Casey calls, and hoots follow from all the hungry men.

I go to get off Ringo's lap to get us a plate of food, but his large hand resting on my thigh grips it, giving it a squeeze.

"Stay right where you are."

A shiver runs up my spine at the gravel in his tone and the way he breathes the words against my ear.

Heck. Why does his warm breath feel so damn good?

Stop it, Abbey. He doesn't actually like you like that.

"Aren't you hungry?" I ask quietly, remaining as still as I can since his lips are still pressed to my ear, lingering, and I can still feel the heat of his breath.

"I'm famished," he rasps, squeezing me tighter, and I can't help it. My lids flutter closed, and I melt into him even more.

"Here's your food, Ringo."

The sweet female voice jolts me from my daze, seeming to have the same effect on Ringo, and I look up to see one of the younger Doxies standing before us, holding out two plates.

"Thanks, Nessy. Pop them on the table." Ringo gestures to the white plastic table to our right.

She smiles timidly and nods, placing the plates down before scurrying away, and I glance at what she brought us.

One plate has an array of cooked barbeque meat items, while the other plate has grilled vegetables.

"Let's get some food back into your body," he mutters, reaching over to the plate and using the fork to stab into a piece of grilled zucchini.

Oh, my… is he going to feed me?

When he holds the fork out, hovering close to my lips, and I don't make a move, his deep voice rumbles close to my ear again. "Open those pretty lips, Angel."

What the…

I shake my head, my gaze darting around the yard to see a few of the big scary bikers looking on, while some of the Doxies pretend not to be looking, but sneak glances every now and then.

"Open. Now," he demands, and just like the other times he's demanded me, my body obeys even though I try to stop it, and my lips part for him to slip the vegetable in.

The moment the flavour hits my tongue, I'm done for.

My lids flutter closed, and I think I even moan as I start chewing.

"Fuck, that's hot."

My eyes snap open at his whispered words, but he pretends not to care about my sudden stiff posture, and he feeds me a grilled piece of carrot this time.

He doesn't even have to ask. My lips part immediately, ready for more, and as I chew the carrot, dread settles in my stomach.

Why do I do that? Why does he demand things, and even when I'm not sure I want to comply, I still do?

The thought makes it hard to swallow the carrot, and before I know it, I'm quickly slipping off his lap, scooping up the plate of grilled veggies, and dashing off to hide in his room.

As I go to close the door behind me and shut the courtyard out, a large hand slaps against the timber, pushing it open to reveal Ringo, his expression now a glare as he once again follows me in.

22

RINGO

The last twenty-four hours have been a lot, and I probably shouldn't be behaving the way I am after what Abbey admitted to last night, but fuck if I can't ignore the way she looks at me.

She doesn't even fucking realise the way her eyes roam over me like I'm something she wants to taste, and I'll be fucked if I can ignore that.

"What are you doing?" she squeaks as I lock the door behind me once again, hiding us away from the rest of my club.

They'll just think we've come in here to fuck, and as much as I'd like that, a fucking feeling I haven't had in years, it's not the reason I followed her in.

"What are *you* doing?" I ask her instead of answering her question, watching how the plate trembles a little in her hands as she stares up at me.

"I…" She glances around, frowning. "I wanted to eat alone."

Ouch.

"Too fucking bad. I don't much feel like leaving you alone."

She huffs, rolling her eyes, and I can't fucking hide my smirk.

These moments, with the eye rolling and the huffing or scoffing, feel like the real girl hiding behind the wall of steel she's erected.

"Why do you feel like being alone? I thought we were having a nice meal together."

She frowns at my words, her gaze dropping to the plate in her hand.

"I'm just not used to being around people."

"Bullshit," I snap, gaining her glare, which just makes me smirk again. "While I'm sure you don't like being around many people, that's not the reason you ran off."

She just continues to glare, so I take a step forward, which seems to snap her to attention, her spine stiffening before she takes a step back.

"What's the real reason, Angel?" I close the distance before she can get much further, taking the plate in my hands and setting it aside on the table. "What did I say to make you run?"

"N-nothing," she stutters, and fuck, there's that flush again, and I watch as her lips part and her chest rises and falls a little faster.

Fuck, I wish she'd take my damn hoodie off so I can see her.

"Was it what I said after I fed you the zucchini and you moaned?" I ask before repeating what I'd said. "Fuck, that's hot."

Her entire face turns red now as she shakes her head. "N-no."

I smirk. She's right. That's not what made her flee.

"Then what was it?"

She shakes her head, refusing to tell me, so I use my dominance to force it out of her.

"Tell me, Angel. Now."

"I don't understand why I do as you demand." She rushes out before her face contorts in annoyance. "Dammit. I did it again." She stomps her foot. "Why do I do that?"

Now we're getting somewhere.

I didn't know she was aware she was doing it, but I don't hate that she's picked up on it.

Yes, I've been using it to get to the bottom of things, but also, I fucking love how she submits to me so easily.

"Does obeying me annoy you?"

"Yes," she admits freely, and I grin.

"All the time?"

She shrugs. "I don't know. I guess maybe not all the time."

"Just some of the time?" I ask, and she nods, her eyes dropping to the floor in shame.

"Eyes up," I order, and just as she hates, her eyes dart up to mine.

Reaching out, I hook my fingers under her jaw, tilting her head back a little more to stare into her caramel orbs.

What is it about her that has me so… intrigued?

"Do you trust me?" I lean closer, noticing her breathing pick up with the rise and fall of her chest before her pink tongue darts out to wet her lips.

Shit. Does she want me to kiss her again?

Fuck, I wonder what she'd do if I just did it without warning.

Even as I ask myself that question, memories of her trauma rush to the forefront of my mind, reminding me that even though we shared a kiss last night, afterwards, she revealed her horror story to me.

Kissing her would be wrong.

Touching her would be wrong.

But fuck, whyyyyy do I want to so badly?

"Answer me. Do you trust me?" I demand, and again, she obeys.

"Yes."

Her word is a breath. A whisper. So silent that if I wasn't looking at her lips, I probably wouldn't have heard it.

"Then I'm going to be brutally honest with you," I admit, staring down at her as she so willingly lets me control her right now. "You're a submissive. I don't know you well enough to know if this is a natural personality trait, or something you were raised to be, probably a bit of both. The fact that you sometimes talk back to me, express your opinion or disagree with things tells me that it's probably more from the way you were raised."

Her eyes drop to my chest, dancing from side to side as she considers my words.

"A submissive?" she asks, although it sounds more like a statement.

"What happened in your home growing up if you didn't do as your parents asked you?" I ask, and those caramel eyes find mine again.

"I was punished. Just like any kid." She shrugs, frowning at me.

"What were your punishments?" I ask, taking her hands in mine and leading her to the couch. When she goes to sit, I stop her, lowering my arse first and then tugging her onto my lap.

"What are you doing?" she asks, stiffening. "There's no one here to see us."

I chuckle at the way she thinks my affection outside is still a ruse.

"I know. Does it bother you to be on my lap?"

For the longest moment, she just stares into my eyes. I almost start fucking squirming from the intensity of it, but then she shakes her head slowly, her lips parting to speak.

"No."

I grin.

Thank fuck, because I'm not letting her run off right now.

"Back to my question. What were your punishments?"

"As a kid, just the typical grounding or going to bed without dinner. Being made to do extra chores. A slap on the hand a few times." She shrugs and I nod, brushing back some of her blonde flyaways.

"And what about more recently? Did your punishments change?"

I already know the answer, but I need her to work through it and come to the realisation herself.

"Yes," she whispers, moving to lower her head, but I lift her chin again, making sure she keeps her head up.

"Don't be ashamed of that, Angel."

Her eyes turn glassy as she fights back tears, and as much as I don't want to see the pain in her eyes, I know these conversations need to be had. Especially now that I know which church she's been attending with her family.

"Tell me how they changed."

She chews the inside of her cheek for a few beats, and I can see she's working hard not to cry.

"Grounded turned into total isolation and being banned from being friends with certain people. Being sent to bed without dinner turned into not being allowed food for the entire week-end sometimes, or only being allowed to eat a certain thing, like porridge." She shudders. "I fucking hate porridge."

I grin. "Angel, did you just swear?"

Her lips spread wide into a grin, and she bashfully bites her lip.

Fuuuuck. I want to bite that fucking lip.

Finally, she relaxes on my lap, resting back on my arm as she continues to analyse her punishments.

"Extra chores turned into complete slave labour."

"How so?" I ask, my gaze falling to her dainty fingers resting on her thigh, and the way they fidget.

Without thinking too much about it—because let's be fucking honest, if I overthink it, I won't do it—I take her hand in mine, stroking my thumb over the top of her hand and watch how her gaze falls to where we are connected.

"Ahhh…" She loses concentration for a moment before she shakes her head and continues. "Instead of mopping the floor, I was forced to clean it with a rag on my hands and knees. Instead of doing the dishes, I was forced to take every dish, glass, and bowl from the cupboards and wash and dry them, even if they were clean." She falls silent then, and I drag my gaze from our hands to her face to see her lower lip wobbling as she struggles with her emotions. "Then there was the night Mum made me cut the back lawn. It was freezing, dark, pouring rain in a storm…" Her tear-filled caramel eyes dart up to mine and she sobs. "She made me cut the entire back lawn with a pair of scissors. It took me six hours. I finished at four in the morning, and even though

I couldn't feel my fingers from how cold they were, they hurt so much from using the scissors for so long. This," she holds her hand up to show me the side of her right thumb where an oval-shaped scar is, "this was raw skin. Blistered and bleeding."

"Fuck, Angel. I'm sorry your parents did that to you."

"That wasn't even the worst thing," she whispers, and my fucking heart sinks. "The times I did something she found unacceptable regarding Daniel were the times that I'll never be able to forget." She shakes her head before swiping at the tears. "I was so clueless the first time it happened. I thought when she brought the Scripture out that I'd have to recite something and repent."

"What Scripture?" I ask, already having an idea.

"The Scripture of Symme."

Fuck. Symme. That's different. Last I heard, the Valley of the Trinity fellowship cults were using the Scripture of Adie. I'll need to update the Marx crew and the Angel sisters about this.

"That's a type of bible, right?" I ask and she nods, leaning into me more and resting her head on my shoulder.

"So what happened when your mum brought the Scripture out?"

"Well… there was some reciting at first. Followed by an admonishment."

"Admonishment?" I ask, not all that familiar with religious terms.

"It's like a reprimand. A warning," she explains, her fingers gently gliding over my open palm, like she's not sure she should be touching me.

"What was the warning?" I ask, gripping her fingers when she goes to pull them away from my palm.

"That each time I dishonour Daniel or my family, my penance will get worse."

A slow, simmering rage bubbles deep in my gut, ready to unfurl and seek vengeance. She hasn't even told me what the penance was yet, and I know without a doubt, I'll crave her parents' deaths a thousand fucking times over.

"What was the penance?" I ask reluctantly, not wanting to hear another word spoken on how such cruelty was dished out to this sweet soul.

"Lashings," she whispers, her whole body beginning to tremble. "Don't make me describe that."

Fuck.

FUCK!

"I'll never make you tell me anything you're not comfortable revealing." I assure her, yet when her eyes find mine, I can see the doubt in them.

"You won't demand me?"

Shifting her to face me better, I cup her cheeks. "I may demand things, but you have the power to deny me. You control what you give to others, not the other way around."

She stares at me for a long moment before giving me a slight nod, and once again my fucking eyes track to her plump lips.

Don't fucking do it.

Control your-fucking-self.

Gently, I force my hands from her face, releasing her and willing my fucking paws to stay the fuck off her.

"Tell me about the Scriptures. Are they the same as Christianity?"

"No." She shakes her head. "There's a lot about worshipping God's vessel, Symme. Followed by guardians that nurture and provide for us."

"Guardians? Like your parents?"

She nods. "That and husbands. Husbands come before parents."

"The Scripture says you have to worship your husband?"

"Yes."

"How?"

"Through wifely duties," she whispers, and I frown.

"What? Like cooking and cleaning?"

"Amongst other things." She shrugs like it's no big deal, but fuck that. I know it's a big deal.

"What other things?"

Again, she shrugs, biting her lower lip as she thinks, probably trying to find a way to sugarcoat it.

Fuck that.

"Angel, be honest. Tell me exactly what other things fall under wifely duties."

Sighing, her caramel gaze drops to her lap where her knees are curled up, and she starts picking at the loose cotton hanging from the bottom of my hoodie she's wearing.

"The duty of the wife is to be at her husband's beck and call. Should he want intercourse," her eyes dart up to mine briefly before looking back down, "a wife should never refuse him, and if she does, as the husband, he has the right to indulge in his wife's body as he sees fit. A husband has the right to choose the penance for his wife if she disobeys him, with the only allowance being that penance must not be something that will affect the wife physically if she is with child and for the first six months of the child's life."

What. The. Actual. Fuck.

Abbey recites the wifely duties like she's been forced to memorise them, and I have no doubt her mother made her do exactly that.

"Eyes on mine," I demand, needing her full attention, and as usual, she obeys, her gaze locking with mine. "You know the Scripture is wrong, don't you? You know no one has the right to indulge in your body in any way you don't agree to and want, right?"

She nods, tears welling in her eyes. "I know. I really do know that, but I had no choice. I was trapped. I… I—"

"You don't need to explain, Angel. You did nothing wrong. That so-called church is a cult. They are nothing more than a group of sick fucks brainwashing people to benefit them. They lie, steal, cheat their way into communities, and it's too late when authorities realise what's happening. The damage is done. They've already got their claws into people that are weak and vulnerable and fucking gullible. They take their money and force their beliefs on their congregation, using them until they get revealed and quickly disappear, only to pop up on the other side of the country as a new religious faction and do it all over again to a new community."

"How do you know that?" she asks, her gaze now wide with interest.

"The Southern Sadists' mission isn't in taking down the cults popping up everywhere, but we help those that make it their mission to try to catch these sick fuckers. I actually thought the one your family has been involved in was already handled, but obviously not if they are still spreading their teachings in the Timber Valley district.”

“Can they go on the list too?”

Her words are so quiet, I almost miss them.

Almost.

A sinister smirk spreads my lips wider, and I give her a nod.

“Yes, Angel. Even if you ask me not to go after them, I will deny you. Death is coming for that cult. Once and for fucking all.”

Slowly, Abbey’s spine straightens. Her eyes appear almost stormy as she takes me in for a long moment before she finally speaks.

“You asked me earlier what I was thinking about that made me blush.”

As her fingers start to fidget together on her lap again, I watch as said blush fucking returns and I almost can’t believe she’s broaching this subject.

“I did. Are you finally going to tell me?”

She nods, taking a moment to mull over her words before she speaks.

“Promise me something first,” she demands, although it carries no fire.

“What am I promising?”

“Not to laugh at me.”

My hairline lifts as my brows do, not at all thinking she was going to say that.

“Why the fuck would I laugh at you?”

She shrugs. “You just might find what I’m about to tell you… funny.”

Using my index finger, I draw a cross over my heart. “I cross my heart and hope to die.” I recite the words we used as kids.

She grins bashfully, taking a moment to study those damn hands of hers again while I wait impatiently.

Then finally she speaks.

"You asked me to go to you." She shrugs like it's no big deal. "Come here, is what you mouthed."

"I remember," I admit, and again she shrugs.

Is that her tell? A nervous shrug?

"Well, you did the same thing the night before… you know."

Oh, I do fucking know, but now I need to hear it from her lips.

"Know what?" I ask, playing dumb.

"You know." She leans in, whispering conspiratorially.

Biting back my chuckle, I shake my head. "I'm afraid I don't."

"Dammit," she mutters, pinching the bridge of her nose as she thinks over her options.

"Just tell me, Angel."

"Fine. Last night in the courtyard when everyone was getting naked. You were…" She gestures her hand to my lap and shoots me a duh glare.

"I was what?"

"Christ, Ringo, you were like… wanking."

Don't laugh. Don't laugh. Don't fucking laugh.

"Yes. I remember."

"Well, that's what I was thinking about that made me do this." She points to her blushing face, her frustration evident in her tone and posture.

"You were thinking about my cock?"

She rolls her eyes. "Yes. Okay. Are you happy? I was thinking about your dick."

I chuckle. "That makes me extremely happy."

"But… Why?"

"What the fuck do you mean, why?" I ask, and she gestures between us.

"This is just a ruse, isn't it?"

"Is it?" I ask in all seriousness and her expression morphs into a deadpan, and fuck, it makes my cock jerk to life.

"Seriously?" she huffs. "You can't keep avoiding answering my questions by asking more."

"Can't I?" I smirk.

"Ugh, stop. You're infuriating."

"Infuriatingly sexy." I shoot her a wink, and when she rolls her eyes once again and goes to move off me, I stop her, delving my hand into the hair at her nape.

She gasps as I tug a little, the action forcing her chest forward, and those tits that I get the feeling are nice and fucking plump despite her bony arms and legs, press against my chest, just begging to be touched.

Sucked.

Fucking worshipped.

I wonder if she'd let me.

Fuck, no. I can't.

"You have the infuriating part right." She breathes and fuck, I tilt her head back even more, hovering over her angelic face, my lips just a breath away from hers.

"I know last night triggered something, but I need you to know, Angel. When I asked you to come over to me, that was no fucking ruse."

I shift a little closer, moving slowly, waiting to see if she'll tell me to stop, or push me away. Our eyes are locked on each other's, her caramel pools darker than I've seen them. My nose brushes hers, so delicate and soft against mine, and I'm pretty fucking certain my bushy mane of a beard is tickling the skin around her lips and chin.

I've kissed women before. Too many to count. But never have I felt my fucking heart beat in my chest so hard and fast that I feel like it's about to explode.

Never has the mere closeness caused such a feeling of anticipation that I don't want to rush over the line just yet, instead, relishing how fucking thrilling it is just to have her here like this, our lips so close that our breath is already mingling, even though our lips aren't touching.

"Angel," I rasp, and she whimpers like she's aching. "I'm going to kiss you now."

23

ABBEY

"Angel," he rasps, and ohhhh, the deep gravel in his tone shoots straight between my legs and I whimper.

Like actually whimper.

How embarrassing.

If he thinks my reaction is funny, he doesn't show it, his dark eyes appearing almost drunk before he speaks.

"I'm going to kiss you now."

I can't breathe, his close proximity seizing the air in my lungs.

Is this really happening?

Is he really going to kiss me without me having to ask pathetically?

And am I going to let him?

Oh, my… I really want to let him, and I don't understand why.

Why does this man, like a real grown-arse man, not a boy like the idiots my age back in Fox Pines, but an actual man that belongs to a scary outlaw motorcycle club who is covered in tattoos and has a beard that I would normally think gross, yet ache to feel graze against my lips again, and who has a gun… why, oh why am I so drawn to him?

Maybe it's because of how safe he makes me feel, even when I'm scared.

I have no idea if that makes sense. Nothing is making any sense right now, but all I can think about is feeling his lips on mine.

Finally, as if time slows, he closes the distance and—

Beep. Beep. Beep.

Stiffening right before our lips touch, Ringo pulls back and hurriedly searches for the source of the beeping.

A shuddering breath releases from me as the spell we were under slips away the moment he finds the source of the noise.

His phone.

"Fuck," he mutters, quickly easing me from his lap a moment before a loud thump rattles the door of his room.

"Ringo!"

The voice belongs to JD, and I scurry to the corner of the couch as Ringo lurches up and opens the door.

"Have they checked in?" Ringo snaps and I notice JD's eyes move past him to glance at me as he shakes his head.

"No, they aren't answering."

"Fuck. Where's Lewy? I need to know if we have eyes," Ringo snaps, turning back to the room and storming to the closet, where he shucks on his leather vest.

"Lewy is working on it now." It's Jols' voice this time as she pushes past JD in the doorway and when her eyes meet mine, she offers me a warm smile.

"What's going on?" I ask timidly, unsure if it's any of my business.

"JD, make sure the men are ready to leave in three fucking minutes. We'll take the tradie vans to avoid attention."

JD nods before spinning on his heel and disappearing, and Ringo comes to me, lowering to one knee as he takes my hand.

"That noise you heard. That was an alert from one of our warehouses. It means something is wrong, and I need to go and check it out."

"Wrong? What sort of wrong?" I grip his fingers tighter, suddenly not wanting to let him go.

"It's happened a few times during lockdowns. Street gangs trying to break in to steal from us. It's nothing to worry about." Even as he says this, he drops my hand and pulls his gun out from the back waistband of his jeans and checks it for something. Maybe bullets? I didn't even know he had a gun on him.

"If it's nothing to worry about, why do you have that?" I ask, my tone kind of snappy.

Those dark eyes of his dart up to meet mine and a sinister smirk spreads his lips wider. "I have this, because whoever has dared to fuck with the Southern Sadists is about to be the ones to worry."

Then he shoots me a wink before leaning forward and pressing his lips to my forehead.

Oh.

It's not exactly the kiss I'd been hoping for, but it makes me feel just as cherished, in a non-sexual way, the simple act warming the inside of my chest, so much so that I'm reminded of how long it's been since someone has truly cared for me in such a way.

Not that Ringo cares. Because he probably doesn't. But the action is something I haven't received from anyone since before everything went down with Daniel.

As he stands, I notice Jols watching on, a small grin lighting her face, which she hides the moment Ringo turns to face her.

"You got this?" he asks her and she nods.

"Always. You leaving the usual men behind?" Jols asks before another body fills the doorway.

"Sarg. Lewy can't access the cameras at any of our warehouses."

"Fuck," Ringo barks as the man I know as Murf glances at me and nods.

"Hey, Charity."

"H-hey," I stutter, confused by everything that's happening.

"Ringo!" The booming voice comes from out in the courtyard right before Murf shifts out of the way and Smitty, the President charges in. "Tell me you have a fucking plan."

"The same as last time, only we take the tradie vans."

Smitty growls. "I hate having to fucking hide like that."

"It's not hiding. It's being smart while the lockdown is on. A group of guys riding motorcycles through the nearly dead streets will draw everyone's attention right now. But plumbers are an essential service for emergency repairs. Even if the vans are seen, no one will think twice. Besides, the vans allow us to carry extra weapons." Ringo smirks and slowly, the furious glare on the President's face turns to a smirk.

"Let's round 'em up, Sarg."

Smitty and Murf charge out the door at their President's words like they are on a mission, leaving Ringo and Jols behind.

"The prospects will remain here, as will Stocky, Barts and Tucker," Ringo tells Jols and she nods.

"Go. I'll look after her." Jols reassures him, and he nods before turning back to me.

"I'll be as fast as I can. Stay out of my drawers." He shoots me a pointed look and my cheeks flare to life at his silent dig at me finding his sex toy last time I snooped.

Then he smirks and leaves the room.

Standing, I follow Jols just outside the door to watch the hordes of men, all wearing black leather vests much like Ringo's, carrying guns, some checking them over as they disappear through the door that leads to the underground garage.

"Should I be worried?" I ask Jols, and in my peripheral, she angles her head in my direction.

"I won't lie. It's always a worry when they have to go off and do business the way only they can. But they are good at what they do. Ringo is smart when it comes to this sort of thing. That's why he's the club's Sergeant in Arms."

I turn to face her now, my brows raised. "Sergeant in Arms?"

"Yeah. Everyone has a role to play in an MC. Some roles are more important than others. Like the President, for example."

I nod, glancing back at the now vacant doorway to the garage. "What does the Sergeant in Arms role do?"

"Well, to put it simply, Ringo's role in the MC is kind of like a law enforcer. There are rules, and his job is to make sure no one steps out of line."

I turn back and study Jols' face, those blue eyes of hers still so captivating. "And what happens if someone steps out of line?"

"They get punished." She shrugs like it's no big deal.

"Punished how?"

Her eyes squint a little as she looks at me now. "You sure you wanna know?"

"Yeah." I nod. "I wanna know."

Jols nods back as she gestures into the room, and I move in, taking a seat on the couch, watching as she closes the door and joins me.

"Just like normal laws, our punishments depend on the severity of the infraction. For something mild, like inappropriate behaviour, it could be as simple as a slap on the wrist and a fine."

I scoff. "The club has rules about inappropriate behaviour?"

She grins. "Yeah. Shocking, I know."

"What does an MC class as inappropriate behaviour?" I ask, truly intrigued.

"Well," Jols sighs, relaxing back against the couch cushion that Ringo had been on only minutes before, "for example, Mex decided to piss on Roadie and Delilah while they were fucking one time without their consent. That's pretty inappropriate. Ringo reprimanded him in a public scolding and fined him five grand."

"What? Five thousand dollars?"

Jols nods. "Yep. He's still paying it off. Taught the fucker a lesson, though. He's been well behaved ever since."

My brows are high on my forehead. "I guess peeing on someone is bloody horrid."

Jols throws her head back laughing, her eyes bright as she watches me. "When these arseholes take a leak, it's not peeing. It's pissing. Trust me. They have zero class when it comes to needing to relieve themselves sometimes."

Smirking, I feel my cheeks heat as I nod. "I've kind of picked up on that."

"It's hard to miss around these thugs."

We smile at each other, and for a moment, it really does feel like I have Lexi here with me.

"So, what's one of the worst infractions?" I ask, and Jols' smile drops.

"There are a few." Her blue gaze drops to her lap, and she seems to be studying her hands for a few beats before she sighs. "You sure you wanna know? It's not nice."

"Yeah, I do," I admit, knowing I may regret it in a moment.

"Let's see." She taps her finger against her chin a few times before her eyes meet mine. "Ringo declared you as his. In our world, it's not just a boyfriend declaration. His declaration makes you his property."

My brows shoot high at that, and dread starts to mingle in the pit of my stomach.

"If one of the members disregards that and tries to do anything with or to you that dishonours Ringo's declaration, the member will pay dearly."

"How dearly?" I almost whisper, not even sure if I want to know anymore.

"There's usually a trial of sorts, done behind the church doors where the members decide as a group how severe the punishment will be, but typically, in the book of by-laws, it states that the member must endure a physical beating until such time that the President grants mercy, or death takes him."

I gasp, my hands flying to my lips in shock. "Couldn't they just like, kick the member out or something?"

Jols shrugs. "I've only ever seen it happen twice. Smitty let one guy live. He was so broken and bloody he had to army crawl his way out the gates. I still don't know what became of him. And well, there was the other time Smitty let a guy die, but I dare say it's because his infraction was against my mum."

"Your mum?" I ask, shocked, my hands falling to my lap again.

"Yeah. Smitty's my stepdad. They met when she came begging him to help rescue me, and well, they fell in love or some shit." She shrugs.

"But… I saw…" Frowning, I shake my head in confusion, and Jols smiles.

"She's his wife. Not his old lady."

"I'm still confused. He was with those women…"

"Like I said. She's his wife, outside the club. Occasionally, he goes home to her, and I guess those are the times he's just a regular man. But in the club, he's the king. And in the life of an MC, the men can have both a wife, an old lady and also enjoy the Doxies, and no one bats an eyelid."

Wendy's words come back to me from our interaction in the laundry room.

"Don't come crying to me when you marry him thinking you've nailed him down, only to find out that I'm his old lady. So while you might end up playing house with him, just remember when he comes to the club, he'll be balls deep in my arse."

The dread coursing through my gut feels too heavy, and anger bubbles in my veins at what that means.

But what does it matter to me? I'm here temporarily. What me and Ringo have is a ruse.

But he nearly kissed you, Abbey. He implied it wasn't just a ruse.

Ugh.

"So they can fool around all they like and it's not breaking their rules?" I ask, needing that confirmed once and for all.

"That's right." Jols nods.

"So what about the wife? Or the old lady? What happens if they fool around?"

Jols' face falls as she deadpans. "They die. Both the guy they fooled around with and the wife or old lady, whichever it was. There's usually a fair bit of torture involved, but otherwise, death is how it ends."

I gulp.

It's a ruse. It's a ruse. It's a ruse.

Shit.

We are lying to the club.

"What about deception to the club?" I ask quietly. "Like lying about a girl that's been snuck in?"

Jols looks away then, sucking in a deep breath as she glances around Ringo's room.

"Jols?" I ask, shifting forward on the couch. "What happens if the President finds out I'm not really Ringo's… whatever, and that I was snuck in?"

Her bright blue eyes return to mine, and this time I can see the worry in them. She studies me, and I wonder if she's going to lie and sugarcoat her response.

"It's hard to say exactly. Smitty and Ringo have been tight since long before I've been around."

"What if it was someone else? What if one of the other members snuck a girl in and lied about her being his?"

"There'd probably be a beating. A fine. And the girl would likely be reprimanded as well."

A huge lump forms in my throat as my heart starts to hammer in my chest.

"Reprimand? Like being told off?"

"Yeah, in the least." Jols nods.

"So… there could be more?"

"Look, Ringo won't let anything happen to yo—"

"I asked if there could be more." I snap, and her brows shoot high.

"There could be. It depends if the girl snuck in is a mole for the cops or another MC or gang, then that would step it up to a physical punishment."

"And me? I'm not a mole, so I won't have to pay a price like that, right?"

For the longest moment, Jols' eyes dance between mine, and I prepare for the lie I know she's gearing up to tell me.

"You may be punished physically." She admits, and as scared and as stunned as I am, I'm grateful for her honesty.

A memory comes back to me from the night I found out it was Lexi who ordered Ringo to kidnap me. He'd stepped outside his room to speak on the phone, and I opened the door to hear his words.

"She'll need to be relocated after the snap lockdown. She's not safe here."

Is that what he meant? If the ruse gets discovered, am I going to be in danger?

Even as I ask myself that question, I already know the answer.

"Look, Ringo won't let that happen. Trust me. He'll protect you."

Tears threaten once again, but I force them to stay put. I'm so sick of crying. So sick of looking weak. So sick of not having control over my own life.

"I know." I force a smile, lying to Jols, because I really don't know her well enough to fully trust her.

Ringo… well, things have gotten a little blurry between us. The lockdown is nearly over, but what happens if someone finds out I'm not actually Ringo's girl—his possession—while we are all locked in together and I can't leave?

I hate the term "possession". Why is it that men want to own women?

I guess it's not all men. My dad never seemed that way. I feel like my mum wanted him to be that way with her, but he's never been like that. She's always been the assertive one. What she says goes. Maybe I wouldn't be in this mess if I were more like her.

Harder. Tougher. Selfish.

But that's not me. I know that's not me.

Even as I think that, I remember the way I was with Daniel in the beginning. I fell hard for him. We quickly became inseparable, and I remember seeing the disappointment on Lexi's face when she'd come to the courtyard at school for lunch, only to find me at the new 'couple's table', already putting a rift between us.

Ugh, no wonder she didn't tell me what was happening to her. I was too wrapped up in Daniel.

Maybe I am selfish.

Suddenly, a red light starts flashing in the room, and the ancient phone on the bedside table starts ringing, making Jols stiffen.

"Shit." She hisses, leaping up, and I follow.

"What's wrong?" I ask, glancing up to see the source of the red flashing light just above the door. "What's happening?"

"Stay here." Jols grips both of my arms, her eyes locking with mine and I see a hint of panic in them.

"What's going on?" I ask again.

"That's our warning system for the pigs." She releases me and moves to the door, cracking it and glancing out.

"The pigs?"

"Cops." She turns back to face me. "They are likely doing a lockdown compliance check, which means all the men that left are going to get into trouble for breaching lockdown rules. But you'll be fine. Just stay in here out of the way. Maybe hide in the bathroom, just in case. I'll come back for you once we get rid of them."

I hear her words, but they sound so far away as the rush of my blood thunders past my ears.

The police are here, and Ringo isn't.

I've already learned my lesson about the police. It was a bitter pill, that's for sure, but when I went to them for help after the first… group attack… they made it very clear that they weren't there for my protection.

No.

They are there to protect themselves and their families. And if they are here and know who I am, then no one can protect me.

Not even Ringo.

24

RINGO

The streets are like a ghost town as we speed through them, our six vans loaded with eight to ten men in each, all armed to the nines with extra weapons stored along the walls of each van.

If we get pulled over by cops and searched, we are fucked. There's no way to hide our tools of trade, so we don't break any speed limits, trying to maintain our cover so we can reach our destinations without issue.

"Are all ten locations down?" I ask from the front seat before Lewy's voice comes through the car's speaker.

"Yes, Sarg. I have my team working on a solution, but it's almost like something is blocking our access. If you could get someone to check the comms controls on site, that will help me figure out what's going on."

Glancing over my shoulder, I eye Murf, who gives me a nod, silently telling me he'll handle that.

"Will do, Lewy. Keep working on it. We'll be in touch," I bark before ending the call, frustration that we are going in blind evident in my snappy tone.

"Lewy's good at what he does." JD reassures me from the driver's seat as he slows the van at an intersection.

"Yeah, I know," I mutter, looking both ways down the road to see them completely vacant. It's fucking eerie seeing the normally bustling streets resemble something I've only ever witnessed in movies.

As we turn onto the main road, three of the vans veer off in the other direction, heading to our northern locations while the other two stay on our tail.

This whole fucking situation doesn't feel right to me. It feels very fucking off.

Leaning forward, I scoop up the CB radio receiver and press the button.

"Van two to all vans, do you receive?"

"Van three receives." Tups, our club Secretary acknowledges first.

"Van one hears you loud and clear." Smitty chirps, sounding way too fucking cheerful to be on a mission. But that's just him. He's an adrenalin junkie through and through. This shit fuels him.

"Van six is present, sir."

The men in my van chuckle at the mocking tone of Spud's voice. He may be our Vice President, but the fucker is a clown.

"Van four, ready," Roadie announces.

"Van five, locked and loaded," Mex practically yells.

"I wish he wouldn't say that over the radio," JD mutters from beside me, and I have to agree, but now's not the time for me to bring that up.

With all vans listening on, I issue my order. "Suit up in protective gear. I have a feeling this plumbing job will be messy."

Groans come from the back of my van, but they immediately start shucking off their vests and slipping the Kevlar vests on, a generous gift from the police commissioner last year.

"You got a feeling about this one?" JD asks, and I nod.

"Yeah. Losing comms and eyes on all ten sites at once isn't a fucking coincidence."

Trunk passes two vests over to the front for us, and as we continue driving, veering off to our destination as van one and three stay south bound, I too suit up.

JD slows the van as we get closer to our main warehouse. This is the one with all the really illegal shit that the cops turn a blind eye to.

Well, the ones on our payroll.

The others are gently steered in another direction by the ones on our payroll, so we rarely have to worry about them.

The street gangs, on the other hand, are a different fucking story.

Last year was fucking chaos. The whole fucking world locking down because of the virus, and all of a sudden, the most valuable items to hit the black market were medical supplies and fucking dunny roll.

Who would have thought that arse paper would be worth so much?

The medical supplies were understandable, and in a group operation with the Marx crew, we very fucking quietly seized an illegal shipment of medical supplies that the Triad tried to get in.

Had they, they would have controlled our fucking hospitals, and we couldn't let that happen.

Hell, even the state premier had a hand in making sure we were the ones to seize the goods. If the cops had gotten it, it would have been held up in red tape. But the Marx family have ties that go all the way to the top, and they needed extra muscle to help not only seize the shipment, but to store it and protect it to avoid more chaos and looting.

"All looks quiet." JD observes as he pulls into the laneway that leads to our warehouse entrance.

He's not wrong. Nothing looks amiss, but that doesn't mean all is well.

Picking up the CB receiver again, I reach out to the other vans.

"Van two on location and ready to go."

I wait a moment, but all we get from the radio is static.

"Van two, does anyone receive me?" I ask, my gaze shooting to JD's wide eyes when we get nothing else but static.

"Sarg. There's zero phone signal," Murf says from the back, so I pull my phone out to see the same thing.

No bars. SOS only.

Fuck.

"What the fuck does that mean?" JD snaps, shucking on his Kevlar.

"It means we have no way of communicating with the others," I hiss, and Trunk grunts from the back.

"So, do we still go in?"

Fuck.

Protocol would say hell fucking no, but we have to check this out.

"Double up on your metal and ammo," I bark, opening the glove compartment to take out another gun for JD before snatching another out for me. "Murf, when all is clear, you and Vender check the comms cupboard and security cameras. Trunk. Bowey. You two do a perimeter sweep. Trigger and Mule, you stay at our six at all times."

A round of yeses sounds from the back and I eye JD.

"You ready, man?"

He holds up his Glock and flashes me a fucking grin.

"Ready Sarg. Lead the way."

With a nod, we all get out of the van, moving quickly but quietly to the entrance door.

JD tries the handle, but it's locked, as it should be, so I key in the code and hear the faint click, releasing the latch.

Swinging the door wide, our guns are raised, ready to shoot anything that moves, but all is clear in the entrance, so we continue in.

For an MC, we aren't quite as thug populated as other MCs in the country. A lot of our men are ex-army, many of which have seen action over in the middle east.

For whatever reason, they left the service and found their way to us, which gives us a unique advantage over most.

Skill and experience.

We move as a unit through the long passage that opens up into the main warehouse, JD and I veering off towards the office just off to the side where the hum of a TV sounds, as well as laughter.

JD eyes me, and he doesn't need to speak for me to know we are thinking the same thing.

What the fuck is going on?

As we reach the door to the office, I glance over my shoulder to see Trigger and Mule on full alert behind us, their guns raised and ready, while the others stand back, fanning the entrance, ready for battle.

When my gaze locks onto JD's again, I give him a nod and he turns the doorknob slowly and quietly before shoving it open.

"Hands in the air!" I yell, scaring the absolute fuck outta the men sitting around a card table playing fucking poker.

"Fuck. Don't shoot," cries Yabbie, his hands darting in the air as his cards go flying.

"Uhhhh, they seem fine." JD voices my fucking thoughts.

"What's going on, Sarg?" Scooter asks this time, his bald head appearing as he accidentally knocks his cap off while raising his hands.

"You all good?" I ask, my gaze darting from my two men, to Patrick and Gerald, who belong to the Marx crew.

"Yeah. Everything is good here," Patrick answers for them and they all nod.

"Lower your guns," I call, relaxing my shoulders and huffing in frustration as I step back out the door to eye Murf and Trunk. "All clear. Get your tasks done."

They nod and hurry off, while I step back into the room, noting that even though I've called all clear, Trigger and Mule remain on high alert with their guns ready.

"We got an alert from this warehouse, but comms and eyes are down," I tell them, and they all lower their hands to pull out their phones.

"Shit. I didn't even notice," Scooter mutters, as Patrick shoots from his seat to check the security monitors in the other room.

Following, I watch as he frowns, clicking a few things before his gaze meets mine.

"The security cameras are down. It doesn't look to be on site, though."

"So the cameras haven't been tampered with?" I ask, and he shrugs.

"I'd have to check, but this shows them still there, but they are somehow not turned on. It's like someone else is controlling them."

Fuck.

"I already have my men checking the hardware, and Lewy can't seem to access them remotely."

"That's weird." Patrick frowns, and right as he opens his mouth to say something else, loud yelling from out in the warehouse has us moving quickly in that direction, guns raised.

"Put your guns down!" a voice booms, over and over, and as I step out into the warehouse where JD retreated with Trigger and Mule, I come face to face with some of the deadliest motherfuckers around.

Marx brothers.

"Lower your guns," I order my team as I step forward, catching my mate Liam's attention.

The cheeky fucker has the audacity to fucking grin as he points his gun at me, kissing the air and shooting me a wink.

"Hey Camy boy."

"Fuck off, you prick. It's Ringo to you." I chuckle and the four Marx brothers, plus Riggs, their head of security, lower their guns as they chuckle too.

"Jesus, do you arseholes sleep in suits?" JD teases as he steps up to my side, and Kendrick shrugs.

"I was born in a fucking suit."

"Speak for yourself," Liam whines. "These fucking shirts choke me."

"What the fuck are you complaining about? I heard you like to be choked." Oswald, the youngest Marx present, snickers, and Liam rolls his eyes.

"Dude. I'm the giver, not the receiver."

"Fucking hell." Conrad Marx, the oldest Marx present, shoves past them and steps forward. "I swear I have no idea how he's still fucking alive." He holds out his hand to shake. "Ringo. Good to see you again."

Taking his offer, I shake his hand before the other brothers step forward and do the same.

It's more formal than what I'm used to. MC members don't exactly shake hands.

Maybe a slap on the shoulder, a fist bump, or even a simple nod is how we typically greet someone, which is exactly the way Riggs greets me. With a nod.

Seth Riggs has been a part of the Marx crew for as long as I can remember. He grew up with Conrad. They were best mates, from what I've been told. When he was in his teens, Ewan Marx, the father and leader of the Marx family, recruited Riggs as one of his soldiers, and after years of loyalty, Riggs was bumped up to the head of the Marx security, watching over Ewan and his heir, Leo as they lead.

This guy doesn't fuck around. He's loyal to a tee, and fucking deadly in the blink of an eye, yet here, now, he re-holsters his gun, not at all finding us a threat.

We are, after all, working together.

"So what the fuck is happening? Why did we get an alert? And why couldn't we access comms?" Kendrick asks, taking the lead on behalf of the family.

"We are trying to figure that out now." I turn to Patrick, who starts filling Kendrick in on the surveillance issue.

Noise from behind us makes the Marx men stiffen, their hands on their weapons in an instant, but I hold up my hand to reassure them.

"It's my men. They were checking comms and doing a security sweep."

"Always got it all covered," Liam chuckles, coming up to my side and bumping his shoulder into mine.

"Always," I agree, watching my men approach.

"Please tell me we are gonna hit a club or two when this lockdown lifts. I could use some Ringo time."

I chuckle, taking in my mate. "I don't think your old man would be too fucking happy about that."

"Nah, he's too busy putting Leo up on a pedestal to notice my clubbing habits. Being child number eight has its perks." Liam grins, wagging his brows, and I can't help but grin back.

I have a feeling he'd like Abbey. Hell, I have a feeling she'd like him too.

My smile drops. Yeah-nah, I don't like that fucking idea.

"Are you sure you're not child number nine?" I ask, trying to cover up my swift mood change at the thought of my Angel being attracted to my mate. "Who was born first? You or Fallon?"

Liam rolls his eyes. "I was born before my twin sister, so that makes me child number fucking eight."

I snicker, already knowing it pisses him off when there's any mention that his twin sister, Fallon, is older than him.

"Sarg. Comms cupboard seems okay, and the cameras are intact." Murf advises as he nears, and I glance at Patrick.

He was right. The problem isn't here, it's online.

"So that means someone else has control over our system?" Kendrick asks Patrick, coming to the same conclusion as me, and Patrick shrugs.

"Maybe. I'm not IT, so I have no idea about that."

"You have Lewy working on it?" Conrad asks me and I nod.

"If there's something to be found, then he'll find it."

"Would whatever it is be blocking our phone signals as well?" Scooter asks and I frown.

"I have no fucking idea."

All of a sudden, my phone starts ringing, scaring the fuck out of most of us since we were just speaking of the lack of signal.

"Speak," I bark, already knowing it's Lewy and putting him on speaker.

"Sarg, I've got control back, and everything looks fine at all warehouses except for one."

My eyes dart to JD and he instantly stiffens.

"Which one?" I snap.

"Warehouse four. I have access again, but the cameras are showing as offline, which means they've been disconnected on location."

"Fuck," Conrad mutters, taking his phone out before texting someone.

Fuck is right. Warehouse four is where the bulk of our medical supplies are kept.

"Thanks Lewy. I want a report on what happened and a contingency plan to make sure it doesn't happen again," I order.

"Yes, Sarg," he says warily, knowing this breach reflects on him and his team as the ones to set up our online security.

As soon as I hang up, I try to conference call all leaders from each van, to give them a quick rundown on what's happened here, but one van won't respond.

Van five.

To the other responding vans, I give them the details we know, only to find out that they had similar experiences at their locations, too. The real concern is that van five, the one that was tasked to check warehouse four, isn't responding.

"Everyone rendezvous at warehouse four. Stay on high alert and approach with caution," I order, and after agreeing, all locations disconnect except for van one.

"Ringo, am I on speaker?" Smitty asks.

"No," I say, stepping away from the others, like that will somehow ensure no one can hear, even though he's not on speaker.

"How do you read Kendrick?" Smitty asks, and I sigh, turning to face the Marx men, a couple on their phones barking orders, while the others talk in hushed tones.

"He was alright until we found out warehouse four is still unreachable."

"Dammit. Why do I get the feeling we have been sent on a wild goose chase?" Smitty asks.

"Because I'm pretty fucking sure we have been. It looks like the Marx crew got directed to this warehouse too, and we split up to check some of the other locations only because Lewy noticed them all down, otherwise we'd all be here where I am."

"I've got a bad fucking feeling about this," Smitty mutters, "try to keep the Marx brothers on side. The last thing we fucking need is them deciding we're their enemy when we fucking aren't."

Although the Marx brothers can be crazy motherfuckers, most of them at least have their heads screwed on right and are fair men. Their old man, on the other hand, well, he's a fucking nutter. Seems to be getting worse the older he gets as well, so Smitty's concerns are understandable, because even if Kendrick and his brothers don't think we have a hand in whatever the fuck this is, it doesn't mean Ewan won't jump to his own fucking conclusions.

"Leave it with me," I mutter before ending the call and rounding up the men.

Why do I get the fucking feeling shit is about to hit the fan?

25

ABBEY

My hands tremble as I peek through the thin curtain, trying to get a look at what's happening out in the courtyard. I know Jols told me to hide in the bathroom, but then I heard yelling through the open window, and I need to listen to make sure everything is okay.

"Come on now. Everyone is sleeping. Can't you come back later?" I hear Stocky's voice, and my eyes find him standing before four cops, whose faces I cannot see, their backs to me.

"Do you seriously think we should believe over thirty men are sleeping at this time of day?" a deep authoritative tone asks, and my spine stiffens.

That voice…

Why do cops all sound the same? Do they teach them that at the police academy? Like a female newsreader is taught how to read the news with the same tone as all the other female newsreaders, are cops trained to sound the same too?

"It's called a siesta." Brody, the young guy that was doing a bad job of watching my door the other night, chuckles like it's a joke, and one of the officers lurches forward and punches him square in the nose.

The crack of it travels all the way over to me, a gasp lodging in my throat as the Doxies standing around all release theirs in loud unison.

"Hey. Hey. Hey." Stocky holds his hands up, gesturing for calm as Brody stumbles back, his hand flying to his nose where blood starts pouring from it.

Oh, my god.

What is happening?

"He's just a dumb kid. There was no need to hit him." Stocky points out, slowly sidestepping to put himself between the officer and Brody.

"Let's stop wasting time." That same deep authoritative voice says, and a memory slams into me.

> *"Let's stop wasting time, Abbey. I know you don't want anything bad to happen to your little sisters. So do everyone a favour, and just leave. If you don't sign the statement, then this little misunderstanding never happened."*

No.

It can't be him.

Surely not.

My trembling morphs into violent shaking tremors as tears prick the back of my eyes.

Calm down, Abbey. It's just your mind playing tricks on you.

"Aligning with the regulations set by the state's governing authority concerning the State of Emergency set in place due to the pandemic," another authoritative voice speaks this time, and I notice how different it is from the first officer. "We have the right to search private premises without a warrant to ensure lockdown compliances. Anyone found to be in breach of the current governing laws could be issued fines up to twenty thousand dollars."

"You can't be serious?" Jols is the one to speak this time, stepping up beside Stocky.

"Oh, we are very serious." The first officer sneers before rolling his shoulders back and yelling. "Start checking rooms!"

His bellow is loud, a few squeaks fly from some of the Doxies huddled together, and I get ready to run to the bathroom to hide, but when I see two of the officers move to the rooms across the other side of the yard, I stay in place, needing to know what's happening.

"Officer, I don't suppose you'd like a drink on this fine day?" an old guy asks, using his cane as he shuffles closer to the officers.

I've only noticed him once in the times I ventured out of the room. He's never been in the crowd for the parties.

"Or perhaps you're interested in something else? Something a little more… exquisite?" The old guy slowly turns, holding out his arm and gesturing to the huddled Doxies.

Oh, my… Is he trying to bribe the officers? With sex?

"Tucker," the second officer says, leaning forward like he's reading the name patch on the front of the old guy's vest. "You wouldn't be trying to bribe a police officer, would you?"

"No. No," Tucker says quickly.

"Because you know, if I want to fuck one of your whores," the officer stands taller, "I don't need to fucking ask."

"You can't touch them!" Brody yells from behind Stocky and Jols, and the two officers start laughing, while the other two keep checking rooms over the other side.

"Anything?" The first officer bellows as he turns to glance at his officers checking the rooms.

That's when I get a decent view of his profile, and all my breath seizes in my lungs.

No.

"Nope. No one," an officer responds, and the main one turns back to face the few club members and Doxies.

"Well, what a surprise. That's a helluva lot of fines."

The officers snicker and turn, starting to walk away, and finally, the air in my lungs comes rushing out.

It's okay.

He's not here for me.

They are going to leave.

I see the Doxies visibly relax too, probably feeling the same relief as me, although for different reasons, but then they stiffen as a group, and I hold my breath again as my gaze darts back to the officers who are now spinning back to face them.

"You know what, I'm feeling generous," the main officer says, stepping back towards the group. "Because I estimate at least thirty men aren't accounted for, and correct me if I'm wrong, but that would add up to six hundred thousand dollars in fines." He leans closer, getting in Stocky's face. "Do the Southern Sadists have six hundred thousand dollars?"

I can see Stocky's face better than that of the officer's, and he has rage written all over his expression, yet he remains quiet.

"But!" the officer yells, and I notice Jols flinch back a little. "Since I'm a reasonable kind of guy, we'll take four blowjobs right fucking here, right fucking now, and call it even."

Oh, my god.

No.

"Now hang on a minut—"

Stocky's words are cut off when the second officer whips out his baton and slogs Stocky over the side of the head.

The Doxies cry out, and I leap back in horror as Stocky falls to the ground with a heavy thud.

"Hey fuck you!" Brody yells, and Barts, the guy who's drunk twenty-four seven, stumbles up from the chair he was perched on, charging the officer.

It all happens so quickly, the officers and the men start fighting, while Jols urges the Doxies back, trying to keep them out of harm's way, but it's no use. The officers overpower the few men left behind, and in a matter of minutes, Stocky, Barts, Tucker, Brody, and another young guy I haven't come across before, are beaten to a pulp on the ground, leaving Jols and the Doxies to fend for themselves.

"Now." The officer I wish I didn't know shouts before spitting off to the side as he slips his baton back onto his belt, and proceeds to undo his fly.

He's not really going to…

Oh shit.

"Which one of you sluts is going to blow me?"

The other officers chuckle, doing the same as their leading officer, and undoing their flies to release their...

This can't be happening.

"How about you, darlin'?" the leading officer asks Jols, but before she can react, Wendy shoves Jols aside and steps forward.

"I can take your big fat cock, officer."

Shit. Did Wendy just do that for Jols?

"Get on your knees then, whore," he snarls, and she hurries forward to do just that.

"Come on, girls. Don't be scared." One of the other officers says this time, and almost like the Doxies have already discussed it and know who is meant to do the deed, Celina who was all over the President the first time I met him, steps forward, followed by, Helina, which was the Doxy Brody had bailed up outside Ringo's door. And the last to step forward is perhaps the biggest surprise because of how young she is.

Nessy.

I look away. I can't watch this. There's nothing sensual about this at all, and although explicit scenes are common outside Ringo's room, this is nothing but vulgar coercion that rolls my stomach.

Ringo.

Come back.

I want to cry, but I know that won't help the situation, and the fact that Officer Allen is out there, the same officer that threatened the safety of my sisters if I proceeded with my rape allegations, reminds me that I need to stay alert. Strong. And ready to run.

What is he doing here, anyway? He works in the Timber Valley district… Doesn't he?

Maybe more police were required in the city to ensure compliance of the lockdown.

Whatever the reason, I hate the thought that it's no coincidence that he's turned up here. Surely, I'm overthinking this.

When I hear the officers cheering a little, I sneak another peek to find some of the Doxies kissing each other.

They can't be getting off on this too, right?

I try my best not to look at the officers getting their appendages sucked, but when I do, I notice Officer Allen forcefully holding Wendy's head as he thrusts into her mouth, and I know, I just know it's choking her. Gagging her. Hurting her.

It's then that some of the Doxies strip their tops off and start sucking on each other's nipples. I'm momentarily shocked that they would be so on board with this, until I notice Casey's face as she turns away from the officers. She's fighting back tears.

Oh… my…

I watch on, assessing every detail this time, and every time the officers get too rough, the Doxies try to catch their attention.

Of course.

They are trying to help.

They are trying to get the officers over the line faster, so they stop hurting their friends and leave.

Tears well in my eyes at how utterly wrong this entire thing is, yet how beautiful it is that friends would go that far to help each other.

I used to have that. Until I betrayed Lexi. Until I helped the girls at school bully her about the secret she'd tried to keep. A devastatingly humiliating secret, much like mine in ways, but so different in others.

Lexi didn't deserve that. She didn't deserve her best friend turning her back on her and helping others harass her. Hell, there was even a physical fight or two.

But I still did it. To save my own arse.

I flop down in the chair, giving my eyes a break from the vile scene outside, and glance around the room.

It's a shitty room. There's nothing special about it and not a hint of personality that speaks to the man Ringo is.

No, to find a peek of that you need to rummage through his drawers.

The corner of my mouth quirks.

I can't believe I found his sex toy and, like… touched it. And he sprung me.

My cheeks heat at the memory.

Sex had been such a hateful thing before I came here. I know it's not about love here, but what I've observed, it's absolutely about pleasure. Most of the time, that also includes the woman's pleasure too. Well, all but the time Brody choked Darla with his… dick in Ringo's bathtub. There's no way that was pleasurable for her.

The knowing sound of grunts has me peeking back out, and I regret that decision instantly witnessing Celina throw up a few mouthfuls of semen, while poor Wendy gets sprayed with thick white ropes of the same stuff, all over her face, hair and chest.

Ew.

I gag.

Shit.

Sucking in a deep breath, I try to ward off my need to hurl right now.

It can wait until these awful officers have left. Then I can purge all I want.

I notice a few of the men are conscious again, but they make no attempt to stand, and as I, and they, watch the Doxies get up off the ground from their knees and scurry back over to the others, the officers tuck their now limp penises away before Officer Allen speaks.

"One last thing." He reaches into the breast pocket of his shirt and pulls out something. A piece of paper maybe. Then he holds it out for everyone to see, walking slowly past them to make sure each Doxy, and then each conscious man gets a good look.

"Has anyone seen this girl? She was kidnapped from her home in Fox Pines last Thursday night. Her name is Abbey Delany, and her parents are distraught."

What?

No.

NO!

This can't be happening.

"What did you say her name was?" Wendy asks, and my heart thrashes wildly in my chest.

She'll give me up. I know she will. She hates me. Has some sort of infatuation with Ringo, so getting me out of the way will solve her problems.

Officer Allen strolls back towards Wendy, still holding the photo up, and I notice Jols subtly glance my way.

Oh, my god.

I have to go.

But I can't.

I'm trapped in here. There's no back door.

If Officer Allen gets me, not only will I be taken back to my parents, but I'll be forced to marry Daniel, and this nightmare will never end.

"I've never seen her before." Jols speaks up before anyone else, and slowly, one by one, the other Doxies shake their heads in agreement.

"Hmmm." Wendy hums, leaning closer to the picture. "I'm not sure why you'd ask us." Wendy shifts back, glaring up at Officer Allen. "We aren't in the skin trade. And besides. None of our men would take a liking to such a plain Jane. Poor thing looks like she'd cry if she saw a cock."

The other Doxies giggle, but Officer Allen remains stoic, glaring at Wendy.

Then he clicks his tongue.

"You won't mind if we search every room for her, just in case."

Gasping, I stumble back from the window, my heart in my throat as panic washes over me.

Ringo.

Help.

Please come back.

Dammit Abbey. He's not here. Only you.

You have to fight for yourself!

Feeling the same desperation I did the night my parents locked me in my room and drugged me, a wildness, untamed and raw, ripples through my veins.

I am the protector now.

I am the only one that can stop this.

Hurrying forward, I pull Ringo's drawer open, rummaging through it, only to find his sex toy.

Ugh.

I hurry to the wardrobe, opening the drawers there, and freeze when I find a gun under a pair of jeans in the second drawer.

Panting from fear and adrenalin, I pick it up in my trembling hand.

It's heavier than I imagined. The metal cool against my skin. It almost feels surreal to hold it. I've never seen one in real life until Ringo came into my life, let alone held one. What with Australia's tough gun laws, I would've thought it would be harder to possess one, yet Ringo left with a gun and has this one hidden in his room.

I have no idea how to work it, but when I hear yelling outside, a small cry lurches from my throat and I rush into the bathroom, closing myself in.

This is it.

I'm going to die today.

Glancing to the side, I see my reflection in the mirror. My brown eyes are wide. Wild looking. Like a crazy woman, and perhaps I am.

My lower lip wobbles and I accept my fate.

"I tried," I whisper as tears fall over, my shoulders slumping before my chin hits my chest in defeat. "I really did try. But I can't go back to them. I can't let that happen. This is the only way."

Glancing at the bath, I decide that's where it'll happen, and I move forward to climb in.

26

RINGO

We are the second van to arrive at warehouse four. Van five, the van we couldn't communicate with, is still here, the doors thrown open and no one in sight.

The screech of tyres from the Marx brothers' two Range Rovers are loud as they come to a halt behind our van, and as we all pile out, Mex steps out from the warehouse entrance, the look on his face grave.

"What is it?" I snap, storming towards him, taking in his slumped shoulders and pallor of his skin which is pale compared to his normally golden tone.

Mex warily glances at me before his gaze travels over my shoulder to the thundering feet coming up behind me.

"Mex. Tell me," I order, and he flinches, his dark eyes returning to mine.

"They're all dead."

My brows shoot up. "All four?"

"Yes," Mex mutters.

"How?" Conrad Marx snaps from behind me.

"Uh, well…" Mex shifts uncomfortably, his gaze darting to mine, and when I nod, he continues. "Two died by gunshot, and two, well… It's hard to tell if it was the bullets or the way their necks have been sliced open to know which killed them."

"Fuck." I hear all four Marx brothers curse behind me.

"Show me," Riggs barks, pushing past me and shoving Mex back through the door.

"Is that fucking necessary?" I snap, turning to Kendrick, who looks fucking pissed.

"Emotions are high, man. And at least two of the dead are Riggs' men, so you'll have to excuse him for caring."

"Alright. Alright. Emotions are high for everyone." Liam intervenes, putting himself in between me and his brothers.

Fuck. This isn't good, and while I should be focusing on what's happening here, all I can think about is returning to Abbey.

Maybe it's because she's so opposite to the lifestyle I lead that has me wishing to be there instead of here doing my fucking job. I only just fucking met her, and really, she's just someone I'm crossing paths with briefly, so why the fuck is it her I'm thinking about continuously rather than the fact two of our men have been killed.

"What the fuck is going on, Ringo?" Kendrick snaps, dragging me back to reality.

"That's what I'd like to fucking know." I snarl over Liam's shoulder to his seething brother.

"Obviously, none of us know what's happening," Conrad barks, thank fuck.

At least he's not automatically blaming us for this breach, unlike Kendrick, who seems to want to point the fucking finger at me.

Liam turns to face me, gripping my shoulder. "Let's take a look." He gestures to the open door, so I suck in a breath that's meant to be calming, but fucking isn't, and turn on my heel to check out the scene.

As soon as we step inside, it's apparent that there was a fight from the start. The first man we come across is one of the Marx security, his throat slashed with two bullet wounds in his chest, and his gun lies mere inches from his fingers.

"Check that." I point down at the gun. "See if he managed to fire a shot. Maybe we were lucky enough that they managed to shoot one of the attackers. We can keep an eye on any reports of gun shot wounds checking in for help at the hospitals."

"Good idea," Liam says from behind me, and he kneels beside the lifeless man, checking his gun with his gloved fingers, before looking up at me and shaking his head. "No rounds were fired."

"Sounds like he was taken by surprise." Conrad grunts, and I nod.

The Marx security personnel are well trained, more so than our men, which means whoever broke in managed to do it without alerting anyone until it was too late.

We move forward, taking in the rest of the scene. The office is a bloodbath, the other three men there, but it's clear there was a gunfight.

"Riggs, get a team here and take samples of every drop of blood in this room," Kendrick orders. "I want to know if there's any blood that doesn't belong to our men."

"On it." Riggs nods, taking out his phone and making the call.

"Do we know what was taken," I ask, dragging my gaze from the horrific scene of our dead men, and face the warehouse, packed with medical supplies.

"At a glance it's hard to say," Mex offers. "Nothing stands out since it looks like nothing was touched, but we won't know until we do a full audit."

Fuck. This will take a few days.

"We'll get a team of ten down here to get started." Conrad suggests and I nod, my eyes catching on Smitty as he strides in with more of our men at his back.

"Someone tell me what the fuck happened!" He booms, and I don't miss the way Oswald Marx rolls his eyes before turning to face my President.

That kinda pisses me off. He should have more fucking respect.

As Mex starts filling him in, my phone vibrates with an incoming call, and I frown when I see Brody's name flashing across the screen.

"JD," I call, glancing up to find my mate.

"Sup?" he asks, stepping around the gathered men to my side.

"Why is your little brother calling me?"

JD frowns, taking his phone out, only to see that he doesn't have any missed calls.

When his eyes meet mine, panic widening them, I instantly hit accept since the only reason he'd ring me and not his brother is if there was something wrong.

"Speak," I snap and at first I hear nothing, so I put it on speaker and step further away from the group of gathered Marx men, trying to hear.

"Ringo," Brody whispers, sounding panicked. "If you can hear me. The cops are here. The compound has been compromised." Brody coughs, and my eyes find JD's again, his panic already setting in. "Help."

The call ends, and for a hot fucking minute, I swear I stop breathing.

Then, at the top of my lungs, I yell. "Code Blue!"

Every Southern Sadist inside the warehouse stiffens, their eyes shooting towards me as a hush falls over the warehouse.

"Code fucking blue. Pigs are at the Western. A brother has called for help."

No more words are needed. Our men charge for the entrance, their heavy feet pounding the concrete like a thundering herd of elephants.

My eyes meet Liam's as he hurries to me. "What can we do?"

"Nothing man. This is our battle. Maybe just get a start on things here. I'll get a team back as soon as I can."

"Okay. Go." He slaps me on the shoulder and I fucking run for the entrance.

The other vans turn up as we are piling in to leave, so Bowey stays behind to fill them in as we speed off.

"Why the fuck doesn't this feel like a coincidence?" JD snaps, no longer caring about fucking speed limits as he plants his foot.

"I was having the same fucking thought," I mutter as I dial Lewy.

"Sarg?" Lewy answers.

"We got eyes on the compound?" I snap.

"Hang on. Just checking now."

My fucking knee bounces up and down like it's having a fucking seizure, my thoughts already on Abbey and how scared she must be, because clearly the pigs weren't there just to say hi. Clearly something has gone down for Brody to call for fucking help.

"Sarg." Lewy speaks again. "Eyes are down at the compound."

"Fuck!" I roar, punching the fucking dash. "What the fuck is going on?! Lewy, you're meant to have a handle on the comms and eyes. Why they fuck don't you?!"

"I-I'm sorry Sarg. I don't know, but I will find out and ensure it never happens again." Lewy promises.

"You'd fucking better. Or you know what will happen," I growl.

"I-I know, Sarg. I promise to get on top of it."

I end the fucking call, no longer wanting to hear his voice.

"Are we about to bury some pigs, Sarg?" Trigger asks from the back of the van, and I nod.

"Seems fucking like it."

It takes us ten fucking minutes to get back to the Western, but fuck, it feels like it takes an hour.

The first thing we notice is the men aren't manning the gates. The second thing is that there are no cop cars in sight.

I leap out as JD drives in, not fucking patient enough for him to pull the van into the underground garage, and the moment my feet hit the pavement, I fucking run.

With my gun ready in my hand, I raise it, prepared to shoot anything in a navy fucking uniform as I leap around the corner of the courtyard entrance and fucking come to a halt.

There are no cops in sight.

"They just left!" Jols calls from the gathered group, the Doxies huddled together, some crying, while my men are fucking battered, bloody and bruised, some on the ground, and a few others limping to chairs.

The others from my van skid to a stop behind me, ready to fucking rumble, but I lower my gun, and so do they.

"What the fuck happened?!"

Smitty's bellow makes everyone stiffen, but I ignore it, moving forward to do a head count.

"Pres, four cops came." Stocky puffs, trying to stand, but instantly tumbles back to the ground, his pants soaked in blood near his shin.

"Get him a fucking chair," I snap, and Darla hurries to get him seated in a chair. "We are two men short. Where the fuck are Morris and Cookie?"

My question results in nothing but blank fucking stares.

"Jols. Have you seen Morris and Cookie?" Smitty asks his stepdaughter.

"No. Last I heard, they were on gate duty."

"She's right. They were manning the gates when we left." I agree, and Smitty picks up a chair and starts smashing it into the ground as he yells.

"Then!" smash, "Why!" smash, "Aren't!" smash, "They!" smash, "On!" smash, "The!" smash, "Fucking!" smash, "Gate!"

Finally, as he heaves, Smitty throws what's left of the chair across the courtyard, the fucking piece of white plastic narrowly missing a window and slamming against the brick wall.

No one speaks, and that's when I know no one has a fucking clue where our two prospects are.

"It's all sounding a bit fucking suss," Spud snaps. "They were there when we left and then all of a fucking sudden, the pigs turn up and they are gone."

"They set off the alert," Jols offers. "But maybe the police took them? Or maybe they ran thinking they'll get into trouble by letting them in."

"Too fucking right, they're in trouble." Smitty hisses. "What the fuck did the cops want?"

"Compliance check." Stocky offers, "Amongst other things."

"What fucking other things?" I step forward, my gun still tight in my hand, ready to fucking kill.

The way Stocky glances at the Doxies, and then at Jols has me fucking grinding my teeth with impatience, so I turn my sights to the one woman I know won't fucking lie to me. "Jols?"

"Look, things got a little out of hand," she gestures to our clearly battered men, "and after checking some of the rooms, the pigs determined that most of the men weren't here, threatening the breach of lockdown fines."

"Those fucking cunts," Smitty snarls.

"Yeah. Twenty K per missing man." Jols continues, before disbelieving murmurs float up around us as the men protest.

"So, they are fining us?" Smitty asks but Jols shakes her head.

"They took payment in another way."

She doesn't have to say more for us to get her meaning, and Smitty picks up another chair and proceeds to break it in another fit of rage.

As he smashes up yet another fucking chair, my eyes dart to my room.

Is Abbey okay? Did she stay hidden?

"Who!" Smitty roars. "Which one of my beautiful Doxies did they defile?"

Dragging my gaze from my room, I watch as Wendy, Celina, Nessy and Helina slowly step forward.

"Fuck!" Smitty rages, even as he steps up to Celina and cups her face. "What did they ask you to do, baby?"

She shrugs, offering him a smile that doesn't meet her eyes. "It was just a blowjob."

He growls. "Their dicks were in your mouths?" Smitty asks, turning his gaze to the other Doxies even as his hands remain framing Celina's cheeks.

"Yes." Wendy speaks up, and that's when I notice how sticky her hair looks.

Those putrid fucking pigs.

Smitty turns his eyes back to Celina. "I'm sorry, baby. I'll clean you up."

"That's not all they wanted," Wendy snaps, her eyes flashing to me before returning to Smitty, who has now stepped away from Celina.

It's then that I notice Jols glaring at Wendy, and all the Doxies shifting uncomfortably.

"Well, what the fuck else did they want?" Smitty snaps, clearly impatient.

"They were looking for a girl that was kidnapped from Fox Pines." Wendy pouts her lips with far too much fucking attitude as she shoots me a glare.

Oh.

Fucking.

No.

My gaze darts back to Jols whose face is turning red in anger, before my eyes shift straight to my door.

I step forward. "What of it?" I snap.

"What did they call her?" Wendy presses her finger to her lips as if the bitch is thinking hard. "Oh. Abbey Delany."

"What the fuck does that have to do with us?" Smitty snaps, but Wendy doesn't even look at him. Her eyes remain locked on mine.

"Well, nothing, except for the fact that the girl in the picture they showed all of us," her claw-like nail points to the Doxies and the men who stayed behind, "looks exactly like Charity."

My eyes widen and my hand fucking twitches with the gun still gripped tightly.

I could fucking kill this bitch.

"Ringo?" Smitty turns to face me, his brow raised. "You know anything about that?"

I ignore him, my gaze moving to Jols. "Where is she? Did they fucking take her?"

Jols shakes her head. "No, they didn't take her. Brody started yelling that you were all on your way back, and the cops just left. She's still in your room."

"The fuck!" Smitty booms, but my feet are moving, and I'm shoving through the gathered men to get to my room.

I need to see her. I need to make sure she's okay.

I shove my bedroom door open, the fucking flimsy timber ricocheting off the wall with a bang, and a quick fucking scan shows the main room empty.

"Ringo! Get the fuck back here!"

Again, I ignore Smitty, knowing too well that I'm walking a very fucking fine line with him.

Storming inside, I head straight for the bathroom, and the moment I shove the door open, a piercing clap fills the air as a bullet slams into my chest.

27

ABBEY

The quaking tremble of my hands holding the heavy metal of the gun is the first thing I see when I pry my lids open, my breath trapped in my lungs as fear grips me.

I just shot someone.

Oh shit.

I really just shot someone.

As my vision slowly unblurs, bringing into focus the now empty doorway, too many things happen at once.

My hearing comes whooshing back, although there's a ringing in my right ear that's not as evident in my left. There's coughing and groaning, as well as yelling that sounds to be getting closer.

That's when I see him. Ringo, laid out on the carpet in the doorway, his feet barely moving as he coughs again and groans.

"Oh, my god. Ringo!" I cry, about to drop the gun, when three large figures jump out of nowhere, guns raised at me.

"Put it down!" one yells.

"Lower the gun or we'll shoot!" another yells.

"Stop!" a female voice calls from somewhere.

Is that Jols?

I cry out, terrified, yet the gun remains in my hands, my grip unmoving, not allowing me to become even more vulnerable as my body trembles violently.

"Ringo!" I cry, tears streaming from my eyes. "Please tell me he's okay." I beg, still aware that I have the barrel of three guns pointed at me.

Cough. "Stand," cough, "down."

A sob escapes me as I hear the muttered rasp of Ringo's voice, and a moment later, he pushes himself up to sit in the doorway.

"But she shot you," one voice says, and through the blur of my tears, I can't focus on the man's face to see if I know him.

"It's alright, Vender. It was an accident." Ringo coughs again, his hands moving to his chest slowly, like their weight is too much to bear.

Then he glances down at his chest, his fingers grazing over something before he chuckles.

"Thank fuck for the Kevlar."

Kevlar?

What?

I'm sobbing now, the gun still pointed in Ringo's direction, yet my determined grip begins to falter.

"My gun will remain on her until she drops the fucking metal, man," Vender snaps.

"You fucking shoot her, and I'll end you!" Ringo booms over his shoulder before his furious gaze returns to me. "It's okay, Angel. You can put the gun down now. You're safe."

Safe?

I'm not safe.

There are still three guns aimed my way, and the police could come back at any time and take me back to Fox Pines.

I'm not remotely safe.

"N-no. I-I can't," I stammer, shaking my head even as Ringo crawls closer.

"Yes, you can, Angel. The police are gone. I'm here. You're safe."

"He's going to come back," I mutter, watching as Ringo's face gets clearer in my vision the closer he gets.

"Who's going to come back?"

"Officer Allen," I admit, as finally, Ringo's face is right at the edge of the bath, his dark eyes boring into mine.

"Who is Officer Allen? Was he one of the cops that came?" he asks, reaching for my trembling hands, but halting before they touch.

"Y-yes," I stammer, studying the inward pull of Ringo's brows as his gaze moves to the gun in my hands.

"How do you know who he was?" Ringo's gaze returns to mine.

"H-he… H-he…" I start sobbing again, and Ringo shifts, leaning closer.

"How do you know him, Angel?"

"I m-met him when I w-went to the Redfield Police Station last year… to report…"

I don't need to finish. Just by Ringo's expression, I know he understands that I'm talking about going to the police to report my rape.

"Angel, I'm going to take the gun now," he says, right before his warm hands encase mine, and I slowly loosen my grip and relinquish the gun.

Sighs flow from the bathroom entrance, and Ringo turns back to talk over his shoulder.

"Some privacy please," he barks and even as the men lower their guns and leave, someone else comes shoving past them.

"Wanna fucking explain what's going on?" Smitty booms, and like the coward I am, a whimper flies from my lips as I flinch back.

"For fuck's sake, man. I will, just give me a damn minute with my girl," Ringo snaps, but Smitty doesn't budge, his glare lethal as it locks onto me.

Sighing, Ringo turns to face his President, standing as he does so.

"Seriously, just let me check that she's okay, and then I'll give you my undivided attention."

Smitty's glare shifts from me to Ringo. "Not just your undivided attention, but fucking answers. No more bullshitting." He jabs Ringo's shoulder, who nods as he shucks off his leather vest with a skull on the back framed with the words, Southern Sadists.

It's then that I see another vest underneath, but it looks more like those bulletproof things the police wear in movies.

"No more bullshitting." Ringo agrees, and finally, the President turns and gives us some privacy.

"Fuck," I hear Ringo mutter quietly as he starts pulling on the Velcro straps holding the vest in place.

I'm still trembling, although it has eased somewhat, yet the familiar coldness that's always present sends goosebumps over my skin. I curl my knees up as tight as I can get them, slipping the fabric of the hoodie over my knees so only my feet are poking out at the bottom.

Finally, turning back to face me, Ringo rubs at his chest like it's tender under his tee.

"That was a good shot, Angel. You familiar with a gun?"

"No," I whisper, shaking my head.

"I guess you got lucky." He chuckles.

"I guess you did, since I had my eyes closed. I could have shot you in the head."

At my words, his shoulders slump as his hand falls from his chest, his eyes appearing almost disbelieving. "You had your eyes closed?"

"Yes." I nod. "I thought you were him."

Lowering himself back to the tiled floor, Ringo rests his forearm on the bath's ledge as he studies me.

"Him, as in the police officer you know?"

"Yes." I nod.

"You know he wouldn't hurt you, right? He would have been here thinking you were kidnapped."

"I was kidnapped." I point out and I can tell by the way his long stubble shifts that he's fighting a grin.

"True."

"He's not a nice man," I say, and his gaze hardens.

"After what I heard happened out in the courtyard, I'd have to agree. Is that what you're referring to?"

I shake my head. "No… I… He…"

"Angel. You know you can tell me."

Lowering my chin to rest on the tops of my knees, I sigh. "When I told the police what happened on my birthday, they kept me in the interview room for hours. Then, Officer Allen walked in. I didn't know who he was at first, and it didn't even click when he said his surname, but then he made it clear that he wasn't there to help me at all."

Ringo shifts, lowering his chin to rest on top of his arm, bringing us to eye level. "How so?"

I hate even thinking about that day. I remember how my faith in law enforcement was so abruptly torn from me with a few simple words.

"He told me that I shouldn't lie to get attention, and when I went to argue that I wasn't lying, he told me that if I proceeded with the rape allegations against his nephew and his nephew's friends, that he can't guarantee the safety of my sisters." A shudder runs up my spine as his face looms in the forefront of my mind, my gaze falling from Ringo's face as I continue. "He asked me to imagine them going through the same thing I was alleging, and to consider if it was really worth it. Then he slid the paper across the desk and asked if I was going to sign the statement or not… So, I stood up and left and I heard him laughing as he tore it up, and called me a whore."

"His name should be on the list, too." Ringo hisses, and I nod. "Angel, eyes up." And like they always do, my eyes obey, locking onto his. "This prick's nephew is Donny Allen, right?"

"How… How do you remember the name?"

He grins. "Your list is stored up here now." He taps his temple. "So yeah, I remember the names of Daniel Stone, Craig McRoe,

Michael Berry, Tim Beck, Darnel Rivers, and, lastly, Donny Allen. And those names will stay there until I've killed each and every one of them, which now includes Officer fucking Allen."

"You can't kill a cop." I argue, but he scoffs, shifting back and standing.

"I've killed cops before, Angel, and this motherfucker will meet the same fate." He reaches out, offering me his hand. "Come on. Time for me to face the music."

"What? Why?" I ask, letting his large hand grip mine and help me to stand.

"Wendy told my Prez about the cops showing them a picture of you, calling you Abbey Delany."

I stiffen, and when Ringo notices, he sighs and cups my cheek. "Don't fret, Angel. I just need to be honest with Smitty. It'll be alright."

Even though he seems to believe that, I remember clearly what Jols told me, and how he may very well *not* be alright. Even so, Ringo leaves me with no time to think about it a moment longer before he's leading me from the bathroom and out into his motel room.

"About fucking time," Smitty barks, shifting forward impatiently on the couch to rest his elbows on his thighs, and in the light filtering in from the window, the grey specks in his hair and beard seem to stand out even more than usual. For some reason, I thought a little grey hair would make a man less scary.

I was wrong.

"You have my undivided attention now," Ringo mutters, dropping down to sit on the end of his bed, dragging me down next to him as he weaves our fingers together.

I'm not the only one that notices this, Smitty's gaze locking onto the action, a deeper frown contorting his expression.

"Start fucking talking," he snaps. "Who the fuck is Abbey Delany?"

I don't know what comes over me. It could be my knowledge of what this man might do to Ringo in punishment for lying to him, or it could be simply because I've gone nuts, but I open my mouth and start rambling.

"My mum was trying to force me to marry Daniel, who is a douchebag, to put it lightly, and I couldn't let her force me into that. I had to escape, and I tried, I really did, but my parents overpowered me and drugged me and locked me away, and well, even smashing my window didn't help because they closed the external shutters, but somehow, Tahli, she's my little sister, managed to reach out to Lexi, who is, or was my best friend, that's still to be determined after what I did to her. Anyway, Lexi sent a bunch of scary men to break in and kidnap me, which was terrifying, but was all worth it when I saw how they were making my parents suffer. It's honestly the best thing I've seen in years but then this arsehole forced me to sit on his lap, which I think was highly unnecessary, and then did the same making me sleep in his bed, but luckily he didn't touch me… not like them… Ringo's just not like that, you know? Of course you know. You know him better than I do, so you know he was just trying to protect me, and well, I wasn't meant to leave the room but, Brody wouldn't stop having sex with the girl to take the phone to Ringo and I didn't want to upset him so I took it myself and then that Wendy bitch was splayed out like a feast for Ringo and that pissed me off more than it should have, and I panicked and I ran and that big guy started touching me and all of a sudden I was back in that room where they did those things to me… and well Ringo claimed me as his, which you know because you were there, and again he did it to protect me, all while I'm nothing but a pain in his arse because he's looking out for me as a favour for Lexi, and don't worry, Mr President, as soon as the snap lockdown is over Ringo's going to send me somewhere else so I'll be out of your hair. But you have to know, we didn't mean to lie about me being his girl, although maybe it all wasn't a lie because I asked him to kiss me and he did and it was really good and well I thought we were gonna kiss again which I'm really annoyed didn't happen because I have this ache, like you know, it's soooo bad, and I have no idea why it keeps happening, but I just really wanted to feel his lips on mine again, but that alert went off and you all had to leave, and again I'm really sorry."

A huge sigh falls from my lips as I finally stop talking, which I think must be the most I've spoken in like a year, and I watch as Smitty's brows, which shot into his hairline at some point during my speech, slowly pull in before his gaze drags slowly from me to Ringo.

"That about cover it?"

"More or less." Ringo shrugs. "I can fill you in on the finer details after, but yeah. I took her as a favour."

"For Lexi?" Smitty asks, and Ringo nods.

"Yes."

"That's the one your good-for-nothing brother saved, right?"

"Yep."

Slowly, Smitty shifts back on the couch, his gaze dancing from Ringo to me and back.

"So this happened when you went to Timber Valley to see Griffin Marx on Thursday?"

Ringo nods.

"And when Charity… or Abbey… When she refers to a bunch of scary men, she's meaning JD, Murf, Stocky and Trunk?"

"Yes, but under *my* order. They didn't break the rules." Ringo offers.

"I decide that, not you!" Smitty roars, lurching up from the couch, making me jump and clutch onto Ringo's arm.

"Yes, Prez. You do." Ringo agrees calmly, like his leader doesn't have the power to kill us.

For a moment, Smitty starts pacing, but then stops to glare back at Ringo.

"Jols was with you. Did she help?" Smitty growls, stepping closer, but Ringo doesn't budge or flinch away.

"Yes."

For a long drawn-out moment, Smitty remains quiet, his glare promising death as his top lip curls.

"My stepdaughter isn't a fucking member!" he yells, his fists balling at his sides. "She shouldn't be assisting with any jobs!"

"It wasn't a club job. It was personal."

"Yet you used *my* members and brought the trouble to our fucking door!"

His roar is so loud this time that I swear the windows rattle, but it still doesn't cause Ringo to flinch. Instead, he stands from the bed, taking a step closer to his President.

"I did. I'm sorry. I thought it would only be for a night or two. I was just trying to help Lexi, and then it became very fucking apparent that Abbey was in real danger, and I knew taking her was the right thing to do."

Peering around Ringo's tall frame, I watch as he and Smitty have a stare off. They are silent for so long that it causes me to shift around feeling awkward, until finally, Smitty speaks.

"Why didn't you come to me?"

"Because I'd already done the wrong thing, and I didn't think she'd be here that long." Ringo shrugs, and my gaze travels up his back to his towering height, and I have the indescribable urge to climb him.

What the hell?

"But you claimed her." Smitty points out, gaining my attention away from Ringo's broad back and the way his muscles look so defined under the fabric of his tee.

"I did." Ringo nods. "To keep her safe."

"From me?" Even though it's a question, it sounds more like a statement.

"I claimed her so you wouldn't have the power to send her out on the street… or force her to be a Doxy or a pass around," Ringo admits.

Man, he has more balls than me.

Obviously.

He doesn't even sound scared at admitting that to his President, yet I'm over here about peeing my pants.

"You really think I'd do that?" Smitty growls and again, Ringo shrugs.

"You have before."

I watch as Smitty tilts his head to the side in consideration, and then his brows shoot up.

"Ahhh, yes, that's right. I have. Now look at Nessy. She loves her life here with us."

"Maybe, but Nessy's situation was different to Charity's."

"Don't you mean Abbey?"

Ringo chuckles at his President. "Yes. Sorry. Abbey."

"So, what's your plan?" Smitty asks, and I start to relax.

Now they just sound like two mates chatting.

"To find her somewhere safe," Ringo admits.

"Where?"

"I reached out to the Angel sisters, but they don't have room, and that's as far as I got."

Sighing, Smitty claps Ringo on the shoulder. "Perhaps you're stalling for a reason, brother."

What does that mean?

"Even so. You know the drill," Smitty continues. "Church tomorrow night."

"Yep." Ringo nods before Smitty sidesteps him and his gaze lands on me.

"Who the hell decided to call you Charity?"

I point to Ringo quickly, more than happy to throw him under the bus for that, and Smitty's brows shoot up.

"I thought it was suitable." Ringo defends himself and I roll my eyes.

"He was being annoying."

Throwing his head back, Smitty laughs at my expense, and when Ringo shifts to face me, I can see the grin lighting his eyes.

I like seeing him like this.

"Right, well I gotta tend to these beaten men and we need to do damage control with the Marx family and find out how the fuck today even happened," Smitty snaps, his mood turning sour again. "And you…" He turns his attention back to me. "While you remain in *my* home, you will continue to be Ringo's girl. What he says, goes. Got it?"

I nod, not wanting to make this man any angrier, and he gives me a curt nod before turning and leaving.

That's the moment that Ringo turns to me with a hard glare, and my mind races to figure out what I did wrong. It could have been the rambling, which in my defence, I didn't mean to do. It just came out, but as he steps closer, I know it wasn't the word vomit.

No. Given the way he starts rubbing at his chest, my guess is he's pissed about what happened before that when I shot him. He was okay about it at the time, but he was on damage control then.

"I didn't mean to shoot you," I rush out, starting to crawl backwards on the bed, right as he grabs the fabric of his shirt at the back of his neck and pulls it off in one swift motion.

"You sure about that, Angel? Look what you did to my chest." His rasp is huskier than usual as he points to the red inflamed skin that looks like it's starting to bruise.

I try scurrying backwards faster, but it's no use. His grip is firm as he grabs my ankles, and in a quick move, he drags me closer, a squeal flying from my lips.

My heart is thrashing wildly in my chest, and I can't tell if it's pounding from fear or anticipation for what he's about to do.

28

RINGO

've learned a few fucking things, not only about my Angel, but myself, in the last few hours.

Firstly, she has bewitched me. That's the only conclusion I can come to that had me thinking of her most of the time at the warehouses, rather than actually the fact that something fishy is going on with our security measures, and the fact we now have dead men.

Secondly, I was ready to fight my way out of the club I've called home for fucking years, just in order to keep her safe. My club has always come first, until now, it seems.

And thirdly, the fact she shot me turns me the fuck on, which is twisted, yet I can't find it in me to care.

And those are just the things I've learned about myself.

Angel, on the other hand keeps surprising me with these little fucking glimpses of a person that might have been beaten down one too many times, but who is still fighting, and probably won't stop.

And she talks too much when she's nervous, which brings me to the fucking word vomit she spewed to Smitty.

Yeah, I could have fucking stopped her, but I was just as curious to hear what she'd say next.

Something akin to pride swelled my nearly dead heart when she admitted to enjoying seeing how we tormented her parents. Just the fact she could stomach that is a sign that even though she looks frail on the outside, she's not on the inside.

Then there was the other stuff.

"You called me an arsehole." I grunt as she tries to kick my grip on her ankles free, and I have to fight back my grin.

"You yourself admitted you were an arsehole the other day." Abbey retorts, still trying to loosen my hold on her with another round of unsuccessful kicks.

"Actually, we agreed I was a prick. That's different." I tease and she scoffs, finally stilling her attempted kicks to glare at me.

"Maybe you're a prick *and* an arsehole," she snaps, and this time I let my smile free, watching as her cheeks flush even more.

"Maybe. But at least I'm not jealous."

Her eyes widen before they turn into slits. "I am not jealous."

"Yeah, you are. You said as much to *Mr President*." I tease, repeating what she called Smitty.

Her lips part to speak, but a second later they snap closed again, and her caramel gaze drops to her lap.

"Oh, come on, Angel. You admitted how much seeing Wendy vying for my attention bothered you. What was it you said?" I ask, squinting as I overdramatise my thinking expression. "Oh yeah. I believe the words were, *that Wendy bitch was splayed out like a feast.*"

"Shut up," she snaps, although her tone holds little venom.

"You told him that we kissed, and how much you really liked it." I tease a little more and watch as if in slow motion, how the apples of her cheeks flare even brighter.

Fuck, she's beautiful like this, her blonde hair tied high, yet a little dishevelled with flyaways, the colour in her cheeks scaring away the deathly pale pallor she typically wears. I bet if I press my fingers to her skin, it'd be searing.

"And you admitted how annoyed you were that our last nearly kiss got interrupted." I tug on her ankles, dragging her arse across the bed and closer to me as I kneel between her legs. "And what about that ache, Angel?" I rasp as I release her ankles and press my hands to the mattress on each side of her head, hovering over her. "Is it the same ache that had you pressing your hand between your legs while you watched me sleep the other day?"

An intelligible squeak flies from her lips right before she curls onto her side and slips out from under me, scurrying off the bed.

"Hey!" I mutter, frowning as I twist to sit on my bed and watch her practically press herself into the wall to pass by.

Is she scared of me?

"What's happening right now?"

"Nothing." She shakes her head as she moves past the bed and gives me her back, but what she doesn't know is that I can see her reflection in the old stained mirror in the corner of the room.

She doesn't look scared, but what she does look is torn.

There's a battle raging in that head of hers, and fuck. What I'd give to be able to hear her thoughts and have the power to silence her chaos.

That thought stuns me momentarily.

I used to feel that way a long time ago about Kylie. About the demons she fought daily that no one could see.

She once told me no one had the ability to quieten the storm inside her head. Unfortunately, there was one thing that silenced it, and in the end, it's what killed her.

"I'm sorry I shot you. I didn't even know it was you coming through the door." Her voice is small. Timid. Filled with shame. "I just knew I couldn't let them take me."

In an instant, I'm up off the bed and standing behind her, my hands gripping her upper arms as I lean in close to her ear.

"Angel, I'm glad you fired that gun. I don't want you to ever stop fighting for your freedom."

Releasing a shuddering breath, Abbey relaxes back against me, and in the mirror, I watch as her lids flutter closed.

She clearly feels safe with me, but she's obviously not ready for a big brute like me to take things further.

Even as I think this, I'm reminded of her admission to wanting to kiss me, and the ache she can't fix.

"I still feel awful about shooting you," she whispers. "What if you didn't have that vest thing on?" Spinning to face me, her glassy, pained gaze falls to the welt on my chest where the bullet hit the Kevlar.

"It's okay," I rasp, loving how close she is to my bare chest.

Fuck, have I ever loved a woman being this close before?

"It's not." She shakes her head, this time her gaze shifting from the welt to the ink on my chest.

"Yeah, it is, Angel. Think of it as foreplay."

Her caramel pools dart up to meet mine, and a small grin tugs at the corners of her lips.

"That wasn't foreplay." She remarks, and fuuuck me, her voice is husky, her gaze is lustful, and even though she's in the fucking huge hoodie, I can still see the rise and fall of her chest with the way her tits press against the fabric as if they want to burst free.

"Fuck, Angel, I need to do something," I admit, my gaze dropping to her plump lips.

"What?" she breathes, almost on a whisper, and fuck it. I'm going in.

Closing the distance, I nip at her lips, feeling the fan of her breath, almost like she sighs in relief to feel my lips on hers.

Darting my tongue out, I glide it over the seam of her parted lips, testing to see how pliable she is, and fuck me, she responds, opening for me to take the kiss deeper as I fist one hand around her ponytail and cup her cheek with the other.

As I moan into her mouth, she responds with a needy whimper that has my cock practically battering at my jeans to be set free and claim her. And fuck, as much as I want to do that, I hold back, knowing she's not ready for that, but knowing she's ready for something by the way she starts squirming on the spot.

"Angel," I rasp into her mouth, not wanting to break the kiss to talk to her. "Does it happen when I kiss you?"

"Does what happen?" she asks into my mouth.

"The ache. Do you still ache when I kiss you?" I nibble at her lips this time, revelling in how she seems to lean closer, chasing my lips.

"Yes," she breathes, and I take a chance.

Easing my hand from her cheek, I graze my fingers down the column of her neck to her chest, noticing how her breath hitches, yet her tits seem to press out further as if seeking my touch.

Deepening the kiss again, my fingers find the hard peak of her nipple straining through the fabric, and when I circle it, her moan is loud, her body sinking into my touch.

My cock is as hard as fucking stone. I want to feel her hands on me. I want to sink into her heat, but I also want to keep wringing out those sweet little moans that keep falling from her mouth and into mine as our tongues dance.

Fuck, she's a good kisser. I can tell she's hungry for this by the way her tongue strokes mine, and by the fever in her nips as I pinch her nipple gently through the fabric.

Needing to see how far she's willing to go, I release her nipple and start to glide my digits further south, but the moment I do that, she gasps and shoves away, her chest rising and falling as her lashes flutter and it's obvious by her panicked expression that she's working to control her emotions.

She looks fucking beautiful. So fucking innocent and pure that I know I shouldn't fucking taint her, yet all I want to do it stain her with my brand of evil.

"We don't have to do anything more than that." I assure her even as my cock jerks like it's trying to slap me but can't, due to being restrained by my fucking jeans. "But will you let me help you with your ache some time?" I ask. "When you're ready?"

For a long beat, her caramel gaze bores into mine, like she's trying to penetrate my cold black soul.

"I'm not sure I can do anything more." She admits in a hushed tone, her gaze dropping to the ugly green carpet between us.

"I don't have to touch you," I tell her, my words forcing her gaze to meet mine again as she frowns.

"I don't understand."

I know she doesn't, which is why I should be walking away. She's too good for me. Too innocent. But fuck, I feel like I've been woken up from a three-year sleep, and she's all I can see.

"You will understand. But right now, I should go out there and help Smitty with the men."

"Oh… yes, of course." She glances towards the door and then back to me. "Can I help?"

"Sure. If you'd like." I grin, happy that she wants to help my family.

"Yes." She nods. "It's the least I can do. I feel like the only reason the police were here was to look for me, which means your men got hurt, and the Doxies had to do…" She shakes her head, anger contorting her expression. "Well, anyway, they all got hurt because of me."

I'm not going to agree with her, even though she's right, but I don't want her blaming herself.

In fact, I get a really fucking bad feeling that the cops, who are clearly not on our payroll, and the security breach and deaths at the warehouse are linked. And if that's the case, we've got a really big fucking problem.

"You didn't make those cops behave the way they did, Angel." I point out, moving to where I dropped my tee and slipping it back on. "Those fuckers are the worst kind of cop, and their behaviour isn't on anyone but them."

When I face Abbey, I can tell she doesn't believe me, so instead of arguing it out, I gesture to the door.

Together, we venture out into the courtyard where the injured men are being patched up.

Despite the angry glares shot Abbey's way by a couple of the Doxies, she moves past me quickly to a commotion where Nola and Darla are arguing over a whining Brody, while JD snaps at them all to shut up.

Following Abbey, I see Brody's leg is bleeding profusely, a huge gash on his thigh the cause of his wailing.

Abbey maneuvers past everyone, and when Nola notices her examining Brody's wound, she falls quiet, her arguing with Darla ceasing.

"Can you move your toes?" Abbey asks Brody, who stops whining like a little bitch, his green gaze locking onto my Angel as he nods and proceeds to wiggle his toes.

"What are you doing?" Darla snaps.

"Take off your belt," Abbey orders, her gaze now trained on JD.

His eyes dart to mine, and I'm not fucking sure what he's silently asking me, but I just give him a nod and watch as he unbuckles the leather strap and pulls it free.

Taking it quickly from JD's grip, Abbey wraps it around Brody's upper thigh and pulls it tight, causing him to cry out again.

"Ouch!"

"Stop it, you cow. You're hurting him," Darla snarls, slapping Abbey's hands to get her away.

Stepping forward, I'm ready to tear Darla apart, but there's no need. Abbey has it under control.

"Of course it's going to hurt. His leg is sliced open and unless we get this bleeding under control, pain will be the least of his worries." Abbey drags her glare away from Darla and back to JD. "He needs this stitched up. He needs to go to the hospital."

"No need." Smitty steps up next to me, gaining Abbey's attention. "Our paramedic is on his way."

"Okay," Abbey nods, turning back to JD. "Come and apply pressure to the wound."

She shifts so JD can get closer, and using the towel they were already using to try and stop the bleeding, Abbey shows JD how to keep pressure on the wound.

"Are you like a nurse or something?" Nola asks, a little in awe, and Abbey shakes her head.

"Not yet. But I hope to be one day."

Fuck. I hope she is too. I can see how good she'd be at it, and how she genuinely cares.

"What are the chances you're gonna keep this one?" Smitty asks quietly from next to me, and reluctantly, I pull my gaze from my Angel to my Prez.

"I can't keep her."

"Why?" he asks, and I shrug, turning back to watch her talking quietly to JD about his injured brother, who is still hissing in pain.

"She's too good for our world, man. She's already been through so much bad shit. She needs to be with someone that can give her the fucking world."

"Damn." Smitty chuckles. "She's been here, what, nearly a week, and she's already got you so wound up."

"Nah, man." I shake my head. "You've got it all wrong. I'm just trying to help her. That's all there is to it."

I want to slap myself for the lie. I don't know if I'm lying to protect her from me or the club. Either way, both options aren't fucking great for me.

"If you fucking say so." Smitty laughs, slapping my shoulder right as my phone starts ringing in my pocket.

Taking it out, Liam Marx flashes across the screen, so I quickly accept the call.

"Speak."

"You know, you could be less of a prick when you answer the phone. Did you get lessons from Barrett? That fucker is always answering calls like that," Liam asks, and I smirk, keeping my amusement to myself.

"Why the fuck would I answer any other way when I know it's you calling?"

"And Barrett would say the exact same thing. You two been hooking up behind my back?"

That makes me chuckle.

"That fucker hasn't been in the country for ages. I can't remember the last time I saw his ugly mug."

"Same. Wait, actually, it was just after Gracie's sixteenth birthday. He flew out the next morning and hasn't been back since."

Barrett Marx is one of Liam's older brothers. His role in the family business is international relations, or something like that. He spends most of his time abroad, brokering deals and making new connections that will help their family, but even so, he's normally home every couple of months.

I guess this fucking virus has kept him prisoner in another country.

"So, what's the update?" I ask Liam, not feeling all that up for a fucking social call.

"Straight to fucking business." Liam chuckles. "We don't have a full audit yet, but it looks like some of the medical equipment stolen was surgical."

"Surgical?" I ask. "Normally it's just virus-related stuff that gets stolen. You're saying someone stole equipment used to perform surgery?"

"Yep, they sure did. That and some nursery equipment."

"Nursery equipment?" I fucking frown, confused as fuck.

"Yeah. You know, for like newborn babies."

"The fuck is going on?" I mutter.

"That's what I'd like to know," Liam agrees. "I'll send through a full list once we have it. In the meantime, we've arranged for your men to go to Morgan's. Let them know if you plan to have funerals. Otherwise, they know the deal. They'll keep quiet."

"Thanks man," I mutter, knowing that Morgan's Funeral Home will do whatever we ask of them. "Can I get you to follow up on some people for me with your contacts?"

"Of course. Always happy to help my Camy boy."

"For fuck's sake. Stop calling me that," I snap, ignoring his snickers. "Four cops were here. One was Officer Allen. I find it a really big fucking coincidence that he turned up just minutes after we left for the warehouses."

"You think he was in on it?"

"I don't know," I admit.

"Okay. Is that all?"

"The other three officers who were with him. I don't know who they are, but I need you to find out. And also, while you're there, anything you can find on some teen fuckwits from Fox Pines. I'll send you their names."

"What do you want with some fuckwits from Fox Pines?" he asks.

"Well, man. I want their fucking heads."

29

ABBEY

"**T**his music is hurting my fucking ears." Ringo protests next to me on the bed, but I saw his foot bopping to the beat of it a second ago.

He's lying.

"Liar. Just admit you like One Direction. There's nothing wrong with that." I grin down at him from where I'm leaning against the headboard with his phone in my hand.

I've been chatting with Lexi and Tahli through the Koala-roo app for the last hour, playing my music on his phone while he pretends to try and nap.

"I will never admit it, because it's not fucking true," he barks, and a second later the corner of his lip twitches.

"Liar. You're about to smile." I call him out and he cracks one eye open, peering up at me.

"Stop perving on me, Angel."

I roll my eyes, and this time he releases a chuckle that works its warm comfort into my bones.

Why does he have this effect on me?

Even after the whole cop thing and me shooting him and then helping to stem the flow of Brody's bleeding leg until the paramedic arrived yesterday, I was so shaken up, but his hand slipping into mine somehow quietened the chaos.

That's the only way I can explain it.

Yesterday was a lot. Almost too much, but the moment Ringo was back by my side, it was like a switch was flipped inside me and the trauma was more bearable.

We went to sleep facing each other last night, and today since the compound has been quieter than usual with some men and Doxies leaving now that lockdown has lifted, while those that remain have huddled together like they are planning something, Ringo and I stayed hidden away, taking the day to just breathe.

"Talk to me about your sister and Lexi. What news do you have from home?" Ringo asks, shifting to slip his hands behind his head on his pillow as he looks up at me.

"Well, Tahli said the police have been by a few times, but it was only to say they hadn't found me yet. She did say that when they were at Monday night's mass a couple of police officers attended and she and Maggie were told to stay seated while they talked quietly with my parents and Minister Banes across the room."

Ringo's brows shoot up. "Interesting. Tell me about Minister Banes."

I frown. "Why?"

"Because I want to learn about this so-called church your family attends. How long has Banes been the minister there?"

"Umm, not long, actually. The other ministers were brothers, and they were killed when the old chapel burned down at the end of last year, but then Minister Banes turned up and took over like he'd been there the whole time, moving the congregation to a new location."

Ringo's eyes squint a little like he's deep in thought before they lock with mine again.

"What's different about that place compared to the old church you grew up attending? Like did they do anything differently besides read different Scripture?"

"Well, yeah. Confession is a lot different."

His brows shoot high.

"How so?" He shifts, sitting up on the bed next to me, and now instead of looking down at him, I have to look up.

"Men's confessions were group confessions. They'd all go into a room with Minister Banes for a while and then come back out. I asked Dad one time what happens in there and he just said confession, so I really have no idea."

"And the women?" Ringo asks, "Did they do the same thing?"

I shake my head. "No, when it was time for women to confess, the men would remain in the pews, and the women were escorted out of the main room, and led back in individually to confess before all of the males."

"The fuck. Did you have to do that?"

My gaze lands on my lap as my cheeks heat, and I nod. "Every time I did something wrong in my mum's eyes, I had to confess before the men. Even if I tried to downplay it or lie, the minister always knew the story from my mum and would call me out."

"Hey," Ringo whispers, his finger hooking under my chin to turn my head back up to him. "You know how wrong that is that they did that, right? That's not the way it should be."

I nod, letting my gaze fall to his lips momentarily to help keep me from crying.

"Was your dad there when you had to confess?"

"Yes," I whisper.

"Daniel? His dad?" Ringo asks, and I nod. "How revealing were the confessions?"

I shake my head, not wanting to think about that, and try to pull away, but Ringo's big hand slides over my shoulders and presses me into his side.

It's not rough. His touch is kind of gentle, but it's enough to tell me he's not letting me get away.

"Nearly every detail about the particular infraction was discussed," I admit.

"So when you were sprung by your mum having sex with that fuckwit, you had to stand before all the men, your dad included, and describe the sex act you did?"

"Kneel." I blurt and Ringo frowns. "We were made to kneel before the men."

His jaw ticks, and his grip on my shoulder tightens as he holds me to him.

"I'm going to kill them all, Angel."

I nod, even though by all, he also means my dad.

It's been a week since Ringo kidnapped me, and now that I'm away from that life, it's even clearer to me how wrong and crude it was.

Why would my dad stand by and let them treat me that way?

Why didn't he ever fight for me?

As if he can't bear to hold himself back, Ringo shifts, cupping my face before pressing his lips to mine.

"I'm sorry, Angel," he rasps between nips, and I kind of forget what we were talking about as his entire presence wraps around me like a security blanket.

Finally, I feel safe. Even after everything that went down in the last twenty-four hours, I feel safe just being in his presence. Safer than I have in years.

With each nip of his lips, heat builds between my legs, that familiar ache that's been building for days returning. I can't believe how horny I am. I never felt like this with dickhead Daniel. I thought I did, but this… this is something else.

Breaking the kiss, Ringo eases back just enough to press his forehead to mine, our eyes locking as we stare at each other.

"I can't seem to control myself around you. But I'm trying really fucking hard to."

His admission means a lot. It reminds me that he, for some reason, wants me too, but also that he won't press for more.

But more is what I ache for, yet I'm too terrified to let him touch me more than this.

"I don't have to touch you."

He told me that yesterday, and honestly, those six words have been bouncing around in my head ever since.

"What are you thinking about?" he asks, slowly drawing back to get a better look at my face.

I open my mouth to tell him, but the words lodge in the back of my throat.

I can't talk about this.

"Angel," he says in warning, yet still I don't say anything because I need him to demand it. I hate that I need that, but it's the only way I can accept revealing what's going on inside my head. I need the choice to be taken from me.

He studies me for a long beat, his dark eyes dancing between mine before his jaw ticks and a low growl rumbles in his chest.

"Tell me, now," he demands, and just like that, the heaviness that was holding me back somehow lifts and I cave.

"What did you mean yesterday when you said you don't have to touch me?"

His brows furrow at my question, but then lift as realisation sinks in.

"You want to know how I can help ease that ache without touching you?"

I nod, biting my lip as heat flushes my cheeks. Ringo must notice because his thumbs start stroking over the searing apples of my cheeks as he holds my face in place.

"The other night out in the courtyard, you liked watching me, didn't you?"

I nod, remembering how he looked sitting with his legs parted wide, his hand fisting his thick, hard dick as he stroked himself. I've thought about that a lot. Like what would have happened if I had gone to him?

I want to tell him that, but the words won't come, my tongue glued to the roof of my mouth, not wanting to say the words, and he smirks.

"Did it turn you on, Angel?"

I nod again, and he sucks in a slow, deep breath.

"Did you see how hard my cock was?"

His deep rasp does something to me. The way he says cock sounds so sensual and not at all dirty in the way I've heard it used in the past.

"Yes," I admit on a whisper, and he presses his forehead back against mine.

"That was all for you, Angel. That's what you do to me."

"I do?" I whisper again, like I can't bear to ask such a thing out loud.

"Fuck yes. For years I haven't wanted anyone to touch me, but then you were watching me, and all I could think about was having your hand wrapped around me."

Heat rushes between my legs at his words. It's almost shocking how much there is, but I don't fight it. I want it. So much.

"Did seeing me like that turn you on? Make that ache worse?" he asks, pulling back and brushing his thumbs over my cheeks again, and I nod quickly.

"Then how about you watch me again?"

I'm the one to pull back this time, Ringo's hands falling away as my gaze darts to the window, and he chuckles.

"Not out there. In here, just you and me." He gestures between us.

For a long beat, all I can do is stare at him.

He's suggesting… just him and me in here, while he…

Ringo shifts off the bed, standing next to it and pointing to the couch.

"I can stand right here so you get a good look, or if you want me further away, I can sit there on the couch, and you can be over here on the bed. You can hide under the blankets if you like, so I can't see what you're doing, and you can watch me while you touch yourself."

All the air leaves my lungs, even as my heart starts to race in anticipation.

"I can't do that."

"Of course you can." He smiles warmly, even as he reaches behind his neck and tugs off this tee.

Oh dear lord, I can't think now.

Abs.

Hard ridges.

Ink.

Skin.

I feel thirsty just looking at him.

When he flexes his pecs, I jerk out of my daze, meeting his intense stare.

"I can't do that… you'll see my face."

He grins wide, and one could almost call it a shit-eating grin.

I think he likes making me uncomfortable like this.

"You don't want me to see your come face?"

He did not just ask me that!

Shit. My cheeks are on fire.

I shake my head. "Not really, that's embarrassing."

"No, it's not really, but we can work on that later." He chuckles and I shoot him a glare. "I'll close my eyes if you like, Angel. Or you can hold the sheet up so only your eyes are uncovered to watch."

Oh. My. God.

Am I really considering this?

My gaze tracks his hands as they move to the fly of his jeans and he pops open the button.

More heat gushes between my legs as the ache flutters teasingly.

I need… something.

"I can't," I whisper breathlessly, not meaning the words in the slightest as I watch him ease down his fly.

"I think you can, and I think you want to, but you don't want to admit it. Why is it so hard to admit to wanting something like this?"

He parts his open jeans just enough to reveal red boxer briefs underneath, and as I watch, unable to drag my gaze away, he rearranges himself, the hard outline of his dick now showing through the fabric.

I shrug, not even remembering his question.

What did he ask again?

"Eyes up," he demands, his fingers gesturing upwards, and in a flash, my gaze is back on his.

"Do you trust me, Angel?"

"Yes," I say easily.

"Do you trust that I won't touch you?"

"Yes." Again, with ease, the word slips past my lips.

"Do you trust that if you tell me to close my eyes when you're going to come that I will?"

I'm not entirely sure about that one, but I also don't know if I care now. "Yes, I trust you."

"Then I'd really like to get my cock out for you, Angel."

Oh.

I press my thighs together as the ache becomes almost too unbearable to ignore.

"Will you let me do that?"

Omg, I can't, can I?

"Can I take my cock out, Angel?"

I lick my lips, and before I realise what I'm doing, I nod quickly.

Instantly, he shoves down his jeans and kicks them off, rubbing the heel of his palm over the hard steel outline of his erection in his boxers before hooking his fingers in the waistband and removing them, too.

All the breath stays trapped in my lungs, my eyes not wavering from the sight before me, this man with strong thighs, rippling abs, and the biggest appendage I think I've ever seen standing before me without an ounce of shame or fear.

God, was it that big the other night?

It's so hard, thick and veiny, and the tip is almost purple. Looks so different up close like this. So tempting compared to what I've seen in my past.

So much better than Daniel's.

"Are you ready to watch me?" he asks, gaining my attention again and I nod, desperate for it.

"You want me on the couch or here?"

"Can you stay there like that?" I ask breathlessly.

"Of course. Are you going to hop under the sheet?"

Oh yeah. The sheet.

Nodding, I hurry to reposition myself, dragging up the sheet to my nose as he watches.

Am I really doing this? This is so wrong, isn't it?

But I ache for it.

For him.

Fuck it, Abbey. Just let yourself feel good for once.

"Do me a favour, Angel. Let go of the sheet with one hand and slip that between your legs."

Oh.

"I can't," I whimper and he sighs before rolling his shoulders back and clearing his throat.

"Hand between your legs, now."

His demand does the trick.

Damn, why am I like that?

As I shift under the sheet, positioning my right hand between my legs, Ringo's eyes flare with something I'm not familiar with but also not scared of, and then he grips his dick and starts to glide his hand up and down.

Damn. That's hot.

Okay, so maybe I can do this. I can be quiet. I can do this.

Gently running my hand over the seam of my shorts, the ache builds at my touch, and I know that this time, even my touch won't repulse me.

"Fuck, Angel. I love having your eyes on me." His abs ripple as he grips his dick before he leans over and opens his bedside drawer.

I frown, wondering what he's doing, but then he brings out a bottle, and I'm not naïve enough to not recognise lube when I see it.

His gaze flicks to mine as he tips up the bottle, squeezing until a stream of the substance shoots from the nozzle. It drizzles over his hardness before he covers his hand with it and starts stroking himself again, the action making a wet sound.

"Are you wet between your legs, Angel?" he asks, his hand busy but his eyes on me.

"Yes," I admit easily, like I'm his puppet.

"Is your hand over or under your clothes?"

"Over," I say as I press a little harder against the ache.

"Put it under."

His demand has me stilling. "I can't."

"Yes, you can. No one can see what you're doing. Just slide it down the front of your shorts and feel how wet you are."

My breathing quickens as my hand obeys him, even as my head thinks this is a bad idea. Shifting the hoodie up just enough, I find the top of my shorts and slip my hand under the fabric into my panties, and the moment I feel my swollen wet heat, I moan.

I gasp in embarrassment, but Ringo ignores that.

"Are you wet?"

"Yes." I nod behind the sheet, and he does another one of those animalistic growls.

"Show me."

30

ABBEY

I still my fingers' exploration. Did he just ask me to show him my wet fingers?

"W-what?" I stutter, my eyes wide.

"Bring your wet fingers out and show me." He smirks as he demands it, and my lips part in an O as once again I obey.

Dropping the hold I have on the sheet, my face becomes exposed again as I use my left hand to hold my shorts open, so my wet fingers don't wipe on them, and I slip them out, holding them up to show him what he wants.

"Fuck, Angel. I want to taste it." His face doesn't hold an ounce of the amusement it did a minute ago. Instead, there's a hunger in his gaze. Want. Desperation.

I can relate.

It's how I feel when I watch him like this.

"You want to taste it?" I squeak, needing confirmation, and he nods.

"Fuck yes, Angel."

Oh.

Can I?

Just do it, Abbey. Give him what he wants. It's what you want too.

"Just reach out and let me lick your fingers," he rasps, his voice huskier than before, and hell, it's so sexy. This man is so… hot. Yes. Hot. There's no other word for it.

Aroused beyond belief, my core flutters between legs, and I find myself reaching out my wet fingers in his direction, desperate to give him the taste he asked for.

Stepping forward, Ringo positions one knee on the bed as he leans in, his eyes locked onto mine the whole time, until the moment his tongue darts out and flicks over my fingers.

His lids fall closed as he tastes me, a groan floating from him before his dark gaze meets mine again.

"Can I suck your fingers clean, Angel?"

Oh, my… that rasp.

I nod quickly, desperate for it, rubbing my thighs together when he growls. Then his lips part, and a second later, he wraps them around my two digits and sucks them into the heat of his mouth.

My left hand presses between my thighs in an instant, the ache there nearly too much to bear, and I have to fight the urge to grab his hand and put it between my legs instead.

That thought is what has me snatching my hand back, and I half expect Ringo to be mad, but he only smiles, licking his lips in a way that has more heat gathering.

How does he do that to me?

Shifting, Ringo stands back beside the bed, hand gripping his dick once again and he starts wanking it faster than before, his grip looking almost painful.

"Hand back to your pussy, Angel."

I'm sure my cheeks are flushing, but I'm past caring at this point, moving my hand back under the sheet and then under my shorts to the wetness between my legs.

I like how he talks. It's kind of dirty, although maybe that's just me because I'm so green.

Whatever it is, I like it. I like the way his voice sounds. The way his eyes devour me like I'm exquisite. The way he demands me to obey him.

Damn, I never thought I'd be happy about that revelation, but with him, I am.

As I start circling my bud with my fingers, my slickness making it so easy, I watch him as he strokes himself, his expression serious, his brows pinched a little like he could be in pain yet doesn't stop his onslaught.

I've tried masturbating recently, and never have I been able to get myself over the line because of the intrusive thoughts.

But they aren't here right now.

It's just me and Ringo and for the first time in a long time, I know that I'm going to be able to give myself what I've been craving.

As Ringo's pace increases, so does mine, and a whimper falls past my lips as my pleasure starts racing ahead, no longer able to hold back.

"Fuck, Angel, I can't wait until you feel comfortable enough to show me how swollen your clit is."

Oh my… His words.

Another whimper meets both our ears.

"Are you close?" he asks, and I nod.

"Yes."

"If I come, will that get you over the line?" His voice is so deep now and there's an edge of desperation to it as he pumps his shaft, his expression pinched a little like he's holding back.

"Yes." I rush out, desperate to see him let go. Desperate to see and hear him come.

"Where do you want it?" he barks, like he's still trying to hold back.

"What?"

"My cum. Where do you want it?" He pumps his dick faster even as my fingers press down, moving on their own.

"I don't know." I shake my head, because I can't think straight right now.

"I can do it neatly in my hand, or I can just let go and come everywhere. How dirty do you want me?"

I whimper again, his words forcing my fingers to move faster as I start thrusting against them even as I struggle to admit what I want.

"Answer me!" he demands.

"Really dirty," I blurt, and his pace gets even faster.

"Fuuuck okay. It's coming, Angel."

He pumps fast, his hips jerking as he groans loudly, and I hardly notice my hand mashing against my mound as the first rope of his cum shoots from his dick, so far that it reaches the bed.

I come apart then, an orgasm I didn't think I'd ever experience again detonates inside me so forcefully that I hear my own cries loud in the room, even though I promised myself I'd be quiet.

With each spurt of his cum, I watch on, my climax intense as I watch him release all over the sheets and floor. Wave after wave zaps through me, more pleasure than I ever remember experiencing before, followed by a tingling numbness that makes me fall slack and languid in Ringo's bed.

I'm panting. Out of breath. I even think my hearing vanishes for a moment.

"Fuck, that was beautiful."

Ringo's words break through the orgasm haze I'm in, and suddenly, embarrassment comes crashing in.

My eyes meet his, mine wide, his still hungry.

I was loud.

I just masturbated in front of a grown man.

Shame.

So much shame comes crashing in.

Why are you so surprised, Abbey? You're nothing but a whore.

Having him see me like this is too much, so I quickly sink down under the sheet and cover my head.

"Angel?"

I don't answer him, my mother's voice in the back of my mind reminding me why this all happened.

Movement through the room is what I focus on, willing my mum's ugly voice away. I can hear Ringo as he goes into the bathroom and runs the tap before returning. Still, I stay hidden away, mortified.

I'm so different from him. Wendy's words from the laundry room remind me of that.

"He can't help it if he likes it rough. He likes to choke his women until they stop breathing. He likes to fuck his women after they pass out. He likes being in full control of their body, able to do to it whatever he wants without them saying no."

She was only trying to scare me, but what if Ringo does like it rough? What if he's into kinks I don't even know exist and here I am scared of touching myself?

He must think I'm so pathetic.

So frigid.

The bed dips, and I feel his form on top of the sheet as he lays down next to me.

"Angel, show me your face."

"No." I utter under the sheet.

"Please don't make me demand it," he says, and guilt gnaws at me.

I'm so pathetic that he has to demand that I do things.

"If you don't mind, I'm just gonna stay here," I say quietly, feeling the weight of my guilt and shame.

"Fine," he sighs, "but I'm coming in."

"What?"

A squeak flies from me as the sheet is ripped up, the fabric parachuting above us as Ringo rolls under, joining me with his head on the pillow as the sheet slowly floats back down over us, trapping us both in together.

His intense gaze locks with mine before roaming over my face like he's trying to see inside my head.

What would he think if he could see the truth?

Would he think I'm foolish? Would he think I'm messed up? Sick perhaps?

"Why are you hiding?"

I don't answer, my gaze remaining on his as he studies me up close. Too close. I can feel his hot breath, which should repulse me, but it doesn't. Nothing about this man repulses me.

It would be easier if he repulsed me.

"Where's rambling Abbey right now?" He smirks.

"I killed her," I whisper, and he barks out a laugh.

"Come on, Abs, talk to me."

Abs.

He called me Abs.

Oh.

"Did I do something wrong?"

I shake my head.

"Did *you* do something wrong?"

I nod this time.

"What did you do?" he asks before his brows draw close in a frown. "You'd better not have been thinking about other men while you watched me jack off."

I roll my eyes.

He sighs. "There's nothing wrong with what we just did."

He knows. I can't hide from him. He always seems to know even when I don't say the words.

Still, I don't say anything.

"Are you freaking out because I'm an old man, as you like to put it?"

I can't help it. I try to hide it, but I'm helpless to fight the grin that tugs at the corners of my mouth, so I shake my head to try and hide it. But he notices anyway, his own lips kicking up.

"So, just a general freak out then?"

I nod and he studies me some more before he speaks.

"Are you ashamed of what we just did?"

I shake my head, but then nod, and change my mind and shake it again.

I don't know how to answer that.

"So what is it, Abs?"

There it is again.

Abs.

My name shortened the way my friends did, when I had them.

I shrug, relaxing into the pillow as we stare at each other, and all I want him to do is call me Abs again.

"You know, sex can be as filthy as you want it to be, as long as both parties are on the same page." Ringo reaches up and brushes back some of my hair the way he does often. "Just for the record, I was definitely into you watching me. I was definitely into you watching me shoot my load everywhere and hearing my grunts, too. Did you like watching that part?"

As embarrassed as I am, I nod, not wanting him to feel ashamed just because I do.

Well, I kind of do.

Shit. I don't even know.

"Maybe one day you'll let me shoot my load a little closer." He smirks even wider, and I know he's trying to make me smile. Trying to turn my mood around.

I want to hug him for that.

"Why do you want to do that?" I ask him bravely, and this time his teeth make an appearance as he smiles wider.

"I'd fucking love to see my cream glistening your skin, Angel."

Oh.

He shifts closer and presses his nose to mine, our breaths mingling under the sheet.

"I'd love to see it oozing from your pussy one day. Hopefully," he admits, and oh wow.

Heat flushes my entire body, and damn it, but horndog Abbey is back.

"Fuck, you're so beautiful like this. Flushed. Glowing." His thumb moves to my lips, gently gliding over the bottom one. "I'm going to kiss you now."

He waits for the first bob of my head and I see the long stubble framing his lips kick up before he leans in and presses his lips to mine.

31

RINGO

I can still feel Abbey on my lips as I take my seat at the table for tonight's church session. I can't remember the last time I kissed someone so thoroughly. Maybe when I was a teenager. Even Kylie and I never kissed quite like that.

Soft.

Gentle.

Savouring.

Something has shifted in me, and I can't fucking figure out what it is exactly, or why the fuck it's happening, and to be fucking honest, I don't want to overanalyse it.

Because the fact of the matter is, I don't know what's going to happen tomorrow or the next day, or next fucking week, when it comes to my little charity case. This was only ever meant to be temporary, and there's a whole world of fucking trouble chasing her tail that could change everything in the blink of an eye.

"Our combined investigations with the Marx crew have turned up the same result for the warehouse raid, although, to what end hasn't been figured out yet." Smitty addresses his club from the head of the table where ten of us sit, and the others lean against the wall around the table listening quietly.

"The only conclusion is that the pigs orchestrated the raid to get us out of the way so they could come in and find the girl."

At Smitty's words, all eyes fall to me.

I don't move, keeping my expression neutral, remaining relaxed back in my chair even though I want to rant and rave that the pigs need to die.

"But medical equipment was stolen." JD pipes up, his frown directed at our President. "Surgical equipment, to be exact. I fail to see why the pigs would go to the trouble of actually stealing the equipment and killing our men just to step foot inside the compound while the women were vulnerable."

"I have to agree with JD," Mex states, while some of the other men nod in agreement.

I want to nod too, but because I have a conflict of interest, I remain quiet. Still. Observing. Yet wanting to beat my chest and demand we burn the city to the ground to find answers.

"Well, we don't have any other theories, and neither does the Marx crew." Smitty lights up yet another fucking cigarette. The second since church started.

"What about the missing prospects? Any word on them?" Spud, our VP, asks, and Smitty shakes his head.

"They are either dead or in hiding. Their families haven't seen them."

"What about our inside men?" I ask, no longer able to keep my mouth shut. "We pay those fuckers on the force a lot of fucking coin. Have they looked at the case file for Abbey? Do they have any intel as to why Officer Allen and his posse stepped foot on our turf?"

Smitty shakes his head. "The file for Abbey is locked. They can't access it."

I fucking frown. "Bull-fucking-shit they can't. What about their hacker?"

"Too risky." Smitty shrugs and I feel like smashing up this entire room.

"Why the fuck would her case be locked? This doesn't make sense."

"He's right, that doesn't make sense." JD snarls, and I know he's thinking about his sister again.

Her case was locked, and the people behind the brutality she suffered were pigs. This feels all too fucking familiar.

"I think the real problem here is that this shit was brought to our fucking front door in the first place." Spud thumps his fist on the table across from me. "There was no order to rescue the girl, Ringo. You not only kidnapped her, but used our club brothers and a fucking sister to help you, and snuck her in here."

Anger washes through me at his fucking tone, but I know I did the wrong fucking thing, so I keep my mouth shut.

"What? You've never used club resources for personal use before?" JD snaps at our VP. "I'm pretty fucking sure you did basically the same thing with your sister-in-law."

"Fuck you, JD! I paid for my infraction." Spud slams both fists on the table this time, his glare lethally directed at JD.

"And so will, Ringo. That's not even a fucking question. You and everyone here knows he won't even try to get out of it, yet you fucking did, didn't you, coward!"

The second Spud flies up from his seat on one side of the table, and JD follows next to me, I stand and slam my fists to the table.

"ENOUGH!"

As my two feuding club brothers breathe heavily in anger, they turn their glares to me.

"JD is right, I will take whatever punishment our President deems fucking fit," I glare at our VP before turning it to my best mate, "and other past infractions by my brothers isn't fucking relevant and should stay in the past." I grit my teeth, fighting for calm.

Slowly, both JD and Spud lower back to their seats, while Smitty remains in place, relaxed back in his chair, taking another drag of his smoke.

"So what's it going to be, Prez?" I ask Smitty, still standing, my knuckles resting on the tabletop.

"Club beating. Public," he says easily, like he decided my fate long ago.

I grit my teeth. "Come on, man, I don't want Abbey to see that."

"Punishment for lying about bringing in an unapproved outsider without revealing her real identity is a public beating." Spud interjects before Smitty nods in agreement.

"Perhaps she needs to witness it, so she understands what's at stake. This is how we live. She's in our world now."

Grinding my teeth, I give my President a nod, not liking this one fucking bit.

I don't care about getting a beating. I can take it. But the thought of her in distress because of it doesn't fucking sit well with me.

"Church is over," Smitty calls, picking up the gavel and slamming it to the table's surface while standing. "Out to the courtyard for a good old-fashioned flogging."

The men hoot, and I can't help but smirk at that.

There are a lot of men in this room who have met my fist from their own punishments, and today, they get to repay the favour.

"Fuck man. I bet it's times like this you wish you were a drinker." JD slaps me on my back, and I chuckle. "Nah, there's nothing like feeling every fucking bit of life. How else will I know I'm truly alive?"

JD scoffs. "Man, you're going to wish you weren't soon."

He bumps my shoulder with his, and we file out behind the others, instantly feeling the hum of energy in the courtyard as the men spread themselves out in a huge circle.

"What's going on?" Jols asks, moving to my side.

I stare down at her, taking in her concerned gaze as it darts between me and the men.

She's seen this circle before. She knows someone's about to get a beating, and the fact she's by my side tells me she has an inkling it's going to be me.

"Do me a favour? Stay with Abbey. Keep her out of trouble."

Jols expression drops.

"Sure." She nods, walking across the circle where I see the familiar sight of golden blonde hair in a high ponytail.

"Listen up!" Smitty calls over the chatter, and everyone falls quiet, the Doxies shifting closer behind the perimeter of my club brothers. "We have rules for a reason. When they are broken, there must be consequences." Smitty starts pacing in the centre of the circle, his expression serious, his shoulders rolled back, his demeanour demanding attention.

Even though I should be paying attention to my President, my gaze won't budge off Abbey, a frown tugging at her brows as I read her lips as she asks Jols what's happening.

Jols doesn't respond.

"Tonight, one of our most respected will endure his punishment. He will receive a beating, publicly, and every fully patched club brother will take part in delivering it."

"What!" Abbey squeaks from across the courtyard, and the moment she goes to take a step forward, Jols captures her arm and starts talking in her ear.

"Every single person will remain present and witness the beating of Ringo. No one will intervene. No fully patched member may refuse."

A round of slaps rise up as my club brothers clap their hands against their shoulders, a sign of respect to our President as he does what he was voted in to do.

Lead.

"Secrets are dangerous. Secrets can bring trouble to our doors. And secrets are why our Sergeant in Arms is receiving a public beating today."

"No wait. You can't do this," Abbey cries out, trying to shake Jols off her.

"Tie his hands behind his back," Smitty calls, ignoring Abbey, and Spud steps forward with the rope, but JD steps in front of him and snatches it from his grip.

"I'll do it."

"Fine." Spud holds up his hands, smirking before he backs away and JD turns to me.

"Sorry man. I don't want to do this, but I'd rather he not be the one to do it."

I chuckle. "How many times have you told me you wanted to tie me up?"

"Dude, only so you couldn't fight off a chick so you could finally get laid." He counters and we both smirk at each other before his grin falls.

"Still. This sucks."

"Just do it." I sigh. "I knew the rules."

Nodding, JD rounds me and I shift my arms, crossing my wrists behind my back as he makes quick work of binding them together.

As he tightens it, I stretch my neck from one side and then to the other, trying to limber myself up as much as I can in preparation for the oncoming bashing I'm about to receive.

When my eyes find Abbey's again, I spot the tears glistening in her eyes as both Nessy and Jols talk quietly to her.

"You ready?" Smitty asks, stepping into my line of sight, and I shake my head.

"Any chance I can have a minute with her?" I gesture my head in Abbey's direction, and Smitty glances over his shoulder before returning his hard glare to me.

"You're pushing your fucking luck, Ringo."

I shrug, knowing I am, but not fucking caring.

"Fucking hell, either I'm going soft, or I really fucking like you," Smitty grumbles before turning around.

"Hey Charity Case. Get over here."

She doesn't even flinch at the words, but hesitates, her eyes going wide.

She probably thinks she's about to get yelled at or something, so when her eyes land on me, I gesture my head backwards, silently asking her to come to me.

My club brothers part, waiting for her to move, and after another moment's hesitation, she does, shifting away from Jols and Nessy, and stepping through the men.

Smitty steps aside as well, and I don't know if it's to make her feel safe, because it's obvious she doesn't with the way she wraps her arms over her chest as she moves, or if he's just being respectful and giving us some privacy.

"Get over here," I demand as she takes her time, and like always, she does what I ask, moving faster until she's standing before me.

"I don't want this to happen," she whispers, those glassy eyes nearly spilling over.

"It's okay, Angel." I take a step closer, fucking annoyed I didn't do this before they fucking tied my hands behind my back. "I know this is hard to understand. We live by our own set of rules in the club. We live differently from mainstream society. But it doesn't mean what's about to happen is wrong. This is the way we do things here, and I will take what's coming to me because I broke the rules."

"But it's because of me," she whisper-yells, stepping up to me and fisting my shirt.

"I don't blame you, Angel. You need to know I'd do it again in a heartbeat if it means keeping you safe."

A tear pops free then, so I lean down, pressing my lips to her ear.

"I need you to stay strong for me. No matter how awful it seems, nothing will be worse than knowing you're in distress."

As I shift back, I drag my lips across her cheek, and by the time I'm nose to nose with her, those dainty hands grip either side of my jaw before she rises higher on her toes and presses her lips to mine.

Hoots and cheers ring out in the air around us, but we both ignore it, trapped in our little bubble as she kisses me with a level of confidence and determination I haven't seen or felt from her before.

"Alright, that's enough. I don't want to get a fucking woody right when I need to swing fists." Smitty chuckles, gripping Abbey's upper arm and dragging her back.

"Let go of her!" I yell, louder than I expected, as red frames my vision at the sight of him gripping her arm.

"Whoa," Smitty laughs, dropping his hold on Abbey and raising his hands in surrender. "Calm down, brother. I wasn't hurting her."

"You fucking touched what's mine. You'd best not do it again."

Smitty's smile drops as he glares at me, calling over his shoulder to his stepdaughter while keeping his eyes trained on me.

"Jols, take the girl."

"Wait," Abbey protests, shoving past Smitty and gripping the front of my shirt again as she drags me back down, her caramel eyes wild and frantic. "I'll be strong. Just for you."

Then she presses her lips to mine again for a quick kiss before pulling back, releasing my shirt, and walking away with Jols.

Damn it, now I have a semi.

I'm too busy watching my charity case walk away to notice Smitty's fist coming my way, the crack loud, the hit making me see stars momentarily as I nearly topple to the ground.

Staggering into some of the nearby men, I hear Abbey cry out in protest before Trunk's voice is in my ear.

"Shake it off. It looks like Prez has more to dish out."

I nod, blinking profusely to clear my fucking vision, before turning to face our leader.

"Thanks for the fucking heads up."

He rolls his eyes. "You should have been paying attention instead of staring at your piece of arse."

I fucking growl, which just makes the fucker laugh, and this time I'm prepared for his iron fist smacking into my jaw, my stance wide and firm as I work to stay in place from the impact.

"Woohoo." Smitty jumps as he shakes out his fist. "Who's next?"

One by one, my club brothers take their swing.

Some go for my face, but most aim for my chest or gut, but the one thing they all have in common is they don't fucking hold back.

I can feel myself grinning throughout my beating. Pride filling my chest at the loyalty in the air, reminding me of why I'm a part of this.

It isn't just about brotherhood, booze and chicks.

It's about family.

Most of the men here, and even a lot of the Doxies, didn't have a family before they came into the fold. Some had people who are meant to be a family but never behaved like it. And others have never known what it's truly like to belong until they joined the Southern Sadists.

I might be getting a hiding right now, but I earned it, and I'm not too fucking proud to admit that.

My eyes wander back to Abbey's each time I right myself from a blow. I can see how hard she's trying to stay strong. This is pure brutality at its finest for her. She's been a victim for so long that it's hard for her to see anything but violence. Hell, she may never see that this is nothing more than maintaining order. Reminding everyone to walk the line. It's something most outsiders can't wrap their head around.

"You know what, I fucking hate you for this," JD snarls at me as he steps up to take his turn. The last man.

"Bullshit. You always want to hit me. Now you can without getting a hiding," I rasp before spitting a wad of bloody saliva to the brick paved ground.

"True, but I'd rather kick your arse in a fair fucking fight." He rolls his shoulders back before cracking his knuckles.

Using my shoulder, I wipe at the blood trickling from my nose, my gaze landing on Abbey again. She looks about ready to jump out of her skin, but she's still watching, and as we stare at each other, I attempt to wink, but I think my eye is already swollen shut.

Fuck it.

"Hurry the fuck up and stop stalling." I snarl at my best mate, turning my one good eye to him. "And you'd better not go easy on me. If you punch me like a prissy, I'll fucking demand everyone go again."

JD's glare turns dark, fury contorting his expression as his fists ball at his sides.

I knew my words would spur him on. He hates seeing this happen to me, so he wants it over with as much as Abbey does.

"I fucking love you, brother." He points angrily to me, emotion thickening his voice, and when I nod, he rears back and takes his swing.

I have to give it to the fucker. He didn't hold back. In fact, I'm pretty fucking sure his hit packed the most fucking punch, slamming into my cheek and spinning me until I fall to the fucking ground.

Cheers ring up, Doxies gasp, and I swear I can hear Abbey scream, "You fucking prick!"

That has me smiling.

Well, on the inside. I don't think the swelling in my face has much give for expression right now.

"Alright! Alright! Quieten down!" Smitty yells over everyone, and within a few beats, the men fall silent. "The punishment has been dealt. The infraction now in the past. Let this be a reminder of the oath you all swore."

Slapping palms against shoulders clap into the air, while I struggle to get up off the fucking ground, what with my hands tied and my arse thoroughly kicked.

"Doxies, help Ringo to his room," Smitty calls before there's a loud protest.

"No!" Abbey hisses, pushing her way past my club brothers and into the circle. "He's mine. I will take him."

Well, fuck if that doesn't make me fucking smile for real this time.

"Get over here, Angel," I mutter, now sitting on my arse, purely fucking exhausted.

Hurrying to my side, my Angel lowers down, her expression pinched, but determination in her eyes as she assesses me.

Fuck. I think we have Nurse Abbey here right now.

My cock twitches.

Seriously, I've just had my arse handed to me and my cock thinks it's time to wake the fuck up?

Behind me, JD quickly unties my wrists and helps me to stand as Abbey slips an arm around me on one side before JD joins in on the other.

"Come on, you old fucker. Let's get you to your room."

I snicker at JD, but Abbey doesn't join in, her focus on each step we take further from the crowd and closer to privacy.

"Shower," I mutter as we squeeze in through the door, and they assist me into the shitty little bathroom.

"I can take it from here," Abbey insists, her eyes trained on my best mate, her stare fierce.

Fuck, I love her like this.

"Okay, I hear you loud and clear. It's fuck time." JD slaps my shoulder and leaves, while Abbey rolls her eyes at him.

As soon as the partying out in the courtyard quietens with the click of the door, I try to pull away from Abbey.

"I can shower myself, Angel."

"No. I've got you."

Huh. She's a stubborn little thing.

"Fine. Help me out of my jeans, then."

She nods quickly, and even though I am perfectly fucking capable of undoing my pants and peeling them off, I fucking let her at it.

Her cheeks turn red as she hurries to pop the button and then eases down the zipper, those big doe eyes shooting up to mine every few seconds, and then she helps me shuffle the fabric down over my hips.

Shifting quickly to her knees, she concentrates on getting my shit kickers and socks off, too sidetracked to realise my heavy cock is swaying near her head.

But fuck. Then she looks up, those innocent eyes locking with mine, before they widen and she can't help but steer her gaze to my growing cock.

Hey. I can't fucking help it. She's on her knees, looking up at me all fucking submissive, and all I want to do is demand she take me in her mouth.

Fuuuck I want that so bad.

But I can't. She's not ready.

"Sorry," I mutter, biting back a smile.

"What for?" she asks, returning her heated gaze to mine, even while her huskier than normal voice gives her away.

I gesture my head to my cock, now bobbing out in front of me.

"I can't help it. Seeing you down there looking up at me… well, you get it."

Her big eyes widen, her gaze shifting back to my cock now at her eye level, which is when her tongue darts out to wet her lips.

Fuuuck.

32

ABBEY

He's so big. Like I already knew that, but up this close, it's something else. I know I shouldn't be thinking about other guys at a time like this or comparing, but I can't help it. Daniel's really does seem so… how do I put this? Immature in comparison.

I mean, he knew how to use it as a weapon, but as I stare at the thick heaviness bobbing before me, veins coiling up to the ridge of the tip, I can honestly say nothing I've seen compares to this.

I should be scared. I really feel like I should. This thing is a weapon. A tool to take. To hurt. To destroy. It wields so much power. Yet as my gaze shifts back up past Ringo's blood splattered tee to lock onto his eyes, so intense as he looks down at me, I don't see a weapon.

I see want.

Perhaps lust.

But I also see restraint.

He may only want me because I'm on my knees before him, but he won't act on it. He won't force me. He'll endure the blue balls that will come from holding back, and I know he won't try to make me feel bad about that.

This place is something else. One could say it's inhabited by a bunch of thugs. Brutes. Monsters.

Sure, Ringo is a monster, but he's the right kind of monster.

My monster.

"Thanks for helping me out of my pants, Angel." He smirks, one corner of his lip kicking up a fraction before he steps back and does that thing again, reaching behind his neck and peeling off his t-shirt.

It's slower than last time, what with his obvious injuries from being beaten.

His eyes don't meet mine again once he's fully naked. This man has no shame, and with good reason. Even battered and bruised, he's a work of art, and where I once saw an old guy, I now see nothing but a man built to protect.

He took that beating because of me. I don't care how he tries to spin it. I'm the reason he's hurting right now.

As he reaches over the bath to turn the shower on, I stand, needing to back away from his dick and the unusual urge I have to reach out and touch it. Here I was thinking I could train myself to only like girls and hope that one day I could find a woman to spend my life with, never wanting to see another penis again.

Cameron Musgrove sure showed me.

Not even waiting for the water to reach the right temperature, Ringo steps over the lip of the bath and under the raining water, while I stand there like a perv watching the way rivers of water run down his tanned skin, making his tattoos appear darker.

"Angel, would you mind finding Jols and asking her to bring some ice packs?"

Ringo's voice startles me out of my perverted stupor, my gaze darting to his face to see that I've been sprung.

"Ahhhh, yes, of course." I nod, spinning on my heel and darting out of the bathroom.

My cheeks are on fire as I step back outside, my gaze searching the crowd for Jols.

I spot her off to the side talking quietly with JD, who is the one to spot me, and gestures for Jols to follow him my way.

"How is he?" JD asks, clearly concerned, which is confusing. I'm pretty sure his punch was the hardest.

"He asked for ice packs," is all I say, not really wanting to tell this man if Ringo is good or bad.

"I'll grab some." JD nods, turning quickly and walking away, leaving me with Jols.

"Are you alright?" she asks, and I nod even as I shrug.

"I don't understand this world."

She nods, reaching out and giving my arm a squeeze. "I know it doesn't make sense to outsiders. But just remember, it's because of the way we choose to live that your friend thought Ringo was the best option for keeping you safe."

Lexi. Yes, she did choose him for that reason, and I guess I can see why now.

"Even so. It's hard to watch someone you care about get hurt and just stand by and not do anything."

Jols' smile spreads wide. "So you do care about him. I knew I was picking up on something between you two."

"What? No." I shake my head, trying to backtrack. "He's just protecting me. Kind of like a big brother."

A deep chuckle comes up beside us and we turn to see JD has returned, ice packs in hand.

"I'm pretty sure it's fucking illegal for a brother to look at you the way Ringo does, kid."

I roll my eyes and Jols giggles.

"Right! And there's no way he's that good of an actor."

Wagging her brows at me, Jols bumps her shoulder with mine, and once again my face heats.

"Thanks for the ice packs," I mutter, snatching them from JD and hurrying back to the room, their laughter following me all the way there.

Back in the room, I stand outside the bathroom door, unsure if I should go back in.

Maybe he sent me to get ice packs so he could have some privacy. Maybe he needed to fix the erection issue.

I step backwards and return to the room, not knowing what else to do, so I sit on the end of the bed, staring at the ice packs chilling my fingers.

A couple of minutes later, I hear the bathroom door open, and when I glance up, Ringo rounds the corner, a trail of water running from his neck, over his peck to bead on his nipple.

I want to lick it off.

Wait. What?

OMG, where is my head at lately?

"Thanks for the ice packs," he grunts, his eyes locked onto me and I nod, quickly standing and holding them out as he approaches, a towel wrapped around his hips, sitting low.

Oh my...

I need to get out of here. I'm feeling way too hot and hungry. So hungry. Just not for food.

"Hey," he rasps, hooking his finger under my chin, and I realise I've been staring at the V that disappears under the towel. "Serious question. You doing okay?"

Am I doing okay?

I consider that.

A week ago, my parents locked me away, forced drugs down my throat, and were determined to make me marry Daniel the next morning. But then this man kidnapped me. Terrified me. Chased me. Forced me to sit on his lap for hours in a car. And then…

Well, then, so much has happened. I've been scared, distraught, angry, aroused more than I'd like to admit, confused, and finally when I started to feel safe, the cops came, assaulted the men and women before announcing they were looking for me, and then tonight, my protector was beaten in front of everyone.

I shouldn't be okay. I know I shouldn't, yet as I stare into Ringo's dark eyes, just him and me in this crappy motel room, I can honestly say that I am, in fact, doing okay.

"I'm alright." I nod. "Just worried about you."

He chuckles. "I don't break that easy, Angel, but if you're offering some TLC, I won't refuse."

I smile at that. "So you'll let me look after you without whining about it?"

"I never said that."

I giggle as he releases my chin and moves to his bed.

"Come and lie down with me. Put on some of that god awful noise you call music."

I roll my eyes at his back, watching him slowly lower himself to his bed.

Shit. He is really hurting.

"I'll have you know, One Direction is one of, if not the best band to ever exist."

He scoffs at that, laying back and stretching out on his bed.

"They're a fucking boy band. No boy band is the best band to ever exist."

This time I scoff. "All four of their albums debuted at number one on the charts. That didn't happen just because they are pretty."

A deep belly laugh rumbles from Ringo as he points at me. "That's exactly why they did so well. Bunch of pretty boys stealing little girls' hearts. They aren't even together anymore."

I glare at him. "I'm not opposed to stabbing you."

His laugh gets louder, the sound infectious, and I have to fight really hard not to join him. "Stop it." I protest and he gives his head a small shake.

"Nope. I'll never stop giving you shit for your music taste."

"I suppose your music is soooo much better?"

"Grab my phone and get your fine arse over here and I'll show you just how good my music taste is."

Why does that sound suggestive?

And why does it excite me so much?

Just like his puppet, I take his phone from the bench near the fridge and move back to the bed, climbing on my side and settling against the headboard next to him.

He holds his hand out for his phone and I give it to him, picking up the ice pack resting on his thigh, and pressing it to the lump on his forehead.

A moment later, music flows from his phone, the strum of a guitar instantly piquing my interest.

"Who is this?" I ask, and he places his phone on the bed between us before picking up the other ice pack and pressing it to the other side of his face.

"Staind. They're a rock metal band."

I nod, hearing the lyrics start and instantly getting ensnared.

"They are good," I admit, feeling the heart and soul in the lyrics.

"Told you my music was better."

I playfully slap his shoulder. "I never admitted that. No one is better than 1D."

Even though I can see the corner of his lips kicking up, Ringo remains quiet, his eyes closed as the music fills the room.

I like him like this. It feels personal somehow. Like not many people get to see him this way.

Playful.

Quiet.

Comfortable.

That's when I realise that I too feel that way.

For so long, I've been in flight mode. Always on edge, just waiting for everything to explode.

And they did, numerous times. But now, even though one could argue that perhaps I'm not in a very safe environment, I do, however, feel safe.

Not even my parents could give me that.

"I've been here for a week," I say quietly, watching Ringo's face for a change in his expression.

There isn't one.

"I know."

"Are you going to send me away?"

This time, there's a slight shift. His lips thin a little, and he sucks in a deep breath.

"No, but I need to find somewhere else to keep you safe."

My shoulders relax at hearing that. I know I'm getting attached to him when I shouldn't be. I'm beginning to wonder if perhaps that's my toxic trait. Becoming too attached. I was like that with Daniel. It happened so quickly, just like now.

"Where?" I ask, not liking the idea of not knowing where I'll be going.

"Not entirely sure, Angel." Ringo sighs, moving the ice pack so he can glance up at me. "I'll figure it out. Can you give me a day or two to recover from this?"

Guilt. It slams into me hard.

"Of course. I'm sorry, I didn't mean to be pushy or—"

"Stop," he demands, and as always, I obey. "You're not being pushy. You're just asking a relevant question. I'm not annoyed about that, Angel." He takes my hand from holding the ice pack at his forehead. "If I sound grumpy, it's only because the pain is kicking in. It's not you, I promise."

"Shit. Do you want some meds or something?"

He shakes his head, still peering up at me.

"What about, like, illegal drugs? I've seen the white powder stuff they've been using out there. Do you need that?"

This time his smile is big. "You'd get me some blow if I wanted it?"

I shrug. "I guess. If that's what you need." Whatever the hell blow is.

He threads his fingers with mine then, and my heart does a little flip.

"I don't drink or do drugs, Angel."

I frown at that.

"You don't? But why?"

He does a one-shouldered shrug. "You've seen how quickly an emergency can happen around here. We need to be alert all the time, and since I'm the Sergeant in Arms, I figure it's my duty to make sure I'm coherent every second of the day."

"That's a lot of responsibility. Don't you want some down time?"

"Nah. I prefer to keep busy."

I study him, wondering if there's more to it than that. He's just so hard to figure out.

Ringo yawns, stretching a little as he does, the towel slipping a little lower on his hips.

"You should sleep." I rush out, dragging my gaze from the part in the towel, like I'm secretly hoping it spreads further to reveal what's underneath.

Maybe I am.

You pervert, Abbey.

"Stay with me?" he asks, and my perverted-ness rushes away at his tone.

He sounds so… vulnerable.

"Of course," I say quietly, shuffling down until my head hits my pillow and I roll on my side to watch him.

There are emotions swirling inside me that I'm not used to. I hate seeing him beaten, yet I love that he likes to share the quiet moments with me. It feels special somehow.

I stare at him until his breathing deepens and evens out, and then eventually, I must fall asleep, too.

I'm not sure how long I sleep for, but when I wake, the night is quiet, darkness is still beyond the window, and Ringo is still sleeping soundly next to me.

I get up and use the bathroom, slipping out of the hoodie for a few minutes to put on some more deodorant, since I'm sweating more than usual tonight.

I can't tell if the air is thicker or if it's just me, but I don't feel as cold as I normally do.

Even so, I slip the hoodie back on, smelling Ringo wrap around me, the simple act somehow quieting any chaos that started up in my head.

Returning to the room, I get a cold bottle of water from the fridge and guzzle half of it down, watching Ringo as I do, still sleeping peacefully.

There's just a hint of light filtering in through the thin fabric of the curtains. Light from the courtyard beyond. There's a streak of it running diagonally across his abdomen and chest before slicing over my pillow.

The way it hits his skin kind of makes the white in his tattoos glow. I move back to the bed, placing the bottle on the side table and shifting to sit on the mattress where I was lying minutes ago.

I'm so tempted to reach out and touch where his tattoo glows. I bet it's hot. And soft. And smooth. Would he feel it if I touched him?

My gaze darts to his face to see he's still sound asleep, his lips slightly parted. I lick my own lips, the urge, no, the desire to kiss him scaring me a little.

Why do I want to touch and kiss this man so much?

The flutter of that ache between my legs has returned. Thoughts of earlier today, or perhaps that was yesterday now, returning to me like a teasing slap.

I watched him pleasure himself. I actually lay in this bed touching myself while he jerked off in front of me. I even let him taste me off my own fingers.

Ohhh, that was so hot. So intimate.

Heat gathers between my legs, familiar and aching.

Why does this man have this effect on me?

I want to touch him so badly. I want to see what his skin feels like. I want to lick it and taste it. I want to be the one to give him pleasure.

It's too late when I realise what I'm doing, stretching my arm towards him, my finger hovering over his hot flesh before it finally makes contact and brushes over the hard ridge of his abs, feeling the satin of his skin, hot and tempting.

33

RINGO

I wake to a gentle brush of fingers gliding up my abs and over my chest. I assume Abbey doesn't know I'm awake since her fingers don't stop exploring, which is why I keep my eyes closed and breathing slow.

I don't want her to stop. I don't want to scare her away and think she can't touch me like this. Fuck, if she wanted to drag a blade over my skin, I think I'd fucking let her.

The graze of her fingers shifts south, going back down over my ribs, moving closer to the towel still secured around my waist.

Of course, my cock starts to wake the fuck up. I feel it swelling, stretching, hardening under the towel, and I have to wonder if she can see it as those delicate fingers linger at the top of the fabric covering my bottom half.

I'm about to ask her to take the towel off when I feel it shift, and I fucking hold my breath, not wanting her to stop as she slowly eases the fabric apart.

A small gasp falls from her, and for a long moment, nothing happens.

I want to open my eyes, but I don't want to scare her off. I want her to do whatever the fuck she wants, without shame, so I keep really fucking still, not knowing what she's doing right now.

Is she looking at my face for a reaction?

Is she staring at my cock?

Does she want to touch it?

That's when I feel the mattress shift a little, the brush of her bare legs against my hip sending a ripple of excitement through me.

What the fuck is happening right now? Am I a fucking teenager? I feel like it with that fucking flutter in my chest, yet still, I don't move. I don't make a sound. I wait.

There's a few long beats before anything happens, and it's too late to prepare myself when her gentle touch presses to the tip of my cock.

The fucker jerks, and she gasps again, the bed shifting like she drew her hand away quickly.

Fuuuck, I want her hands on me.

Come on, Angel. Do it again.

As if she can hear my thoughts, the mattress shifts again, and this time when she touches my hard length, I'm prepared.

Her fingers start gently gliding up and down over my straining flesh, the feather-like touch teasing the fuck outta me before her palm presses to it and she slowly wraps her hand around me.

Fuuuck yes.

Gritting my teeth, I will my body to remain completely still and not get carried away by the fact my Angel has my cock in her hand. There'll be time to celebrate later, but for now, she just needs to explore of her own free will.

Slowly, my heavy length is lifted upright before her grip tightens and she starts to ease her hand up and down my cock.

Fuck. I'm quickly losing my control, and I know my breathing has quickened, which she must notice because she speaks.

"Are you awake?"

"Yes, Angel," I rasp, keeping my eyes shut.

"Should I stop?"

FUCK NO!

"Only if you want to," I say instead, fucking surprised by my self-control.

"I don't want to," she says, and I swear, I relax and let out a breath I didn't know I was holding.

"Then don't," I say through clenched teeth as she starts working her dainty grip over my cock again.

"Will you keep your eyes closed?" she asks, and even though her words are soft and quiet, she doesn't sound as timid as I thought she was.

"If that's what you prefer?"

"Yes." She squeezes my cock tighter this time, right from the tip to base and back up again.

Fuuuuck. I'm going to arrive too fucking fast at this rate.

"Okay, Angel," I groan as she works over my length again.

It feels fucking fantastic having her touching me like this. To be honest, I didn't think she had it in her. And not because she's a prude or anything, but because she's been abused. The very thing she's stroking has been used against her by other men and

I would think it's fucking natural to be turned off by it, or never want to touch one again.

But here she fucking is, blowing my mind, and I'm not about to take this away from her. If I can do this for her and give her back some of the power she's lost, then I'll do it a thousand fucking times over. And not just so I can get off. Hell, if she stopped right before I came, I wouldn't fucking care. All I care about is how she feels.

Risking a glance, I part my left lid slightly since it's the one least swollen, letting my eye adjust to the darkness, and the low hue of the courtyard light filtering in through the curtains.

She's sitting on the bed next to me, probably with her legs crossed, if I have to guess. It's hard to tell with my fucking hoodie engulfing her. I wish she'd take it off. She wears it like armour, and while I do like her wearing my clothes, I kind of wish she'd take it off around me.

Her hand squeezing my cock as she slides it down has me moaning, Abbey's eyes transfixed on my erection in her hand, rather than my face where she'd spring me watching.

Fuck, she's beautiful.

Granted, the light is low, but she's always beautiful, and the last few days the colour has started to return to her skin, and she's been eating more, the sustenance already making her look healthier.

Her tongue darts out to wet her lips before she bites down on her lower one, moving her hand a little faster as she pumps me.

"Fuck, Angel. Your hand feels so good." I tell her, wanting her to feel good about what she's doing.

Abbey's head darts in my direction, but I manage to close my eye before she springs me watching, and she shifts on the bed like she's trying to get closer.

"I'm not hurting you?" she asks, curiosity lacing her tone.

"Fuck no." I grit through clenched teeth. "I've been aching to feel you touch me like this."

"Really?" she asks, my admission clearly surprising her.

"Fuck, yes, really."

Not able to control myself, I thrust up, meeting the pump of her hand and she starts working it faster.

Parting my single lid again, I see her focused on my cock, her eyes hungry from what I can see of them. Watching. Anticipating.

Her breathing is rapid. Her chest rising and falling quickly, like she too is struggling to maintain her control.

What I'd give for her to let go.

Fuck, just the thought has my nuts tightening, the familiar tingling at the base of my spine preparing me for my pending climax.

"Fuuuck, Angel. That feels so good." I admit, unashamed. "Can I come?"

"Yes, pleeease."

Oh fuck. The beg in her tone is what undoes me.

"Grip my cock tighter," I demand, and she does, obeying quickly.

"Pump faster," I demand, and she does that too.

"Fuck yes. Your hand feels so good around my cock, Angel."

She whimpers, her hand pistoning around my erection, and pleasure erupts deep inside me, drawing my balls high as I roar.

I force my eyes wide, not wanting to miss this, and I watch my cum shoot from my cock, so fucking high it must be a new fucking record, and Abbey's eyes widen brightly, watching as each rope of cream jets from the eye of my pulsing cock.

"Fuck, Angel." I pant as the waves subside, my breaths loud in the room. "That felt amazing."

My white seed is oozing down over her hand and back down my shaft to pool at the base, while more of it remains in its splatter pattern where it came to rest from the first few explosive eruptions over my abs, thighs, and even some on Abbey's bare knees.

A small grin kicks up her lips as she looks at me, her hand still wrapped around my cock as it starts to soften.

"That was… something else," she admits before dragging her gaze back to my cock and gently laying it to rest on my lower abdomen.

"A good something else, or a bad something else?" I ask, wanting to keep her here in this space of confidence.

"Good. Definitely good," she admits, running her fingers through the white substance coating my skin, making my cock jerk from its sensitivity.

"You wanna taste it?" I ask, daringly, loving the way her cheeks flush red.

Yeah, she does. She just doesn't want to admit it.

"It's okay. You can if you want." I gesture my head to my cock when she looks at me in surprise.

Biting her lip in thought, she releases it and brings her coated finger up to hover before her lips, her caramel gaze shooting back to mine as she flicks her tongue out and tastes my cum.

Her brows shoot up, meanwhile my cock is reawakening, for fuck's sake.

"Not so bad, huh?"

She smiles and nods. "Better than I remember."

Fuck.

Just hearing that makes me want to fucking kill.

The thought she has tasted anyone else's cum is bad enough, but I have a really fucking bad feeling that her experience wasn't consensual.

Grinding my teeth, I work for control as she returns her stare to my cock.

Okay. Calm the fuck down. I can't change the past, but I have her right here, right now, clearly curious about sex, which is a good thing. She obviously feels comfortable with me or she wouldn't be doing this.

One thing is for sure, over the past few days, she's been really fucking randy. Being in this environment where sex, especially open-door sex, is such a regular occurrence, it's no wonder she's been feeling this way despite her past.

She bites her lip again as she glides her finger through my cooling cum, and I wonder if biting her lip is a tell for her. An arousal tell.

I'll have to keep my eye out for that.

"Are you horny, Angel?" I pry, hoping she'll be honest.

"Yes," she admits so quickly that her brows shoot up again, surprising herself.

I bite back my smirk as she eyes me warily, like she's worried about how I'll react to her admission.

"Do you want *me* to touch *you*?"

Her frown is instant at my words.

"I-uh… I'm not sure."

"You can control my hand if you like," I suggest, holding up my hand closest to her. "Pretend my fingers are yours, and you can move them however you want. I won't do anything but give you my hand."

She stares at me for a long-drawn-out beat, and I can't tell by her expression what the fuck she's thinking.

"You won't move your fingers?" she asks, and I shake my head.

"No. You can move them. Have full control over them. Place them wherever you want."

She considers this. "And you won't try to touch me anywhere else?"

"No, I won't even look if you don't want me to. I'll lay on my side, keep my eyes closed and you can just use my hand."

"On my bare flesh?" she asks to confirm, her brows high again.

"Whatever you want. It can be over the top of your clothes if you want. It can be touching your bare flesh. It can be sinking inside you. Whatever."

She squirms the moment I say, '*sinking in*', and I know she's imagining the feel of my fingers stretching her.

"You promise not to touch me anywhere else?"

"I promise. I'll even give you my gun if it makes you feel better."

Her shoulders relax at that offer, and she smirks. "No, that's not necessary."

Smirking back, I nod and wait to see what she'll decide, and a moment later, she rolls off the bed.

"Let's clean you up first."

There are fucking bugs or butterflies or something in my chest, because I'm pretty fucking sure something is dancing in there the moment she just agreed to my offer.

Disappearing before I can say anything, Abbey returns a moment later with a damp washcloth, coming to stand next to my side of the bed, eyeing my still semi hard cock laying in its own filth.

Grinning, I snatch the cloth and make quick work of cleaning myself, using the towel to dry myself before tossing both on the floor, too fucking worked up about what's about to happen.

"Get in here, Angel," I say, half demanding, half playful, hoping she doesn't change her mind.

She rounds the bed, not looking at me, her brows drawn together deep in thought. I want to tell her to take her clothes off, but I get the feeling her clothes, like my hoodie, are an armour. If she's wearing them, she'll feel safer. Less exposed.

If Abbey needs that, then I won't try to strip her bare.

Slowly, she slides into the bed, pulling up the sheet, hiding her body away.

I'm completely naked now and wonder if I should perhaps put some clothes on, but then she glances down at my cock, hard again just from the idea of her letting me touch her, and her cheeks flush with arousal.

Yeah, she can fucking look all she wants.

"How should I… what do I…" she trails off, and I hold in my grin, not wanting to make her feel self-conscious just because I find her uncertainty adorable.

Rolling to my side, I offer her my hand, my eyes trained on what I can see of her expression in the dull light.

"It's yours to do with as you please, Angel."

Her gaze darts to mine, and a flicker of fear flashes in her eyes.

"I want you to know if this doesn't work… like if I freak out or can't get over the line or…" she sucks in a deep breath. "It's not because of you. It's because of me." She stabs a finger to her temple in frustration.

Shit.

"I won't take anything personally, Angel. Don't worry." I offer, reaching forward to remove her finger from her temple. "Before we begin, can I kiss you?"

Her breath hitches and her lips part, her dark gaze snapping to my lips.

"I don't want to hurt you," she whispers, obviously looking at my split lip.

"Angel, it hurts more not to kiss you."

This time her lips part in an O before a smile breaks through and she nods.

I don't waste another fucking second, closing the distance and pressing my lips to hers.

She's so soft and timid at first, but when my tongue darts out and brushes into her parted lips, she melts into the mattress and gives herself over to the kiss.

Fuck, I love kissing her.

I know I shouldn't be doing this. My job is to protect her, not bed her, but how can I refuse her if she needs this from me?

A soft moan falls from Abbey's lips and into mine when I deepen the kiss, and I shift closer, my body nearly flush with hers, but not quite. I don't want to make her feel smothered, but I want her to feel the heat of my body. I want her to know what she does to me.

Reluctantly, I break the kiss, knowing all I want to do is lose control with her, and I'm right on the edge of doing that.

"Can I touch you now?" I rasp, holding up my hand again, and she nods, accepting it in hers.

For a long moment, she just stares at the pads of my fingers, holding my hand up between us. I can't tell what she's thinking. Maybe she's trying to figure out how to get out of this. Or maybe she's trying to figure out if she wants me over or under her clothes.

Whatever her thought process, a moment later she comes to her decision, and directs our hands under the sheet and between her legs.

Even though she's the one guiding my hand, she gasps and jerks at the first contact over her shorts, but when I don't do anything, my fingers remaining relaxed and at her disposal, she sighs and presses my fingers to the seam that runs through the centre of her mound.

She holds it there for a moment, and small trembles rattle from her hand and into mine.

She's scared.

Nervous.

Yet determined.

I feel privileged that she trusts me enough to try this.

"Do you need anything else from me, Angel? Do you want me to put a pillow over my head?"

"No." She giggles, her eyes darting to mine before she turns serious. "No, I need to see you."

"Do you want me to talk, sing, whisper?"

"Definitely talk… but like…" she bites her lip before whispering, "dirty."

"So, it's okay for me to tell you how much I ache to feel how wet your pussy is?"

"Yes," she rushes out breathlessly, her fingers pressing into mine, which puts more pressure between her legs.

"I can't wait to taste you again, Abs. You have the sweetest nectar."

She moans quietly, and I feel her pelvis shift under my fingers, pushing against them, seeking more.

"I really want to feel what it's like to slide my fingers into your tight cunt," I rasp, and she stiffens, her half-lidded eyes snapping wide.

Fuck. She obviously doesn't like that word.

"Forget I said that," I demand, and she nods, although she's still as stiff as a board, so I try again.

"I really want to feel what it's like to slide my fingers into your tight pussy."

She relaxes, thank fuck, and starts moving my hand with hers, rubbing my fingers over her mound.

Okay, so cunt is a no, and pussy is a yes. Noted.

Shit. This is a lot of pressure.

What if I do or say something that is a real trigger for her?

What if I make things worse for her?

Even as I think it, she moves our hands so my fingers run over the seam again, another whimper of a moan falling from her parted lips.

Fuck. It's okay. She's here with me. She wants this.

"Do you think you'd like to feel my fingers inside you, Abs? To feel my skin on yours. Gliding through your wet folds and spreading you wide?"

Her rubbing speeds up as she whimpers incoherently.

Fuck yes. I want her to take what she needs. Lose control and let herself go.

"I want to sink my fingers inside you, while I lick your clit," I rasp, shifting closer so I can feel her panting breaths over my lips, and then I get really fucking game. "Fuck, baby, I want to fuck you with my tongue."

I flick my tongue out then, grazing her lips, and she gasps before latching onto it and sucking it in.

Fucking hell, my cock jerks, and need slams into me, making my whole fucking body vibrate with the desire to claim her.

Before I realise what's happening, Abbey shifts under the sheet, her other hand dragging her shorts down before she desperately presses my fingers to her bare, wet flesh.

I moan, claiming her lips as we both start fucking each other's mouths, and I have to remind myself to not do any more than this, because this wasn't part of the fucking deal I made her.

But she's going with it. Taking my lips and devouring my kiss, all while she uses my fingers to drag her slick juices from between her folds to her clit before she finally lets go.

"Fuck, Abs. I'm going to come again," I admit against her lips, and she whimpers a loud yes, mashing her clit with my fingers so fast that I'm surprised a fire doesn't erupt from the friction.

"Cam," she cries, using my real fucking name, which I gotta admit, does something to me, and then she goes silent, as if she's holding her breath, fighting to get herself over the line.

"I'm coming," I lie, because I know that's what she needs, and just like I predicted, she gasps right before she explodes in a shattering orgasm.

My lie is no longer, my balls tightening, my spine tingling, and pleasure rippling through me for the second time before I'm covering the sheet between us with my seed.

She doesn't let up on her clit, using my hand, my fingers to wring every rippling wave of pleasure from herself, until she finally stills, pressing my fingers between her folds as her slickness pools at her entrance.

Fuuuck, my fingers are so close. How easily I could sink them in and take control.

I'd make it my mission to replace every awful memory she's had there with new ones, and then some.

But I can't. Not now. Not yet.

Never have I had to have so much restraint.

34

ABBEY

This morning I woke up in Ringo's arms. He was still naked, and I was still fully clothed, but everything felt different.

I know we didn't have sex. That's still a hurdle I'll have to figure out, but what we did share together means so much more than anything I've experienced.

He gave me control.

I didn't have to demand it. Fight for it. Beg for it. He just gave it to me, because he knew that's what I needed.

I wonder if he'll ever truly know how much that means to me.

I guess I could tell him, and maybe I will tonight, when we are alone again. Just him and me hidden away in his bed.

I hope he lets me touch him again like I did. I know I shouldn't have done that without asking first. I'm feeling guilty about that, especially since I feel so strongly about consent. I don't even have an excuse for it other than I was driven by this insatiable need churning deep inside me that controlled my actions.

Still, it doesn't make it right.

"What's the frown for?" JD asks, bumping me with his shoulder as we stand in the shade, our eyes trained on the chaos in the middle of the courtyard where the Doxies are lined up with white t-shirts that are ten sizes too small for them as some of the men squirt their chests with huge water guns.

"Shouldn't they be like working or something? Lockdown ended on Wednesday night. Surely, they have better things to do."

JD chuckles. "Yeah, you would think so, wouldn't you? But it's Friday."

Glancing up at the towering man, close to the same height as Ringo, I take in his mussed beard and hair. "What happens on Fridays?" I ask and he points to the giggling Doxies whose tits are clearly visible through the thin fabric.

"Shit like this," JD offers, like that makes total sense, and I shake my head in disbelief.

"I guess every day is a party, hey?"

"Now you're getting it." JD nudges my shoulder again.

"Stop chatting up my woman." Ringo's gruff voice comes from behind us, so we turn to see him glaring at JD, as much as his bruised face will let him.

"I don't remember you being this possessive with—"

"Shut the fuck up." Ringo snarls, cutting JD off before his eyes settle on me and soften. "Hey, Angel."

My grin is from ear to ear. I can feel it. My cheeks are on fire too as he smiles at me.

I kind of want to ask him who JD was just referring to, but I love the way he's looking at me so much. I don't want anything to take it away.

"What the fuck is going on here? Lovey dovey eyes?" JD snickers and darts out of the way when Ringo tries to whack him. "Too slow. You look a little battered there, brother."

"I wonder why," Ringo scoffs, reaching out to me absentmindedly and tugging me to his side.

We fit together so naturally. It should be weird, right? Nothing about how we met or our pasts fit. We are polar opposites. It's safe to say Ringo comes from the wrong side of the tracks compared to me.

Yet, still, the way he holds me, the way this thumb brushes back and forth absentmindedly over my nape before he runs his fingers through my hair, all while he continues talking shit with his best mate, it feels so easy.

"You should have woken me when you got up," Ringo rasps against my ear when JD heads to the centre of the courtyard to join the wet t-shirt competition, or whatever it is they are doing.

"You looked so peaceful. I wanted to let you get some sleep since I kind of woke you through the night."

His eyes meet mine as he turns me, pressing me back against the porch post, bracing one hand above my head as he leans in close.

"You can wake me anytime you want something like that, Angel."

His nearness has me feeling dizzy, but in a good way. My heart races and my tongue darts out to lick my lips as he closes the distance.

I swear I melt the moment our lips meet. My heart thrashes in excitement and something that feels like hope blooms in my chest.

I'm not sure what the hope is.

Hope for more with Ringo? Or just general hope that perhaps I'll be okay.

I have no idea what my future looks like. There's so much yet to figure out. The reason I was desperate to flee my home is still a situation I have to face. And soon.

But today, right now, I'm here with Ringo. I'm here at the Western, somewhere in the outer suburbs of Melbourne, and I'm safe.

Threading his fingers into my hair, Ringo deepens our kiss, angling my head back as he draws me flush with him.

I can feel his erection pressing against me. A hard rod that doesn't seem so scary now that I've had my hand wrapped around it until he came.

Oh man, just remembering that moment has heat pooling between my legs, and I moan into our kiss.

"Ahhh, Ringo?"

The male voice has Ringo growling into my mouth this time, and he barely pulls back, instead speaking against my lips.

"What the fuck do you want, Brody?" he snaps, but then pulls back abruptly to glare at the guy. "Why the fuck are you still here? I thought I told you to fucking leave."

"Prez wants you. We found Morris."

I stiffen as Ringo shoves back off the post.

"Where is he?"

"In the garage," Brody gestures his head behind him, and my eyes dart to the door that leads to the underground parking garage.

Ringo starts storming towards the door, JD hurrying to his side, obviously having seen something was up, while Brody and I stare at each other for a beat.

"Who is Morris?" I ask quietly as we start following behind.

"Morris was a prospect like me. He was one of the guys manning the gates when the pigs showed up the other day."

My brows shoot up, mainly because Brody used the term 'was' implying he is no more.

Surely, I misunderstood him.

Ringo's long strides are hard to keep up with, him and JD hurrying out of sight so fast that I find myself nearly jogging to catch up.

"I don't know if you want to go in there," Brody states as we come to the garage entrance but feminine crying meets my ears and I can't help it. I push past Brody and hurry inside.

The first thing I notice is the smell. It's pungent and vile, and I immediately gag.

Lifting the neck of the hoodie, I hide my nose inside, moving towards the gathered men and the few Doxies all standing around the back of a car with the trunk open.

"Who found him?" Ringo asks, his gaze shifting from the trunk to Smitty.

"It's my car." Casey sobs as Celina tries to comfort her. "I was going to drive to the store, but something smelt off, and I opened..."

That's the moment I step up behind Casey and Celina and see a body crammed into the trunk, the greying skin and smell telling me that Morris is, in fact, dead. Right there.

"I'm going to be sic—" Casey spins, vomit spraying from her mouth, and all down the front of my hoodie.

I gasp, Celina diverts Casey to the side where she keeps hurling, and I stand wide eyed, covered in puke as I fight not to join in.

"Fuck, Angel." Ringo takes a step towards me, but I shake my head, moving back, waving my hand dismissively at him.

"No. It's fine. I'll just go and clean myself up." I rush out, needing to get out of there before this becomes a puke party.

Ringo nods, concern clearly etched across his face, and I spin, hurrying for the door where a smug-faced Wendy is leaning against the wall.

"Looks like you got a little something on you." She snickers, and I shoot her a glare as I pass by.

"Fuck off, Wendy," I snap and Wendy gasps.

"Rude." She scoffs, and oh my god, I can't believe I just said that to her.

Even though I'm covered in puke, I can't help but inwardly smile at how much more I feel like the old me today. It's a good feeling, reminding me that once upon a time I was stronger, and that perhaps I'll be strong again one day soon.

Rushing into Ringo's room, I grab a new hoodie from his drawer on my way past and duck into the bathroom, trying to figure out how to get the damn thing off without getting it all over my hair.

Draping the clean hoodie over the towel rack, I ease my hands into the hoodie before using them to wiggle the neckline up and over my head without getting the vom on me.

The moment the fabric is free of me, I toss it into the bathtub and sigh.

"Shit," I whisper to myself, even as I grin.

That could have been worse. I'm grateful it wasn't.

Sighing, I take a moment to access my lower half.

Since the hoodie was so long, my shorts were saved, but there are some puke splashes on my legs and runners.

Getting a washcloth, I quickly clean myself up, wondering if perhaps I should have just had a shower. And maybe I will after I figure out how to get the hoodie clean.

It's hot, and with this moment of freeness without the hoodie engulfing me, I take a moment to splash some water on my face and neck.

"I knew it."

I gasp and jump, startled at the female voice, my head darting to the open bathroom door as I spin to face the woman filling it.

Wendy.

Oh shit.

"He doesn't know, does he?" she snaps, her eyes dropping down my body.

For a moment I just stand there stunned, not sure what to do, but then panic sets in, and I spin and lurch for the towel rack where the clean hoodie is hanging.

"It's too late, Abbey. I've already seen." Wendy steps into the room as I hold the hoodie in front of me before she lurches forward and snatches it from my grip.

"Give that back!" I screech, but smug-faced Wendy just scoffs, shaking her head as she steps backwards.

"Fuck no. I'm not missing this."

No. This can't be happening.

The sound of male voices outside Ringo's room has me stiffening while Wendy beams.

"Give it to me," I whisper-yell at the bitch, but she laughs like I'm a fool.

"How long did you think you could hide that?" she asks, but I can tell her question is rhetorical. "He's going to lose his shit. Let's see how fast he kicks you out."

The voices get closer, coming into the bedroom, and I know one of them is Ringo's.

Shit.

What do I do?

It wasn't meant to happen like this.

I need more time.

Panicked, I lurch forward and try to snatch back the hoodie, gripping the fabric and pulling, but Wendy widens her stance and holds on for dear life, a battle of tug of war taking place in the small space of Ringo's bathroom.

"What the fuck are you doing, Wendy?"

Ringo's menacing growl meets our ears, my eyes widening as Wendy smirks at me.

And then she yanks hard, pulling the hoodie from my grip before stepping aside to reveal Ringo behind her.

"I thought you should see this." Her tone is nothing but smug. Pleased to finally have one up on me, but I no longer care about her. I only care about the man filling the doorway as his eyes scan me.

All of me.

My breathing becomes shallow as his brows draw in, the secret I've tried to keep hidden until I could figure something out, revealed too soon.

Feeling exposed, I reach across my swollen stomach, trying to cover myself, but it's grown too big over the last few days. It wouldn't have been long before even the hoodie wouldn't be able to hide it.

"Did you know she was pregnant when you saved her?" Wendy asks like the child growing inside me is a vile thing.

And I guess, with how it came about, most would think it's an abomination. How could I ever want to keep it when it was created with hate? Violence? Depravity?

Slowly, Ringo starts shaking his head, his face contorting with what can only be described as pain.

"No." It's a whisper, Ringo's eyes glued to my stomach.

"Ringo?" I whimper, not understanding exactly what's happening here.

He's angry. I get it. I lied. Or at least I didn't tell him my whole situation. But this, whatever this is, is different.

Ringo takes a step back, and then another before he's quickly backing away, his expression morphing into fear as he shakes his head.

"I'm sorry. I was going to tell you, but I didn't know how," I cry out, taking a step towards him, but he continues to retreat.

"No." He shakes his head over and over as he gets to the mouth of the wardrobe, which is when the man I thought I knew vanishes. "NO!"

His roar is deafening, and he spins and starts punching the wall by the open shelves.

I squeak and jump back, my heart about leaping from my chest as his rage unleashes, and Wendy turns back to me, grinning.

With another loud animalistic roar, Ringo surges into the bedroom out of view, and things start smashing before JD hurries in, frantically trying to access the situation.

"What happ—" he stalls, skidding to a stop just outside the bathroom door, his eyes wide as he takes me in. "Oh, fuck."

Turning quickly, JD darts back out into the room, his voice floating in as he calls for more of his brothers.

"I need some help in here!"

Tears burst from my eyes, my chest hurting right in the centre like a hand is reaching in and squeezing it.

"You stupid bitch. You really think you could fool Ringo?" Wendy snarls, coming to stand before me.

"I was going to tell him, I…"

"He doesn't want damaged goods, Charity Case. You need to fuck right off and take your bastard pregnancy with you. He has no interest in raising someone else's kid."

And there they are. The words I knew I'd hear once word got out.

No one will understand why I'd choose this. Why I'd willingly have the child of a rapist.

It's not their choice though, it's mine.

Those men may have left me wounded, but no one will break me, not when my child needs me.

Still, Ringo's reaction stings, bad, and a sob lurches from my throat as I remember the words he said but clearly didn't mean.

"There's nothing you can say that would make me want to turn my back on you. Nothing would stop me from wanting to protect you."

"Why the fuck are you still here?" Wendy leans close and whispers in my face. "If you don't run, he'll fucking kill you."

She shoves the clean hoodie at me, and I brace it to my chest as I stumble forward, hurrying from the bathroom.

She's right.

I have to go.

I can't stay here.

I'm not safe.

And if I'm not safe, my baby isn't safe.

Without a second thought, I slip the clean hoodie on and run through the bedroom towards the open door. In my peripheral, I see three men holding a roaring Ringo face down on the bed, and once I'm out the door, I run like I've never run before.

Holy shit!
Are you ready to find out what happens next?

Find out in
BEAUTIFULLY RECKLESS
SECRETS AND SCARS BOOK 2
https://geni.us/secretsandscars2

JOLS & JD

Want to know if Jols and JD end up hooking up?

Get your bonus copy of
SAY THE WORD, AND I'LL ROCK YOUR WORLD
now.

Secrets & Scars Book 1 Bonus Scene - SAY THE WORD, AND I'LL ROCK YOUR WORLD
https://dl.bookfunnel.com/1g4mslv0ra

By downloading a copy of SAY THE WORD, AND I'LL ROCK YOUR WORLD, you will be signing up to Sarah JD's Darker Shades of Romance Newsletter.

HEAVY – CHAPTER ONE

My bedroom door rattles on its hinges, threatening to fly open as my good for nothing half brother beats it from the other side. My lungs betray me, seizing up so no air can get in, and I slap my hand to my chest a couple of times, trying to force them to work. A cough escapes me as my body fights to breathe past my fear, and I hurry to my window, my fingers fumbling as I struggle to get it open fast enough.

"Open the fucking door, Ali!" he bellows, and a squeak escapes me as I panic and jump in fright, worried he's about to break through.

"Shit. Shit. Shit." I whisper, feeling hot tears burn my eyes before I finally manage to get the window open.

Hurrying to climb over the sill, I slip out onto the rooftop, desperate to get away before it's too late.

Even though my heart is thrashing against my ribs, being out here in the open helps me to think clearer, knowing he can't trap me. I carefully balance my way across the tiled roof as fast as I can, desperate to escape without notice before I climb down over the edge.

This has been my escape route for a little while now. It used to be my way of sneaking out to go and have fun with my friends. I never imagined I'd have to use it to flee, but that all changed when my half brother moved in unexpectedly, and the strange boy I used to know growing up, is now a sinister man.

As my feet land on solid ground, I can still hear him beating on my door, yelling. It's not as loud out here, but it makes me wonder if our neighbours have heard the noises that come from my house lately. Or perhaps they are none the wiser, thinking us to be the happy family my mum tries to portray.

My phone vibrating in my pocket reminds me that Abbey keeps calling, so I hurry along the side of my house and out onto the path before I call her back.

"Lex. Where are you? I've been trying to get a hold of you for ages."

"Sorry. I must have fallen asleep." I lie as I hurry to the end of my street, checking over my shoulder to see if Mike is coming.

"Only you would fall asleep when everyone else is already half drunk at a party." Abbey laughs, and I laugh too, glad she can't see my face and the lack of smile on it.

"I'm on my way. I'll be there in twenty minutes."

"Okay. You'll find me at the beer pong table. Or by the fire, although that's close to the shed where all the stoners are sucking on bongs which I'd prefer to avoid."

This time, I do smile, although it's only slight. "You already sound drunk Abs. Maybe steer clear of the beer pong?"

"No way. I'm the champion." She sing-songs. "Oh, I have to go. It's my turn. Byyyye."

The call disconnects, and I stop on the path, taking in a deep breath.

Fuck.

How the hell has my life come to this?

Looking down at myself, I shake my head. I'm still wearing my skinny jeans and hoodie from earlier, and I can only imagine my blonde hair is a mess. The dress I was going to wear was in the laundry, but I couldn't get to it. As soon as Mike saw me, he was in my face, too close, behaving too fucking inappropriate that my only other option was to get back into my room and hope he'd go away.

He didn't.

My hands are still trembling even though my heart rate has eased, and all I want to do is go to the party and pretend for the night that I'm just like all the other seventeen-year-olds there. I need to pretend I'm happy. That I'm carefree.

After all, it's what everyone expects from me. Lexi West. The pretty blonde popular girl with a perfect life.

They don't know.

No one knows. Not even my best friend, Abbey.

Needing to keep moving in case Mike discovers me missing and decides to come looking, I press forward, taking the back streets where I can, and make my way to the party.

It's at Tasha's house, one of my friends. And I mean that loosely. Tasha is in our circle of friends, but I endure her more than I like her, which I know is fucked up, but if I want to hang out with my best friend Abbey, I need to learn to deal with Tasha.

The party has been going for hours now, everyone is completely smashed, and I get hugs from people I don't even know as I weave through the crowd in search of my best friend. Unfortunately, when I find her, she's a little preoccupied in a dark corner with Daniel. Her new boyfriend.

Great.

"Lexi!" Allison runs into me, throwing her arms around my neck and sending us both backwards, tumbling to the floor from the force.

"Jesus, Allison. How drunk are you?" I ask, trying to shove her off me, and she rolls off, laughing before Tasha stumbles over and pulls her up off the floor.

"What are you wearing?" Tasha asks, screwing her face up, not at all trying to hide her disgust at my clothing choice. "You've known about my party for months, Lexi. Why the hell are you wearing that?" She points a claw-like finger at me.

"What's wrong with wanting to wear pants and a hoodie?" I ask, standing up after she doesn't even bother to offer me a hand up.

Her brows shoot high, and she cocks her hip, ignoring Allison who runs off to hug-tackle some random guy across the room.

"You look like a homeless person. Jesus, Lexi. My party has standards. If you're going to dress like a pot head, you may as well go and hang out with them."

My cheeks heat at her insult, and my top lip threatens to sneer at her, but I hold it back. Like always, I keep my real feelings in.

"You know what?" I step up into her personal space. "I think I will go and join the potheads."

I want to say that at least they aren't stuck up bitches like you, but I don't. I just turn my back on her exasperated expression and push my way through the crowd, heading to the shed where the stoners hang out.

I don't know why I do it. I don't know why I go inside. Or why I snatch a bong off some guy who starts cackling at me when I press it to my mouth and suck the damp smoke in. And I don't know why I drop my arse onto the old, tattered couch and accept a joint off some other random guy I don't know.

All I know is that I just want all the fucking noise in my head, and in my life, to stop.

Just for a while.

As I sit in the shed, with a haze of smoke hovering in the air, I finally relax and just be. I drag back on the joint, loving the burn as it seeps into my lungs, and the longer I hold it, the lighter I feel.

In fact, everything feels lighter now as I continue to smoke the joint. People talk to me, but I don't acknowledge them, and I don't even care.

Time slows, or maybe it speeds up. Lights are brighter but then they are duller. Sounds are muffled and it all just seems so easy.

It's peaceful. Moving, walking, it feels both harder and easier at the same time. I feel tired, yet wide awake, and the stars in the sky look huge.

Wait? The stars?

When did I come outside?

It doesn't matter. It's nice out here. Less people. No one around.

Where did everyone go? Is the party over?

I glance around, fairly sure the streetlights I'm looking at are lining a different road to where Tasha's house is.

Did I leave the party?

There's someone here. I don't feel alone. I can't really see them, though. He—I'm pretty sure it's a he—is more like a shadow. I can't seem to see his face.

Smashing glass echoes through the silence, forcing me to sharpen my attention. It's a hard task, given the fuzzy feeling in my head and the way my eyes struggle to focus. I blink fiercely, trying to clear my vision, my eyes locking on to the blurry shape of a hand pulling back through the now shattered window. As the scene before me comes into clearer view, the moonlight filtering from above allows me to see tiny droplets of blood splattered across the pale skin of a dainty hand.

Ouch, that has to hurt.

Normally, the sight of blood turns my stomach, especially when it's not mine. Right now, though, I find the way the crimson beads over the ivory skin quite fascinating. I watch, transfixed, as the molten juice starts to ooze and trickle over my hand and down my wrist.

Wait…

My hand?

My wrist?

What?

"You're such a badass!" A deep voice interrupts me. "A sexy badass!"

Forgetting about my hand, I drop it lazily to my side and turn to whoever dared to interrupt me while I examine the nectar seeping from my body. The shadow I saw earlier is here again. Definitely a guy. Why is he here, and where did he come from? Where did we both come from? And where are we exactly?

He's laughing at something he said as he walks away from me, and the view of his broad shoulders gives me no clue as to who he is. I should probably ask him, but the fuzziness in my head is making me too tired, and I just can't be bothered talking.

Through the haze clouding my eyes, I watch as the guy climbs through the smashed window into the building, being careful to avoid the jagged shards of glass protruding from the frame. He disappears into the darkened room, which kind of resembles a classroom. It's hard to tell from outside in the shade of night and my lacking ability to see straight. The room doesn't look as vibrant and as full of life as a classroom normally would, especially with the artworks lining the walls that are now devoid of colour. In this light, everything appears to be monochrome.

My feet shuffle on the concrete path just outside the building and I curiously watch the guy through the shattered windows as he lifts his leg and kicks a few chairs out of his way. Walking up to the wall of art, he laughs and rips piece by piece down, tearing some in the process as they float down to the floor.

I frown.

This isn't funny. I know I should tell him to stop, but I don't have the energy to speak.

Once he finishes destroying the artwork, he turns and stalks towards the chairs he kicked out of his path. I still can't see his face from where I stand outside, and I squint, hoping it will help. I can't tell if the reason why I'm unable to see him is because the night shadows his features from me, or if my head is really just that fucked up. I can, however, make out his form, which is now lifting a chair over his head.

What the hell is he doing now?

I get an answer to my silent question when he hurls the chair towards the bank of windows next to where I'm standing.

Time slows to sloth speed. The moment the chair leaves the guy's grip, and sails across the room seems to take forever. The intense shattering of glass fills the silent night again as the chair explodes through it, coming to a crashing thud as it lands outside on the concrete path below.

The boy jumps and fist-pumps the air, calling out a loud "whoop." He then turns his sights on me, his face shadowed in darkness except for the white of his teeth spreading into a smile.

"Your turn, Lexi," he encourages.

How does he know my name? Do I know him? His voice isn't familiar to me. Surely, I would remember his voice if I knew him. Come to think of it, why am I here again?

I should care about these things, I know, but I don't. My body feels heavy and numb, yet light as a feather, and if a bed were close by, I'm pretty sure I could fall asleep before my head even hit the pillow.

Even as I think this, my mind flutters to what the guy did, and oddly enough, the thought of it makes my heart race a little. Throwing the chair through the window did kind of look like fun. If there's one thing I like, it's fun.

The chair that was hurled through the window only moments before catches my eye, and I find myself approaching it. It's laying on its side on the path surrounded by shards of glass. Reaching down, I clasp the cold metal legs and lift the chair above my head. Turning towards the windows that still remain intact, I toss the chair with a grunt, keeping my eyes on it as it sails through the window, before tumbling to the floor inside the classroom. The sound of the shattering glass sends a spike of adrenaline rushing through my veins while the guy repeats his jumping and fist-pumping as he leaps out through the glassless window.

"Damn, girl, that was sick!" He appears in front of me, and the moonlight touches the side of his face, giving me a better glimpse of dirty blonde hair and brown eyes. He has a faint smattering of freckles across his nose that makes him look more boyish than manly.

Who is this person?

I tilt my head to study his familiar face, but I keep coming up blank. My brain flutters with the knowledge, but it's not playing fair and won't divulge the secret.

"Who are you?" My voice rasps, feeling dry and unused.

Confusion flits across his face briefly. Then he throws his head back as he laughs hysterically. "Oh man, Lex, you're baked as fuck!" His grin is wide and pleased as he places his hands on my shoulders, turning me into the moonlight to examine my eyes.

I shrug him off, not wanting him to touch me. I'm not sure why I don't want him to touch me. He seems to know who I am, and he's decent looking enough, but for some reason, I can't stand the thought of his hands on me.

A loud gurgle rumbles in the silence between us, and then he laughs, throwing his head back again.

"Damn girl, was that your tummy? You hungry?"

I shrug, "Yeah, I could eat."

"Me too. Let's crash the canteen before security turns up." The boy nudges my shoulder, and we quickly lose interest in the classroom we just demolished.

A canteen with food sounds like the best idea, so I nod and follow him as he leads the way. As I stagger slowly behind, I gaze lazily up at the stars, trying to tune out his annoying yapping. After stumbling a few times, I reluctantly draw my eyes away from the twinkling sky and look around at my surroundings.

There's an Australian flag floating in the breeze, and it looks familiar, much like the one we have at school. Cometo think of it, this place really does look like a school. I'm sure I'd be able to confirm that if my fuzzy vision wasn't making it so hard to see clearly.

If this is a school, then why am I here at night? And why am I with this weirdo whose incessant yapping is irritating the crap out of me? He won't shut up. I don't know what he's saying, and while I want to tell him to stop, I can't find it in me to bother. My eyes are too tired, and my stomach won't stop growling at me.

Am I getting *hangry*?

The stupid thought makes me giggle as we come to a stop in front of two glass doors with the word 'Canteen' displayed overhead.

Oh good. Food.

"Shit, the glass looks thicker than the classroom windows. I'll break my hand if I try to smash it." The boy, who I shall name Weirdo, has a point, although his head looks thick enough to do the job. I giggle again, and he grins at me like he's the one who just thought that hilarious thought, even though he has no idea what's going on inside my head.

"I love this version of you, Lexi. Who would have known such a bad girl was inside this gorgeous prim and proper body?" He chuckles, giving me a lopsided smirk, which I think is meant to come across as sexy, but it looks the opposite and just makes me laugh again.

Eventually deciding that food is more important than talking to this weird guy, I look around the dark yard to find something to help us break through the doors. Keeping in line with the theme of the night, I spot a chair under the covered eating area and walk lazily over to collect it. Lifting it seems like too much effort, so I drag it, and the normally irritating sound of metal on concrete doesn't bother me in the slightest.

As I approach Weirdo, I witness idiocy at its finest when he tries to take matters into his own hands by repeatedly ramming the glass doors with a flimsy tree branch. Backing up, he charges towards the doors with a grunt and nearly face plants the concrete ground when the branch snaps.

The laugh rips from my mouth before I have time to stop it, and his reddened face turns to me in fury, which only makes me laugh harder. Dusting himself off, he starts towards me, his hands balling into fists at his sides.

I get the impression he thinks he's going to intimidate me.

Huh! Not likely. I have bigger monsters than him in my life.

I repeat my earlier actions and lift the chair above my head. Weirdo, using his brain for once, freezes in place, his heated face turning worried. Ignoring him, I lunge with force, letting the chair fly from my grip. Weirdo's eyes widen right before he drops to the ground to duck out of the way as the chair sails mere inches from his head, before the knowing sound of smashing glass greets us again, and I grin.

Even though I don't seem to feel much at the moment, I feel my grin. That was legit good!

"Fuck, Lexi!" Weirdo hisses as he rises and turns to me. At first, I think he's going to try and act angry and intimidating again, but he surprises me and laughs. "Seriously, can I kiss you?"

I look at him, now advancing on me with a determined look in his eyes. I don't answer, and before I can react, his hands delve into my hair, tugging my head close as his lips close over mine.

I kiss him back… I think. It's hard to tell because I feel nothing. My face is numb, and my mind is fuzzy. I don't typically let random guys kiss me, but then again, I don't typically break into schools and throw chairs through windows, either. I'm not sure why I'm doing any of this. I can't remember how I got here. My memory is nothing but a haze of fog.

"You're a great kisser." Weirdo draws away, his eyes flicking back down to my lips as he licks his own.

I think about his words and realise I must have been kissing him back. It seems strange that I didn't feel it.

I shrug, not caring if I'm a good kisser or not, and step around him to climb through the broken glass doors of the school canteen. My food of choice is chocolate cake and juice boxes. He chooses potato chips and a can of cola. We don't speak now that food is in our hands and filling our mouths, and when we are all stocked up, I follow him out of the canteen.

Walking in silence, we're both too ecstatic with the food we've scored to care much about anything. I probably should care about a lot of things right now.

Like who the hell he is, and if kissing him is something I would normally do. I should probably care that we were just in a school instead of the party. And as we make our way towards the back of the school, where the shadows are at their darkest, I should care more that at any point, I could run into my brother, and if that happens, I should really fucking care about what he will do to me.

**Continue reading HEAVY – Heavy Hearts Book
1 today to find out what happens next.
https://geni.us/heavyhearts1**

READ MORE BY SARAH JD

Sarah JD's Books

https://sarahjdauthor.com/books

STALK SARAH

Want to join the conversation about your fav characters?

Join my Facebook Readers Group
SARAH'S VICIOUS KITTENS

JOIN HERE!

https://www.facebook.com/groups/
sarahjaneduncanreadersgroup

For more information on books & book signing
events please visit:
https://sarahjdauthor.com

STALK SARAH HERE:

Sarah JD

Sarah JD, also known as Sarah Jane Duncan, is an Australian dark romance author living her best life with her high school sweetheart, Mr Duncan.

Sarah can be found in her writing room plotting out her next smut filled romance, packed with angst, violence, and themes so dark you should probably question why you love it so much.

Sarah enjoys torturing her characters. There's nothing easy about their stories. They are hard, gritty, and painfully heartbreaking at times. But what doesn't kill us makes us stronger, right? And when you throw in a swoon worthy guy, or an alphahole you just want to slap, but also fall to your knees and obey, it's the recipe for a rollercoaster ride.

So buckle up. Read the warnings. And let yourself get lost in the dark stories Sarah creates.

SOUTHERN SADISTS MC